F

C000175676

Rosemerryn

Gloria Cook

First published in the United Kingdom in 1995 by Headline Book Publishing

This edition published in the United Kingdom in 2020 by

Canelo Digital Publishing Limited
Third Floor, 20 Mortimer Street
London W1T 3JW
United Kingdom

A CIP catalogue record for this book is available from the British Library.

Print ISBN 978 1 78863 809 8
Ebook ISBN 978 1 78863 647 6

Look for more great books at www.canelo.co

Printed and bound in Great Britain by Clays Ltd, Elcograf S.p.A.

*This book is dedicated to the memory
of my friend Linda
and love to Peter and the children*

Chapter 1

Laura Jennings opened a bedroom window of Tregorlan Farm and looked anxiously down the muddy track that led to Rosemerryn Lane. With a heavy mist spreading gaunt fingers all the way down to the black moorland earth, she could see no sign of the midwife heading for the old and solid farmhouse on her bicycle.

'Hold on a little longer, Tressa, for goodness sake,' Laura implored, returning to the young woman nearing the last stages of labour on the huge double bed. She forced a confident smile. 'The midwife shouldn't be much longer now.'

'Are you sure Andrew's coming home?' Tressa Macarthur gasped between deep pants as a strong contraction subsided slowly.

'We've told you over 'n' over,' Joan Davey, on the other side of the bed holding her hand, said chidingly. 'We phoned Andrew's office and he left at once. If you hadn't been such a silly girl and told me or your father you were having pains at dinner time we would have got Andrew and the midwife here by now. 'Tis a good job Andrew had a phone put in and I was able to ring Laura at the shop.'

Tressa smiled at her aunt. She knew how nervous Joan was of the telephone, a 'new-fangled contraption', to her, and she had shaken visibly when she'd dialled the number of the village shop, which Laura partly owned, to alert her of what was happening.

'Thanks for coming straight away, Laura. I didn't want to cause a fuss. First babies are supposed to take hours to arrive,' Tressa grunted, gritting her teeth as the next contraction racked her body. 'I was hoping Andrew would be home before anything really hap— ohhh!'

Laura grasped her other hand. 'Breathe deeply, Tressa, like the midwife told you. Don't tense your body. That's it. Good girl. Breathe out on the count of five.'

The contraction seemed endless and when it was over, as Laura wiped the perspiration from Tressa's face with a damp flannel, she caught her own reflection in the dressing-table mirror. She was flushed, her deep blue eyes were sparkling brighter than usual with excitement, and although she was getting more nervous by the moment and there was an uncomfortable quivering in her lower stomach, she looked as steady as a rock. She hoped her confident manner would give Tressa all the reassurance she needed at this critical time.

When Tressa was comfortable again, Laura switched on the light and lit the bedside oil lamps to dispel the gloom the mist was casting on what otherwise would have been a fine spring afternoon. It added cosiness and warmth to the pleasant surroundings for Tressa to give birth in. Andrew, her devoted husband, had completely refurbished the bedroom, one of the largest in the farmhouse, when they had married nearly a year ago. The floor was carpeted from wall to wall in a plush pink and dotted with Turkish rugs. Pretty chintz curtains contrasted well with rosebud patterned wallpaper. With a wealth of nursery equipment, a padded rocking chair waited by the fireside for the new mother to nurse her baby in. Another addition was a sink on a pedestal, and fluffy new white towels were there in readiness to be used after today's occasion.

'I want to push!' Tressa shouted, instinctively drawing up her knees.

'You can't!' Joan screamed in panic. 'Laura and I don't know how to deliver a baby.'

'Calm down, Joan,' Laura ordered sternly, although her own heart was racing at twice its normal speed. 'We'll manage. We'll have to.' She pulled back the bedsheet and looked between Tressa's legs. She was electrified at what she saw but forced herself to speak normally. 'I can see the baby's head. Let this pain go gently if you can, Tressa, then on the next one you'd better start pushing, but not with all your might.' Laura had read a lot of books on childbirth since Tressa had become pregnant and she knew each stage of labour was better taken gently at first.

There was a sudden loud rap on the bedroom door and Joan shrieked in fright.

'Is everything all right in there?' It was Jacka Davey, Tressa's father. Before coming upstairs he had been anxiously pacing the kitchen floor of his and Joan's share of the accommodation on the farm.

Hearing his strong, caring voice gave Laura another boost of confidence. 'Tressa's about to have the baby, Jacka,' she called out while swiftly tying back her shoulder-length blonde hair. 'Could you bring up some hot water so we can wash her afterwards?'

'Oh, my goodness!' Jacka opened the door and peeped round it, taking off his floppy hat. He was holding a bunch of daffodil buds he had picked for Tressa. He was built like an ox but had a gentle disposition and a heart of tenderness for his only child; tears were misting his eyes. 'Yes, yes, of course.' He didn't look at his daughter, but asked her, 'You all right, my handsome?'

'I'm doing fine, Dad.' Then Tressa screwed up her face and bore down on the next contraction. Jacka beat a hasty retreat.

Laura had already put out on the bedside cabinet the things the midwife had left during a routine visit. She rolled up the sleeves of her silk blouse then tossed Joan a dry cloth to wipe Tressa's brow. It would be wise to keep Joan occupied; she may have helped many a calf into the world, but being a quiet, unmarried, middle-aged woman, she was nervous about childbirth.

The contraction eased and Tressa allowed her heaving body to fall back onto the pillows. Breathlessly, she uttered, 'I could do this much easier if I was standing up.'

'Don't you dare, Tressa! Whoever heard of such a thing?' Joan wailed. She was trembling and pulled the hairnet she always wore over her grey hair more firmly in place.

'I can manage by myself if you want to leave the room, Joan,' Laura offered in a firm voice. The arrival of the baby was imminent, but her nerves felt as strong as cold steel. She stroked the bare bump that stuck out almost grotesquely from Tressa's skimpy body, feeling for the start of the next contraction.

3

'No, no,' Joan muttered belatedly as Laura's words finally sank into her confusion. She willed herself to be calmer. 'Don't worry. I won't let you down.'

Tressa grinned at her aunt encouragingly. Despite the pain and effort, and the niggle of worry felt by every mother that her baby would not be born strong and healthy, she was enjoying the process of giving birth. Her only regret was not informing Andrew earlier so he could be in the house with her father.

The next contraction started, and as if she had delivered many a baby, Laura moved to a position where she could more easily assist this one to be born.

A few minutes later, after much granting and heaving on Tressa's part, the baby's head slid into Laura's eager hands.

'One more push, Tressa, and it will all be over,' Laura stated with authority, her eyes rooted on the little wet human roundness in her hands.

Tressa's small face was filled with determination. She reached for Joan's hand, took in a long lusty breath, then pushed down with all her might.

Laura pulled very gently on the baby's head, easing the final part of its journey into the world. In moments she was exclaiming, 'It's here, it's born!' and had to control the urge to shout in exhilaration. She carefully raised the baby for Tressa to see and it let out an almighty bawl.

'It's a boy,' Laura breathed in awe.

Then all three women burst into tears of elation.

Tressa held out her hands for her son. Laura tied the cord in two places with lengths of sterilised string and cut the cord cleanly between the string. Wrapping a soft towel round the baby she reluctantly handed him over to his mother.

'He's just like Andrew,' Tressa said softly, gazing at him tenderly, a new love, deep and strong, welling up inside her.

Joan agreed with her. 'Aye, he's got the same blue eyes and sandy hair, even his stubborn-looking chin.'

Laura couldn't speak. As Tressa cradled her son to her breast, Laura stroked his damp, downy head. This day, the fifteenth of March,

1949, would never have come about if Laura hadn't brought her late husband's body back home to be buried in the village of Kilgarthen, nearly a mile away from the farm. On that fateful day, her solicitor, Andrew, had informed her that Bill Jennings had bankrupted her father's building company, and Laura had decided to stay on in her only remaining property, the cottage where Bill had been born and bred. A few days later, Andrew had travelled down from London with papers for her to sign and to check on her welfare. He had got hopelessly lost in fog and had come across Tressa in the muddy potholed track that led up to Tregorlan Farm. He had instantly fallen in love with Tressa, then an unapproachable tomboy who'd lived in a private little world of her own, spurning all contact with reality, her family so poor she'd worn her dead brothers' clothing as she'd worked the moorland farm with her father and aunt. It had taken a lot of determination on Andrew's part, and a near tragedy, before he had overcome the differences in their backgrounds and broken into Tressa's heart and won her for his own.

Laura was proud to have delivered their first baby safely. She couldn't control her tears. Neither could she stop the intense feelings which often gripped her, that filled her whole being and threatened to overwhelm her – the longing to have a child of her own.

Andrew and the midwife burst into the room together and Laura found herself being shunted out of the way as the midwife took over from her.

Much to the annoyance of the midwife, Andrew hugged his proud, radiant wife. 'Oh, darling. Was it awful? Are you all right? Are you sure? You should have called me sooner.' Tressa smiled triumphantly and moved the towel aside so he could see they had a son. 'He's beautiful! You're beautiful! Oh, well done, you've given me a wonderful little boy.'

The strident tones of the midwife broke into Andrew's bliss. 'Move back from the bed, Mr Macarthur! In fact you should leave the room altogether. I don't like having fathers in the way. It is not good for mother or baby. Perhaps Miss Davey and Mrs Jennings would like to take you downstairs and make us all a nice cup of tea.'

5

Laura was peeved that she should be dismissed too; after all, she had successfully dealt with the most important part of the delivery, but she obediently took hold of Andrew and, with Joan's help, pulled him away from Tressa and their baby and out of the room. Jacka was lurking outside on the landing, on tenterhooks to be told about his first grandchild.

The group made their way downstairs to Jacka and Joan's kitchen. Because of Jacka's past financial difficulties, and an unsuccessful under-hand deed by Harry Lean, the village womaniser, Andrew now owned Tregorlan Farm which had been the Daveys' home for generations, and although an extension had been added to provide the young couple with their own kitchen, bathroom and sitting room, they automatically made their way to what was the hub of the house. It was a dark and dull room but everything in it was comfortingly familiar, the old furniture, the faded checkered oilcloth on the huge square table, the ragged rush mats on the flagstoned floor; the only concession to modern living that Jacka and Joan had allowed in their part of the farmhouse was electric lights when Andrew had installed a generator.

'Never mind tea for a minute,' Jacka said, his voice heavy with emotion. 'I have a bottle of wine put by for this very day.'

They raised their glasses, all odd ones, to the new mother and arrival.

'To my first grandchild,' Jacka toasted with pride.

'To my great-nephew,' Joan chirruped, her voice thick with tears. 'I've never seen anything so marvellous in all my born days. And to think I was half scared out of my wits at what was going to happen.'

'To Guy Andrew Macarthur,' Andrew said, shining with happiness and feeling somewhat stunned now. 'And to my beautiful, wonderful Tressa.' He suddenly hugged Laura and kissed both her cheeks. 'And all my grateful thanks to you, Laura.'

'To the Macarthurs and the Daveys,' Laura said in a small voice, pulling herself away from the others. It was the most momentous event to happen on the farm for many years, but while she shared the others' joy, she felt deeply lonely, an aching sense of melancholy, and she knew that she was desperately jealous of Tressa's motherhood.

'That makes two new babies in the village in one week in time for Easter,' Joan remarked dreamily.

'What other new baby?' Laura asked sharply, so sharply the others looked at her curiously.

'The one in the young family that moved into the village next to the Millers the other day. Uren, they're called, Dolores and Gerald Uren. They have five boys, the youngest a two-year-old called Rodney, and one little maid of four months called Emily.'

'I suppose Ada Prisk told you all this,' Andrew smiled, referring affectionately to the village gossip.

Joan nodded. She did not add that Ada Prisk had also said the Urens were dirty and scruffy and 'like ruddy gypsies' and Gerald Uren was a 'lazy so-and-so who's never known an honest day's work and shirked his national service'.

Andrew sipped his wine and looked at Laura sympathetically. She had gone quiet and looked as if all the spirit and energy had left her, rather like the way she had become in the five disastrous years of marriage she had endured with the cruel, amoral Bill Jennings, a man whose true nature hadn't been known to the villagers who had hero-worshipped him as their 'local boy made good'. Andrew knew about the dream that Jennings had denied Laura.

'You knew the Urens were moving into Kilgarthen, didn't you, Laura?'

His question broke through her pensive mood. 'What? Oh, yes. I served Mrs Uren in the shop only this morning, but I didn't know she had a baby girl as well as the five boys who trooped in with her. She must have left her at home with her husband.'

'Well, you're too busy with young Vicki to take in everything that goes on in the village,' Joan said, taking the battered tin kettle off the ageing black wrought-iron range and pouring boiling water into a huge brown teapot.

Mention of Vicki Jeffries brought a smile back to Laura's classically beautiful face. Her vitality returned, and with it the proud bearing with which she carried her tall, shapely figure. Her moment of self-pity evaporated and she was filled with joy at Guy's birth. She couldn't wait to cycle on to Rosemerryn Farm and tell the little girl whom she adored all about the baby.

When the midwife had gone, Laura slipped upstairs to say goodbye to Tressa.

'I've phoned Aunty Daisy in the shop and told her the good news. It will soon be all round the village.' Laura glanced at her watch. 'It's a good thing Spencer was collecting Vicki off the school bus today and not me. I was due there over an hour ago.'

Going to the cradle beside the bed she gazed down at Guy's pink face peeping out of the white shawl she had knitted for him herself. 'You coped exceedingly well, Tressa. Are you sure you're feeling all right?'

'Nothing to it really,' Tressa replied breezily. 'I don't even feel tired. Andrew reckons it's all the moor air I've consumed from childhood.' Laura thought that was probably true. Tressa was sitting upright in a new pink silk nightdress and fluffy bedjacket, the complexion of her pretty round face glowing, her long brown hair brushed glossily over her slender shoulders. 'I was very lucky. You can pick Guy up if you like.'

'Are you sure you don't mind?'

'Of course I don't. You delivered him, Laura. You held him first. If anyone deserves to hold him, it's you. I doubt that things would have gone so smoothly if I'd been here alone with Aunty Joan, bless her.'

Putting her hands gently under his little warm body, Laura lifted Guy out of his cradle as if he was as fragile as thistledown. She held him tenderly to her body. 'He feels a lot heavier with clothes on,' she said.

'Well, he's a big baby. He weighs eight pounds, twelve and a half ounces,' Tressa said proudly. She watched with feeling as the wistful expression on Laura's face turned to tears. 'Andrew's asked you to be his godmother, hasn't he?'

'Yes. You've both made me feel very proud.' Laura lowered her face and brushed it lightly against the baby's cheek.

Tressa wasn't an emotional woman but she felt she was about to cry for the second time that day. 'There's plenty of time for you to have a baby of your own, Laura,' she whispered softly.

'It's what I want so very much.' Laura smiled wanly, placing a tiny peck on Guy's forehead.

Tressa wasn't given to handing out advice, at twenty-one years old she was four years younger than Laura who was sophisticated and much more worldly-wise than she was, but she felt this was one time when she should speak her mind. 'Well, I'd have thought the answer to that was obvious.'

Laura took her eyes off the baby and looked at the young woman, frowning. 'What do you mean?'

'You have an understanding with Spencer Jeffries, haven't you? Marry him and have a family.'

'Just like that, Tressa?' Laura was astounded. 'But—'

'But nothing. You're already as much a mother to Vicki as any woman can be. When you're not working in the shop you spend practically every minute on Rosemerryn Farm. You'd like to be Vicki's legal stepmother, wouldn't you?'

'Yes, of course I would, but...' Laura was at a loss to know what to say. She tenderly kissed the baby's cheek. 'I love Vicki more than anyone else in the world. I quite like Spencer – well, I like him a lot, he's saved my life twice, but...'

'If you're worried about sleeping with him, don't forget Spencer is very good-looking,' Tressa pointed out.

This was unexpected from the new mother who hadn't harboured a single romantic thought until she'd fallen in love with Andrew. Laura countered in grudging tones, 'And he's stubborn, inclined to be bad-tempered, and despite it being his idea that we have this understanding, he can get jealous of my closeness to Vicki.' She sighed at the irony of life. 'Sometimes I think that if only Vicki was Ince's child, it would be so much easier.'

'Well, she isn't,' Tressa said, sounding like a stern matron. 'Granted Ince is a kinder and gentler man altogether but your brief romance with him didn't work out, remember? And you must have seriously considered marrying Spencer, you wouldn't have an understanding with him otherwise. Think about it. It could be the answer to all your prayers.'

Laura looked at the alarm clock on the bedside table and chided herself. 'I must go. Vicki will be getting worried about me.'

'Don't change the subject, Laura.'

'I wasn't going to, Tressa,' she said, handing Guy to her. She grinned ruefully. 'But it isn't as easy as going up to Spencer and saying, "Hey, I want a baby, let's get married now." But if it makes you happy, I promise I'll go away and think seriously about it.'

When Laura had gently closed the door behind her, Tressa listened to the light steps descending the stairs. She pictured Laura running into Rosemerryn Farm and hugging and kissing the six-year-old girl with the perfect heart-shaped face, flawless skin and white-gold hair, a girl so like Laura she could be her own daughter. Tressa gazed down adoringly at the child in her arms, and after the fierce new feelings she had experienced within the last hour, whispered knowledgeably, 'A woman will do anything for the child she loves.'

Chapter 2

Laura had to wait to share her joy over the new baby with little Vicki Jeffries. When she leaned her bicycle against a granite wall at Rosemerryn Farm, she was frightened to hear Vicki screaming and a lot of urgent shouting coming from the kitchen.

First, however, she had to get past Barney, Spencer Jeffries' irascible big Border collie who made a point of leaping out at her from behind barns, farm vehicles and the tops of grey moorstone walls. Strangely, Barney was nowhere in the yard but thoughts of Vicki being hurt or terrified would have given Laura the authority needed to order him off today.

She ran through the mist into the farmhouse and found Vicki, Spencer, and Ince Polkinghorne, Spencer's farmhand and closest friend, at the sink.

'Keep your hand under the water, Spencer!' Ince was saying roughly. 'It's the best way to stem the bleeding.'

'No, it isn't,' Spencer returned angrily, struggling to get free of Ince's strong grasp. 'You're supposed to tie a cloth or something round it.'

'What's going on?' Laura raised her voice over the hubbub.

Vicki, who was still screaming and jumping up and down, turned round first. 'Laura!' she squealed, running to her. 'Help Daddy! He's nearly cut his hand off.'

'What?'

Her heart in her mouth, Laura rushed to the sink to see for herself. Spencer had a deep gash across the back of his left hand and due to the men's struggles, blood-streaked water was splashed on them, all over the sink, the mat under their feet and the well-worn linoleum. There were spots of blood on Vicki's cotton dress and cardigan too.

'Let go of him, Ince,' Laura ordered, tugging on Ince's hands. 'You're thinking of the right treatment for a burn. You need to put pressure on a cut that deep.'

'Oh.' Ince let the arm go so abruptly that Spencer lost his balance and fell to the floor. He roared with rage. Vicki jumped in fright and clutched Laura's skirt. Laura hugged her close.

'That's enough of that!' Laura shouted at Spencer. 'You're frightening Vicki.' She wouldn't allow any behaviour that was detrimental to the peace and security of the little girl she had grown to love so much. She snatched a tea towel off the draining board and tied it swiftly and tightly round his hand. 'You'll have to take him to hospital and have it stitched, Ince.'

'I'm not going to the damned hospital,' Spencer bellowed, using his good hand to lever himself to his feet.

'You'll have to,' Laura asserted, ignoring the fury building up behind his stone-grey eyes. 'Don't be silly. You can't work on the farm like that and you'll have to have treatment to stop your hand getting infected.'

Spencer muttered something foul under his breath; he hated what he felt was Laura's occasional superior attitude with him.

'Daddy said a bad word!' Vicki exclaimed, putting a hand to her lips.

Laura wanted to dig him cruelly in the ribs; Vicki overheard a few too many 'bad words' from her father. It was time she had a word with him, but not right now.

Ince had heard it too, wasn't prepared to wait, and tut-tutted at him. 'Watch your mouth, Spencer.'

Spencer was sorry his daughter had heard him swear but was too stubborn to admit it to the two adults.

'Oh, very well, I'll go to the hospital if I must,' he uttered ungraciously. Then he turned on Laura in a tone that was designed to make her feel guilty. 'Where have you been? You should have been here ages ago. If you had then this wouldn't have happened.'

Laura glanced guiltily at the ormolu clock on the mantelpiece but she was cross that he should blame her. Rather than argue with him, she looked at Ince for an explanation. He shot Spencer a look full of pique and shook his head scornfully.

'He collected Vicki off the school bus then left her in here playing. We're going to pull down the old trap house, it's getting far too dangerous, and he came to help me with some junk I was turning out. He was complaining he was hungry and was peeved that you were late cooking the meal. He was tossing things about in a temper—'

'I wasn't!' Spencer protested tartly.

'You were.' It showed in Ince's honest, dependable face that he wouldn't be shifted from his own irreproachable stance. 'And that's when a box of old rusty nails and tools fell from the top of a wobbly shelf and hit him. He put up his hand to save his head and was struck by a chisel. He's probably got bruises on his arms and shoulders as well.'

Spencer retreated into an indignant silence. He felt that his best friend had betrayed him and made him look a fool in front of Laura and his daughter; Vicki had adopted the same exasperated expression on her sweet little face.

Laura was wondering, as she sometimes did, how she could ever have seriously considered marrying this man.

'Would you run upstairs and fetch Daddy a clean shirt, please, Vicki?' Laura said in an imperious tone. 'He can't go to the hospital looking like that.'

'I'll go up and change my shirt too,' Ince murmured.

When Ince and Vicki had left the room, Spencer let out a loud huff.

'What was that for?' Laura asked, surveying him impatiently.

'I don't like being treated like a bloody child.'

'That is not my intention,' Laura said in a voice as if she was trying to explain something to a difficult adolescent. 'You've received a serious injury and you need all the help and consideration you can get. You're trembling. You're probably shocked. Let me help you sit down.'

Spencer realised he was shaking from head to toe. If he didn't sit down soon he'd probably fall down. Laura put her hands firmly about

13

him and he was grateful for the warmth and comfort they gave. Feeling ashamed of his outbursts and bad language, he allowed her to lead him to a chair at the table.

Relieved that he was at last acting sensibly, she began to unbutton his shirt. 'This is ruined. There's oil on it and it's badly torn.'

'Better than losing my hand,' he sighed, gazing at the blood-soaked tea towel wrapped round it. He grimaced as a sharp pain shot through his hand. It would have been good to rest his face against Laura's soft, fragrant body, but their relationship hadn't progressed in twelve months beyond the friendly understanding that one day they would get married for Vicki's sake, the understanding coming hard on the heels of Laura's rescue of Vicki and eight other children from the village school which had been burnt to the ground.

Easing off his shirt, Laura looked at Spencer's broad shoulders and muscular torso. 'You've got a few grazes and bruises and a small cut on your neck. The nurses will clean you up.' She could have washed off some of the dust and oil from his body and his thick fair hair herself but felt it might not be appreciated. Most of the time he was unapproachable and it seemed too intimate a thing to do.

Spencer sighed in contrition. 'I'm sorry I shouted at you. You were only trying to help. I shouldn't behave like that in front of Vicki.' For Vicki's sake he always brought their arguments to a quick end. Vicki adored Laura and her constant presence at Rosemerryn gave his daughter, peace and security. And while he wanted this beautiful young widow's influence in his daughter's life, he was also greatly attracted to her.

'No, you shouldn't, especially using such bad language,' she replied, then her face softened. 'But I understand how you must have felt, Spencer.' She never stayed angry with him for long. When he dropped his habitual guardedness, like now, and relaxed his chary bearing, his bold fair features, weathered arrestingly by thirty-seven years of moorland life, looked so much more like Vicki's. She had a sweet outgoing nature and Laura felt a similar one in Spencer lurked not too far below the surface.

The nation was in the grip of tight petrol rationing but Ince calculated there was just enough in the tank of Spencer's old but reliable Ford to get them the nine miles to Launceston and back.

While the men were at the hospital, Laura cleaned up the messy sink area, scrubbed the mat and washed the bloodied clothes. She had a meal cooked and keeping hot for all of them when the men got back.

Vicki, now in her nightclothes, made a fuss of her father, who in her imagination, instead of suffering an accident, had got the wound on his hand by bravely fighting off a screeching spirit that had risen from the marshes on the moor. She climbed gingerly up onto his lap as he sat in his chair by the fire, while Ince helped Laura dish up the pork casserole.

'Did the doctor sew up your hand the same as when Laura darns our socks, Daddy?' Vicki asked softly, cuddling into Spencer's neck while staring at his expertly bandaged hand. The love between father and daughter was deep and manifestly clear.

'Yes, pipkin, but he gave me something to take the pain away.' He kissed the top of her white-gold hair.

'Does it hurt now?'

'No,' he lied.

He glanced at the pair at the table and was extremely irritated to see a warm look pass between them. He had seen them exchange many such looks, too many for his liking, and he wondered if the brief romance they'd had soon after Laura had moved into Kilgarthen was really over. There was definitely a spark of something left between them and he feared it might be rekindled. Ince was quiet and unassuming but he must know he was stepping on Spencer's feet, and as for Laura, she had no right to flirt. It might be old-fashioned, but she was promised to him and maybe it was time he did something to remind them of it.

He forcefully interrupted their cosy talk. 'Why were you late getting here today, Laura?'

Vicki suddenly sat up straight and her sharp movements hurt his hand. 'I can tell you that, Daddy,' she piped up excitedly. 'Laura told me all about it. Tressa had a baby boy and Laura fetched him for her.'

'The Macarthurs have a son?' Ince said delightedly, looking at Laura as he carried the empty casserole dish to the sink. 'That's wonderful. Praise the Lord. Did I hear Vicki right? You delivered the baby?'

'That's right,' Laura replied, once more washed over with the emotions she had experienced a few hours ago on Tregorlan Farm. 'The baby arrived just before the midwife and Andrew did.'

'Goodness. Jacka must be over the moon. Male kin on his farm again since his sons were killed in the war.'

'That's good news,' Spencer said unenthusiastically, narked that Ince had taken over the conversation. Seeing the food was ready on the table, he motioned for Vicki to get down off his lap. 'You and Vicki should have eaten,' he chided Laura as they approached the table. 'It's late for Vicki. She has to go to school tomorrow.'

'Sorry,' Laura said, but she wasn't really. 'We didn't know how long you would be at the hospital and she wouldn't have been able to go to sleep until she was sure you were properly patched up.'

She wasn't prepared to eat under Spencer's disapproval and talked to Ince, mindful of what she said because young ears were listening. Vicki thought she had brought Guy to the farm in her shopping bag and she felt it wasn't her place to tell her anything different. 'I think it's got to be the most moving experience of my life. Thankfully Tressa had an easy time. The baby was well over eight pounds and is the image of Andrew. They've called him Guy.'

'Guy?' Spencer said mockingly, inadvertently sprinkling too much salt on his meal. 'A bit highbrow for a farmer's daughter's baby, isn't it?'

'Andrew chose names for a boy and Tressa for a girl,' Laura retorted, vexed by his sourness. 'What's wrong with Guy? It's a nice name.'

'I like it,' Vicki said innocently.

'You can't do better than choose a name from the Bible, I think,' commented Ince.

'Talking of that,' Spencer said, 'you were thinking of offering to help out one of your Methodist friends at his smallholding this evening, weren't you?'

'Yes, Les Tremorrow's hurt his back, and as he's getting on a bit I thought he might be grateful for a hand round the place. But the work here comes first. You won't be able to do anything much for a few days, at least not until you've had the stitches out.'

This hadn't occurred to Spencer and he dropped his fork which clattered to the floor. 'How are we going to manage? There's ditching and harrowing to do, then the tilling.'

'I'll help of course,' Laura said, fetching him another fork.

'Thanks, but you can't do everything I do.'

'We'll manage,' Ince said soothingly. 'Felicity and Harry will almost certainly come over from Hawksmoor and when folk find out what's happened, there will be plenty of offers from the village.'

'And I break up from school tomorrow,' Vicki added, yawning. 'I'll help too.'

'Right now, darling,' Laura said, smiling tenderly at her, 'you'd better go up to bed.'

Vicki got up from the table, rubbing her eyes. She moved to her father and he bent his head to kiss her goodnight; it was taken for granted Laura would put her to bed. 'Tressa's a mummy now, Daddy. I want Laura to be my mummy. Say she can. I want her to live here all the time with us. And I want brothers and sisters like the other children at school.'

This was a plea that Vicki brought up often. Although a part of him had wanted to do something about it, Spencer had always withdrawn at the thought and made an excuse, but smarting under the display of affection he'd witnessed again between Laura and Ince, tonight his answer was totally different. He replied in an assertive voice, 'I'll see what I can do, pipkin.'

Laura tried not to show her astonishment as she headed for the door that led immediately to the stairs. Ince excused himself with an embarrassed look on his rugged face and went outside to get on with the evening milking.

Laura managed to get Vicki into bed but the little girl was very excited after what her father had just promised her. 'You will marry Daddy, won't you?' she squeaked, clinging to Laura's neck when she kissed her goodnight. 'Say you will.'

'It... it's not as simple as that, Vicki,' she answered, flustered: even though Tressa had said it was.

17

She felt like thumping Spencer for dropping his dramatic sentence on them like that. It struck her then that she often wanted to thump Spencer over his grumpy or contrary behaviour. She had been reading an article in *Woman's World* last night about one's behaviour having hidden motives; the magazine suggested her motive was a secret desire to touch the man in her life. Rubbish, she told herself. But her cheeks were crimson when she asked Vicki, 'Now what story would you like me to read, darling?'

'I don't want a story,' Vicki said, putting on the appealing face that usually resulted in her getting her own way. 'I want you to say you'll be my mummy.' She held up her favourite doll. 'So does Lizzie. You do want to, don't you? Can I call you Mummy now?'

Laura's heart was torn. She would love to be her mother but there was much to consider before marrying Spencer. She had one bad marriage behind her. Bill Jennings had despised her, using her only as a springboard to the board of directors of her father's building company. Six months after her father had died in 1947, Bill had choked to death in a hotel fire and it had turned out he had bankrupted the company. Laura had been left with Bill's cottage in Kilgarthen, a small amount of savings and some valuable jewellery. Months later it had transpired that she also owned half the village shop so she was financially secure. Marriage to Spencer wouldn't change that but a great many other things would change. She would have to give up her independence, being able to please herself as she came and went. She would be much closer to Vicki, of course, but if life with Spencer proved to be incompatible it could hurt Vicki most of all.

She picked up a storybook and tried to look determined. 'I can't stay up here long, Vicki. I have the dishes to do and then we have to sort out the workload on the farm now that Daddy's hurt his hand. Settle down and we'll talk about it another time.'

'Promise?'

'I promise.'

Vicki was content with that and when the story was finished she settled down to sleep.

Laura prayed Ince would be back in the kitchen when she went downstairs but Spencer was alone, sitting in his chair, drinking a glass of whisky – to steady himself after the accident or because of an attack of nerves following his sudden declaration? she wondered. Self-consciously she crossed the room and did the dishes, putting them away without a single word passing between them. Her mind was full of questions. Why had Spencer suddenly said that to Vicki? If taking the next step regarding their understanding had been on his mind, why hadn't he spoken to her privately instead of blurting it out, exciting Vicki and embarrassing her and Ince? As he had nothing to say now, was he regretting it? She knew she should address these questions to Spencer but she couldn't bring herself to ask him.

Leaving aside her feelings for Vicki, she felt frightened at the prospect of marrying again and turned her thoughts to Guy's birth. Standing at the oak dresser with a dinner plate in her hand, she went into a sort of trance as she recalled the feel of his tiny wet body in her hands as he'd emerged into the world. She heard again the sound of his first cry. She could almost smell the wonderful baby scent of him when she had held him after he'd been washed and dressed. Tressa would have fed him twice by now, changed at least two nappies. Laura was consumed with her old longing to prepare a nursery for herself, to knit baby clothes, to choose names and godparents, to hold and love and cherish her own baby, to watch it grow up. Tears were only a moment away.

She didn't realise Spencer was beside her until he touched her arm. 'Laura, are you all right?'

'What?' She flinched and Spencer was horrified that she had recoiled from him. 'Oh, yes. Sorry, I was miles away.' She put the plate in its place. 'I was thinking about Guy's birth. It's silly, isn't it? How we women come over all emotional at a baby being born.'

'No,' he said softly. 'I won't ever forget how I felt when I first saw Vicki.' After a small pause he added, 'And how Natalie cried with joy.'

'I'm sorry, Spencer. I didn't mean to bring up old memories.'

'I don't mind any more, Laura. I've accepted now that Vicki's birth led to Natalie's death.'

Dejectedly he returned to his chair. He had been thinking over what he'd said to Vicki. It hadn't been a slip of the tongue even though he'd said it out of jealousy. When he had suggested the understanding to Laura, he'd thought he would be happy to allow things to ride until Vicki grew up, simply accepting the love and attention Laura would give her. Just lately he had been thinking differently. He had always desired Laura, even when she'd first arrived in Kilgarthen and he had hated her unjustly over Bill Jennings' past behaviour to Natalie. He had been a widower for over six years and now he wanted to put an end to that kind of loneliness.

Forcing a small smile, he said meekly, 'I'm sorry if I make you feel you have to tread on eggshells over my feelings whenever we're together.'

Laura smiled back, feeling a little shy, but she liked these moments when Spencer was kind and considerate. She felt guilty at the description she had given of him to Tressa. She would try to remember the next time they clashed, as inevitably they would, that he wasn't entirely an ogre. She gave him a few moments to say something about his earlier declaration. With nothing forthcoming, she reached for her cardigan. 'I'd better be going. I'll be over early tomorrow.'

Spencer knew she had wanted him to say something to her but he could only clear his throat. 'Thanks for all your help,' he said sincerely, as if he was talking to someone no closer than a kindly neighbour.

'You're welcome,' she answered in the same manner. 'I'll see Vicki on and off the school bus tomorrow. I'll stay here throughout each day until things are back to normal.' She stressed the word normal. 'I'll get Joy Miller to do my stints in the shop with Aunty Daisy.'

Joy Miller was a young mother who had been Rosemerryn's daily cleaning woman until Laura had taken over her job, unpaid, so she could spend more time with Vicki. She employed Joy on a part-time basis in her place in the shop.

With that sorted out, Laura left hastily.

Spencer lit a cigarette. For Vicki's sake he usually smoked outside but he was troubled. He couldn't get the look on Laura's face as she had talked about the Macarthur baby out of his mind. It was plain she desperately wanted a child of her own. If he didn't get things worked out with her quickly, there was the danger she might marry someone else to have a baby.

He got up and paced the floor restlessly then looked out of the window over the sink. He was shaken to see Laura hadn't gone yet but was involved in a close conversation out in the yard with Ince. She seemed to like Ince more than she did him, that was even more obvious after the way she'd recoiled from him. Ince might only earn a farm labourer's meagre wage but with his dark good looks, black curly hair, his hard-working and gentle character he would make any woman a good husband. Laura probably realised that. One reason Spencer had been dragging his heels over Laura was the difference in their finances. Laura was well placed, while the farm was just breaking even and Spencer had no spare money to build the much-needed new outbuildings and maintain his all-important tractor. Ince had fallen in love with Laura soon after she had come to Kilgarthen, he probably still was in love with her. He might not be too proud to take a wife who was so much better off than he was.

Spencer screwed up his face in anguish and banged his good hand on the draining board. Suddenly he wanted Laura Jennings with all his being and he realised he was running a great risk of losing her.

Chapter 3

Harry Lean alighted from a first-class carriage at Liskeard railway station and, humming softly to himself, made his way towards his red and black Vauxhall sedan. As he put the key in the door he felt a light tap on his shoulder.

'I wonder if you can help me?'

It was a young female voice, with a distinctly cut-glass accent. Harry turned round with a smile stretching the full extent of his wide mouth and he wasn't disappointed. The woman smiling up at him was exceedingly well-dressed. The day had begun with a hard frost and she was wearing a fur stole. She was muskily perfumed, expertly made up if a trifle overdone, not a natural beauty, but a stunning redhead. She gleamed with natural confidence.

'I promise I'll do my utmost,' Harry replied smoothly, raising an inquiring eyebrow. 'Miss…?'

'Celeste Cunningham,' she answered, making her voice throb while looking him up and down with a twinkle in her green-flecked eyes. She smoothed her white-gloved hands over the narrow hips of her long flowing skirt. 'And you're right, it is miss.' She put on an appealing frown and glanced about helplessly. 'There doesn't seem to be a taxicab about and I'm making my way to a place called Kilgarthen. It's a little village apparently, on Bodmin Moor. Would you have any idea where it is? Mr…?'

Harry put out his hand. 'Harry Lean,' he drawled, thinking the gods were decidedly on his side this morning to throw him this divine piece of fluff. 'Not only do I know where Kilgarthen is, Miss Cunningham, but I also just happen to live there. Allow me to give you a lift.'

Celeste placed her hand in his and summed him up: an animal of practised charm, about thirty years old, carelessly handsome, dark active eyes, an interesting three-dimensional fleshy circle in the centre of a strong chin, almost certainly an utter beast where women were concerned – but she could handle his type. Mmmm, perhaps the village wasn't going to be a boring little backwater after all.

'I'm delighted to find Cornwall can so quickly offer such a gallant gentleman. The guard is collecting my suitcases.' She returned Harry's firm clasp before gently withdrawing her hand.

Harry saw her into the front passenger seat of his car then supervised the loading of her luggage into the boot. There was a lot of it. She had slipped off her stole and was checking her make-up in a silver compact when he got in beside her.

'There's no need. You look immaculate,' he said, lingering over her full cherry-red lips.

'Thank you. I must say I'm surprised at how well I've survived the long overnight journey down from London. Where have you travelled from, Harry?'

Harry was pleased with her familiarity but his face showed disappointment. 'The same as you, Celeste. What a pity we didn't meet on the train.' He was sure she would have made a much more enjoyable companion than the mousy little woman who had got off at Plymouth; he'd had to work hard to encourage her into his sleeper and the result had been far from satisfying.

'My sentiments exactly,' Celeste returned, eyeing him in the compact mirror.

They pulled out of the railway station and were soon bowling along narrow country lanes.

Harry glanced and smiled often at his delightful companion. She gave him a perky smile. 'I'm down here making a surprise visit to a friend.'

'Don't tell me,' he said, grinning, as he swerved expertly to avoid them ending up in a ditch. 'Mrs Laura Jennings. I can't quite imagine you visiting anyone else.'

Wisely hanging on to a strap above the car door, Celeste replied, 'Unless it was someone like you, eh, Harry?'

23

'Absolutely.'

Celeste just managed to read the typically Cornish names of the little picturesque villages and hamlets they passed through. She caught glimpses of cattle and sheep in the fields. She gazed at the hedgerows, some high, some low, some made of earth, foliage and trees, others made of stone in curious slanting patterns. She tried to get a good look at the patches of pale yellow flowers adorning them as they flashed by. Spring came late to the upland but there were whispers of it to be seen in the bright yellow of celandines, the rich purple of wild violets.

'These must be the primroses Laura's been enthusing about in her letters. She says they smell divine. They're very pretty. Everything's so green at this time of the year. I spend so much time in the city I seldom see this much greenery.'

They were now looking at a wild stretch of country, wide open spaces divided by straggling stone walls, softened in places by stretches of gorse, fern and brambles. 'Oh, look, that's the moor, isn't it? It's breathtaking. I can see a big hill up ahead. Laura tells me the moor you live on is the most beautiful place on earth.'

'It is,' Harry said, and he was sincere about that. He scanned the stony horizons and pointed to where a number of men could be seen working and a deep depression had been cut out of the moor. 'That's a china clay works. It's ugly but gives some necessary work locally.' As the journey progressed he pointed up ahead. 'That big hill you referred to is called a tor, in this case Hawk's Tor on Hawkstor Downs. It overlooks Kilgarthen. You must come riding with me, Celeste. I can show you some riveting sights.'

Celeste eyed him sideways under mascaraed lashes. 'I'm sure you can, Harry, I'll look forward to it. Laura will be surprised to see me turn up on her doorstep, she has absolutely no idea I'm coming down.'

'Any special reason why you have, Celeste?'

'Oh, you know, just a spot of chronic boredom. I simply fancied a change.'

'I'm glad you did. It's unlikely you'll find Laura home at the moment. She'll almost certainly be at Rosemerryn Farm. I'll take you there. I'm going there myself actually before I go home. The farmer happens to be my brother-in-law and my mother telephoned me last night to say he's had a minor accident. Laura adores his little girl, my niece, Vicki, and she'll be helping out there. I had a little more business in London but left it to come down and help out myself.'

'You're lucky to have close family ties,' Celeste said. She looked out of the window to let her envy wash over and leave her. 'I know about the little girl. She's six years old and lost her mother at birth. I take it that was your sister?'

'That's right. Natalie had a kidney problem. It was terribly sad. Vicki's father blamed my mother for not telling him about Natalie's weakness and it's only because of Laura that he came round at the beginning of last year and allowed my mother and me to have anything to do with Vicki. I'm keen to keep a good relationship with Vicki, make up for the lost years.'

Celeste sifted through the names mentioned in Laura's letters. 'Spencer Jeffries, that must be the name of your brother-in-law. He sounds like an absolute rotter to me.'

'We loathe each other,' Harry said, meeting Celeste's flashing eyes.

Celeste pulled off her deep-brimmed hat and let her hair curl round her neck. 'Let's not talk about him. Tell me something about yourself, Harry.'

He opened his mouth to oblige but instead out came the words, 'Oh, damn!'

'What is it?' Celeste asked, wondering if she should get alarmed. Harry looked so angry.

'From a twist further up the lane I saw a pony and jingle heading this way. It's being driven by the village madwoman, known as Ma Noon. I'm sick and tired of having to pull in for that fat old crow when I'm driving to and from home.'

Celeste patted his arm and tutted. 'More haste, less speed, Harry.' Then she looked shamelessly into his dark eyes. 'You'll get everywhere you want to go in the end, you know.'

Laura was upstairs in the farmhouse, collecting bed linen for the copper, mulling over the best way to ask Spencer if he would like to come to her cottage for supper with her; she had decided that would be the best way to get closer to him and try to find out what was truly on his mind concerning their future. After what he had said in front of Vicki and Ince last night, things had to be brought to a head. Nervous as she was about making a permanent relationship with Spencer, the present arrangement was no longer satisfactory. If it didn't change it might have to end and the thought of seeing less of Vicki saddened her.

Looking out of the landing window with a bundle of sheets in her hands, she wasn't surprised to see Harry's car jolting over the granite cobblestones, chickens and ducks scuttling out of its way. Felicity Lean had said yesterday she would be informing her son about Spencer's accident. However, a lady was getting out of the sedan and this made Laura run downstairs and dump the washing out of the way in the back kitchen.

'What is it?' Vicki asked, looking up from the few things on the kitchen table Laura was allowing her to dust.

'It's your Uncle Harry, he's just pulled up in the yard in his car with a lady.'

'It must be Grandma,' Vicki said, using the tone grown-ups employed to explain difficult things to her.

'No, it isn't her.' Laura held out her hand. 'Come with me and meet them.'

Everyone entered the farmhouse by the back door and Laura and Vicki were stationed there as Harry approached with the mysterious lady who was holding on to his arm and picking her way carefully over the cobblestones to avoid the mud. Laura frowned, puzzled. Then letting go of Vicki's hand she ran to the newcomer.

'Celeste! Good heavens! It's you of all people. What are you doing here?'

Harry picked Vicki up and kissed her and they laughed as the two friends hugged one another excitedly.

'Well, what are you doing here, Celeste?' Laura demanded again, looking her friend in the face. 'You look wonderful, as usual.'

26

'Of course I do, darling. As I was telling Harry, whom I was fortunate enough to meet at the railway station and who offered me a lift, I was bored and I decided to look up my dear friend tucked away at the bottom of the country. And I must say you look pretty good yourself, but darling, these clothes,' she fingered Laura's apron and plain blouse disdainfully. 'You wouldn't have been seen dead wearing something like this eighteen months ago.'

'I've changed a lot since then, Celeste. I've got a new life now and I've never been happier. Come and meet Vicki.'

Celeste regarded Vicki in Harry's arms critically for some moments. 'I agree with you, Laura. She's absolutely beautiful, just like you said in your letters.' Then, as if losing interest in the child, she looked around. The low farm buildings lay in a natural dip of the moor and were almost completely circled by small fields which had seen the plough or on which cattle were grazing. A few leafless trees sheltered the buildings, oak, sycamore, ash, all aslant, having lost the fight to stand upright against the prevailing east wind and winter gales. She turned her nose up in distaste at her immediate surroundings. 'So this is Rosemerryn Farm where you spend so much of your time. It's just what I expected, muddy everywhere, heaped with junk and it smells appalling.'

Laura grinned resignedly. She wouldn't expect someone like Celeste to appreciate it but she had grown to love all the familiar sights of the farm, the crumbling outbuildings, hayricks, spare granite gateposts and animal troughs, the Ferguson tractor, ploughs and rollers, the old well which had provided the farm with all its drinking and washing supply before water was piped into the house. The kitchen garden where she cut and dug up vegetables to cook for the household. She loved every patch of randomly sprouting weed and nettle, even the endless black mud that got everywhere, some of which she carried away with her on every visit.

'I don't like her, Uncle Harry,' Vicki whispered in his ear.

Harry chuckled. 'Never mind, poppit. Let's go inside and make Miss Cunningham a cup of tea, then Uncle Harry will show you what he's brought you back from London.'

'Show me now, please,' Vicki squealed in delight as they disappeared into the house.

Celeste drew Laura's attention from them. 'Delightful she may be but there's got to be more than just that little girl keeping you down here, Laura Farraday,' Celeste asserted, calling Laura by her maiden name and using the silly adolescent voice they'd invented for themselves at boarding school. She clutched Laura's arm. 'So where is he?'

'Why has there got to be a man involved, Celeste?'

'When isn't there, darling?'

Barney came dashing towards them and Celeste shrieked and gathered in her skirt, afraid the dog would jump up and muddy her. Laura pushed Celeste protectively behind her.

'Spencer! Where are you? Come and call Barney off this instant. Stay behind me, Celeste. I can't get this dog to do a thing I say. Spencer!'

Spencer was in the cows' shippen, working one-handedly. He had let out the water from the granite trough that kept the evening milk chums cool, tidied away the udder buckets, pails and milking stools and was putting dippers of cowcake into the feeding troughs. It wouldn't be needed until the evening but he was doing as many small clean jobs as he could, plus it was dark and quiet in here which gave him the chance to think straight.

He intended to ask Laura to have a drink with him at the village pub tonight, just the two of them, an open declaration to the village that they were courting. She must be wondering what would come next after his sudden promise to Vicki last night and, strangely for him, a deeply private man, inclined to keep his own company, he didn't feel particularly shy about asking her to marry him and setting a date; they were halfway there already. His thoughts drifted over her attributes. She was as good as a mother to Vicki, the one thing at Vicki's age that she needed most. She was pleasant, although she wasn't afraid to speak her mind and he had found himself at the sharp end of her tongue more than once. Today, however, she had been very kind to him, fussing over him because of his injury and making him feel special. He liked that very much.

It was her physical attributes he was mainly attracted to. She was blonde and beautiful, tall, shapely and graceful, and owned the same natural sophistication his late wife had possessed. He had not missed the special intimacy of husband and wife all that much, not until soon after he'd met Laura. Now it bothered him and he wanted Laura with an urgency that unnerved him at times.

He heard Laura shouting to him to call Barney off.

'All right, I'm coming,' he shouted back, grinning mischievously. One of these days he must train Barney to stop tormenting her.

He wasn't pleased to see the female stranger who looked as out of place in a farmyard as full evening dress would in the village pub.

'You only have to order him away from you, Laura,' he said grudgingly, scowling at Celeste who was cowering behind Laura while Barney barked and jumped about in front of them.

'Barney, down, boy! Off!' The scruffy Border collie gave a parting yap and raced away.

'Who's this?' Spencer asked ungraciously.

Celeste emerged from behind Laura with her white-gloved hand extended, a heavy gold charm bracelet chinking on her wrist. 'I'm one of Laura's old school friends actually, Mr Jeffries. My name's Celeste Cunningham. I've just met your darling little daughter.'

Spencer raised his eyes to the heavens as he shook hands with her and Laura knew he didn't approve of her friend's name, her voice, her clothes, or her being here.

'Harry's gone inside to make tea,' Laura said before he could make a biting remark. 'Shall we all go in? Celeste's come down to visit me.'

'Obviously,' Spencer grunted, leading the way to the kitchen. He was fuming. There would be no cosy drink for two at the Tremewan Arms tonight.

Celeste held Laura back from following him. 'You sly little cow, Laura. Now I can see exactly why you stayed down here after you'd buried Bill's body. First I meet the tall, dark, handsome, if somewhat sleazy, Harry Lean and now your very own fair-haired hunk. I'd never have thought to find two gorgeous men in such close proximity. What's he like in bed?'

Laura shook her head ruefully at her friend's question and replied patiently, 'I haven't been to bed with Spencer.'

'You haven't? Why ever not? Are you half dead or something? What about Harry?'

'Oh, Celeste, you know I wouldn't dream of going with an out-and-out womaniser like Harry.'

'You know me,' Celeste giggled, 'I can hardly wait.' She sighed heavily and put her arm round Laura's waist and Laura did the same to her as they moved indoors. 'I'm looking forward to some tea though, my throat's parched and these damned heels are killing me.'

Laura frowned down at her friend's strappy high-heeled shoes. 'You won't have to be such a slave to fashion down here, Celeste.'

'I suppose I ought to be grateful for that. I haven't packed my Hartnell or Dior creations, and judging by the way you are dressed, the local women wouldn't know what they were looking at if they saw one. Anyway, I intend to get up to a lot of new things while I'm here. I take it I can stay with you at this cosy little cottage of yours?'

'That goes without saying. Harry will have to go home and change before he can start work here. I'll ask him to drop us off at Little Cot on his way and get you settled in. We'll take Vicki with us.'

Celeste turned her head away and made a face. 'Wouldn't she be better staying here with Spencer?'

'One of the reasons I'm here is to look after Vicki.' Laura's ears picked up a familiar sound. 'Ah, I can hear Ince coming on the horse and cart. He must have smelled the teapot.'

'Ince? What a funny name. I presume he's some wrinkled-up local character.'

Laura turned her friend round, pointed and waved to Ince. 'If you weren't so vain and wore your glasses, Celeste, you'd see that Ince is about the same age as Harry.'

Moments later, when she got a clear view of the man in question, Celeste gasped. 'He's absolutely wizard.' Forgetting she was a lady she whistled through her teeth. 'Oh, I just love curly hair.'

'You won't get anywhere with him,' Laura said, much amused. 'You're not his type.'

'Don't you count on it, old girl. Before I leave Kilgarthen I'll have this Ince fellow eating out of my hand.'

'How come you sleep in a back bedroom?' Celeste asked Laura as she came down the dark oak staircase that led directly into the front room of Little Cot. She had been unpacking her things in the main bedroom. Fearing she would have to use a primitive convenience like the one at Rosemerryn Farm, which flushed but was located outside in the yard, she was greatly impressed with the modernisations installed by Laura's late husband, particularly the fully fitted bathroom.

'I prefer it,' Laura said, pouring Celeste a nightcap of brandy. 'Bill used to sleep in your room.'

Taking the drink to the settee, Celeste curled up on it, sombre now. 'Do you still hate his memory?'

'I don't have any strong feelings about him now,' Laura said truthfully, sitting in the rocking chair and looking completely comfortable; she was one of those women who seemed to fit in wherever she went. 'The five years I spent married to Bill were the worst of my life. I'm grateful they're over and now I just look forward.'

'Good for you. I'd hate to think you were wasting time moping about on account of that utter swine. I must say the cottage is very nice.' Celeste gazed up at the black beams of the low ceiling. Typical of the village dwellings, Little Cot had extremely thick walls to stave off the cold winds. It was painted in warm colours, and a tapestry-covered three-piece suite and several horse brasses gave it a rustic charm. 'As I remember, Bill didn't always have good taste.'

The women hadn't seen each other for nearly two years and Laura was eyeing her friend as much as she was her. 'You never met anyone who took your fancy enough to marry then, Celeste?'

'There was one man during the war, Laura. He was killed in action.' There was a slight hesitation. 'There's been nobody special since.'

'I'm sorry.'

31

Celeste shrugged her shoulders philosophically. 'You get over it. Would you ever consider marrying again? With a village full of desirable men, a woman like you must be spoilt for choice.'

Laura's thoughts were never far from her desire to be a mother. She smiled. 'I might.'

'What do you mean, you might?' Celeste's eyes shot wide open. 'I recognise that mysterious look. You've been keeping something from me. So there is a man in your life. Who?'

'Well, I'm sort of engaged to Spencer. We have this understanding, you see.'

'Mmmm, I'd have guessed it was either him or Ince. The way you and Ince reacted towards each other, I'd have put my money on him. You look so content in this new life of yours I'd say you'd be happy settling for a farm labourer. I suppose this understanding with Spencer came about because of Vicki.'

'That's right, it did, but I'm very fond of Spencer. He despised me when I first came to Kilgarthen. On the second day, curious about him because he didn't attend Bill's funeral, I went to Rosemerryn Farm. He saw me off and even threatened to set his dog on me.' Laura smiled. 'But we ended up as friends, I'm glad to say, and a little more.'

'Well, that didn't come across to me when we drank tea in his farmhouse. He sat there looking disgruntled all the time and hardly said a word. He scowled every time I said something and made me feel like a silly little schoolgirl.'

'Spencer's not as approachable as Ince or Harry, that's all,' Laura retorted, springing to his defence. 'He's a bit of a loner by nature.'

Sipping her brandy thoughtfully, Celeste passed the glass from hand to hand, watching Laura with beady eyes. Laura recognised the joyfully wicked look that always preceded a cheeky remark. 'I bet you haven't even kissed him.'

'I have.' Laura coloured.

'Really? Long and passionately?'

'Celeste!'

'Don't protest. I know you, Laura. You've never been forward with men. Goodness knows how you married when just a mere girl. I

32

bet that is the extent of your experience with men, as Bill Jennings' wife. You're rather shy in that department and you say Spencer Jeffries is unapproachable, so at that rate you'll never get married.' Celeste laughed salaciously. 'Want me to warm him up for you? He's very attractive. I'd be very pleased to.'

'Don't be silly, Celeste.' Laura had never quite come to grips with her friend's looseness where men were concerned. She was amused to think how astounded Celeste would be at how far her short romance with Ince had gone.

'Do you seriously mean to marry him, the fair-haired hunk of a farmer?'

With the amount of time she spent at Rosemerryn Farm, the villagers had been speculating on the possibility for some time. Ada Prisk had asked bluntly when the, wedding was going to take place. Faced with the question from someone not from Kilgarthen, Laura saw the answer clearly. 'Yes, I do.'

Celeste raised her thickly pencilled eyebrows. 'You do surprise me. Well, what are you going to do about it?'

Laura pursed her lips. 'I was going to invite him for a meal here tonight.'

Celeste pouted. 'What a great idea. A candlelit supper for two and I've put the kibosh on it. Never mind, darling. Do it tomorrow night instead. I'll make myself scarce, probably end up somewhere quiet and cosy with the delectable Harry Lean. Get Spencer to consume a couple of good bottles of wine, take him upstairs, get yourself pregnant to make sure he takes you to the altar, and there you are, the baby you've always wanted as well as a ready-made family.' Celeste was rolling about the settee with mirth.

Laura viewed her wryly. Life wasn't going to be dull while Celeste was around.

Chapter 4

Early next morning two women were heading towards Little Cot. Halfway up the steep hill of the village was the shop and sub-post office, and Daisy Tamblyn was hastening down from there to beat the village gossip-monger, Ada Prisk, who was speeding along from the bottom of the hill. Ada had the disadvantage of having to cross the road and Daisy beat her by two full strides.

'Who's Laura got in there with her, Mrs Tamblyn?' Ada barked. 'I saw her go in with Vicki and the most extraordinary-looking creature yesterday. Someone down from London, is it?'

'I've really no idea,' Daisy returned, deliberately sounding puzzled. 'Laura's been so busy since Spencer hurt his hand she hasn't had a spare moment to tell me anything.' Actually Laura had popped into the shop and told Daisy, who was Bill Jennings' aunt, all about Celeste Cunningham so Daisy wouldn't fear there was an intruder in Little Cot. Daisy could lie perfectly to Ada; most of the people of Kilgarthen had found it necessary to perfect the art.

The difference in appearance of the two women was striking. Ada was dominant and overbearing, her eyes constantly searching, like a hawk's on the lookout for a tasty morsel. If she could be compared to a hard-backed chair, Daisy was like a lumpy comfortable armchair. Daisy was round, kindly faced and good-natured.

Ada adjusted the black turban-style hat on her iron-grey bun and, being a lot taller than Daisy, lowered her thin face suspiciously towards her. 'I hope Laura isn't overdoing it. I've offered to help her out but she usually refuses me. If she's got a fancy visitor as well as all the work she does on Rosemerryn to tire her out, then this time I shall insist.' Ada prodded a flower basket hanging from the eaves. 'This could do with a good watering for a start. Spencer Jeffries is taking advantage of Laura's good nature, if you ask me. It's about time he did the honest thing by her.'

'I'm sure Laura will be very pleased to have your help, Mrs Prisk,' Daisy said, sidestepping the other woman's favourite topic of speculation although she herself had been wondering about the true nature of Laura and Spencer's relationship. She hoped they would settle down together.

She lifted the ancient latch, called out, 'Cooeee, it's only me, and Mrs Prisk is with me,' and stepped inside the cottage.

Ada followed on her heels. Laura had avoided the nosy old woman like the plague when she had first stayed in Kilgarthen, but Ada was welcome in her home any time now. When the village school had burned down and Laura had rescued Vicki and eight other small children, Laura had been overcome with smoke fumes as she'd tried to push the last boy out through the smashed window. Ada, standing on a dustbin, had grabbed her and with Spencer's timely help had saved her and the boy.

Laura appeared from the kitchen in her dressing gown. 'Good morning, Aunty Daisy, Ada. Come in here and I'll pour you both a cup of tea.'

The cottage door opened straight into the front room. Before moving into the kitchen, Ada swept her formidable black eyes round it, noting the frivolous bolero cardigan on the settee, the long silk scarf draped over the large ornament of a sleeping ginger cat behind the brass fender of the hearth. She wrinkled her nose at the gold cigarette case and matching lighter, the empty brandy glass on the table, and grunted at the strong smell of wanton perfume. More money than sense here!

'Still in bed, is she?' Ada asked, nose prying everywhere like a bloodhound on the scent as she took her seat at the small round kitchen table.

Laura smiled. 'You'll never catch Celeste up before nine o'clock, Ada.'

'Nine o'clock? Scandalous. 'Tis a bit early in the year for anyone to be taking a holiday. Ill, is she, this Celeste woman? Come down for some good country air?'

'No,' Laura answered patiently, toasting a slice of bread at the grid in the range. 'She's an old school friend of mine. We've always kept in touch. She came down here to look me up. You'll like her, Ada. She's very friendly.'

Ada looked delighted, a friendly stranger wouldn't be shy about answering questions. Before she could pump Laura further, Daisy took the opportunity to plunge in. 'I've got Rosemerryn's groceries all packed up—'

'I hear food's going up again,' Ada interrupted. 'And beer's coming down. It'll suit that lazy good-for-nothing Gerald Uren.'

Daisy looked vexed. She was getting fed up with the grumbles she received almost daily in the shop and didn't appreciate getting them elsewhere. She wasn't responsible for what the government did, any more than it was her fault that there were still chronic shortages following the war, and prices inevitably rose. Returning to the matter in hand, 'Bunty's offered to do some ironing for you, Laura.'

'I can do that,' Ada interjected. 'You poor maid, you'll be wearing yourself out running around after that man. How's his hand? Shouldn't take more than a week before it's healed up, surely. I saw Harry Lean driving his wretched noisy car through the village yesterday so Rosemerryn will have his help. Andrew Macarthur and Bert Miller's been helping out and Andrew Macarthur a new father too! He needs the time to spend with his wife and baby. If you ask me, it's Spencer who's enjoying a holiday.' Ada grunted disapprovingly then fixed a hard stare on Laura's face. 'Got a wife without a wedding ring, if you ask me.'

Feeling rather wicked, and taking the opportunity to shock Ada, Daisy remarked stoutly, 'But he isn't having all the wifely benefits, is he, Laura?'

Laura dropped her head and let her shoulder-length hair fall over her face to hide a huge grin.

'Of course he isn't!' Ada rose splendidly to the bait. 'Laura's not in the least bit like that. As her aunty, Daisy Tamblyn, I can't see how you could mention such a thing.'

Daisy drank from her cup and looked innocently over its rim. 'That's what I've just said, Mrs Prisk.'

Ada gave Daisy an indignant look then wagged a finger at Laura. 'Now, dear, I'm insisting today, what can I do to help you out?'

'I haven't done my brasses for ages,' Laura replied, thinking it a nice easy job the elderly woman could do sitting down. She knew it would delight Ada, she could ply Celeste with questions when she finally surfaced, and Celeste, used to having things done for her, would be grateful for the breakfast Ada would, no doubt, insist on making for her. 'You can do those for me if you like.'

Ada beamed. 'I'd be pleased to. That's what we're all put on earth for, to help one another.' She got up without a moment's delay, took off her coat, pulled out the apron she just happened to have in her bag, and went to a cupboard to find rags and the Brasso.

–

Tressa Macarthur leaned over from the bed to Guy's cradle and felt about gently on the baby's neck. Andrew sat up in bed beside her. 'He's all right, isn't he?'

'He's lovely and warm,' she replied, and Andrew could see her muscles relaxing. 'I can't stop myself from checking that he's still breathing.'

'Only natural, I suppose,' Andrew said, gathering her tenderly into his arms and kissing her soft brow. 'I can't get over how clever you are, darling, bringing him into the world.'

Tressa returned the kiss and cuddled in close. 'You had something to do with it too, Andrew.'

'We're both clever then, the cleverest, luckiest parents in the world. I don't want you returning to slogging it out on the farm again,' he added seriously. 'I won't forget how hard it was making you take it easy at the end of your pregnancy. Besides, it's good for Bert Miller to have a job since he lost his on the plantation. We'll need him for good now.'

'I couldn't bear to tear myself away from Guy at the moment but I'm looking forward to getting a breath of fresh air. Shouldn't hurt to put him out in his pram for a little while this morning. I can sit beside Dad and watch over him.'

'That's the ticket, darling. I don't want to go to the office worrying about you both. I hope Jacka's not overdoing things. I'd hate him to have another heart attack.'

'You needn't worry about Dad. He's so determined to watch Guy grow up he won't do anything silly.'

Guy made a strange little noise and Tressa sprang upright and bent over his cradle again. She put a hand to her pounding heart. 'It's all right, it was only a cough.'

Andrew flopped back on the pillows. 'Phew, you nearly scared the life out of me. Daisy Tamblyn was right when she congratulated me yesterday; she said apart from the love and joy they bring, children are a lifelong worry.'

—

Kilgarthen reckoned it had seen many a wondrous sight and happening but it had never boasted a visitor who moved in royal circles before today, if the gossip put about by Ada Prisk was correct. It wasn't true and Celeste didn't know what Ada had said about her when she took a morning stroll in the bracing air. She was wearing full make-up, a natty black hat, her fur stole and a tailored suit which accentuated her generous bosom, the tight skirt making her hips and bottom sway. Most of the people who greeted her nudged each other afterwards and declared that for a friend of royalty she seemed 'a bit common'.

Celeste tottered over the road on her unsuitable shoes and studied the sign of the pub, the Tremewan Arms. She decided that, like the rest of the large square granite building with its window boxes, small-paned windows and low porch, it had character. She wondered if Ince ever went into the pub. If she didn't receive an invitation to dinner from Harry Lean tonight she would spend the time here so

Laura could entertain Spencer alone. The door opened and a man and woman came out. He was broad in the body with a cheery, brown, whiskered face holding twinkling pale eyes, and she was small and neat and seemed full of energy. Both were middle-aged. The man stuck out a large paw.

'Mornin' to 'ee. I'm Mike Penhaligon and this is my wife, Pat. Pat was cleaning the windows and saw you coming up the hill from Little Cot. We reckon you must be a friend of Laura's. We always like to welcome newcomers. We're the landlord and landlady here.' He had a loud friendly voice.

'Pleased to meet you, Mr and Mrs Penhaligon,' Celeste said, smiling graciously. She was met with a good-natured protest and the couple insisted she call them by their first names. 'The people in the village are so friendly. I've met a few already. Laura went to Rosemerryn Farm very early this morning and a dear old lady made my breakfast.' She told the Penhaligons about her friendship with Laura and why she had come to Kilgarthen.

'We hope you enjoy your stay,' Pat said kindly and genuinely. She made a mental note to fetch her shopping bag and hurry to the shop to learn the gossip that Ada Prisk was no doubt spreading. 'You must call in soon. First drink will be free.'

'I'll look forward to it.'

Pat thought Celeste an unusual friend for Laura; they were so different, and she remarked so to her husband the moment Celeste turned and tripped back down the hill.

For a moment Celeste gazed at the ornate iron pump which provided most of the villagers with their only drinking water. Most people admired it; she thought it was archaic. The pump stood in front of an empty cottage. Next to an arch for rambling roses stood a 'For Sale' sign which bore the name H. Lean. Laura had told her that Harry was an estate agent. It was a pretty little building, seemed to be in good repair and like some of the other dwellings around, it was long, low, whitewashed and had a thatched roof. No doubt Harry would get a good commission on its sale, but Celeste couldn't understand how anyone could live in such an impossibly small house.

She headed for the telephone box. It was a nuisance, Laura not having a telephone in Little Cot.

A piercing wolf-whistle stopped Celeste in her tracks. She pursed her lips into a smile and looked about for the giver of the compliment. Every other householder seemed to have been on their doorstep a few moments ago but now there was no one to be seen. Celeste walked on.

There came another loud wolf-whistle. She kept walking. And another wolf-whistle.

'Nice bit o' leg.'

Celeste spun round. On her heels was a boy, frecklefaced, ginger-haired, his nose running, his clothes including a knitted slipover full of holes, worn-down boots lagged in mud. His pert features made him about ten years old and he was small for his age. He must have jumped out from behind the hedge. Screwing up his grubby face he stared blatantly into Celeste's eyes.

Lifting her chin and putting her head to the side, Celeste asked demurely, 'Was it you who whistled at me?'

''Es, you're a smasher.' His eyes dropped to the twin swells of her bosom. 'You've got nice everythin'.'

Most of Celeste's contemporaries would have swiped a hand across the boy's face and stormed off. Celeste was much amused by him. 'What's your name?'

Wiping his dripping nose with the heel of his hand, the boy gave her a semi-toothless grin; his large brown eyes appeared to be perma-nently wrinkled at the corners. 'Alfie Uren, that's me,' he replied, stabbing a dirty finger at his thin chest. 'I know who you are. Miss Celeste Cunnin'am. Everybody in the village are talkin' about you.' A look spread over the boy's face which Celeste could only describe later to Laura as 'definitely lecherous'.

She wanted to take her handkerchief out of her skirt pocket and wipe the mixture of black jam, mud, and blood from a deep scratch off his chin.

'I'm pleased to meet you, Alfie. I'm going to the telephone box to look for a number for a taxi. I couldn't possibly travel into Launceston or Bodmin on the bus.'

'Double four, two. That's the taxi number. That'll save 'ee lookin' for it in the box.'

'Thank you, Alfie,' Celeste smiled. Taking a scrap of paper and a tiny pencil out of her skirt pocket she wrote the number down.

'You b'lieve me?' Alfie gasped incredulously, scratching his unruly long hair.

'Of course. Why shouldn't I?'

Alfie pulled a face which made him look like a pug dog. 'Most people don't b'lieve nothin' my family say. They call us scruffy and gyppos. They say me old man's bone idle 'cos 'e don't work and me mum's disgustin' 'cos she's had six kids nearly one after the other. Me mum's half gypsy, she'll tell your fortune for you for a shillin'. She says there's a big black cloud hangin' over this village,' he ended dramatically.

'Well, I'm not narrow-minded like those people,' Celeste announced loudly, outraged on Alfie and his parents' behalf. 'You have no reason to lie to me about the telephone number, have you, Alfie?'

'Nah.' He looked away bashfully.

'Then I shall reward you with threepence for your trouble. I've only brought enough money for the telephone call. You can walk to Little Cot with me.' Celeste looked around as if she was hoping for a big audience. 'I don't mind you talking or walking with me. I'll just book a taxi first.'

'Thanks, miss,' Alfie said. When Celeste emerged from the telephone box he fell into step beside her, his hands stuffed in his pockets. 'I 'aven't 'ad no money for sweets for ages. We 'ardly use our sweet coupons. You gotta car?'

'Yes, I've got a Mercedes in London.'

Alfie was much impressed. He walked backwards just in front of Celeste so he could see her face. 'You ever been to car races?'

'I have, a few times.'

'Wow! Aeroplanes are me favourite. You ever been in an aeroplane, Miss Celeste?'

'Lots of times,' she smiled down on him.

'Wow! Lucky thing. Take me with you next time? I can't wait to grow up and do me national service. I'm goin' to join the RAF and fly all the time. If we 'ave another war I'm goin' to be a fighter pilot. The Yanks built an airfield on the moor during the war, at Davidstow. One of their aircraft crash-landed on Langstone Downs. No one was killed. I'd like to see the place where it 'acked up the moor. The Yanks were nitwits. Do you know why it was a stupid place to build an airfield there?'

'No,' Celeste replied, but she was sure the chatty boy was about to tell her all about it.

'Well, the moor is often covered in thick mist.' Alfie crossed his eyes in incredulity. 'You can't fly in mist. You'd think they would've *asked* someone! Did you know anyone who was a fighter pilot in the war?'

'I had a friend who was killed in the Battle of Britain.'

Alfie looked as if he would burst with pride. 'We ain't lived in the village long but I don't think they've 'ad anyone as famous as you 'ere before.'

'I'm not famous, Alfie.'

'You are t'me,' the boy stressed, carrying on with his precarious backwards walk. 'Can't wait t'tell me brothers.'

'How many brothers have you got, Alfie?' Celeste asked. She had enjoyed listening to Alfie's chatter all the way back to Little Cot and was holding her purse on the doorstep. She had kept Alfie outside but only because, it didn't seem fair to Laura to let such a mucky child inside her home.

He counted on his fingers. 'There's me first, then Colin, Graham, Maurice, Rodney and I've gotta baby sister called Emily.'

Celeste put a silver coin in the palm of his hand. 'Here's half a crown. That should be enough for sweets for all of you.'

'Wow! Thanks, Miss Celeste. You're a smasher, all right.'

As Alfie ran back down the hill, his arms spread out and flapping like an aeroplane's wings, making a loud engine noise, Celeste watched him thoughtfully.

Laura was taking her time pegging up one of Spencer's work shirts on the washing line. She was deep in thought. Now would be the ideal time to ask him to supper with her. Ince and Harry were muck-spreading in the fields and Vicki was playing with Joy Miller's six-year-old son Benjy in her playhouse in the huge garden. Harry's mother Felicity wasn't due to arrive until just before lunch.

Although Spencer had been unusually friendly and responsive since she had arrived at the farm this morning, Laura was nervous. The invitation would declare her hope of them permanently sealing their relationship but perhaps he was content with the way things were. She could be risking the comfortable familiarity they had attained since he had hurt his hand.

She took two steps in the direction of the outbuildings, was over-come with fear and doubt and instead made her way indoors. She realised she had carried the washing basket with her and dropped it on the back kitchen floor. Coward, she scolded herself. If she didn't arrange the supper date, Celeste would never let her hear the last of it. The terrible thought that Celeste would brazenly arrange it herself gave Laura the courage and determination she needed. She went outside in the bright spring sunshine and headed for the irregular sounds of an axe being wielded on dry wood.

'Damn and blast it!'

Laura very nearly gave way to cowardice again. Chopping wood with one hand wasn't an easy task and Spencer was losing his temper.

'Why don't you leave that for now?' she said soothingly.

He paused, holding a piece of half-split wood in his gashed hand. The axe had flown out of his other hand and was lying some three feet away. He looked down guiltily at the dirty bandage, dropped the wood and hid his hand behind his back. When he grinned at her sheepishly, Laura wanted to burst out laughing. Spencer brought so many moods out in her, sometimes she felt she was mothering him.

'Time for a mug of tea, is it?' he said to ward off a chastisement.

'Time you found yourself an easier job,' she couldn't resist pointing out. 'There's plenty of kindling chopped anyway.'

'Don't I know it.' Harry had chopped several bundles last night and it didn't please Spencer that his brother-in-law was so efficient about the farm. He retaliated, 'I hope you aren't overdoing it. You're not an unpaid slave here, you know.'

'I know that, Spencer. I'm happy doing what I do here for—'

'Vicki's sake,' he ended for her. He had heard that so often it ground on his nerves. 'Where's this tea then? Have I got to go inside for it?'

'What tea?' She was looking at him strangely. 'Spencer... I was wondering if...'

'Yes?' he said eagerly. He sensed she was going to say something out of the ordinary, hopefully about the same thing he had been steeling himself all morning to ask her.

This beating about the bush was prolonging the agony so Laura plunged straight in. 'Would you like to come to my cottage for supper with me tonight? Just me, I mean. Celeste won't be there. She'll be going out.'

He could hardly believe his luck. Her invitation gave him that last little bit of boldness he needed and he blurted out, 'Laura, I was about to ask you out for a meal myself.' Bright colour spread all the way up his neck and face and he went on with a little tremor in his voice, 'Look, why don't we race on a bit, put an end to our understanding and the villagers' expectations and get married?'

'Spencer!' Laura dashed her hands to her face and laughed like a young girl asked out for the first time. 'I – I thought it was going to be so difficult...'

He was laughing too. 'I've gone nearly out of my mind rehearsing what I would say to you. So that's settled then?'

'Yes... I... yes.'

He was still smiling but he ran his hand through his hair uncertainly. 'There is one thing you ought to think about before you're absolutely sure.'

'What's that?'

'Life's going to be rather basic after what you're used to. No electricity or proper bathroom. You might not find it very comfortable here, specially in the winter. I – I thought it was only fair to point it out.' Spencer was genuinely worried about this, he wanted to provide well for Laura but couldn't afford to make modernisations to Rose-merryn.

Celeste had pointed out the same things to Laura, asking how she would cope without her modern conveniences if she ever married Spencer. Laura felt she could put up with any circumstances to be Vicki's stepmother, and she hoped Spencer would allow her to spend some money on the house after they had settled down.

'I don't think I'll find it a problem,' she said confidently. 'What do we do now? Tell Vicki and the others, I suppose.'

'And go down into the village to see the vicar.'

'I want a quiet wedding, Spencer.'

'Of course. I mean so do I.'

There was still several feet of cobbled yard between them and neither had moved, although their eyes were locked tight. Both realised they had a lot of boundaries to cross.

Laura was aching inside. What should she do? It seemed daft to say something like, 'Well, fine, now we've settled that, I'll put the kettle on.'

Spencer could almost read her thoughts. He'd been bold once and it was up to him, on his home ground, to be so again. He strode up to Laura and took her hand. 'You won't regret it, Laura. Rosemerryn needs you.'

He was about to plant a kiss on her cheek and see what progressed from that when Vicki and Benjy came running up to them. Tears were streaming down Vicki's face and she grabbed Laura's skirt. 'Laura,' she piped up in her fiercest voice. 'Benjy said you don't really want to be my mummy. Tell him you do.'

Laura pulled her hand free from Spencer's and picked Vicki up in her arms and dried her tears. 'I do, darling. Your daddy and I have just been talking about it and I'm going to become your mummy very soon.'

Chapter 5

The following Sunday afternoon Ince Polkinghorne knocked on the shabby front door of Les Tremorrow's dreary small cottage. Ince was dressed in the clothes he'd worn to chapel but he carried a bundle of work clothes and his boots. He had been careful about the time of day he'd come to the smallholding. The Methodist minister, the Reverend Brian Endean, had told him Les's back was worse, but although he might be grateful for some help he couldn't abide people calling on him during mealtimes.

Receiving no answer, Ince knocked again, louder. There was a cough and a long complaining grunt, a shuffle of heavy feet.

'Who is it? What do 'ee want?'

'It's Ince Polkinghorne, Mr Tremorrow. I heard at chapel this morning that your back is worse. I thought you might be glad of a hand about the place. I've brought my work clothes with me.'

After several moments the door was opened cautiously. Les Tremorrow peeped out through the crack he'd made. He looked as if he had been woken from a long slumber. Poking out thin ragged lips between a stubbly unshaven face, he regarded Ince with his habitual expression, hostile suspicion.

'I hope the Reverend Endean didn't blab out my business to all and sundry.'

'No, Mr Tremorrow. He mentioned your name in his prayers and I asked him quietly how you were. He only spoke to me about you.'

'I should think so, 'n' all.' Les was wearing a pair of very old flannel trousers over a striped nightshirt, his loose braces hanging down to his knees. Slippers with holes in the toes were on his feet. A small humpbacked man with scaly skin, a squashed red nose and shrewish eyes in deep sockets, he had his greasy green and grey flat cap on.

Gazing up at Ince, he looked as if he was counting. 'Well, as it happens I could do with a strong young back and arms like yours, boy. I've tended to my goats and pigs, I've never neglected them. But there's ground in want of teeling and weeding, the lawn needs mowing, paths need weeding and you can draw some water for the house and animals. The timber on the goathouse needs creosoting and the galvanise tarring. You'll find all you need in the tool shed. Knock on the door when you've finished and I'll give 'ee a mug of tea and slice of saffron cake.'

Ince wasn't concerned about his small reward, his offer of help wasn't based on what he could gain, but he didn't like the door suddenly being shut firmly in his face. Few people would offer to help Les Tremorrow. He was too grouchy and inclined to find fault with men and was downright rude to women; both sexes complained that he was smelly. But the main reason that most people wouldn't come anywhere near Carrick Cross was because they were too scared.

Carrick Cross was said to be haunted, not least by Tholly Tremorrow, Les's grandfather, who the locals swore had 'ridden with the devil'. It was well off the beaten track, approached through the back of the village first by an impossibly narrow lane unsuitable for large traffic, then along the ancient moorland track that crossed it. Suicides were rumoured to have been buried where the two byways crossed. The smallholding was situated half a mile along the track, out of sight in a small natural basin, and was completely surrounded by a high granite stone wall to offset the extremes of the weather. The air was so clear here that the walls were covered with numerous species of mosses and fungi but Ince could imagine this place bleak and isolated in the winter snows. One side looked up to the remains of a small nameless quoit, an ancient burial chamber whose huge slabs of stone had fallen and shifted from their table-shaped position aeons ago. Hawk's Tor reared up on the horizon and seemed to throw a dark shadow over the smallholding. Some thirty years ago, an unwary walker who had got lost in the mist on Hawkstor Downs had been found dead just outside the boundary wall, his arms stretched out as if he was pleading for help, his face apparently frozen in horror. Ince put the stories down to wild fancies – in the daytime.

He went to the tool shed, which was knocked up from scraps of wood and galvanised sheeting long turned rusty, and changed his clothes and pulled on his boots. He flexed his muscular arms and looked about for tools. They were scarce and ill kept. It was just as well he had been well fed by one of Laura's succulent roast lamb dinners if he was to get much work done with the rusted, battered and broken tools at his disposal.

The shed door was suddenly thrust open and a shaft of strong sunlight streamed in.

'Is it true your boss is marrying that fancy London woman in the village?' Les asked, squinting at Ince and reminding him of a peculiarly ugly toad he had come across sitting imperially on a granite rock in a stream yesterday.

'Yes, Mr Tremorrow, Spencer is marrying Laura Jennings,' Ince replied, looking busy so as to ward off early criticism of his efforts.

'When?'

'The first Saturday in May, the seventh,' Ince said, picking up a half-moon spade that had a quarter of its handle snapped off, and rubbing dried earth off the blade.

'Don't make a mess of my shed!' Les snapped, making his bushy white eyebrows leap together. 'Take it outside and do that. Bit sudden, isn't it? Is it a shotgun wedding?'

'No, nothing like that,' Ince answered, remembering the remarks of some of the Methodist congregation that it was a wonder the crotchety old man with his nasty unforgiving tongue had the nerve to set foot inside the chapel. 'They've been engaged for a long time.'

'Have they?' Les returned, doubt in his croaky voice. 'Well, 'tis news to me. Get on with your work then, or it'll be time for you to leave for the evening service and you won't have anything done.'

Les shuffled out of the shed and Ince shook his head and reminded himself of the Bible passages that exhorted a believer to love his neighbour, whatever he was like.

48

Apart from the lack of good usable tools, there was no oil or rags Ince could use to clean them and nothing to mend them with. He was forced to 'mow' the small lawn of coarse field grass with a pair of wobbly hand shears of which the screw that held the blades together needed tightening every few cuts. The ground round the vegetable crops, which Les supplied to a small market trader, hadn't been tended to for weeks and was hard and unyielding.

The pulley rope in the well broke and the dented bucket went hurtling down into the watery depths. Ince had to search about for a long nail and fashion it into a hook then let it down on the knotted rope to retrieve the bucket by its handle. It took the better part of half an hour and then Ince found there were small holes in the bottom of the bucket and he lost a lot of water as he filled the animals' drinking troughs and the tall pitcher for household use that Les had dumped outside his door.

The only real work Les seemed to have managed in months was the husbandry of the two fat pink and grey pigs and the small healthy herd of white and brown goats. The pigsty was in reasonably good repair but the goathouse was the only building that was really well maintained, dry and draught-proof. It was set at a good distance from the back door of the house, in a sunny spot and sheltered from the north and the prevailing east wind. The four nanny goats and billy browsed or chewed the cud in their paddock as Ince painted their dwelling.

There were flowerbeds either side of the little path which led to the front door and against the walls. Ince recognised several typical 'cottage' species, hollyhocks, snapdragon, marigolds, wallflower, lily of the valley. There was also flowering quince and delphinium and sticks had been put in the soil for sweet peas. Some weeding had been done amongst the flowers.

Ince only paused from his dusty, sweaty labour to snatch gulps of cold water, but he knew that as he worked Les was watching him. At first he didn't mind, then it began to annoy him that he wasn't trusted. Time stretched into three interminable hours, and at the end of them Ince felt there were eyes on him wherever he went. When he

49

straightened his aching back and wiped the sweat from his brow, he felt the atmosphere had turned rather eerie. The black curly hairs on the back of his neck were standing up stiffly.

Telling himself not to be so silly and hoping Les would be satisfied with the amount of work he had finished and how he had done it, Ince washed his hands at the well and wiped them on his shirt front then knocked on the door for his promised mug of tea and slice of saffron cake.

'Wait there!' Les shouted to him.

And he did wait. For fifteen minutes, spending the time admiring his handiwork, the straight rows of black earth mounded round the potatoes, the other vegetables all neatly hoed and weeded, the flat lawn and the strong repairs he had done to the boundary wall.

The door was opened and Les plonked a small tin tray which had the remains of a Christmas scene painted on it on the dusty ground. Ince ducked his head under the low granite lintel and saw a shabby but clean and tidy kitchen. 'Here, and don't break the mug, it's one of my best ones.' Les peered up at Ince and gave him a twisted grin. 'Coming again, are 'ee?'

Ince picked up the mug and took a welcome sip of the strong tea to wet his parched throat. He tried to extract some manners out of the old man. 'Would you like me to, Mr Tremorrow?'

'Well, not if it's too much trouble,' Les grunted, making to close the door.

Ince was sure he was going to regret another act of Christian charity but he had been taught to help not only those he liked and got along with. 'I can come again one evening this week, after I've done my work on Rosemerryn.'

'See you on Tuesday evening then,' Les said, and he shut the door with a bang.

Ince would have banged his fist on the wall in sheer frustration but he felt Les was watching him.

Tressa had been enjoying the same warming sun that Ince had been toiling under, and she sighed at the hazy signs that spoke of a mist coming. Never mind, she was on her way back from the village having shown off her baby first to Daisy Tamblyn and then to Pat Penhaligon who had been Andrew's doting landlady until they'd married, and she would get home long before the mist blotted out everything.

Tressa preferred simple things but she was proud of the big carriage-built pram that Andrew had insisted she have and she was thinking there was plenty of room for a new baby in it next year with Guy sitting at the foot. She wanted lots of children. To fill Tregorlan Farm with noise and laughter. To raise strapping, hard-working sons and daughters to take the place of her two beloved older brothers who had been killed in the war.

She heard a horse clip-clopping towards her but instead of meeting someone she could proudly parade Guy to she was dismayed to see it was Harry Lean. As expected, rather than doffing his hat and carrying on his way, he jumped down and, leading the horse by its reins, walked along beside her, going back the way he had come.

'Had your baby then?' Harry said, a hint of humour in his voice.

'You can see for yourself, can't you?' Tressa replied shortly. She despised Harry Lean. He had tried many times to seduce her before her marriage and she was in no doubt that he was still after her. She didn't trust him in other ways either. Jacka had nearly died from a heart attack when despite his having paid off their mortgage interest arrears on the farm the bank had insisted they'd received no postal order and were seizing the farm. Tressa had the uneasy feeling that somehow Harry had been involved.

'Aren't you going to stop and show him to me?' Harry persisted.

He wasn't looking at the baby's head peeping above its covers but was eyeing Tressa intimately. She was wearing a simple button-through cotton dress, a cardigan resting on her shoulders. She had got her delectable willowy figure back and he was itching to get his hands on it, all of it. Her breasts were fuller due to her motherhood, making her all the more desirable. He was also longing to take Laura Jennings to his bed, but this young woman, who retained a virginal aura about her, was still top of his list for seduction. He had been angry when his plan to have the Daveys evicted had failed, thanks to Macarthur's intervention, and for a while he'd hoped to see the family, including Tressa, brought down to the gutter, but his desire for her had not deserted him for long. He wanted her so much it hurt him, and if he ever got the chance to take her, there were times he felt it would need a lot of restraint to stop himself from hurting her.

'Why should I?' Tressa challenged him, speeding up her steps.

'I thought you young mothers loved to show off your offspring. Can I take a look at him, please? Just a quick one. I'm most curious to see if he's turned out looking like you.'

'Oh, very well,' Tressa said curtly, thinking that the only way to get rid of this wretched man was to let him take a quick look at Guy.

She stopped walking and pushed the hood of the pram down, making sure the sun wasn't shining on the baby's face. Gently lifting the top cover, she exposed a third of Guy's little body.

Harry leaned over the pram and stared at the baby. To him all babies were ugly wrinkled creatures and this one looked much the same as any other. Very carefully he caressed the boy's cheek with a fingertip and was surprised at the downy softness there. Tressa gasped briefly in fear for her son. Harry took his hand away and looked into her eyes.

'I'd never hurt the child, Tressa. Don't forget I'm a doting uncle.' His attempt to impress her failed. Tressa was glaring at him and it angered Harry. He might be a bit of a cad but he wasn't evil.

He said huskily and somewhat dangerously, 'Macarthur's not done a bad job, but if you ever want a proper brat you know where to come.'

'Leave us alone, Harry Lean!' Tressa snarled, positioning herself protectively in front of the pram.

Harry clenched his fists to stop himself from clutching Tressa to him. It wouldn't be the first time he had grabbed her, he had even forced a long passionate kiss on her in the past, but this time he didn't trust himself to stop. 'Sometimes your purity makes me sick.'

Tressa shivered. 'I'm just not interested in you,' she pleaded. 'Can't you accept that?'

He gave her a dark, lingering look, then turning swiftly on his heel he mounted his horse and rode on to the village.

Shaken, but in no way defeated, Tressa went on her way. She couldn't tell Andrew what had happened. He had clashed with Harry before, over that forced kiss, and there would be one hell of a fight. She could tell Laura but she had enough on her mind making her wedding preparations. Guy stirred and Tressa smiled at him, trying to shake off a sudden feeling of foreboding. Harry was sexually immoral but nothing more than that had ever been proved against him. He wouldn't do anything to hurt her or Guy, surely.

–

Harry pulled up Charlie Boy at the church lych gate, opposite Little Cot. Laura would undoubtedly be at Rosemerryn and he had seen Celeste Cunningham at an upstairs cottage window as he'd ridden by a while ago. The minx had offered sex to him on a plate but, unusually for him, he had not taken up the offer yet. Now he felt his loins would burst if he didn't get relief.

He did not knock but walked straight inside. There was nobody about. Tossing off his hacking jacket and hat, he took the stairs three at a time and looked into the main bedroom. Wearing very little, Celeste was dozing on the bed. Harry went to her, sitting down close and running a hand over her silky thigh.

Celeste woke with a fright.

Harry put his hand over her mouth. 'It's all right. It's only me.'

'Good heavens, Harry,' she rasped between her painted lips when he took his hand away. 'You nearly gave me a heart attack.'

Harry glared at her for a second. 'I did read *you* right, didn't I?'

Celeste wound her arms round his neck. 'What took you so long?'

'Don't worry,' he swore, ruthlessly helping himself, his mind else-where. 'I won't be so slow again.'

Laura's hopes of a quiet wedding were lost the moment the villagers got wind of the occasion. Led by Daisy, aided and abetted by Ada, they took over completely. Daisy, thrilled as if Laura was her own daughter, booked the village hall for the reception and put herself in charge of the catering, begging ingredients from her customers and staying up all night to bake the wedding cake. She assured Laura that despite the harsh post-war shortages the villagers would club together and provide the guests, which looked more and more likely to be the whole village, with a feast. Ada was in charge of church cleaning and promised that it would be fit for a queen to get married in.

Spencer complained bitterly and Laura, who could see it was no use but to go along with all the kindly-meant intentions, had a difficult time stopping him from cancelling all the arrangements. A quiet ceremony with Vicki, Ince and the Leans, then a small celebration with a few more close friends at Rosemerryn was what he'd had in mind.

Celeste insisted Laura have a bridal outfit specially made and Vicki a bridesmaid's dress, and with clothing rationing ended she planned to dazzle the guests herself as matron-of-honour, and no amount of pleading from Laura would put her off.

After a mist-drenched start to the day, the sky cleared. Bluebells were sweeping through the woods and hedges, the may trees were budding, larks soared over the fragrantly sharp and fresh moor. Laura would have felt it a perfect day for her wedding but she was in the worst panic of her life. She looked every bit a lovely and radiant bride in a royal blue full-skirted suit with self-covered buttons and pointed sleeves, white silk–satin blouse, and white netted hat. Standing back from the curtains in Celeste's bedroom, watching the villagers gathering across the road in their best clothes, the odd new hat here and there, she was asking herself what on earth she thought she was doing.

From the moment of Spencer's proposal she had been swept along on a fast tide of excited arrangements. It was only now that she realised she had hardly spent a moment alone with Spencer. They had never got round to taking a quiet drink or cosy supper. They hadn't even touched each other or passed one single endearment, and tonight she was expected to sleep in his bed. This marriage could be nothing but a disaster. She was about to make the second biggest mistake of her life and enter another miserable marriage. If the villagers hadn't taken over the event and turned it into the biggest occasion Kilgarthen had witnessed since V-E Day, she would have seen the inadvisability of it, the stupidity of it, the madness of it.

'I expect Spencer's just as scared as you are,' Celeste said, floating into the room in a concoction of chiffon and tulle and noting Laura's harrowed face. 'Zip me up, will you, darling?' She chuckled. 'Lucky old you will have a man to do this for you after tonight.'

Laura couldn't move. She stared at her friend's smooth freckled back, her blue eyes looking three times their normal size. 'I – I can't go thr-through with it, Celeste.'

Celeste turned round and hastily snatched up a handkerchief to wipe away the tear running down Laura's burning cheek. 'It's only pre-wedding nerves, Laura. Pull yourself together. Oh, darling, we've let this get all out of hand for you, haven't we? Never mind, it'll soon be over and you can settle back and enjoy the reception. The villagers have been very kind. Think how they're going to love the spectacle of you, me and Vicki walking down the aisle. You're lucky they've gone to so much trouble, our old set would have done nothing like this.'

'Bugger the villagers!' Laura cried vehemently, using a rare swear word. 'It's my life we're talking about here, my future. I'm glad none of my family are coming down from London, they would have thought me mad!'

Taking her by the shoulders, Celeste gave Laura a hard shake. 'I've just seen Spencer going into the churchyard with Ince. He looked terribly nervous. Now if he can turn up with everything going on contrary to his nature and wishes, so can you. I'm going to pop downstairs and pour you a stiff brandy.'

'But Celeste,' Laura clung to her to stop her leaving the room, 'I've got to sleep with him tonight.'

'Is that all that's worrying you? You dolt, Laura. You don't have to do it tonight. Spencer will probably be understanding and I bet he's just as nervous about it as you are anyway. Just let things happen naturally in their own good time.' Celeste was getting flustered. 'Oh, do stop fussing, Laura. You're ruining your make-up.'

Laura dropped her hands and took the handkerchief from Celeste. Sniffing loudly, she dabbed her eyes and blew her nose. She was about to start crying and pleading again when there was a knock on the door.

Unaware of the drama, Daisy entered, her broad, kindly face abeam with happiness. 'Take a look at this,' she breathed, moving aside and pointing out of the room.

Celeste gasped in wonder and a strange peace settled on Laura's heart. Vicki was standing there. She was dressed from head to foot in beribboned pink satin and silk, a coronet of ivory wax flowers sitting on her white-gold hair, a pompom of camellias, anemones and columbine, which Laura had made herself, hanging delicately from her net-gloved fingers.

Here was the reason Laura was getting married today. 'Oh, Vicki.'

'Are you nearly ready, Laura?' Vicki said, proudly twirling round in tiny dancing steps to show off her dress. 'Andrew's come to give you away.'

'I only have to get my flowers.' Laura gave her a watery smile, picking up her bouquet. She turned away to make a quick repair to her make-up and Celeste exchanged an emotional look with Daisy.

Spencer was sitting on the front pew on the right-hand side of the large granite church, almost paralysed with numbness outside, the jitters within. He clutched Ince's arm as if it was a lifeline. 'H-have you got the r-ring?'

Ince produced it from his pocket. 'Safe and sound, stop worrying. It's a good job I remembered you had to have one and we had time to go to Launceston yesterday.'

'I hope it fits.'

Ince turned the gold band between his finger and thumb. 'It looks the right size to me.'

'How would you know?' Spencer snapped. Even at this time and in this place he was jealous of Ince and Laura's special closeness. That had better stop after today. 'Do I look all right?'

'Course you do. You've got a new suit.' Ince thought that in his nervousness, his fair hair cut and slicked back, Spencer looked much younger than his thirty-seven years, but owing to his present mood Ince kept the thought to himself.

'Do you think I'm doing the right thing?' Spencer whispered, tightening the grip on his friend's arm. Jealous of him or not, he valued Ince's honest opinion.

'You're the luckiest man in the world,' Ince replied, then fell quiet. To have a wife and family of his own was his burning desire. While he had not had any luck finding the right woman, his introspective friend was getting a second bite of the cherry. To Laura, too. Ince's torch for Laura didn't shine as brightly as when he'd fallen in love with her but he would have jumped at the chance to change places with Spencer right now.

Roslyn Farrow, the vicar's wife, and one of the new hat brigade, came up to them and whispered, 'The bride's at the door. When my husband gives you the signal, come up to the altar.'

The Reverend Kinsley Farrow was determined to give Laura and the villagers a wedding they would never forget. When the organist struck up the Wedding March, he followed the cross-bearer and the nine-strong choir up the aisle, a few feet in front of the bridal party. When he reached the altar he beckoned Spencer and Ince to come forward and this they did, Spencer on shaky legs.

Subdued exclamations of delight and a good deal of female sniffing into snowy white hankies accompanied Laura and Andrew as they proceeded up the aisle, followed by Vicki and then Celeste. Spencer thought Laura looked every bit as beautiful as Natalie had on their wedding day over seven years ago and he was bursting with pride to see Vicki looking like a fairy princess in her wake. With a tapping of heels on the cold stone floor, Celeste stepped forward elegantly and took Laura's bouquet.

Laura was struck, like Ince, at how young and vulnerable Spencer looked and it helped to soothe her taut nerves. Neither of them remembered singing the hymns, exchanging their vows or kneeling for the prayers, but it must have happened because they were being propelled along to the vestry to sign the register. Laura signed her old name away for the second time in her life, camera lights flashed and there were calls for the bridegroom to kiss the bride. Spencer obliged, pecking Laura on the cheek, and a cheer went up. Then it was time for them to walk down past all those people together, not two separate people any more but a bound and wedded couple.

Spencer smiled broadly for the photographs outside the church then relaxed and allowed himself to feel important on what was, after all, his special day. He proudly escorted Laura to the village hall and she held out her free hand to Vicki. Vicki skipped happily along as the new family led the way to the festivities.

'Why's Aunty Daisy crying?' Vicki asked, much puzzled.

'Women often cry at weddings,' Laura explained. 'They cry when they're happy as well as when they're sad.'

'That's silly,' Vicki snorted and she knew by the look on young Benjy Miller's face that he thought so too.

It hit Laura then that now she was Vicki's stepmother she had the right to explain many things to her, but how would her new husband, who was a very possessive father, react? She looked at Spencer. He smiled at her. She smiled back.

Five minutes into the reception Celeste got bored with being the matron-of-honour and the moment the speeches were over she made a beeline for Ince. The fact that he was deeply religious and unlikely to fall under her spell, that up until now he had only been quietly polite to her obvious overtures, added zest to the chase. He was standing in the corner by the piano, holding a glass of wine, talking to an old man. Celeste had already consumed a large quantity of champagne which had been supplied via Harry, but picking up a glass of lemonade she sauntered over to them.

'She makes a lovely bride,' Celeste purred, motioning to Laura. 'Things will be different for you now, Ince, with Laura living at the farm.'

'I shall enjoy her regular cooking,' Ince replied in a quiet voice. He found Celeste unsettling and wished she would talk to someone else. 'When it was just me and Spencer we sometimes didn't eat until the middle of the night.' He looked at the eager-faced old man with him. 'This is Johnny Prouse, by the way. Have you met him yet? He lives round the corner from Laura's cottage, in School Lane. Johnny, you probably know this is Miss Celeste Cunningham, a friend of Laura's.'

Celeste shook Johnny's hand. 'Ah, an old sailor, if I'm not mistaken. I've seen similar tattoos to the one on the back of your hand, Johnny.'

Johnny was delighted. 'Got this one done in the Pacific. Been all round the world, I have. I've seen the lady about,' he told Ince, 'but haven't had the chance to speak to her before.' He turned back to Celeste. 'I was just saying to Ince, if he ever feels he must leave the farm, what with a new wife being there, he's welcome to come and lodge with me. He used to backalong, until Spencer's first wife died. You staying in the village long, Miss Celeste?'

'For a little while longer, Johnny,' she said, sipping her lemonade then gazing into Ince's eyes. 'I haven't got any definite plans. I'm going to rent Laura's cottage.'

'She'm a lovely woman, is Laura,' Johnny rattled on. 'Been some good to the village.' Johnny told Celeste some of Laura's good deeds and ended with, 'She walked out with Ince for a while when she first come here, but it wasn't to be, was it, boy?'

Ince blushed blood-red. 'N-no. If you'll excuse me, I want to have a word with Mr Tremorrow.'

Celeste was happy to chat for a bit longer with Johnny but her eyes kept creeping over to Ince by the food table. It was stuffy in the hall and his black curly hair was plastered by moisture to the back of his neck. She knew she made him feel uncomfortable; my, but he was going to make the most scintillating of partners when he gave in to her. He was probably still a virgin. Her eyes narrowed. She'd had no idea that there'd ever been anything between him and Laura. There might have been a few chaste kisses but presumably it had been too soon for Laura after Bill's death for her to form a lasting relationship. It made Ince Polkinghorne all the more interesting.

Ince felt mightily relieved to have made his escape. Celeste was attractive, in a tarty sort of way, and seemed a pleasant, patient woman; she was happy to spend time chatting to the sick and elderly of the village. Her intentions for him stood out a mile but she was worlds apart from him, with her lah-de-dah voice, highly fashionable clothes and strong perfume. Certainly not wife material.

'I'll come over tomorrow afternoon then, Mr Tremorrow,' he said over Les's bent back as the old man, wearing his ill-fitting suit and flat cap, piled his plate high with food for the third time.

'Eh?' Les said, turning round when he'd finally claimed enough to eat. 'Oh, 'tis you, boy. Bring over a strong mallet with 'ee. I want a bit of fencing put up. And mind you don't come before dinnertime.'

Vicki had grown tired of being on her best behaviour and was sitting on her Uncle Harry's lap, twisting his silk tie and threatening to cut off his air supply.

'It's all settled then, Spencer?' Harry said earnestly to the bridegroom. 'Vicki's spending the night at Hawksmoor House with me and Mother?'

Sitting beside her son at the top table, Felicity Lean affectionately rubbed her granddaughter's back. 'You needn't worry, Spencer, we'll take good care of her. We'll take her to church and bring her home after lunch, when she's had a good ride with Harry.'

Felicity had a lump in her throat today. It had been heart-rending to watch her son-in-law marry another woman. A little while ago Vicki had called Laura 'Mummy', as if it was the most natural thing in the world. It had torn at Felicity's heart but she loved Laura in the same way as the other villagers and she was glad it was her who had taken Natalie's place rather than another. What had hurt the most was being the one to suggest to Spencer that he move Natalie's things out of his bedroom to make room for Laura's. Spencer was hurt too and hadn't been able to do it until three days ago when he had lovingly packed up Natalie's clothes and personal things and taken them to Hawksmoor

House. 'It was like saying goodbye to her all over again,' he had said with tears in his eyes. Felicity would keep them for Vicki for when she grew up.

'I'm not worried,' Spencer said, but he looked doubtful. 'It will feel strange, that's all.' Felicity had asked him many times in the sixteen months her relationship had been established as Vicki's grandmother if she could have Vicki to stay at Hawksmoor House and Spencer had always refused. He'd agreed this time because it would make his wedding night easier; Ince was discreetly staying the night at the pub. He ruffled Vicki's hair, dislodging the coronet. 'You be a good girl for Grandma and Uncle Harry, pipkin.'

'I want to play outside with Benjy,' Vicki said, seeing him through a window where he was tearing about the yard with a group of children. She pulled the headdress off her hair and plonked it on the table.

'A bit of fresh air will do her good,' Laura said, having observed several minutes ago that Vicki was looking hot and bothered.

'I'll take you, poppit,' Harry said, and he carried her outside.

On the other side of the double doors he met Tressa carrying Guy through from the kitchen where she had been feeding him. He looked so rapt with the niece he adored she dropped her guard and thought perhaps he wasn't such a bad man after all.

'I see we have a similar task,' she remarked, speaking first to Harry for the very first time.

'I suppose Vicki is too big to be carried really,' he replied.

Eager to be outside to join in what looked like a rough game of tag, Vicki wriggled out of his arms and ran off. 'Mind your dress, poppit,' he called after her, then pleased that he'd extracted a positive response from Tressa at last, he said with a big smile, 'Your baby's growing well. I would like to have seen Vicki at that age but Spencer kept her under wraps.'

Tressa moved Guy's weight to her other arm. 'They grow up so quickly.'

'Yes, they do,' Harry agreed, then he thought he would box clever and not linger over Tressa today. 'Well, if you'll excuse me I promised my mother I'd help with the clearing up.'

As he went back into the hall, Andrew came out. 'Was that man bothering you again, darling?' he asked, holding out his arms to take his son.

'No, not this time,' she was glad to tell him. 'If you put Guy in his pram, darling, I'll get Dad and Aunty Joan. 'Tis time we were getting home.'

Joy Miller, Laura's friend and stand-in assistant at the shop, shyly approached Laura as she stood looking over the wedding presents with Daisy.

'I know this is hardly the time to bring it up, Laura,' Joy said nervously, wringing her plump hands and running them down her shapeless floral dress. 'But you've been so busy and I haven't had the chance to ask you before, but I was wondering how things stood for me at the shop.'

'Oh, I'm sorry you've been kept in the dark, Joy,' Laura said, feeling guilty that her marriage plans had made her neglect Joy. 'Aunty Daisy and I discussed it days ago and I meant to speak to you about it. I want to be a full-time mother – and wife – and we'd like to offer you a permanent part-time job in the shop. The hours will be the same as they were when Spencer cut his hand and we'll raise your wages to a pound a week. Is that agreeable to you, Joy?'

The young mother was delighted. 'Oh, Laura, that will be wonderful. With Bert working regularly at Tregorlan, things have been getting better for us lately. This means we'll be able to make plans for the future and the children will never go without shoes again.'

Joy went off to tell Bert the good news, and Laura, sensing that Daisy was dying to talk about her wedding night, excused herself to thank her guests for the wedding presents.

The afternoon was drawing to a close and the women were washing the dishes and packing up the remaining food while the men folded and put away the trestle tables. Celeste baulked at doing anything domestic. She glanced out through the doors and saw Alfie, in his usual grubby and scruffy state, with his brothers, whooping like a Red Indian as he chased some other children round the yard. Celeste realised that none of Alfie's family had attended the wedding or reception. She knew this would be none of Laura's doing and angrily assumed some spiteful snobbish villagers had told them they couldn't come. Picking up a large plate she piled food onto it, cut off a huge slice of wedding cake and went outside.

'Hey, Alfie,' she shouted through the noisy game. 'Come here. I've got something for you.'

Alfie was inclined to ignore her at first, he was a master at tag and liked to show off his running prowess, but seeing the feast in the lady's hands he abandoned the game. His brothers, all replicas of him in varying sizes, except for the youngest who was blonde and quite beautiful, immediately trotted after him hoping for a share of the goodies.

Celeste held out the plate to them. What the Uren boys couldn't clutch in their grubby fists they stuffed into their pockets.

'Thanks, miss,' Alfie spluttered, food toppling out of his chomping jaws.

'Why didn't you and your family come to the wedding, Alfie?' Celeste asked, frowning in indignation on the Urens' behalf. 'It was an event for all the villagers.'

'Mrs Jennings saw Mother and asked us 'erself but we 'aven't got any good clo'es to wear,' Alfie replied matter-of-factly. 'This is smashin',' he declared, stuffing a whole sausage roll into his mouth. 'Anyway, Mother won't step foot inside a church, being half gypsy, and Dad says all the church wants is money out of people. He told the vicar to bugger off when he called the other day to see if we'd been baptised.'

'I see.' Celeste thought this was likely to be the only food the children had eaten today. She leapt back when she noticed something crawling about in at least two of the boys' greasy hair. She made up her mind to talk to the vicar about the Urens' circumstances. 'Run along back to your game, boys. Vicki and the others are waiting for you.'

Celeste reckoned playing with the rough and tumble Alfie was probably the best fun the village kids had ever had but she hoped he and his brothers wouldn't touch Vicki. She wondered if she ought to warn Laura of their uncleanliness. As Vicki's stepmother she had the right to know if another child was likely to infect the little girl with head lice.

Ince had come outside and had been watching Celeste for some time. 'That was a kind thing to do. I was about to bring some food out for the children myself.'

'Poor little things,' she said, looking wistfully at the youngest boy, aged about two years, toddling on bandy legs as he tried to join in the fun. 'I know they probably don't want pity but I feel sorry for them. During the war I did some voluntary work among some of the poorer families in London. You don't really expect to see kids living under the same conditions in the country.'

Ince saw Celeste in a new light. 'I wonder if something could be done for them.'

She took the opportunity to rest her hand on his arm. 'Will you leave it to me, Ince? I'm going to have a word with the vicar, perhaps your minister too. I'll let you know if we come up with any suggestions.'

Ince thought this over. He spent his spare time helping out at Carrick Cross since Spencer's hand had healed, and he was glad someone else wanted to do something for the Urens. And perhaps the young family would accept help more readily from someone not of the village. There was already tension between the family and some folk and Celeste had formed a friendship with Alfie.

'All right,' he said. 'I'll leave it to you.' He made to go, to get on with the evening milking at Rosemerryn so the newlyweds could be left alone.

Celeste held on to his arm. She liked the look of his hands, rough but sensitive. There was no whiff of aftershave about him and she liked his natural male smell. He stirred her vitals like few men could. 'That horrid little man is taking advantage of you.'

'I know.'

Amazed, Celeste raised her pencilled brown brows. 'And you let him get away with it?'

'It's the Christian thing to do,' he answered simply, then his dark features deepened. 'Would you like to come to chapel with me tomorrow?' That would either do her some good or stop her making advances to him.

Celeste raised her chin as if accepting the challenge. 'What time does the service start?'

'Eleven o'clock.'

'Mmmm, not too early. I might come along.'

That will make him think, thought Celeste as Ince walked away. There was a sharp tap on her shoulder.

'I saw what you did for those children,' Ada Prisk's deep voice boomed. 'You don't want to mix with the likes of they. No good will come out of that household. The children rarely attend school. They're always hiding away from the authorities or debt collectors. Their mother tells fortunes and consults the dead. She'll be drumming up evil spirits to stalk the village next. It was a sorry day when that lot moved in among us.'

Celeste controlled her temper only because it was Laura's wedding day. She stated through clenched teeth, 'I take your point that fortune-telling is not always desirable, Mrs Prisk, but although the family are poor and not particularly clean they are human beings with feelings. And doesn't God call us to love our neighbour, no matter who they are?'

Ada bristled but she had been put in her place. She scanned Celeste's frothy dress, her face working like a cow chewing the cud. 'You look very nice, although the dress is too young for you. You can come back in now – the clearing up's nearly done and Laura's preparing to leave.'

Laura and Spencer appeared at that moment and the guests piled out of the hall. Laura passed her flowers to Daisy, to be put on Bill Jennings' grave, a gesture for the villagers' sake. Felicity had already put Vicki's flowers on Natalie's grave.

Spencer lingered over kissing Vicki goodbye and watched avidly as the Leans led her to Harry's car. 'I hope he doesn't drive too fast,' he said to Laura, her eyes also rooted on Vicki's excited face peeping out from the back seat window. 'The man drives like a maniac.'

'I'm sure he'll be careful today,' Laura returned. She knew part of her wifely duties would often involve placating Spencer.

A floral decked trap with ribbons, boots and old tins trailing behind it was brought round for the bride and groom to travel home to the farm. The villagers had been disappointed the couple wouldn't be taking a honeymoon, but neither of them would leave Vicki, except for tonight.

To a chorus of cheers and good wishes, and a few wedding-night innuendos, the newlyweds were driven by Bert Miller to Rosemerryn.

A taxi pulled up. A stocky, bearded man in his early forties, wearing a checked, fleece-trimmed jacket got out and silently watched the villagers wave goodbye to the bride and groom.

—

Ince hadn't come into the farmhouse to bid them goodnight and at about seven o'clock Laura and Spencer were suddenly uncomfortably aware that they were totally alone. Until then they had pottered around the kitchen and had a cup of tea, talked about Vicki and pretended all was as it usually was.

'I hope Vicki's enjoying herself,' Spencer said for the umpteenth time. He was leaning against the sink, a place he often parked his bottom when thoughtful or nervous, his jacket and tie off, arms folded.

'It'll make a nice change for her,' Laura replied, coming up with yet a different reply to his worry. Her hat lay on the table, shoes in front of the hearth. She was sitting in Ince's chair beside the range; it would most likely become her chair now.

Every now and then Spencer cast his eyes over her. Vicki's happiness wasn't his main worry tonight. It was seven years since he'd spent the night with a woman. Laura had been married before. She knew what to expect. If he was a failure he couldn't bluff his way through it, promise things would be better the next time they tried. His eagerness was still there, it had built up to a fine pitch. Laura had endured an unhappy marriage, physical relations had probably ceased before Bill Jennings had died. Jennings might have been as cruel in bed as he had been in every other respect to her – she might not be interested in the physical side of marriage. On the other hand she wanted a baby so she would have to make love with him. But did she want to tonight? He

66

could kick himself for being so reserved. He would have discussed this delicate subject with her otherwise.

At half past nine Spencer put on his work coat and went outside to make his final check in the yard. He smoked a cigarette then, as always, ended up in the cows' shippen. He took comfort in the familiar sight of the eight milkers, their noses wet in the warm, steamy atmosphere, their feed bowls long empty. Spencer patted Luby's rump where she was tied up in the corner; he did it carefully for Luby was a kicker. He was thinking how easy life was for the cows, their days ruled by a comfortable routine, when he saw a note nailed to the wall with his name on it. It was from Ince.

'When you go back in, go into the sitting room.' What the hell was Ince playing at? This was hardly the time to be sending his mate cryptic messages.

Spencer swiped the note off the, nail, crumpled it into his pocket and stamped indoors. He banged the door of the kitchen and Laura looked at him curiously.

'Sorry,' he said shamefacedly.

'Do you want a cup of tea?'

'No, thank you.' He spread a smile across his face for Laura's benefit and surprised her by going into the sitting room.

'What's he up to?' she whispered to herself. Her nerves had never been so on edge. This was one of the worst evenings she had spent in all her life. She hoped she appeared relaxed but she just wanted the night to be over, for it to be past lunchtime the next day and for Vicki to be running from Harry's car to tell her all about the night she'd spent at Hawksmoor House. What was going to happen between now and then?

She could see Spencer was nervous too. If only they had spoken of the intimate side of married life, said a sentence or two; that would have been better than nothing. Perhaps she should go upstairs, undress and get into bed and leave it up to him to make a move – or not. Why had he gone into the other room?

In the sitting room, Spencer smiled to himself. Good old Ince. He must have known this was going to be a difficult time for them both and he had left a tray with a posy of flowers, glasses and a bottle of wine in the sitting room. Spencer could present this to Laura and it would say he wanted to be her lover as well as her husband without a single word passing his lips. If she shunned him, at least he would know where he stood. The subject would be brought out into the open and they could talk about it at some later date.

He carried the tray through to the kitchen. 'Would you like some, Laura?'

She was thrilled by his thoughtfulness. So he had a little romance in him after all? 'Yes please, Spencer.'

He lowered his face to hide his relief. So she wanted him too. He could slake his thirst for her and it would make their relationship so much easier.

They drank standing close, the occasional glance at each other gradually turning into a long searching look into each other's eyes.

'We did it then,' he said, tentatively reaching out for her hand. That sounded suggestive and he blushed. 'I mean, we got married.'

'Yes,' she smiled at his boyishness. 'You did really want to?'

'Oh, yes. Did you?'

'Yes.'

He held his breath, waiting for the inevitable addition of 'for Vicki's sake'.

But Laura had forgotten his daughter for a moment. Spencer's eyes had turned warm and smoky. He was moving closer to her and his eyes were continually travelling from hers to her lips. His hand was warm and rough, tightening round hers, and he was pulling her nearer to him. Now they were touching. She looked at his wide mouth. His lips parted slightly.

Spencer slid his arms round her waist. Laura placed her hands on his chest. He closed his eyes and let instinct take over.

Laura didn't want to think about what she was doing, only to concentrate on what he was doing to her. She shut her eyelids and the next moment his lips were brushing over hers. Her response was immediate and so intense it shocked her. It was a long time before he released her. She had never enjoyed a kiss so much before. Spencer's lips had been tender yet demanding, rough but somehow velvety, warm, moist, totally sensual.

'That was easier than I thought,' he whispered huskily into her hair.

'Yes,' Laura replied dreamily, her face pressed against his chest.

He gathered her in again, possessively, intimately. His mouth consumed hers, hungrily, exploring and feasting while he ran his hands knowingly all over her in light, lingering movements. Unused to such a frank and pleasurable exploitation of body, Laura was thrilled in all her most hidden places. She became so aroused she was forced to cling to him to stop herself rocking on her feet.

'Shall we take the wine upstairs?' he asked, nuzzling her neck with hot breath-laden kisses, leaving a delicious tingly wetness on her skin.

She couldn't trust herself to speak and nodded in reply, climbing the stairs as eagerly as he did.

The day before, Felicity had unpacked the small suitcase Laura had brought to the farm – just overnight things, Laura couldn't bring herself to move in all her belongings until after she had actually married Spencer – and she had put Laura's brush and comb and washbag on the dressing table, her dressing gown on a chair and nightdress on the bed. Except it wasn't the rather demure nightdress Laura had packed but a lacy figure-hugging creation with a plunging neckline – Celeste's devious work.

Laura didn't have time to hide the nightdress as Spencer put the wine down on the bedside table. He ran his hand down over it.

'Want me to wait outside for a few minutes?'

Laura laughed and looked deeply into his eyes. 'Why bother? What's that going to hide?' She couldn't believe she could be so brazen. She could have blamed it on the wine or on Celeste for exchanging her modest nightie for a flimsy one. But she knew it was Spencer himself, the total maleness of him, the scent of his heated skin, the assurance she felt that he was experienced and sensitive and enjoyed giving pleasure that was bringing out this forwardness in her.

He tapped the tray and came to her. 'Well, we'll finish the wine later then, much later.'

Chapter 7

'I still can't believe you're here, Bruce. When you got out of that taxi yesterday I'd never have guessed it was you if you hadn't spoken to me. I was flabbergasted. What a pity Laura and Spencer were driving off at the time. I'd like you to have met her. What can I get you for breakfast?'

Daisy Tamblyn hadn't seen her son, the middle one of her three children, for twenty-nine years. He hadn't changed much in appearance. He had always been a few pounds overweight, his complexion florid, and even at the age of fourteen when he'd left home he'd had nicotine-stained fingers. His fairish brown hair was closely cropped showing off his bull neck. There was still a hungry look in his hazel eyes; Bruce had never been satisfied with his life as a boy. He'd been the one most like her husband Sidney, jealous and sullen, deliberately causing squabbles with his sisters, but with his full, neatly-trimmed beard he reminded Daisy of her late father who'd been a quiet-natured man. The most notable difference was the aura of confidence about him and it was strange listening to the broad Canadian accent he had developed.

He was smoking his third cigarette since rising and she pushed the ashtray closer to him on the kitchen table. He was well dressed, casual this morning in immaculately creased trousers, a blue shirt with cufflinks, navy blue tie and sleeveless pullover. Daisy was so glad to see him, she had not slept a wink last night thinking about him and she couldn't tear herself away from him now.

Bruce Tamblyn basked under her proud scrutiny. 'I'll eat whatever the rationing allows me, Mother,' he said, using his deep gruff voice softly.

'Why have you grown a beard, Bruce?' Daisy prattled on, happily fetching eggs and bacon. Her son was welcome to her weekly ration. 'It spoils your good looks.'

A dark look crossed Bruce's face. He thrust out the wide span of his jaw and rubbed at the rough bristles there. 'I like it. I've been travelling about the last couple of years and found it easier not to shave. I can't match the thatch of the landlord of the pub though.' Bruce guffawed and slapped his knee. 'That was a great celebration we had last night. 'Twas a pity I missed young Billy's widow though. You wrote me she was a rare beauty when he married her. I guess I'll catch up with her at her new home.'

Daisy hadn't wanted to be dragged off to the pub last night. She'd wanted to stay in and talk to Bruce and catch up on the news of all those lost years. 'You received my letters then?' she muttered while cutting bread, unable to hide the hurt in her voice.

'I never was much of a letter writer,' he retorted moodily. 'Anyway, Carol used to write to you.' He changed the subject. 'I didn't live here long, don't suppose many of the villagers will remember me, except that nosy old Prisk woman. She had plenty to say to me yesterday. Wasn't there someone living next door you were friendly with?'

'Bunty Buzza,' Daisy said sadly, putting dollops of dripping into the frying pan. 'She died suddenly a few months ago. I've been quite lonely since, will be even more now that Laura's married and won't be working in the shop any more.'

Bruce looked rather pleased. 'What a shame. This place hasn't changed much since Granddad's day. Same Cornish range and dresser, and lino and mats on the floor, same old toffee tins on the mantelpiece. It even smells the same, of yeast buns and coal tar soap.' He got up from the table and took a photograph of a child off the wide windowsill.

'Is this Malcolm?'

Daisy's heart sank. 'So you haven't been in Canada for at least a year then? I thought not. Carol sent that to me. It was taken on his fourteenth birthday. She didn't mention that you'd parted. Well, son, did you leave her or did she kick you out?'

Daisy had never been close to her children, Bruce in particular. She was completely taken aback when he burst into tears and sobbed into his hands. 'She was unfaithful to me during the war, Mum. While I was away fighting, slogging it out in the desert, she was whoring round with every man left in town. When I was demobbed from the army I forgave her. I said we could start all over again. But she'd tasted the good life and I wasn't exciting enough for her.

'I came home early from the lumber yard one afternoon and found her in bed with a trucker. She encouraged him to beat me up. She screamed and shouted at me and said I was no good to her like that any more. I couldn't take it, Mum. The kids didn't want to know me. With me being away fighting for so long, Carol had let them run wild. They showed me no respect. I was all washed up, so I packed my bags and left. I wandered about Canada at first, then further afield, trying to get my life together, looking up army mates, taking a string of jobs, but I couldn't settle. Eventually I thought of you, Mum, and Cornwall and you living here in Kilgarthen. I liked it when we came to live with Gran and Granddad after the old man cleared off.'

Bruce ran out of breath and collapsed in the little armchair Daisy used at the fireside. He looked up appealingly at her through his tears. 'C-can I stay here with you, Mum? At least for a bit. I won't be a burden to you. I'll get a job and do my bit round the house, I promise.'

Daisy went to her son, moved by his plight, and placed a firm hand on his shoulder. 'You can stay as long as you like, Bruce. If I'd known what a hard time you were having of it I would have suggested it a long time ago.'

—

Laura carried a pot of tea to the breakfast table and checked that she had everything needed for three places.

Spencer came in, rolled up his sleeves and washed his hands. He stood behind her, wound his arms round her waist and whispered close to her ear, 'Thank you for last night... and this morning.'

'This morning' had actually been the middle of the night, when Laura had woken up and found herself facing Spencer. They had drifted off to sleep leaving the lantern on, and in its low light she had admired the top half of him, bare above the covers. She had seen him with his shirt off many times while working outside in the sunshine or washing at the kitchen sink. After a few cursory moments of curiosity, she had taken it for granted. Now she drank him in. His shoulders were broad and well set, the muscles there and on his chest, stomach and all the way down his arms were tight and work-formed. His chest was dusted with strong fair hair, the skin lightly tanned and smooth.

She touched his face, skimming her fingertips over his cheek and the firm contour of his chin, sliding them down his throat to his chest, letting her hand rise and fall with his breathing. She looked at his closed eyelids to see if he responded to her in his sleep. He woke up and, without a word, and unlike their first slow and measured coupling, they made love with urgency and passion, their bodies moving convulsively in perfect timing, becoming spent and released at the same exquisite moment.

They had lain awake. It wasn't worth going back to sleep, he would have to rise very soon and she wanted to be part of the farm's daily ritual of hard work and long hours from the first full day. Loving with Spencer had been different to her past experiences. Bill Jennings had been brutal on the first night, uncaring of how much it had hurt taking her virginity. He'd been the same every time he'd sought her bed. Marital relations had ceased, thank goodness, long before he'd died. Her next time, the one occasion she had made love with Ince, had been performed in a gentle, self-giving harmony. It had been too soon for her to form a lasting relationship and they had drifted apart, Ince being the one to bear the brunt of the hurt. And now she had given herself to Spencer, had positively encouraged it! Despite his long abstinence he had been sensitive, skilful, masterful, bringing her to her first real intense feeling of total fulfilment. She would seek that pleasure again.

Laura marvelled at how this most intimate of things had turned out for her. She had thought she might have given a wife's duty to Spencer, regularly and willingly, because he was an attractive man. They might even have developed a mutual enjoyment and understanding. She had not expected the physical side of their married life, on her part anyway, to be based on lust.

Now in the kitchen she giggled and pushed him gently away. 'Ince will be here in a moment.'

Spencer kissed her on the cheek before she moved away to the range. He watched her. She looked just right there, wearing an apron over the skirt and blouse of her bridal outfit and the slippers she kept under the sink next to the dustpan and brush.

'Pity you had to get up at four thirty the day after your wedding. I should have insisted you lie in for a couple more hours. I'm sorry I never asked you if you wanted a honeymoon but we didn't talk about anything much, did we?' Then he grinned, pushing out his chest, his hands in his pockets. He was in high spirits this morning. 'But we managed to make love all right. We should have got married ages ago.'

She turned and smiled at him. 'I was just thinking that.' She was also wondering how he felt about taking another woman into Natalie's bed but felt it wasn't the right time to ask him. Perhaps she never should. But she wanted everything to be out in the open between them; they should talk more.

'It will be good for Vicki to see us getting along so well, right from the start.'

'Yes, it will. I wonder how she slept at Felicity's. It will be lovely to have her back home.'

'Seems like she's been gone for ages.' Spencer would have tossed and turned all night worrying about his beloved daughter whom he loved more than his own life, but while he'd thought of her, other things had taken precedence in his mind for the first time since her birth. Laura lying next to him. The silky ivory smoothness of her skin as he'd touched her while she'd slept. Breathing in her feminine scent and subtle perfume. Wanting her again. He'd closed his eyes and his skin had leapt deliciously to feel her touching him. He had only been able to hold out for a moment…

Laura gazed at the array of photographs of the little girl at various ages that Spencer had put up on each wall. 'I've never spent the night here before but I'm missing her dreadfully.'

There was a tap on the door, it was opened slowly and Ince came in in his stockinged feet. He looked pink and embarrassed.

'You don't have to knock before coming in, Ince.' Spencer was aghast. 'For goodness sake, this is your home. You're my best friend.'

'Well, I just thought... Good morning, Laura.' Ince was feeling awkward. Spencer had done his share of the milking in a decidedly jaunty manner, had even cracked a joke, so evidently the wedding night had gone well. Ince had been worried about that. It hadn't been easy for Laura settling into the village and she had turned to him after a particularly harrowing time. When they had gone upstairs in Little Cot, it had been a natural progression of their romance. Her marrying Spencer had been more of an arrangement than anything else and last night could have gone badly. But Ince knew his friend was a very possessive man. What would Spencer say if he ever found out he and Laura had been lovers?

'Breakfast's all ready,' Laura said jovially to break the tension, but in these circumstances she found it hard to face Ince, similar thoughts to his now running through her mind.

The three sat round the table, and when Spencer realised his friend's and bride's embarrassment, he too felt discomposed. The food stuck in their throats, tea making a noisy follow-up journey.

Spencer had a sudden thought which would have saved them all this awkwardness had it occurred to him earlier. 'It's Sunday today,' he said. 'You should have had the day off, Ince.'

'I don't mind. I would have woken up early anyway.' Ince closed his eyes for a moment. He was feeling the most strained of the three. When Vicki came home later it should be a strictly family occasion. 'But if you can do without me, I have some things I'd like to do in my room before chapel, then I'll go straight over to Les Tremorrow's. Don't worry about dinner for me. It's a lovely day. I'd prefer to take some sandwiches and eat them on the moor.'

'That's settled then,' Laura said, clearing away dishes. 'I'll make them for you and a flask of coffee as well.'

–

Celeste didn't go to chapel but presented herself at the vicarage at twelve fifty-five in the afternoon. She sniffed the air and smiled under her pillbox hat. Lunch was cooking and smelled as though it was not long off serving.

Roslyn Farrow rushed from her kitchen, hoping a pan of greens wouldn't boil over before she could get back. 'Oh, Miss Cunningham. Is everything all right?' People usually only called at the vicarage at such an inconvenient moment if they had an urgent problem or were terribly lonely.

'All is well, Mrs Farrow,' Celeste replied politely. 'I was wondering if I might have a word with the good vicar.' Celeste took in Roslyn's apron, nicely permed but scatty thick black hair and slightly harassed face and smiled sweetly. 'But only if it's a suitable moment, of course.'

'Well, Kinsley is out in the garden going over his sermon for even-song. I daresay he will welcome the interruption,' Roslyn said doubt-fully. Kinsley would be looking forward to his meal, as ravenously hungry as their three young children who had been popping into the kitchen every few minutes to ask if the meal was ready.

'Something smells delicious,' Celeste said meaningfully as she was being escorted through the large square-roomed house, decorated in muted colours and containing shabby but solid furniture. Wild and cultivated flowers, from cowslips and crab apple blossom to camellias, which looked as if they'd been thrown into every imaginable recep-tacle, added charm. Celeste was reminded that Laura did the church flowers, the vicar's wife obviously not having a flair in that direction.

A gawky fat girl aged about ten or eleven with stiff black pigtails looked up appealingly from where she lay sprawled on the sitting room floor gluing magazine pictures of animals into a scrapbook. 'Is the dinner nearly ready, Mummy? I laid the table ages ago.'

'It's almost done, darling. This is my daughter Rachael,' Roslyn murmured to her unexpected guest, keeping a keen ear open for hissing and boiling sounds in the kitchen.

'How sweet,' Celeste purred, thinking she had never seen a plainer child, hoping she wouldn't be subjected to tales of boring trivia about the girl's hobby.

Roslyn led the way through the French windows and shouted to Kinsley at the other end of the wide lawn. He was pacing up and down with a piece of foolscap paper in his hand. 'Kinsley! Miss Cunningham is here wanting a word with you.'

'Eh? What, dear?' Kinsley was stopped in full flow, propounding a point on the certainty of the afterlife for all believers. He folded his sermon and hastened over to the two women, thrusting out a welcoming hand. 'Good afternoon, Miss Cunningham. Nothing wrong, is there?'

Celeste returned his firm handshake and looked him straight in the eye. 'As I told your wife, Mr Farrow, my reason for being here has nothing to do with doom or disaster. I would like a word with you, concerning a family in the village actually, but I can see I've called at an inopportune time. I shall leave and call back later, perhaps tomorrow if that is better for you.' She rarely cooked for herself and fancied a free meal and was daring the vicar and his wife to allow her to leave unfed.

'No, no, you mustn't go. We wouldn't hear of it, would we, dear?' Kinsley protested. In his vocation there were a lot of calls on his time and he was concerned for his one precious day off each week, Monday.

Roslyn readily offered hospitality to anyone but she liked Sunday lunch to be just for the family. However, she smiled resignedly, it would give her a chance to find out something about this painted creature who she was sure was more than a mere social butterfly. Right now Roslyn could smell the water of her greens scalding on the top of the range. 'If you haven't already eaten, Miss Cunningham, perhaps you would care to join us for lunch. There's plenty to go round, it's roast lamb, local meat.'

Celeste smiled disarmingly, 'Well, I don't want to be a nuisance...'

'Do join us, Miss Cunningham,' the vicar urged. 'It will give us the ideal opportunity to get to know you better.'

'Put like that,' Celeste purred, 'how can I refuse?'

With that agreed, Roslyn rushed off to save her range from further spoiling.

Celeste accepted a sherry from Kinsley and sat down in a clumpy oft-recovered armchair in the sitting room. She was uncomfortably under the scrutiny of all three Farrow children, the other two being

77

chubby boys, one younger, the other older than their sister. The boys had inherited their father's brown hair and large expressive dark eyes. There was a hint they might grow up to make rather attractive men, their father wasn't too bad, Celeste observed. He was somewhere in his forties and had weathered well, was straight-backed, no paunch sagged out of his shiny old suit. His wife had left the room but he seemed perfectly comfortable in her company.

Kinsley was wondering if the lady wanted a private interview. He hoped it was something simple that could be brought up over the dinner table, then he wouldn't have to forsake his Sunday afternoon snooze, and if the children took themselves off to roam the bit of moorland they were allowed to play on, Roslyn would probably join him on the bed...

He was in luck. After grace, when the family and their guest were sitting round the long oval table in the dining room, their plates laden with steaming, delicious-looking food, Celeste brought up the purpose of her visit.

'I've made an unusual friend since arriving in the village – Alfie Uren. I'm concerned, Mr Farrow,' and she included Roslyn in the conversation, 'that he and his brothers, and probably his baby sister, are undernourished and somewhat neglected. I would like to help them and you were my obvious first port of call for suggestions.'

'That boy smells,' Richard, the elder boy at twelve years, spouted disgustedly. 'They all do.'

'He can't help it!' Rachael responded heatedly. 'He's just as important in the Lord's eyes as we are.' She was apt to take her father's sermons on board and she had a desperate crush on the wild-natured Alfie Uren, even if he did spit and swear and did his wee-wee in the ditches. He didn't tease or thump her, or hide her toys away, like her big brother sometimes did.

'He let me play with his slingshot,' Ross, the third child, remarked, helping himself to mint sauce, then grinning impishly at Celeste. He was in love with Celeste, seeing her as a film star type who rivalled his favourite heroine, Rita Hayworth.

'I've noticed your kindness to Alfie,' Kinsley said after swallowing a big mouthful of food to deal with his hunger. 'I've tried to welcome

78

the Urens into the village but have only been met with rebuffs. I offered to help them in any way I could and I said I'd give all the children a quick private baptism but they only saw my efforts as interfering, I'm afraid. Someone like yourself, not from the village, could have more luck. I would like to see the children in better circumstances.'

'We could collect some good used clothes for them,' Roslyn said enthusiastically. 'There are certain kind folk who would be glad to help. I'm thinking of Tressa Macarthur. She's a pleasant young woman. We could ask her to try to befriend Mrs Uren, as one young mother with another.'

'That sounds like a very good idea,' Celeste said. She had a man's appetite and had almost cleared her plate. 'But isn't Tressa very quiet and reserved? She hardly spoke a word to anyone at the wedding.'

'She is rather quiet, but very kind,' Kinsley said. 'We can but ask.'

Celeste sipped from her glass of water, wishing it was wine. 'If I can keep Alfie's trust then perhaps I can call at his home and do something positive. I worked with underprivileged children during the war. I found that if one approached the family in a way that left them their dignity, one was invariably successful. If only to find out if the little ones have had their inoculations, that sort of thing.'

Roslyn could hardly believe this woman had actually worked with children, she seemed uninterested in her three children and even Vicki Jeffries, but she did have a way with Alfie who could be a difficult child, sharing his parents' distrust of 'do-gooders'.

Kinsley sighed, he had been recalling some spiteful gossip he'd heard about the Urens in the churchyard this morning. Two of the boys had impetigo and mothers were warning each other not to allow their offspring to play with them. Kinsley could sympathise, impetigo was very infectious, but those concerned had made it sound as if the Urens had the plague. 'If we could get them cleaned up a bit and get some decent clothes for the older boys to go to school in it might dispel some of the prejudice against them.'

Looking round at the three clean, tidy and well-fed children at the table, Celeste fixed them each in turn with a hard stare. 'Not one word from you lot about our plans for the Urens or they'll slam the door in our faces and the children will suffer. You wouldn't like that, would you?' She looked down at her empty plate, wishing Alfie and his family had eaten so well today. And she vowed to deal very severely with any villager who thwarted her plans to help them.

Chapter 8

Ada Prisk was fetching water from the village pump. Her arm was slower these days, owing to her arthritis, but she still managed to make the steady rhythm of creak, squeak, creak, squeak. She could only carry half a bucket at a time the short distance to her house but she didn't mind the extra journeys, it gave her more opportunities to ensnare someone and pass on the latest news. This afternoon she was hoping to chew over yesterday's wedding. A victim was coming down the hill at that very moment and she straightened up, easing her stiff back, making the alarming figure that so many of the locals feared. This one wouldn't try to slip past her hastily though – Ince Polkinghorne was too nice a man for that and she would get more than 'Good afternoon, Mrs Prisk' out of him.

Ince was just as glad to see Ada. After carrying a full bucket of sparkling clear water into her house he lingered in her spick-and-span back kitchen which smelled pleasantly of stored apples.

'I'm on my way to Carrick Cross, Mrs Prisk,' he volunteered.

Ada sharpened all senses. She had been going to ask him about that.

'People say it's haunted,' Ince continued, watching the old woman equally keenly. 'I've heard all the rumours about Tholly Tremorrow, about how he's supposed to have ridden with the devil and haunts it himself as an earthbound lunatic spectre. Apparently he was a rotten man.'

'He was,' Ada snorted indignantly. 'When I was a girl he used to ask me to…' Ada coloured and put her hands together primly, 'to see what he had in his trousers. When I ran away screaming he'd shout after me laughing that it was only a ferret, but everyone knew Tholly

Tremorrow never kept ferrets! He was a disgusting old man. He'd do anything to lure young girls onto his smallholding.'

Ince knew nothing had been proved against Tholly Tremorrow but Ada wasn't the only woman to have complained about his habits. 'What about the other ghosts? Do you know any of the stories?'

'Why?' Ada thirsted to learn more. Ince wasn't the sort of man to take legends and rumours seriously. 'Has something happened to 'ee there? Have you seen something strange?'

'Well, I keep getting this feeling that someone is watching me. First I thought it was Les, but I've heard him snoring in his chair and seen him sitting outside in the sun, his face leaning in a different direction, and I've still felt like something is watching me. It gives me the creeps.'

'*Something* watching you?' Ada shuddered. 'There's the ghost of the lost hiker who died clawing at the wall. He's said to wail on windy nights.'

He would, Ince thought impatiently. 'Anyone else?'

'There's Les's late wife, Ruby. She was a good woman, quiet and ordinary, dark in looks, a wonderful cook. We all thought it a great shame she married that miserable so-and-so. Treated her like a slave, he did – well, you should know, he's got you breaking your back for him in your spare time when you should be out looking for a wife.' Ada had noted that Ince had spent a lot of time dating available women in the last few months, and had mentally ticked them off her list when nothing had come of it. She ignored the blush that rose in Ince's face and cuffed his arm. 'I know just the woman for you. My cousin Myrtle's maid, Penny. She's a bit older than you at thirty-five but she'd make you a fine wife. She lives down Camborne and goes to chapel. Is a lovely cook and hardworking, still young enough to have children. I'll invite her to tea then you can meet her. How about next Sunday? That'll give me time to write she a letter and her to answer it. I'll make my specialty, apple crumble with lots of clotted cream.' Ada's mind shot to her sideboard and her best white damask tablecloth and matching napkins.

Ince put up his hands as if he was pulling up a wayward horse. 'I'm too busy at the moment but thank you for the thought. You were telling me about Les's wife.'

'Ruby? She died of a broken heart, poor woman. Les was such a swine to their only child, a daughter, always picking on her, making her work like a skivvy, that she left home and went to live in Plymouth. Angela, she was called. She never came home again, not even for Ruby's funeral. Well, that same night Johnny Prouse was out walking his dog on the moor - you remember Admiral before he got run down and killed? Anyway, it was dusk as Johnny passed Carrick Cross and he'll swear blind, you ask him yourself, that he saw Ruby sitting outside the front door in this brown spotted dress she often wore, with her arms folded like she was angry or something. We believe she'd made up her mind to haunt Les to get her own back on him for making Angela leave home through his constant moaning at her.' Ada looked around warily and rather fearfully, as if this talk was tempting fate and her own home would be filled with the supernatural. Then she whispered, 'You be careful, Ince. It don't do to stir up the dead. Maybe Ruby don't like you helping out Les and making life so easy for un.'

Ince felt a cold tingle run down his spine. He shook himself, telling himself not to be so silly. He'd known Mrs Tremorrow at chapel. She had been a friendly, pleasantly mannered woman to those who'd taken the trouble to speak to her, and she was decently buried in the Nonconformist graveyard in a nearby village. He thanked Ada, dodged the question of her cousin's maid again and went on his way. Not to be put off, Ada wrote a letter to her cousin, then she went out to get more water.

Using the narrow path that ran beside the telephone box, Ince went by way of the moor, stopping by a narrow tinkling stream to eat the picnic Laura had packed for him. Mayflies and dragonfly nymphs, some preparing to emerge, flitted over the water and the long grasses. Having spoken so recently of ghosts, Ince was reminded of one of the dragonfly's ancient names, devil's darning needle, the innocent creature being credited with flying into a person's ear and sewing it up. Usually Ince would have felt content with these familiar sights and the warm raw smell of the moor, but his position on Rosemerryn Farm had changed and he was unsettled, and now Ada's tale was running through his mind.

The smallholding seemed dreary and bleak when he walked through the little wooden gate he had repaired, the hinges for which he had bought himself and was still waiting reimbursement for. The Celtic roots so deeply entrenched in him made him stand perfectly still, absorbing the atmosphere, his senses alert for dissonance.

Les came flying out of the front door and shouted heatedly, 'What the hell are you doing here so early?'

Ince took umbrage. Before he'd left Rosemerryn both Laura and Spencer had pointed out that Les Tremorrow was only using him. Spencer had called him a fool. Ince himself had begun to think that there was really little wrong with the old man's back.

'What I'm doing here at all is what I should be asking myself,' he retorted stiffly. Then he was angry. Before spending so much time here his main quest in life had been to seek a wife. He was in two minds whether to march back across the moor and take Ada Prisk up on her offer. 'Of all the ungrateful… don't worry, I'm going and I won't be bothering you again.'

Les shot across the few yards between door and gate to him. 'No need to get so het up, boy. I'm sorry I went for 'ee. I, um, you see, the truth is, since me wife died I've got this thing about eating on me own. Don't go. Put your bag in the shed so you can have that flask of tea later on, then come inside and I'll make 'ee a nice fresh one.'

Ince felt he would be wiser to go but he was curious to see inside Les's home. He nodded curtly and went to the tool shed. True to his word, Les had a mug of tea ready for him, but it wasn't fresh. Sitting down on a rough, unvarnished, high-backed chair at the kitchen table, Ince took a good look round. Les grinned sheepishly at him but he was disinclined to speak.

The kitchen hadn't been modernised since Tholly's time and was drab and empty, the furniture sparse and riddled with woodworm. There was not a single ornament or picture on the thick, uneven, whitewashed walls to brighten up the room. The fireplace took up almost all of one wall. A solitary old goatskin rug lay in front of it and the only aid to keeping the fire going was a battered black shovel. Slabs of peat were neatly heaped in one corner. Ince had cut more peat on his last afternoon off and it was drying out in a stack outside. A small broken black-faced clock sat in the middle of the high mantelpiece, letters were heaped behind it and threatened to send it crashing to the floor. The curtains at both windows were threadbare and moth-eaten but scraps of cloth were hung over the top of the strings to make the room dark and private. The room was clean but there was a mouldy smell. The place was utterly cheerless; it held little incentive for the daughter to stay.

Ince was still feeling rebellious. Taking a sip of the bitter tea he muttered, 'I can't stay long today. What do you want done?'

'Aw, not much, boy,' Les returned soothingly. Ince knew he was afraid of losing his unpaid help. ''Tis too nice a day for working. Just put me up a new clothes line, I've left it out for 'ee, and tidy up the tool shed.'

Ince didn't expect gratitude and he didn't get it. He didn't want another drink so soon after his picnic and left the tea undrunk. When he got up he noticed there was only one other door in the room; it must lead to the stairs and two bedrooms. He was puzzled. The shape of the house spoke of another downstairs room. His eyes were drawn to a faded thick red curtain fixed to one of the walls by two nails and a piece of sagging string. A sense of foreboding filled him, and while he wanted to know if there was anything behind that curtain, he longed to get outside into the fresh air.

Les distracted him. 'You'd better get on, then you'll have some afternoon left to yourself.'

Ince was happy to beat a retreat. The 'new' clothes line Les wanted put up turned out to be an old length of rope which was none too clean. Ince secured it between a blackthorn tree and a hook on the tool shed.

Despite the lack of thanks he'd received, Ince felt satisfied with the results of all the hard work he'd put in before today. There was a marshy wet patch at the bottom of the garden and he had cleared away the weeds that choked it, revealing a pool of clear water where wild cress grew. He'd come across the body of a dead cat, not someone's beloved moggy but a wild-looking mangy stray. He'd buried the cat and burnt a heap of old chicken bones with a lot of other rubbish on a roaring bonfire. The paths he'd worked so hard on were immaculate, the holes filled with cinders, nearly as good now as the ones at Hawksmoor House. He'd brought the vegetable garden under control, the runner beans, broad beans, carrots, peas and potatoes and strawberry plants were growing healthily. Les was partial to celery and Ince had dug a trench, spaded in some well-rotted compost, filled it in and planted the seeds.

Ince didn't work with the animals but now, as he often did, he went to his crib bag and took out some titbits for the goats, standing well back because if they didn't like the offerings they would spit them out. He didn't know their names but they were his friends. Les kept them well, their coats shone and they smelled fresh.

It wouldn't have taken long to clear up the tool shed if it had only housed usable tools but there was a hopeless tangle of empty paint pots, cracked and earthy flower pots, nails, screws and hinges of every description, dust-laden tins of turps, oil and paraffin with just a dribble slopping around inside them. There were empty wine bottles and jam jars from Ruby Tremorrow's sloe gin, jam and chutney making days – Ince remembered she had been famous for them in the village. There was broken glass, corks, yellowing newspapers going back a decade, decaying seed potatoes, half a sack of hard cement, a rusted watering can with a huge hole in it, even a broken tennis racket. Nails and hooks hammered in the walls and roof stuck out dangerously and Ince's cheek was scratched and his shirt ripped at the back. Mummified creatures in dusty cobwebs were everywhere. In a corner he found a long-forgotten rag doll made out of a man's sock.

It was humid and sticky in the shed; Ince propped the door open with a huge lump of shapeless rusted metal. An hour and a half later he was still at his task. Hot and breathless, he reached for his crib bag to pour some coffee, intending to go outside for a breath of fresh air, when out of the corner of his eye he saw something moving. He whipped his head round to the doorway and his breath locked tightly in his lungs, his heart lurched wildly.

Before him was a woman wearing a brown spotted dress. She gasped and a hand flew to her face. Ince's mouth dropped open. He couldn't gather his wits together to speak but mouthed a silent prayer for help. He stared, expecting at any moment she would disappear. His flesh crawled in icy stinging pricks from head to foot. He was terrified. He was looking at the ghost of Ruby Tremorrow and her eyes were boring into him.

Ruby Tremorrow turned on her heel and vanished. Not into thin air, she was running away and Ince could hear her footsteps. Ghosts didn't usually run away, they dematerialised. Some life flooded back into Ince's limbs and he forced himself out of the shed. He couldn't see her but somehow he knew he'd find her in the house. He was inside the front door in a trice.

The kitchen was empty. He could hear loud snores coming from upstairs - Les was taking his Sunday afternoon snooze. Ince pulled the double curtains away from the windows and glanced outside. There was no sign of the ghost out there. Spinning round, he faced the curtain fixed to the wall. Drawing up his courage, he crossed the room. Standing in front of the curtain he found his fists were tightly clenched. Uncurling them, taking a deep breath, he pulled the curtain aside and found a door. A low door of bare wood. He put his hand on the brass knob and turned it.

He stepped into what was a small, square sitting room. The difference between this room and the bare kitchen was astonishing. It was carpeted and well furnished. A big vase of garden flowers stood on top of a china cabinet. Heavy velvet curtains were drawn over at the window but he could see Ruby Tremorrow through the gloom. She was standing behind the settee, trembling hands on its back, staring wide-eyed at him. The room was stuffy but through the musky odour of the flowers he detected a faint smell of violet scent which he knew came from her. He could hear her harsh breathing. He had frightened her too. His work had taken longer than expected and she must have assumed he had gone home. She was no ghost.

'Mrs Tremorrow?'

She didn't answer, nor did she take her eyes off him.

'I'm sorry if I scared you. You scared me too. I'm Ince Polkinghorne. I've been helping Les out about the place.'

He stepped closer to her and she moved to the middle of the room. Then, as if admitting the game was up, she spoke in a tone that sounded like resignation. 'He won't be happy that you've seen me.'

'Why? Because you're not really dead?' An insurance fraud was running through Ince's mind.

'You're talking about my grandmother,' the woman said in a quiet and unemotional voice, then going to the window she thrust back the curtains and Ince saw the truth of her words. Sunlight flooded in and illuminated her, a plain young woman in her early twenties. If this had been Ince's first sight of her, he would not have doubted she was a ghost and he would have hightailed it from the room. Her skin was very pale, like that of someone who spent little time outdoors, large brown eyes stood out darkly above high, tight cheekbones. Her hair was short and straight, a simple style with a full fringe, framing an impassive, longish face. He could see the dress was too big for her, disguising any figure she had.

'You're wearing your grandmother's dress,' he stated.

'And you thought I was her ghost,' she replied.

'How long have you been living here?'

She looked away, obviously not wanting to answer questions, but Ince felt he had the right to know something about her.

'What's your name?'

'Eve Tremorrow. Please go. If Grandfather finds out you've seen me he'll be furious.'

'I don't care if he is. What are you hiding from? Are you in trouble with the police?'

'Of course not.' She looked down with a hint of a sigh, as though she was used to being ordered about, but there was also a marked dignity about her movement, cutting her off from him.

Ince wasn't prepared to be dismissed. Things were falling into place. 'Why doesn't Les want me to see you? I was never allowed to come here at mealtimes. Was that because you were eating with him? Knowing that lazy so-and-so, I imagine you cook the meals, serve it up then do the dishes. I bet it's you who looks after the animals and flowerbeds too. How long have you been here like this?'

88

Eve Tremorrow stood stock still, saying nothing. There was something wrong here. Was the old man keeping his granddaughter a prisoner? Ince ran upstairs to demand the truth.

Les was lying on top of a double bed, covered with an imitation watered silk bedspread that was badly snagged. He was in the middle where the mattress sagged. A nearly full chamber pot gave off a fetid smell and no windows were open. Marching across the bare creaking floorboards, Ince flung up a window, making it shudder against its sashes.

'What's goin' on?' Les wailed, waking up with a start. He was stung to fury to see Ince in his room. 'What the bleeding hell are you doing here? Get out! Get out at once or I'll have the law on you!'

Ince stood his ground and pointed a finger. 'I'm not going anywhere until you tell me why you're keeping your granddaughter a prisoner here.'

'You've seen the maid?' Les blinked rapidly, throwing aside the bedspread and wriggling off the bed, dressed only in his patched woolly combinations. 'What the hell's been going on while I've been up here?'

'Nothing's been going on,' Ince snarled, angered at the old man's outrage. 'I've seen Eve and I've spoken to her. She thought I'd finished in the shed and was shocked to see me still there. I followed her into the house. Now you explain to me what's been going on here or I'll get the police.'

'Bah, you interfering young bastard! How dare you make assumptions. I'm not keeping the girl here against her will if that's what you're inferring.'

'Mind your language, you old swine.' Ince towered over him and Les was suddenly intimidated.

'I – I've done nothing wrong, Ince. Go down and ask Eve for herself.'

'I will.' Ince barged out of the room. 'It had better be a good story.'

When he closed the door to the stairs, he found Eve in the kitchen. She was standing in front of the huge fireplace, her hands clasped together. Now he could see her in a natural light she cut a dignified figure.

'I'll tell you what you want to know, then you must go,' she said, her voice soft and mellow, the words finely and precisely pronounced.

'I'm sorry for chasing around the house but I was worried about you,' he replied, somewhat humbled now. He was as curious about this young woman as Ada Prisk would be.

Eve retained eye contact with him. Her chin, firm and well shaped, lifted, just a fraction, but he saw it. He sensed a stronger character here than he'd first thought.

'My mother died three months ago. When I was going through her things I came across my grandparents' address. I've known all my life that she was estranged from her parents and we only found out by chance that my grandmother had died several years ago. Anyway, I wrote to Grandfather and asked him if I could visit him, just for a few hours. He wrote back saying that he wanted nothing to do with me, but as he is the only relative I have left, I persisted with my letters. He finally relented and agreed we could meet.

'When we met at the railway station we got along well and he said I could stay with him for a few days so we could get to know each other. My employer allowed me to take my annual holiday. While I was here, my employer had a stroke and was put in a nursing home. Her son dispensed with my services. Grandfather said I could stay longer and I've been here ten weeks altogether. I might stay on or I might apply for a new position. It all depends...'

'Depends on what? And why do you want to stay out of sight?'

'They're both personal reasons and I hope you won't say anything about me in Kilgarthen.'

Ince shook his head. 'It's an odd thing to be asked.' Her explanation had sounded truthful but it was a very strange situation.

'Please, Mr Polkinghorne,' and a little pleading came into her voice. 'At least will you say nothing until we make up our minds whether I stay or not?'

'Oh, Les will want you to stay all right, as an unpaid slave.'

His bitterness wasn't lost on Eve but she didn't react to it. 'That's our business.'

'Yes, I'm sorry, forgive me. I'm forgetting myself. I'd better go.'

'Don't leave thinking I'm not grateful for all you've done for my grandfather, Mr Polkinghorne,' Eve said, following him to the door. 'Will you do as I asked?'

Ince saw that Les had come into the room. He was fully dressed. 'All right,' Ince said grimly. 'I won't say anything. As you've said, it's none of my business anyway.'

'You coming again?' Les asked, and there was no gratefulness or friendship offered in his voice.

Ince shrugged his shoulders. 'I don't know.'

He cut across the moor on his way back to Rosemerryn. It was a long walk but he needed the time to be alone, feel the bracing fresh air, the sense of timelessness, the solitude. Laura had insisted he come home for tea but he wasn't looking forward to it.

Suddenly Ince was tired. Tired of living without a real home, a real family; he felt like a cuckoo in the nest at Rosemerryn. He was physically tired with all the hard work he had put in on the farm and smallholding for the last six weeks. He was tired of being good old reliable Ince, never stinting himself for other people and never getting anywhere himself.

He would never go back to Carrick Cross. Yet if he didn't, how would he find out more about the quietly dignified and mysterious Eve Tremorrow?

Chapter 9

Several people were making their way to Rosemerryn for tea that afternoon; two were uninvited, but one of the two was sure they would find a welcome. Daisy was walking with Bruce along Rosemerryn Lane, her arm proudly tucked inside his.

'I'm really curious to meet Billy's widow,' Bruce said, idly pulling at cow parsley sticking out from the hedge. 'Are you sure she won't mind me turning up like this, Mum? Her wedding night was only last night, after all.' Daisy was eager to show off her son. With his confident manner, good-quality clothes and regimental walk, he cut a refined figure in comparison to many of the local men. She overlooked his conceit; his conversation had been full of boasting.

'When you've known Laura as long as I have, Bruce, you'll know how much she'll love to meet you. Anyway, if she and Spencer wanted to be really private they would have gone away on honeymoon.'

'I guess so. I hope they like me. I want to get along with all the local folk.'

'I'm sure you will, dear. It will be lovely having you around. The house and shop were broken into two years ago. I sometimes get a bit nervous at night.'

Rather than look for a job, Bruce had suggested he help his mother in the shop. Wanting to catch up on all those lost years, Daisy had readily agreed.

He rubbed her hand affectionately. 'You won't have no worries on that score now, Mum. Just let 'em try. I've never served in a shop before, it'll be fun. And you won't have to lift anything heavy now I'm here. I saw for myself how big some of the boxes in the storeroom are. I can cook too so you won't have to slave over a hot stove for me every day. I'll make a start on the garden tomorrow. It needs a man to give it a good digging over.'

Daisy laughed heartily. 'I'll be quite the most spoiled woman in Kilgarthen.' She was certainly one of the happiest right now.

They could hear a pony's hooves coming up behind them and moved in close to the hedge of the narrow lane to allow room for a jingle to pass. Bruce stared at the extremely fat woman driving it. She was an awesome sight in a voluminous tartan cloak and Victorian bonnet.

Daisy spoke to her. 'Good afternoon, Mrs Noon. Out for a little drive?'

'I am, Mrs Tamblyn,' the elderly woman replied airily, only slowing the tawny pony down a little as she drove straight past.

'I remember that old lady,' Bruce said, gazing at the back of the jingle which was badly in need of fresh paint. 'She never was very friendly. We used to call her Ma Noon. You didn't like us going near her or her place because you thought she was mad. We kids used to sneak onto her property to tease her and, I'm ashamed to admit, throw stones at her pig and goats and bang on her chicken run. It was untidy on the outside but there were rumours about her being filthy rich, that her house was like a palace inside. That's what we kids used to say, anyway.'

Daisy was thinking about the strange old woman who had never had anything to do with the village since the days of her marriage; she had been a widow for forty years. 'I never knew it at the time, but when Billy was a boy he used to go there a lot. He got on with her quite well. He was the only one she was friendly with. He never said anything about her having a posh place. She hasn't had any livestock for years now. I expect it got too much for her. She must be in her seventies. Her pony doesn't look as if it's got many years left in it. She could have money, I suppose. She must have come from rich people in the first place, you only have to listen to her speak to know she's not one of us. People said she married beneath her when she came to Kilgarthen. Mind you, she never spends much money in the shop.' Daisy chuckled. 'Perhaps she's got heaps of money hidden under her mattress.'

Bruce looked at his mother deeply. 'You really think so?'

'I was only joking, silly,' she answered, taking his arm again.

Celeste heard the car pull up with a screech of brakes and beckoned to Harry from Little Cot's doorway. He got out, but before he asked her what she wanted he ogled her voluptuous figure in slacks and a tight sweater. Her breasts stuck out like overripe melons as they vied for room on her chest with several long strings of bouncing beads. Her hips and bottom looked as if they had trouble being contained in the sleek material.

'I forgot to tell you yesterday that Laura wants some of her things taken over to the farm,' she said, enjoying his appreciation of her. 'Would you be a darling, Harry, and carry them to the car?'

Harry stepped inside the front room and ran a hand over her shapely bottom. 'I will – if you'll be a darling to me later tonight.'

Harry had been quite rough in his lovemaking the other day but she was happy to comply. She missed Laura's company and would be glad of his. 'If you're sure you're not seen coming to the cottage. I won't be living here for long but I don't want to make enemies.'

'I'll be careful,' Harry promised, grinning salaciously.

Felicity and Vicki were sitting in the back of the sedan. As they watched Harry pile two suitcases and some bags into the boot, Vicki wrinkled up her nose and declared petulantly, 'I don't want that awful woman coming with us. She tries to take Laura away from me.'

'But she's Laura's friend,' Felicity explained, smoothing the girl's shiny hair. 'Laura said she could come to tea with us today. She can't leave Miss Cunningham alone all the time, that would be unkind.'

Felicity had not missed the amorous looks passing between Harry and the other woman and she had also seen Celeste's interest in Ince. She noticed that Celeste had sensible flat shoes on today; if Ince went out in the yard alone… 'I don't expect she'll stay long,' Felicity added tartly.

Harry opened the front passenger door and Celeste got in in a flurry of exaggerated feminine movements and strong musky perfume. Vicki waved her hand in front of her face and coughed rudely. Felicity tapped Vicki's arm chidingly. They set off with a roar of engine and squeal of tyres. Johnny Prouse heard the racket from his back garden where he was feeding his bantam hens. 'One of these days,' he told them, 'that young man is going to kill someone rushing round the lanes like a mad hound.'

Moments later the car flashed past Daisy and Bruce, tossing up dust and grit and disappearing round the next bend. Bruce had heard it coming and quickly pulled Daisy to the comparative safety of a ditch. He shook his fist at the sedan, his face furious. 'Bloody damned idiot! What's he trying to prove?'

They heard a screech of brakes.

'I think he's stopped for us,' Daisy said, her heart dancing from the fright as she pulled bits of twig and bramble off her dress. She could smell wild garlic where her legs had been squashed against it.

'Good,' Bruce snapped, marching off along the lane. His face had turned red and his body was shaking. 'I'll punch his bloody nose for him.'

'Oh, Bruce,' Daisy rushed after him. 'I don't want no unpleasantness.'

On rounding the bend, Harry had brought the car to a halt. Felicity and Vicki were flung about and Celeste fell forward and bumped her head on the lacquered dashboard.

'I'll see if they're going to Rosemerryn,' Harry said, reaching for the door handle.

'I shouldn't think they'd want a lift anywhere with you,' Felicity said angrily. 'And if you don't drive carefully in future, neither will I. Don't forget you have Vicki in the car. What would Spencer say if she was hurt?' She saw Celeste rubbing her forehead. 'Are you all right, Miss Cunningham?'

As Harry looked in horror at what he had done to Celeste, his door was pulled open and he was hauled out of the car. 'What the bloody hell do you think you're doing? You nearly killed me and my mother,' Bruce screamed. His face was contorted with rage.

'I – I'm sorry,' Harry gulped. He was truly sorry because it hadn't registered there was someone on the road until he'd nearly ploughed

95

into them. But he would not be manhandled and he tore Bruce's hands from his sports jacket and pushed him off.

Bruce's back hit the hedge but he promptly sprang back. 'People like you should be bloody hanged. Driving around like you own the bloody road.'

'Bruce!' Daisy reached out a restraining hand which he shrugged off. He wasn't finished yet.

Felicity had wound the window down. 'Would you please stop swearing? There's a child in this car and she can hear every word and you're frightening her.'

Bruce shot Felicity a look of pure venom. She wound the window up rapidly and pulled Vicki protectively into her arms.

'I stopped to ask you if you were walking to Rosemerryn and to offer you a lift,' Harry said, unafraid of this glowering stranger and angered by his aggressive attitude. 'I wish I'd never bothered.'

'I wouldn't ride in your damn car if you paid me,' Bruce spat. Glancing at the child staring at him on the back seat, he dropped his voice. 'Hoity-toity bastard.'

'I won't fight in front of the women but any other time you like…' Harry said dangerously.

Bruce poked him viciously in the chest. 'Our turn'll come, you can count on it.'

Daisy was nearly in tears. 'We can't go on to Rosemerryn now, Bruce. We'll have to call on Laura another time.'

'Better still, wait till she calls at the shop,' Harry said acidly. 'I don't want him anywhere near my niece.'

'We'll go where we bloody well like,' Bruce snarled, raising his fist again.

'Bruce, please,' Daisy pleaded, tugging on his arm. 'Let's go home.'

Bruce's head jutted forward a few times like a turtle trying to slip off its shell then he reluctantly gave way and the company parted. Bruce strode back to the shop, his bull neck bent down, hands rammed in his pockets. Daisy's joy in the afternoon had been ruined.

The three adults in the car knew they couldn't give a watered-down version of what had happened in the lane, for Vicki was a forthright child who liked excitement and would blurt out the truth. She hadn't been afraid as Felicity had said, certain that her Uncle Harry could easily fend off the horrible man. After she had excitedly kissed her father and new stepmother and gleefully told them she hadn't gone to sleep last night until after midnight, Vicki brought the subject up and even elaborated on the story. Spencer took a lot of consoling. He was more angry with Harry for his reckless driving than with Bruce Tamblyn's foul language and outrage, which he thought was justified in the circumstances. He extracted a solemn promise from Harry that he would never drive like that with Vicki in the car again.

'It's a pity for Daisy,' Laura said, putting food left over from the reception on the table. 'She must have been so upset at not being able to come here and introduce her son to me.'

'What do you want to meet a character like him for?' Spencer asked disbelievingly, helping her lay the table. He might sympathise with Bruce's right to rail against Harry but he didn't like the sound of the man.

'Well, he is Daisy's son. She hasn't seen him for years. I'm curious about him.' Laura looked at Celeste who was sitting in a fireside chair holding a damp cloth to her head. 'Are you sure you're all right, Celeste?'

'It's just a little bump,' Celeste replied as if she was trying to be brave.

Four pairs of accusing eyes alighted on Harry. Fed up with being treated like a criminal, he went outside for a cigarette.

Ince didn't appear for tea and Laura put a plate of sandwiches, cake and tiny sausage rolls aside for him. Spencer went outside to do some work and Vicki tagged along happily with Barney. Celeste said she was going for a short stroll. Felicity dried the dishes as Laura washed them.

'I did so enjoy having Vicki last night,' Felicity said meaningfully, pausing as she carefully wiped the bottom plate of a three-tier cake stand, a wedding present.

'I'm sure Spencer will let her do it again,' Laura said, peering out of the window, not paying much attention.

'But you've got some influence now, Laura,' Felicity pointed out.

'Yes, I suppose.' Laura pulled aside the curtain and leaned over the sink to get a wider view of the yard.

'What are you looking for?'

'Ince. I can't help wondering why he didn't come home for his tea.'

'Oh, Laura, you're not actually worried about him?' Felicity was amused. 'Ince is a big boy now. He doesn't need a mother.'

'I know that, Felicity. But you didn't see him this morning. He looked so out of place. This is his home. I don't want him to think he's not wanted any more because I'm Spencer's wife and living here now.'

'Well, you seem to have got used to your new situation as Spencer's wife very quickly. It took me a whole month to get used to the idea of being a married woman.'

Laura looked at Felicity. It must be difficult for her having another woman take her daughter's place. Felicity didn't return her gaze; she busied herself putting the cutlery in the drawer. 'Don't worry,' she said without looking up. 'I'll get used to it.'

Celeste lit a cigarette and leaned against the low granite wall of the small paddock where Spencer's horse, Splendour, and the farm nag Brindle were kept. She watched the two horses for a while, both of them having the characteristics suggested by their names, and she envied them their companionship. Gloomily she ran a finger in and out of the rough speckled grey contours of a large stone. Laura wasn't the only one to be disappointed that Ince wasn't here. But what was the use if he was? Nothing could come out of a liaison with him or any other man. Did she really want the same sort of relationship with him as with Harry? Celeste sighed, asking herself why she had been man-mad all her life. Men had brought her nothing but trouble so far, but she had to admit that the situation she was now in was her own fault.

She saw Ince coming through the gateway of the next field when she was stubbing out her cigarette. He was plodding along dejectedly, his crib bag in danger of slipping off his hunched shoulder. Celeste entered the paddock. She didn't want her chase to be too obvious and she knew Ince was too caring and polite to ignore her. Splendour trotted up to her and she stroked his glossy black mane.

Ince was dismayed to see Celeste. He was in no mood to fight off the bait she dangled so brazenly in front of him. 'Hello, Celeste,' he said cagily at some distance away.

'Hello, Ince.' Celeste pretended nonchalance to put him off his guard. 'Laura's quite concerned about you. She was expecting you for tea.'

Pausing for a moment, looking her squarely in the eyes, he muttered, 'I felt like roaming the moor.'

She was determined to hold a conversation with him. 'You've scratched your face.'

He put his fingers to the stinging spot on his cheek. 'It's nothing.'

'You look tired.'

'I feel tired.'

He started walking again and Celeste, seeing him slipping through her fingers, ran up to him. She took his hand. 'I could make you feel better.'

He pulled his hand away roughly. 'Look, Celeste, I'd like to be friends with you, nothing more. Got that?' She would have tried a little gentle persuasion, he was such an attractive man and in his present inexplicable mood, his rugged face furrowed, he looked more appealing than ever, but she sensed a rawness, an intensity about him. She knew he wouldn't be trifled with. And he would be good to have as a friend; she might be glad of someone she could turn to in the future.

'Very well,' she smiled softly. 'Friends it is. Brindle's a sweetie and Spencer's horse is magnificent, isn't he? I understand you moorland farmers herd your cattle using horses. I've seen Spencer's stock of little wild moorland ponies, they're fascinating,' she glanced at Hawk's Tor, 'like the moor.'

'It's how I find it,' Ince said, sounding a little more friendly. 'I'd better go in, to stop Laura worrying about me.'

'I'll come with you,' Celeste said, rubbing her forehead. 'I've got a bit of a headache. Perhaps Laura's got an aspirin.'

Ince eased his long strides and took a closer look at her and realised that despite her make-up she was rather pale. 'You don't look very well.' He took her arm to help her along.

'Harry pulled up sharply in the car and I bumped my head on the dashboard. Come to think of it, I feel a bit dizzy too.' She leaned heavily on Ince's arm.

'Do you want me to carry you?'

'I think you'd better. I—'

Her legs gave out and Ince had to move fast to support her limp body or Celeste would have crumpled to the ground. He gathered her up in his arms and rushed to the farmhouse. Laura, who had seen them from the kitchen window, came hastening outside to meet them.

'What's happened to her?'

'I don't know. One minute we were talking, the next she just keeled over. She told me she'd banged her head in Harry's car.'

'It's all his fault,' Laura said crossly. 'You'd better carry her inside and I'll send Harry to get the doctor. Lay her on my bed, Ince.' Then Laura tutted, 'We need a telephone here. I'll talk to Spencer about it.'

Felicity had followed on Laura's heels. 'I'll fetch Harry,' she said, feeling guilty on her son's behalf.

Celeste came round at the same moment Ince laid her on the double bed. 'What happened?' she mumbled, trying to sit up. 'What am I doing here?'

'You fainted,' Laura explained softly, brushing red hair from her flushed cheeks and gently removing her rows of beads. 'We're going to send Harry for the doctor.'

'I don't need a doctor.' Celeste chuckled and Laura was afraid she was getting hysterical.

'Yes, you do,' Laura insisted. 'You were hurt more than you thought when Harry suddenly stopped his car.' Celeste laughed loudly and clutched her head as it ached dully. 'Ooh. I'm telling you I don't need a doctor. The reason why I fainted has nothing to do with Harry's careless driving.'

Fearing he was about to hear something private and feminine, Ince excused himself, saying he'd make some tea.

'You'll find some food I've left for you on a plate in the larder,' Laura said, giving him an encouraging smile. 'You haven't had a cooked meal today. I'll make something for you later.'

'I'm fine, you look after Celeste,' he replied, and Laura got the impression he would not be argued with.

She turned her attention to Celeste who was now lying with her eyes shut and an arm crooked across her brow. 'What's the matter, Celeste? What is it?'

'There's no need to go on about it, Laura. It's nothing much, just a short-term problem.'

'Oh, that? Do you want me to fetch something for you while there are no men about?'

'No, I'm all right, Laura. I just need a little sleep, that's all.'

'You must stay here tonight.'

'I most certainly will not. I'm not in the least bit ill and you're on your honeymoon.' There was another chuckle. 'And incidentally, it stands out a mile that the wedding night was a roaring success. If I stayed here it would mean turning Ince out of his bed and that wouldn't be fair. He seems down in the dumps over something as it is.'

'Poor Ince, I feel terrible over the way he feels so lost in his own home. I never stopped to think how my marrying Spencer would affect him.'

Celeste moved her arm and opened one eye, its mascara all smudged. 'You're really fond of him, aren't you? Exactly how far did your romance with him go?'

Laura turned her face away from that penetrating eye. 'How can anyone not be concerned about Ince? He's so kind and gentle, a thoroughly nice man. He doesn't deserve to be made to feel ill at ease.'

'He would make the ideal husband. You'd think someone would have snapped him up by now. Oh, well, no use me putting a bid in. I'm not his type at all.' Celeste half sat up. 'Listen, I feel better already. I'll get Harry to drive me home in a little while but I insist, Laura, no doctor.'

'Well, if you're sure you'll be all right,' Laura said doubtfully, getting up from the bed. She knew from way back that Celeste would hit the roof and be intolerably rude to the doctor if he came. 'I'd better run downstairs and catch Harry before he leaves for the telephone.' Alone, Celeste lay down again and putting her palms on her stomach gazed thoughtfully at the ceiling.

—

Spencer was always the last one to bed in his household and that night, when he was satisfied the farm was secure, he climbed the stairs hoping for another night of passion. He wouldn't have been so bold normally, reckoning on making love two or three times a week, but he had pleasant memories of just a few hours ago and he and Laura had got on well all day. This marriage looked like it was going to work. He was taken aback to find Vicki in bed with Laura.

'What's the matter, pipkin? Are you feeling poorly? You should have been asleep hours ago.'

'I wanted to give Laura, I mean Mummy, another cuddle,' Vicki replied, yawning and rubbing her eyes then snuggling in tight to Laura.

To counteract his rapidly forming frown, Laura said, 'It's been an exciting time for Vicki these past few days, Spencer. She couldn't settle down to sleep tonight.'

'Well, she can't sleep in here.' Things would be very awkward if this went on every night.

'She knows that. I was just about to take her back to her own room.'

Laura had one of her own nightdresses on tonight, a sensible garment rather than the piece of nonsense Celeste had put in her overnight bag, but it was silky and feminine, and she was pleased to feel Spencer taking a keen interest in her as she walked out of the room. She tucked Vicki up in her little bed and padded back to her own room ten minutes later. As she crossed the short landing, she noticed light coming from under Ince's door.

Spencer was sitting up in bed, wearing just his pyjama bottoms. He had turned the lantern light down to a warm rosy glow. When she got in beside him, he put his arm round her shoulders and pulled her close.

Laura eased herself away and picked up a book she had unpacked from her belongings and put on the bedside cabinet.

'I usually read for a little while,' she said, opening the book at its bookmark.

Spencer took it from her hands. 'Agatha Christie? Mmmm, we've got a lot to learn about each other. I like Thomas Hardy myself.' He put the book down on his side of the bed and nuzzled her neck. Laura liked it, alarmingly so, but she tried to retrieve her book. Spencer pushed it out of reach and began to undo the buttons at the front of her nightdress while taking her lips in a hungry sensual kiss.

Laura would have welcomed this if they'd been in the house alone or with just Vicki sleepy and across the landing. But Ince's little room was connected to theirs and she couldn't bear the thought that he might hear them.

Realising he wasn't getting the response he wanted, Spencer stopped. 'Is something wrong?' he asked, his voice husky, ready with a score of different comforts and inducements.

Laura felt embarrassed to admit it but she didn't want him to think she was rejecting him personally. 'I'm sorry, I'm just afraid that we'll be overheard.'

Sighing heavily, he lay back on his pillows and linked his hands behind his head. 'I understand.'

'Do you, Spencer? I don't want there to be any misunderstandings between us.'

'Yes... this time. But we can't always wait until we think the others are asleep. It'll take the spontaneity out of it.'

Laura patted his arm. 'We'll work something out.'

Spencer murmured something in agreement but he couldn't see how, not with Ince living under the same roof.

Chapter 10

Laura was up early again the next morning and Spencer and Ince assumed she had come into the milking shed to ask them what they wanted for breakfast. She was dressed in very old clothes and they were surprised when she put a white coat on over the top of them, rolling back the long sleeves which hung down over her hands.

'What are you doing, Laura?' Spencer asked after exchanging a puzzled look with Ince.

'I'm determined to learn to do everything on the farm and I want you to teach me how to milk the cows,' she replied breezily, and she struck a defiant stance in the lantern light to show them she wouldn't brook any arguments or male patronising.

Ince felt it was a good idea but it wasn't his place to say anything, so he kept quiet.

Spencer raised his fair brows but was careful to keep his face perfectly straight. 'Well, all right, but you don't have to learn right now, Laura.'

'Don't worry, I'll still make your breakfast. Vicki is sound asleep so I've slipped out for my first lesson.'

Spencer wasn't bothered about Laura learning the ropes round the farm; Natalie had always done a farmer's wife's share of the work despite growing up in a privileged household and having trained as a personal secretary. Shrugging his shoulders, he said, 'You'll need a cap as well.'

This had gone smoother than she'd anticipated; Spencer could be very stubborn if he didn't agree with something. Laura took a white cotton cap off its hook and placed it on her head. She had made up her mind long ago that if she ever married Spencer she would be a farmer's wife to the full. She was more likely to enjoy her new life and it would make things easier in times of illness, holiday or accident.

Spencer strode up to her and turned the cap round so the peak was at the back of her head; he made a display of touching her affectionately, to hammer home to Ince that she was his woman and that she didn't mind close attention from him.

'Right then,' he said, 'the cows are all in their places. You already know their names and that Luby's a kicker. Ince or I will milk her. We've just started to feed them with cowcake mixed with barley. You can see how much we're putting in their own bit of trough.' He handed her a dipper. 'You can carry on.'

Laura had not closed the door as she'd come in and after she plunged the dipper into the sack of barley, the meal swirled round in the draught and hit her in the face. She coughed and sneezed and wiped gritty bits from her eyes. Taking a quick glance at the men, she was infuriated to see them grinning at each other in amusement. Ince closed the door and she thanked him rather tartly. He got on with his work quietly. Pursing her lips, she carried on with her task.

'You have to wash the teats next,' Spencer said, resisting the desire to brush husks of barley out of her hair which she'd tied back with a red scarf. 'Go fetch an udder bucket. No, not that one, that's a milking pail.'

Laura duly took back the pail and brought an udder bucket which was different in shape and size. He handed her a clean cloth. 'Right, you wash each teat separately and check it for signs of soreness and disease. I'll show you how to do it on old Maisie, she's the quietest girl we have.'

Laura copied his careful actions successfully and found the teats softer and smoother than she had thought. On her husband's patient instructions, she took back the udder bucket and picked up the pail again and a little three-legged stool. She sat down close to the animal at its side, near the tail end.

'Now you can see why I turned your hat round,' Spencer said. 'You have to get very close to the cow and the peak would knock it off. Now, face up under her body and take a firm hold of two teats.'

Flexing her hands a couple of times and hoping she wouldn't scratch Maisie with her long fingernails, which she guessed rightly wouldn't last long that way, Laura took a deep breath and put her fingers round the two nearest teats.

Putting a hand on her shoulder, Spencer looked up under Maisie's body. He pushed Laura's hands further up the teats and tightened their grip. 'Don't be afraid of hurting her. You won't get the milk out if you go about it too gently and she won't like it.' He squeezed and pulled over her hands and two small streams of creamy milk skitted downwards and sang in the bottom of the pail.

'I did it!' Laura cried delightedly in the same way Vicki would.

'Carry on by yourself,' Spencer said, taking his big rough hands away.

With her cheek pressed against the cow's warm body, Laura squeezed and pulled on the teats. Nothing happened for several moments then she produced a double stream, irregular ones at first, but she was getting milk from the cow.

Spencer stroked Maisie's back. 'Make sure the teats are empty before you go on to the next ones. I'll come back and see how you're doing in a little while.' He moved to the other side of the shippen to sterilise the churns.

Laura gritted her teeth and nearly forgot to breathe in her determination to milk the cow properly. As the milk gradually covered the bottom of the pail and began a tentative journey up its sides, she got red in the face and prayed Maisie wouldn't shift about or drop a large smelly pat which might splash her, but Maisie seemed content to chew on her morning feed. Laura had done many jobs about the yard, some dirty, some requiring a lot of physical effort, but working with a warm live animal was exhilarating.

When Ince had finished milking Luby who was tied up at the other end of the stalls, he crouched down beside Laura and watched her efforts. She was on the other two teats now.

'How do you think I'm doing?' she panted.

'Very well,' he replied, smiling at her. 'Some cows give us one or two full gallon buckets, others you're lucky if you get a jugful. Maisie's usually a good milker, you'll get a full bucket out of her today. Takes about ten to fifteen minutes altogether.'

No more milk would come and Laura took her face away from Maisie, rubbing her neck which had acquired a painful crick because she had been so tense. Ince squeezed all four udders to make sure they were empty. 'You've done a good job here.' He patted her shoulder in congratulation. 'I'm proud of you. Vicki will be some excited.'

He and Laura had their faces close together and something made them look up. Spencer was standing over them, his face as black as a thunderstorm over Hawk's Tor.

–

Andrew Macarthur had a day off from his solicitor's office. He had done the milking on Tregorlan Farm with Bert Miller and he had taken the chums down to the stand they shared with Rosemerryn for collection by the milk company. He was on his way home on a new tractor and trailer for breakfast, feeling happy and fulfilled. He had given up a high-flown life and lucrative career in London to settle down in Cornwall when he'd so unexpectedly fallen in love with Tressa and he didn't regret a moment of it.

The wife whom he adored more than life itself had given him a healthy thriving son, and their lovemaking since Guy's birth was the same wonderful experience each time as their romantic wedding night. He had the challenge of his job in Bodmin and he had built Tregorlan Farm up into a successful business. The rundown parts of the farm had all been fixed or dismantled, and modern machinery produced quicker and more profitable results. Jacka's weak herd of cattle had been replaced with a fine breeding stock. Everything in his life was perfect and nothing could spoil it.

The dawn light was just forming and Andrew's heart did an uneasy flip when the tractor's headlights caught a strange shape heading towards him in the lane. He pulled into a passing place and laughed with relief and amusement at his foolishness when he saw it was only the Reverend Kinsley Farrow on his bicycle. Andrew turned off the engine and the vicar stopped pedalling.

'Good morning, Mr Farrow. You gave me a terrible fright. I thought at first you were a floating ghost of some poor lost soul on the moor or perhaps one of the small people grown to a grotesque size.'

Kinsley chuckled. 'Well, perhaps if I can get you to believe in the supernatural, Mr Macarthur, I'll see you more regularly in church for spiritual succour. Tressa rarely misses these days.'

Andrew sidestepped the friendly admonition the vicar gave him every time he saw him; he didn't need anything else in his life. 'You're up early. Couldn't you sleep?'

'You're absolutely right. My wife calls it my spring fever. But I can't sleep on in the mornings at this time of year, there's always such a feel of promise in the air.'

'Would you care to come back to Tregorlan for breakfast? Tressa will be pleased to have you join us. I've got the day off from the office so I'm in no hurry to be off anywhere.'

Kinsley was addicted to fresh air but he didn't have to think twice. Coming from a middle-class family on its uppers he had starved in his student days and fared little better when he was called to take the cloth and went to theological college. Kinsley never refused a meal and he would do justice to whatever Roslyn put in front of him.

'Thank you for your very kind offer. Actually I was going to call on Tressa later today so this will suit me very well.'

The two men and Tressa, who was a hearty eater, tucked into a large plateful of food, augmented by big, wild fried mushrooms. When they had cleared their plates, Kinsley brought up the subject of Celeste Cunningham's visit to the vicarage and her concern for the Urens.

'I agree they need help, Vicar,' Tressa said, pouring them all more tea, 'but I can't see what I can do.'

'Roslyn rather thought you could try to befriend Mrs Uren. You have something in common, you both have new babies.'

'I see.' Tressa was thinking about what she could say to break the ice with Dolores Uren. In the circumstances she could hardly ask her for advice on child care.

'Roslyn thought you might be at a loss as to how you could approach Mrs Uren. She's got an idea. Good used clothes are often handed into the vicarage and Roslyn passes them on to where they are most needed. Recently a bag of girl's baby clothes was handed in. Would you, I wonder, mind telling a little white lie? I'm sure the good Lord won't mind in this case. You could say they were given to you, before little Guy was born, and as you had a boy you wondered if she would like them for her little girl. They are very nice clothes, apparently. They shouldn't offend Mrs Uren in that respect.'

'I think it's a very good idea, Vicar,' Tressa said enthusiastically. 'I'll pop along to the vicarage discreetly and pick the clothes up today and call on the Urens afterwards.' She noticed Andrew was looking dubious.

'Don't you want me to do it?' she said, going to him, and he immediately put his arm round her slight form and held her close.

'It isn't that, darling. I don't like the sound of Gerald Uren. He sounds a bolshie character to me if he can't be bothered to get work and I'm afraid he might get stroppy with you.'

'Oh, you need have no worry on that score, Mr Macarthur.' Kinsley ruefully remembered his ill-fated excursion up to the family's front door. 'The man really is bone idle. He told me to, well, to something off, but he couldn't even be bothered to come to the door to tell me.'

—

A little later that morning, just before opening time, Bruce Tamblyn took it upon himself to rearrange some of the merchandise in the shop. He wasn't impressed with its contents. The shortages made for empty spaces on the shelves, the packaging was dull and dummies were used in place of goods in the window. The place was dreary, out of date, smelled musty and needed brightening up. Who still bought Partridge's Remedial Stomach Mixture? he asked himself. Or Mrs Cox's Magic Gravy Mixture?

'You can't put margarine in the window, Bruce,' Daisy said, glancing up from behind the diamond mesh of the little post office corner. 'It needs to be kept cool. The sun shines right into the window about midday.'

'Oh, sorry, Mum. I wasn't thinking,' he said jovially, taking three packets of margarine back to their original place in the cold cabinet.

'You will remember that you can't serve in the post office, dear, won't you? You need a licence for that. There's one or two who'd report you and get me into trouble, I can tell you.'

Bruce turned his back on his mother and a harsh look distorted his ruddy features. 'I won't forget.' He breathed out long and hard. He saw a woman heading for the door. 'Ah, here comes our first customer. I'll tell her we're not open for ten minutes yet.'

'You can let her in, Bruce. That's Joy Miller who I was telling you about. She works here for a couple of hours on Monday mornings and afternoons when I'm busy after the weekend.'

Bruce unlocked the shop door and the bell rang out its friendly dinga-ling over Joy's head as she walked through the door. She was an ordinary, eager to please sort of woman, nearing thirty, with weak, plump features, who had let her hair, figure and dress sense go since having her four children. She was shy and embarrassed when introduced to Bruce. She was wearing an overall, her hair in a scarf twisted in turban fashion, ready for work.

'I heard you w-were here, Mr Tamblyn,' she stammered, her nondescript eyes on the floor, a hand with bitten-down nails smoothing at straying wisps of hair. The newest arrival in the village was nearly as sophisticated-looking as Harry Lean or Andrew Macarthur; what wouldn't her Bert give to wear clothes like his? And his Canadian accent sent shivers down her back, it was very close to the burr of an American airman she had taken a secret shine to during the war. 'I don't expect you'll find many changes to the village since you were here last.'

'Only the village hall which my cousin Billy had built, Mrs Miller,' Bruce replied, looking into her flushed face and seeing the once pretty girl she had been. 'I'm very pleased to meet you. I'm sure you and I and my mother will get along just fine working together.'

'I'm sure we will. Well, then, I… I'll make up Johnny Prouse's little order that he always picks up on a Monday morning.'

Late in the afternoon, after school was over, Laura came in with Vicki and Daisy bustled them through to her sitting room to meet

Bruce properly, leaving the intimidated Joy to manage alone in the shop. 'Just give me a shout if someone wants stamps or a postal order, Joy,' Daisy told her.

'So you were married to Billy?' Bruce drawled, taking his time shaking Laura's hand. 'I'm sorry I never met you then.'

He seemed reluctant to let go of her hand. Laura pulled it free and moved away from him; he was standing so close he seemed to loom over her. Laura could not have said why but she took an instant dislike to him. There was something false about this man and she didn't like his boldness. She was certain she had just met a braggart.

Wanting to distance herself from him, she said in her coolest voice, 'A pity you missed my wedding. Your sudden appearance must have taken Aunty Daisy by surprise.'

Daisy had told Bruce the true nature of Laura's marriage to his cousin. He would have tried to charm the beautiful widow so recently turned bride but as she seemed as friendly as a snake to a racoon, he returned to the subject he was sure she must loathe. 'Billy did a lot for Kilgarthen. You can see his mark everywhere. You must be proud of his memory.'

Laura merely nodded. She knew he was taunting her.

Vicki had been staring at Bruce since they'd arrived. He looked familiar and when he scowled she remembered where she had seen him. Running to Laura, she clutched her skirt and buried her face against her waist.

'That's the man who was horrible to Uncle Harry, Mummy,' she whispered nervously. She hadn't been afraid of the man while sitting in the car but it was different being in a room with him.

'I'm sorry I frightened you yesterday, Vicki,' Bruce said, putting on a mellow voice. 'Your uncle scared the wits out of me and your Aunty Daisy. We ended up in a ditch. How about I take you into the shop and treat you to some candy – I mean sweets?'

Laura instinctively drew Vicki closer to her and Vicki shook her head. 'Perhaps on the way out, Bruce. She's a little shy at the moment.'

Bruce ruffled Vicki's hair and she shook his hand off. His face hardened but he spoke casually. 'As you said, if I'd arrived earlier on Saturday I would have seen your wedding. Congratulations.'

'Thank you.'

Daisy didn't notice there was a strained atmosphere between her son and the two visitors and she was disappointed when Laura said they couldn't stay long. After buying sweets for Vicki and a few groceries, they were soon walking back to Rosemerryn.

Glad to get away from the 'nasty man', Vicki chattered happily all the way back but Laura couldn't get the dark brooding look of Bruce Tamblyn's face out of her mind. She hoped he wouldn't spell trouble for Daisy. His wasn't the only disgruntled male face she'd had to put up with that day and the moment Spencer came in from the fields for his evening meal she tackled him over his.

'I want a word with you before Ince comes in.'

Spencer was washing at the sink with his shirt off and he dried his torso slowly, eyeing his wife warily. He hadn't missed the edge of discontent in her voice.

'What's the matter?'

'To put it bluntly,' she said, tossing her hair away from her face and putting her hands on her hips, 'I want to know why you are being so unkind and offhand with Ince. You've been irritable with him all day.'

'No, I haven't,' Spencer said defensively. 'And you can't say a thing like that. We haven't been in the yard for most of the day.'

She wasn't going to let him get away with that. 'In the milking shed this morning then. Don't split hairs.'

He narrowed his grey eyes and tightened his mouth. 'Why are you so angry with me?'

'Don't be evasive, Spencer. Ince is your best friend yet you're treating him like a worthless menial. You've been short with him and impatient, he can't do a thing right for you.'

'You don't know what you're talking about,' Spencer muttered sulkily. He wasn't about to admit his jealousy – or that he had suspicions.

Ince came in at that moment and after grunting to Laura passed through the kitchen to his bedroom without a word to his 'best friend'.

'There,' Laura said triumphantly, going up close to Spencer so their vexed voices wouldn't alert Vicki, who was upstairs playing, that they might be on the verge of their first row. 'Neither of you spoke. What's going on?'

'If something's going on, why does it have to be my fault?' Spencer said, raising his voice.

'Because it's you who's being nasty and not Ince, and you can't deny it, can you?'

Spencer was in a corner here. He could turn on Laura and demand to know why she was so keen to take Ince's part but after his surliness with Ince, she was asking a reasonable question. He knew he wasn't being fair. It could be successfully argued that Ince was only being friendly to Laura, he was a kind, helpful man. Spencer didn't want to fall out with Laura, he was very fond of her and he wanted her to be obliging in his bed. She was a strong-minded woman and there would probably be none of that if he upset her too much.

He told a blatant lie. Smiling disarmingly, he went on drying himself. 'You're not used to us yet, my sweet, we're often like this. I get huffy with Ince. He takes no notice of me. He knows I don't mean anything by it. But if it makes you feel any better I'll try not to sound like I'm having a go at him.' Bending forward he kissed her cheek and gave her a boyish grin. Then he turned away and whistled gaily as he put on his shirt.

Laura stared at his back, not sure whether she believed him.

When Ince came downstairs he thought that after a day of either being ignored or picked on, the meal would be eaten in stony silence. But Spencer seemed to have got over his bout of jealousy in the cow shed and he laughed and talked as though everything was normal.

Ince responded in the same manner and he saw Laura visibly relaxing. But he knew things were not normal. They never would be. He and Laura had been too close, were still too close, and there was more than a feeling of awkwardness here while Laura established herself as the mistress of Rosemerryn. Ince knew, looking sorrowfully at Vicki whom he had helped to rear from birth, that for the sake of his friends' marriage he must move out of the farm.

Chapter 11

Tressa collected the baby clothes from Roslyn Farrow and felt very nervous as she walked along School Lane, half expecting that she, too, would be sent on her way by the Urens. Their house was the second in a terrace of four council houses and it was a striking contrast to the Millers next door and the other two. There was no tidy garden or well-cut lawn. The front of the house looked like a scrapyard and the Urens had only lived there a few weeks.

There was no sign of Alfie but his four younger brothers were raucously playing cowboys and Indians and Tressa found herself having to duck missiles used as bullets and arrows on the way up the front path. She took it all in good part although she was glad she had Guy's pram hood up. The boys stopped racing about and whooping at the tops of their voices and stood and stared at her. None of them had shoes on. All four of them were dirty and had impetigo. The two new cases had small red spots and blisters round their thin lips, the other two had loose crusts over weeping sores round their mouths and on their hands and knees. Tressa shuddered at the sight and felt sorry for them.

'Got any chewing gum, missus?' the oldest of the boys asked, copying Alfie's form of cheek; not unexpectedly he was viewing her with suspicion.

'No, I'm sorry,' Tressa replied, hoping none of the children would try to pull back Guy's covers and touch him. She wished she had left Guy at home but it would have made her errand more difficult. 'Is your mother at home?'

'She is,' a terse voice said from the doorstep. 'And what do you want with me?'

Tressa turned to see a tall, dark, well-set woman in long floating clothes which had seen better days. She was holding a scrawny, almost naked baby who was feeding fretfully from her bare pendulous breast. Dolores Uren looked about thirty years old and despite having borne six children in quick succession she had an enviable figure and a proud beauty about her. A thick plait of long black hair hung over her chest, getting in the way of the baby's suckling, gold-hooped earrings glittered in her ears, her nails were exceedingly long, pointed and varnished crimson red. Her black eyes seemed to bore deep into Tressa's soul and she knew she would have to be careful with her little white lie.

'I'm Tressa Macarthur, Mrs Uren.' Tressa pushed her fine pram up to the doorstep and the other woman looked in at Guy who was stirring from his sleep. 'I live at Tregorlan Farm on the outskirts of the village. I hope you won't be offended at why I've come here.' She couldn't help herself colouring. 'You see, when I was expecting Guy, people were very kind and passed on some of their baby clothes to me. I, um, wondered if you would like to have the little girl's clothes I was given.' Tressa lifted up the bag of clothes she had only just put at the bottom of the pram.

'What are they like?' Dolores Uren asked, regarding Tressa with a twist to her full red lips.

Tressa gulped, heartily relieved that Roslyn had unpacked them at the vicarage so she could see them. 'Little dresses and cardigans mainly. There's ever such a sweet little pink and white dress with smocking at the front. And there's leggings and a winter coat and bonnet. They're in good condition or I wouldn't be offering them to you.'

'Don't you want to keep them for yourself in case you have a girl next time?'

Tressa had already thought out answers to possible questions she might receive.

'There's no guarantee I would ever have a girl,' she said, 'and I thought it a shame to have them lying about in a cupboard when they could be put to good use.'

'Do you know why I reckon you're here?'

Tressa made ready to run back down the front path with the pram. 'No, why?'

'You're lonely.' Dolores' voice dropped a tone, the aggression which seemed a living part of her went out of her eyes. 'It often happens to new mums. Your man's at work and you can't lead the active life you're used to, or see your friends when you want to with a baby in tow everywhere you go. You don't know what to do with yourself all day, do you? So you've come looking for company.'

Suppressing a deep sigh of relief, Tressa admitted that was the truth, although it wasn't; she was perfectly happy caring for Guy and had her father and aunty for company when Andrew was at the office.

'Want a cup of tea? Come inside and bring your baby with you. I'd like to have a good look at him.' When Tressa hesitated, worried what the condition of the house would be like inside, Dolores smiled reassuringly. 'Don't worry, I'll make sure the kids don't touch your lovely pram.'

She shouted at the four boys who had gradually edged closer to them and were hanging on to their every word, hoping a treat of food was in the offing. 'Carry on with your game, you lot, and don't you dare touch this nice lady's pram or I'll stram your arses bloody hard. Mind you stay in the garden.'

The boys ran off, hooting and screaming, and Tressa wanted to put her hands over her ears. A glance down the garden and she saw the predatory figure of Ada Prisk watching her. Ignoring the old woman's beckoning hand, she lifted Guy out of his pram and carried him inside the house after Dolores.

'That old hag's been spreading some tales about we,' Dolores said over her shoulder, leading the way down a narrow passage. There was a nice shade of blue paint on the walls from the previous tenants but it had a line of small grubby handprints on it.

'I shouldn't take any notice of Mrs Prisk, she does cause trouble but she's really kind-hearted,' Tressa said.

They reached the kitchen at the back of the house. It contained a table of sorts, two bare wooden rocking chairs and the crib which the baby slept in. A very old dog of indeterminate breed left an old bone it was trying to gnaw on and wobbled its way over to Tressa.

'That's Woody,' Dolores said, holding her daughter in one arm while still feeding her and expertly tipping tea leaves from a tin teapot one-handedly into the sink and making a fresh brew. 'I've had him for years. As you can see, he's on his last legs now.'

'He's lovely,' Tressa said, gingerly patting the dog's matted thin grey head. 'I've got a dog. Meg. She's a big brown mongrel.'

'She must be useful on the farm. Do you take milk? Don't worry, it's fresh. I try to give the kids a little bit most days. I haven't got any sugar though.'

Dolores poured out three mugs of tea, one mug was huge and she excused herself to carry it out of the room.

Tressa put the bag of clothes on the table then sat down in one of the rocking chairs which was very comfortable. She had been hoping she could report back to Roslyn and Celeste Cunningham that the Urens weren't really dirty, that Dolores just allowed the children a free rein to roam about and get grubby, but the kitchen hadn't seen a broom or mop in weeks, dust was thick everywhere, the cloam sink was stained brown and smelt offensively. There was a general smell of rotting food, dirty nappies and baby sick.

'There,' Dolores said when she came back with little Emily. 'That's got my man settled. Now we can have a nice little chat. I'll tell your fortune if you like, but I'll have to charge or 'tis unlucky.'

Tressa didn't want her fortune told but she would be glad to give Dolores all the money in her purse if it meant putting some food on the table for the children. Guy was stretching and puckering up his face in Tressa's arms, threatening to cry at any moment.

'If it's his feed time don't be afraid to feed him here,' Dolores said, sitting in the other rocking chair and switching Emily to her other breast. 'The kids won't come in and Gerald won't be getting out of bed for ages.'

'Is your husband poorly, Dolores?' Tressa asked.

'He's not ray husband,' Dolores said bluntly. 'We never got married. He's not the father of my first four either. Gerald doesn't come round till much later in the day – he's what you might call a night person.'

Tressa could guess why Gerald Uren had difficulty getting out of bed. Amongst the other smells, she recognised the dank odour of stale alcohol. She wondered how the Urens managed for money but of course she couldn't ask. Guy woke up and began to bawl. Tressa opened the front of her dress and unselfconsciously fed him.

'He's a fine baby,' Dolores remarked, ferreting about in her dress, coming up with half a cigarette and lighting it. 'He's nearly as big as my Emily already and he's weeks younger.'

'He was nearly nine pounds born,' Tressa said to make Dolores feel better about her under-developed offspring.

'Do you want any more?'

'Oh, yes. Andrew and I would like four. Two boys and two girls would be nice.'

Dolores gazed into her eyes for several long, unsettling moments. 'You'll have them too, believe me. I always wanted a girl. I'm expecting another one at the end of the year. I hope it'll be another girl.'

'That will be lovely,' and Tressa could have kicked herself at how lame and insincere she sounded. Poor child was what she was thinking.

'Your husband's a good-looking, sandy-haired man, isn't he?'

'That's right. He comes from London originally.'

'I've seen you together, it's obvious how much he adores you.'

Dolores suddenly leaned forward, dislodging Emily from her nipple and making her whine as she searched about desperately for it. Tressa felt disturbed. She trembled. Dolores' eyes had become huge and intense, there seemed to be sparks flashing from them. The room seemed cold and eerie now.

'I'm going to give you a warning now, Tressa, and I hope you won't take it lightly.'

'What?'

'This may sound like a typical gypsy's warning, but beware of a black-haired man. He means you harm.'

Tressa tried to laugh it off but she felt frightened and found herself blurting out, 'Oh, you mean Harry Lean. He's been trying to seduce me for years but he never gets anywhere. I'm not afraid of him.'

'Be afraid of him, Tressa. Be very afraid of him. The danger will come in an unexpected way.'

With a shaky hand Tressa sipped her tea. She wished she had never come here. She had come to help and had received a lot of frightening mumbo jumbo in return. She couldn't tell Andrew about this. He was so protective of her he would be furious with Dolores for upsetting her. She thought about what Andrew would say to comfort her. It would be something along the lines of the other woman finding out all the information about the villagers that she could to help her charlatan purposes to make money out of gullible people. Everyone knew what Harry Lean had been up to over the years concerning her. The obvious danger from him was that he'd go too far one day and rape her. Tressa couldn't believe Harry would ever do that but she couldn't stop a violent shudder. Guy stopped feeding and began to cry pitifully. She had a hard task comforting him.

Dolores said very little else. She crooned softly to Emily when she'd finished feeding her then put her in her crib without changing her wet nappy. Tressa cut Guy's feed short. She refused to let Dolores look at her hand for a full reading but gave her two half-crowns to ward off bad luck, and as an extra precaution thanked her for the warning.

Dolores was still in a serious mood when she thanked Tressa for the baby clothes and showed her out of the house. Tressa saw a tiny bottle on the doorstep and stooped to pick it up. It was filled with purple liquid. She handed it to Dolores.

'It's gentian violet,' Dolores said, twisting the bottle round in her long, tapered fingers. 'Someone must have left it for the kids, to paint on their impetigo.'

'That was thoughtful,' Tressa replied, trying to regain her sense of perspective in the mild sunshine. 'It's very effective.' She believed the act of kindness had come from Ada Prisk.

'A two-edged sword,' Dolores said, and Tressa was fearful she was going to announce a prophecy of doom and gloom. 'This stuff will make the kids' skin go purple and that's just as embarrassing as the impetigo. It's not necessarily caused by uncleanliness, you know,' she finished defensively.

'Of course not,' Tressa agreed. 'Well, I must be going.'

'Drop in any time,' Dolores called after her as Tressa wheeled the pram out into the lane.

Tressa waved goodbye. She would call again, but not for a long time and certainly not with Guy.

Dolores slopped back to the kitchen and gazed down on her sleeping daughter. She rocked backwards and forwards on her feet. 'Poor baby, poor baby,' she murmured over and over again. 'Poor Guy.'

Andrew wasn't the only one to take a day off from his office. Harry was out riding on the moor with Celeste. They had followed the Withey Brook which ran at the back of the village and through Hawksmoor property, then they had trotted on to Twelve Men's Moor to look up at the half-mile ridge of granite that made up the summit of Kilmar Tor. Celeste declined the scramble to the top and they finally stopped for a picnic at a quiet little spot Harry knew.

They sat on a blanket. Harry unpacked the food hamper. Granite boulders lay embedded in thickets of gorse and fern and on the open heath. Here and there was a pink or purple or yellow or blue splash of small-headed moorland flowers. A crow, its feathers ruffled by the steady warm wind, seemed to be watching Celeste from its perch on an old wooden post that stood aslant. The bird reminded Celeste of a particular stern, gowned schoolmistress from her past, who because of her high jinks and pranks had declared to both staff and pupils that Celeste was the bane of her life. Miss Forsythe wouldn't be at all surprised at the many twists and turns her life had taken.

Celeste leaned back and looked up at the sky. 'There's quite a few clouds up there. Are you sure we won't suddenly get caught in a mist? Laura wrote to me about the time she got lost on the moor out riding and nearly died.'

Harry put a sandwich box down on the blanket and gazed about. He sniffed the air. 'We'll be fine. I've lived here nearly all my life and you get a sixth sense about the weather changing. Here, have something to eat. I'll open the wine.'

'Did you happen to bring any lemonade or something? I don't want any wine, thank you.'

'No wine?' Harry was mortified. 'This is a very good hock. I chose it specially.' He rooted about in the hamper. 'I've brought some water in case it was a hot day. If I'd known I would have packed a flask of coffee.'

'Water will do fine, darling.' Celeste munched delicately on a ham sandwich. 'Mmmm, food tastes so much better out of doors and best of all in a setting like this.'

'It's also one of the best settings for making love in,' Harry drawled. 'See that post over there? The one the crow's on? Just past it there's a deep depression in the ground and a sort of natural cave. You come across it almost by accident. The opening is very small but it's quite wide once you're inside it. I first went in it when I was a boy and found it was safe. It's shored up and roofed by moorstone. I used to show it to my friends – in fact I made my first conquest inside it.'

'I don't doubt it,' Celeste muttered, and he missed the hint of sarcasm.

'But making love outside is better. We'll be all right, there's no one around for miles.'

'Maybe so, but I'm not in the mood, Harry.'

'That's disappointing. I felt certain you were going to make this a day to remember.'

He brushed away a large black and red insect stinging his arm and smiled while pouring himself a generous glass of wine, confident she would change her mind. Celeste made love with an abandon even he had a hard time keeping up with. He would make this their last time; regular sex with a woman usually gave her the notion he was making a commitment to her. He intended to get married one day, perhaps in about five years, to provide an heir for Hawksmoor. Until then he wanted to enjoy his freedom.

'How much longer are you staying in the village?' he asked.

Celeste was glad he didn't try to talk her round or get moody with her. She hadn't enjoyed making love with Harry the last time and she'd had to work hard to achieve satisfaction. Her body needed the rest. It would have a very important job to do quite soon. If only Harry, or Ince, were different sort of men, they might get involved, but Harry saw women only in terms of how he could get sex, and how much of it, out of them, and Ince was too honourable.

'Oh, just a few more weeks,' she replied. 'Then I have something pressing to do. Of course it's not the same now Laura's married. I thought we'd go around together, but she's become all domesticated and so far we've only gone on shopping trips to Launceston, Bodmin and Liskeard and one afternoon we drove to Dozmary Pool in Spencer's clapped-out old car. I'm keen to do something for the Uren family before I go though. Do you know them?'

'The dirty lot? The mother looks as if she might have been a rare beauty in her day but I couldn't fancy it with her now.' Harry would in fact have made an overture to Dolores if she'd kept her family clean. 'I don't see you as the crusading type, Celeste.'

'It's the children I feel sorry for. The poor little things don't stand a chance in life. I've approached the vicar. He and his wife are getting a few people together to try to help – Tressa Macarthur's one. I hope she can overcome her shyness or she won't be much use.'

'Tressa? She's not shy, just very quiet. Has she agreed to help?'

'Yes. I saw the vicar's wife as I was leaving the cottage and she told me Tressa would be calling on the Urens today and would be letting me know how she got on. I've made friends with the oldest boy, Alfie, he's quite a card. I think he's an intelligent boy. Given a better home life he could go far. I've made inquiries as to whether they are entitled to any government help, what health checks there are for children now, that sort of thing. As soon as I know I shall call on the family myself.'

Harry leaned back on his elbow and stared into his wine for a long time. 'I suppose people in our position should help those who aren't so fortunate. Is there anything I can do? I'd ask my mother but there's a gymkhana and fete at Hawksmoor House soon and she's busy organising that.'

Celeste had seen the way Harry looked at Tressa. She didn't want any complications in her attempts to help the Urens. 'If I think of anything I'll let you know.'

'Don't worry, Celeste,' he returned, aware of her coolness and considering this picnic a damned waste of his time. 'I'm sure I shall think of something myself.'

Chapter 12

One of the first things Laura did as Vicki's stepmother was to accompany her to the school at Lewannick and introduce herself to her headmaster and teachers. Before, she had mainly cared for Vicki's practical needs, now she did more personal things. She chose new clothes for Vicki. She taught her how to arrange flowers and sew simple doll's clothes. They soon fell into a pattern where they did everything together, baking cakes, tending the flower garden, feeding the ducks and chickens, pegging out washing, roaming the moor on foot or pony; Benjy Miller became quite forgotten, and sometimes so was Spencer.

As far as Laura could see, Spencer seemed to be settled with the changes their marriage had brought him and she overlooked his odd spark of bad temper. When he wanted to be quiet, which was a big part of his nature, she left him to it. Sometimes she thought he must be thinking of Natalie. He had obviously trained Barney to behave; not long after the wedding, Barney had stopped leaping and barking at her unless he was glad to see her. Spencer congratulated her on the progress she had made with the milking and other manual jobs and she was pleased with this and with herself.

On one subject she encountered difficulty – money. One evening Spencer was impatiently filling out some government forms at the kitchen table. Laura had not yet learned that he was best left alone while he was applying himself to this task which he hated with all his heart, and she mentioned that she wanted to make some changes to Vicki's room. With Vicki's help she had taken the measurements for new curtains and they had talked about fresh paint, borders and bedding and she had the details jotted down in a notepad.

She hid the notepad behind her back when he sighed heavily, staring down at the pen in his fingers. 'We can't afford it. The tractor needs overhauling first and some of the outhouses need repairs. I can't do it all from moorstone and odds and ends.'

'But I could pay for it, Spencer,' Laura said coaxingly, adding quickly when he glowered at her, 'The things needed for Vicki's room, I mean.'

'There's nothing wrong with Vicki's room,' he said in a decidedly frosty tone. 'Natalie decorated it right through just before Vicki was born.'

Hurt and feeling something of an intruder in her own home, Laura turned away.

'It's my responsibility to provide, Laura,' he muttered, returning to the forms. 'For all of us.'

Catching him in a better mood a few days later, after reminding him of Celeste's faint and how she might have needed the doctor quickly, she persuaded Spencer to agree to having a telephone installed. He had got better prices for some calves at market than he'd anticipated and he insisted that he would pay half the cost. Laura thought that although the outhouses could wait, it was a pity he didn't spend the money on the tractor instead.

Both Laura and Spencer appreciated Ince making himself scarce. As soon as his work was done he either made his way to extra chapel meetings or to Johnny Prouse's to do a few repairs to his little cottage. Sometimes they worked so late Ince stayed overnight. Laura and Spencer noticed that he didn't go to Carrick Cross any more. Spencer's irascible attitude towards Ince eased and for the most part they resumed their old easy-going friendship, but every now and then, when Ince had a smile or kind word for Laura or she for him, Spencer would glare at them.

Laura was intimate with Spencer any time he wanted, which was often, when Ince wasn't there, eager to conceive a baby and enjoy the physical contact. She looked forward more and more to these times as her attraction to Spencer grew, sometimes initiating them herself. She had great hopes for the future, but her optimism had a setback at the beginning of June. She was collecting eggs in the hen house when she felt a familiar niggle of discomfort in her lower stomach. She hurried to the toilet and her disappointment was immense when her fear was confirmed; there was to be no new baby on Rosemerryn yet.

She felt thoroughly miserable and was glad Vicki was at school, wanting to be alone. She had said she would finish off in the shippen that morning but forgot all about it.

'Milking no longer holding an attraction for you?' Spencer asked teasingly as he came inside for lunch. A large number of orchid-like wild flowers grew in the field where he had been herding his cattle and he held out a bunch of the creamy white and rose-pink blossoms to her.

'No,' she replied astringently, putting a plate of bread and butter on the table with a thud.

'I didn't mean anything by that remark, Laura.' The flowers were dropped limply at his side. 'I'm quite happy if you just want to look after the house and Vicki. If you've been getting tired and feel I've been taking advantage of you then I'm very sorry.'

He had spoken so sincerely, tenderly, his face reflecting his words, it made Laura search for her hanky and dab at the tears that seared her eyes.

Spencer went to her. He put his arms round her and she pressed her face against his chest. Caressing her hair, he said gently, 'What's brought this on?'

'I – I'm just being silly,' she sniffed, feeling very foolish.

He lifted her face and kissed her hot cheek. 'Silly about what?'

'I've got my monthly.'

'Is that all?' He ruffled her hair and held her tighter.

'I want a baby so much, Spencer. Don't get me wrong, I love Vicki dearly but it's something I've always wanted. Sometimes it hurts so much, like a terrible physical pain.'

Tenderly he brushed away the tears falling down her face and smiled warmly. 'Think about it this way, darling. In a few days' time we can have a lot of fun trying again.'

She laughed and sobbed at the same time, then taking his floral gift from him she wound her arms round his neck and clung to him.

'You look nice today, Joy,' Bruce Tamblyn said, taking another long appreciative look at her. They were at the back of the shop which had just closed for the lunch period. Joy was fetching her cardigan. Daisy had left to walk to Rosemerryn to spend the afternoon with Laura; she welcomed these little breaks Bruce's presence allowed her.

Joy's appearance had seen a few subtle changes of late, and the more observant among the villagers had noticed they had occurred since Bruce's arrival in Kilgarthen. From her regular wage at the shop she had saved up and treated herself to a permanent wave. She had lost several pounds in weight, practically starving herself to do so, and the ten stones, four pounds she was down to suited her large frame. She had started to wear the outfit she'd worn at Laura's wedding and some beads when she went to work. Today she had put on a little lipstick and powder.

Joy stroked her small sweeping waves with a coquettish but self-conscious movement. 'With Celeste Cunningham charming all the men in the village I… I thought I ought to take stock of…' Bruce was looking at her closely and her face burned. 'Of my looks.'

'You've done an excellent job, Bert must be very proud of you.' He lowered his voice to a husky whisper, 'I'd much rather have your looks to that London woman's, Joy.'

'You would?' Joy squeaked, twisting her cardigan in taut hands.

She wanted to linger here before going home. On the second day she had worked in the shop with Bruce he had told her all about his unhappy home circumstances. She had sympathised. He had seemed grateful and she had felt less in awe of him. She found him rather dashing compared to the rapidly receding charms of Bert who had grown stouter and more boring by the year, his only idea of an outing a weekly trip to the pub without her. Bruce was always courteous to her and paid her compliments. He hastened to lift heavy boxes for her. He sent sweets home to her children. Joy began to resent the mediocre life she led, tied down in a small village miles from the nearest town, with a man who belched at mealtimes and rarely uttered a word of gratitude. Bruce made her feel young, attractive and alive again. He had given her the incentive to make the most of herself.

'How about having a cup of tea with me before you go?' Bruce said nonchalantly. 'Your kids are at school. Bert's at work. I haven't got anyone to talk to now Mother's gone out. I could make us a sandwich.'

'That will be very nice,' Joy replied in the careful tone she'd adopted to lessen her natural warm Cornish burr. She was crimson with embarrassment as she followed him into the kitchen. She knew full well Bruce Tamblyn was a man of the world and that agreeing to stay here alone with him meant more than sharing a spot of lunch.

Bruce hardly took his eyes off her as he made the tea and cut a plate of Spam sandwiches. Joy sat meekly at the table. She thought she was sitting there in a regal manner, like someone who was used to being entertained, but after a few moments she realised she was sitting on her hands and leaning forward in the habit of one of her small daughters who was always eager to eat. Horrified, she snatched her hands off the chair and sat up straight. She took a sandwich off the plate with all the decorum she could muster, making the tiniest bite in the bread and thick-cut meat.

Bruce munched away completely at ease. He smoked a cigarette, keeping it in the ashtray between puffs, turning it round and round and slowly tapping off the ash, watching Joy, contemplating, anticipating.

Joy's throat wouldn't receive more than the first bite of sandwich and the tea would only go down in an obvious nervous gulp. She didn't want anything to eat and drink anyway. Her stomach was churning. She glanced at Bruce, smiled, gazed down shyly, then did it all again.

'Not hungry?' he asked, raising his thick eyebrows.

'Not really.' She looked down at her hands, shaking at each side of her plate.

'Would you like a chocolate biscuit?'

'No, thank you.'

'No appetite at all?'

'No, I'm sorry.'

'I'm not, Joy.'

'Oh?' She couldn't bring herself to look at him now.

'You feel it too, don't you?'

'Wh-what?'

'The attraction we have for each other.'

Joy got up so hastily she knocked her sandwich to the floor. She picked it up, threw it on the table and fled.

But Bruce caught her arm.

'Don't fight it, Joy. We like each other, a lot, perhaps even more than that. I can't get you out of my mind for a single moment, day or night. I know you feel the same.'

He pulled her into his arms and Joy struggled – for a little while.

She became still, feeling the broadness of his body, the brute strength of his thickly-muscled arms, smelling the manly scent of his aftershave. He was looking into her eyes and she felt weak and dizzy. His face was coming closer to hers. His beard was tickling her cheek. His lips were on hers and she went wild with desire.

They panted like old dogs, clinging to each other, finally breaking into adolescent giggles.

Bruce bit her neck. 'That was great. Let's go upstairs for some more.'

'We'll have to be careful someone doesn't come,' Joy replied, feeling coy as the full force of their actions washed over her. She pushed him away and straightened her skirt.

'Mother won't be back for ages and if someone comes to the shop we'll just ignore them. Come on, Joy, don't let me down. I think we're about to start something that'll be really good for both of us.'

Bruce was jolly and businesslike in the shop that afternoon. People came and went in dribs and drabs, impressed with his efficiency and chattiness, but one customer in particular caught his special attention. He dashed to open the door for Ma Noon who hobbled her great weight inside and bought two ounces of plain flour, gravy browning and a bar of coal tar soap.

'It's a lovely day, Mrs Noon,' he said breezily, packing the shopping into her basket.

'You remember me then?' Ma Noon said, handing him a ten shilling note.

'Yes, I remember you. I'm ashamed to admit I wasn't the nicest of children. My mother tells me that you got on very well with my cousin, Billy. Apparently he did little jobs for you. If there's anything I can do for you I hope you won't be shy in asking.'

'You were a despicable child, Bruce Tamblyn,' Ma Noon replied with a deadly calm, her shrewd eyes glaring at him as if he was so much rubbish. 'You used to throw stones at my goats and jeer at me. You called me a big fat witch and dared me to put a spell on you. You encouraged the other children to do the same. I despised you then and I certainly don't want you on my property now.' Shuffling round, her folds of fat wobbling like ripples on a river, she stuck her bonneted head in the air and made for the door.

Bruce beat her to it and opened the door for her with a smile disguising the rage bubbling under his stone-hard exterior. He hoped she would trip over the step. He watched her heave her bulk onto the trap; it was accomplished with a considerable struggle. He hoped her pony would drop dead in its shafts, toppling the old woman onto the ground. He swung the shop door shut and the bell jangled in protest.

'Stupid old bitch,' he scowled. His good manners might have been lost on her but he had noticed she'd been wearing a good quality cameo brooch.

Les Tremorrow watched his granddaughter as she put a loaf of home-made bread on the table for their midday meal. He licked his chapped lips when she added the dish of pilchards he had bought from the fish cart which stopped at the crossroads for his custom. Eve had marinated the pilchards in vinegar and herbs, and after years of plain food, hastily prepared since Ruby had died, he was looking forward to the treat. He was getting used to having Eve around, even if she did have rather fine manners and wouldn't allow him to swear and disapproved of him smoking his pipe indoors.

He'd had good reason to throw his daughter, Angela, out of his home. His wife, Ruby, had never forgiven him, and although he'd suffered the almost total silence she'd treated him to for the next twelve years until she'd died, he missed her and had been terribly lonely. He'd had mixed feelings when he'd received Eve's first letter about Angela's death and her request that they meet. He was glad that he'd relented and had agreed to meet her. He'd seen from the very first moment that she was a different kettle of fish to her mother. Eve was respectable. And she was kind. She was quiet, but it was a different sort of quietness to what he'd endured with Ruby. She was a willing worker and her tasks were accomplished quickly yet she seemed to move slowly and gracefully, and while he didn't encourage questions about Angela's childhood and youth (the truth was too terrible even to think about) she chatted in her soft melodious voice and told him about her life in Plymouth. He didn't want her to go back. He didn't want to live out the rest of his days alone. He had worked out a suitable story about her existence to present to the villagers.

'Do you like it here, Eve?' he asked her suddenly.

'It's very peaceful, Grandfather. You soon get used to the wind.'

'We hit it off all right from the start, didn't we?'

'Yes, we did. You can come to the table now.'

'Aw, can't I have it down here in my chair?'

Eve thought to argue but seeing her only living relative screwing up his wizened old face appealingly, she gave in, even though he had manners like a pig and without the use of the table a lot of his meal would end up on his shirt and trousers. 'I'll bring it over to you.'

Les chuckled happily. He liked to be pampered. 'You're a good maid. Don't forget the salt 'n' pepper, m'dear.'

'You really shouldn't eat so much salt, Grandfather,' she said chidingly, passing him his meal served on the tray he had used for Ince the first day he had worked here.

'Why not? What's wrong with salt? I can afford it. I'm not short of a bob or two, you know.' He hoped that would impress her.

'It's not good for you, that's why.'

''Tis nice to have someone to worry over me again after all these years. Don't know how I stuck it for so long, all alone here, after your grandmother died.'

'Why did you never get in touch with my mother? She might have come to you.' Eve knew very little about why her mother had become

131

estranged from her parents. All she had ever got out of Angela, who had flown into a rage at her probings, was that she didn't blame Ruby but Les was an 'evil man'. There were many things Eve wanted to know. If Angela didn't blame Ruby, why didn't they keep in touch? In what way was Les evil? He was lazy, he readily took advantage of her, as he had the good nature of Ince Polkinghorne. He spat and swore, he was none too clean and she often had to remind him to wash and shave, to fetch a clean handkerchief, to change his underwear and socks. And it had to be admitted that it was Les's grouchiness and ingratitude which had stopped the man with the gentle brown eyes from coming here. That was a pity.

'You know why,' Les muttered, tucking into his food, not looking at her. ''Twas too late to be sorry then and 'tis the same now. What your mother did was unforgivable! Your mother was poison, and she tried to spread it. Don't ask me about it again.' If Les wasn't so keen for Eve to stay he would have flown into a terrible rage with her. 'At least we've got each other. We must be grateful for that.'

Eve said nothing in reply. She became resigned that she would never know the whole story. Les Tremorrow was a strange, secretive old man, but when you had no one in the whole wide world, you were grateful to be related to anyone, and she did like her grandfather.

Les scoffed down his food, drained the teapot dry, wiped his mouth noisily on his shirt sleeve, and settled down for a snooze. Eve was washing the dishes when he gave a groan and got up out of his chair. 'Think I'll go upstairs and lie down for a bit, m'dear. Got a bit of a headache. What are you going to do for the afternoon?'

Eve looked at a bundle of clean laundry she had put aside on one of the deep windowsills. 'I'll look for some needles and cotton and mend your clothes, Grandfather. You've hardly got a button on your shirts. Did Grandmother keep a button jar?'

'In the sitting room, I b'lieve. Like I said, 'tis nice having someone here looking after me.'

Curiosity got the better of Ince and he made a visit to Carrick Cross that evening. He had often thought about Eve Tremorrow in the quietness of his soul. It helped take his mind off his unsettled life, off having to move out of Rosemerryn. Johnny Prouse had said he could move back in with him any time but Ince was waiting for the right moment to tell Spencer to avoid hurting him. In the meantime he filled his mind with images of Eve. A longing grew in him to know if she was still at the smallholding and to learn something more about her.

It had occurred to him today while out haymaking that if the quiet young woman was called Eve Tremorrow, then it almost certainly meant that her mother had never married. Perhaps the reason why Les wanted to keep her a secret was because she was illegitimate. A few careful remarks in the village revealed that no one knew what had happened to Angela Tremorrow when she had upped and left home. It was assumed she'd had enough of Les's constant moanings and went off to seek her fortune. Les hadn't been to chapel since Ince had discovered Eve so he had been unable to ask the old man about her.

The days were getting longer and it was still light as he stepped off the moor. The sky was streaked with fluorescent pinks and oranges, a bank of clouds was building up on all horizons, promising rain in the night. When he reached Carrick Cross Ince did a double-take before going through the gate. It was now painted in black gloss and the name Carrick Cross was scripted with a flourish in yellow paint. An oval-shaped plaque had been nailed to the front of the gate, and a picture of a fox and badger surrounded by moorland flowers was expertly painted on it. It looked as if Eve was still here and that she had an artistic streak in her.

He saw her in the garden, taking in washing, and strode straight up to her. 'Good evening, Miss Tremorrow.' There was none of the shock, fear or indignation in her eyes that he had first seen in them. Now they were softly bright, like a kitten's.

'Good evening, Mr Polkinghorne. So you've come back then?'

'I see you're wearing your own dress.' It was a simple cotton gown, ruched at the bodice, with plain sleeves and a small, neat, white collar. It gave a little roundness to her angular figure and suited her perfectly.

She smiled lightly. 'When you saw me that day I had few of my own things here.'

'And have you all of them now?'

'If that's a question to find out whether I am staying here for good, I cannot give you an answer.' She started walking towards the house, the washing basket held on her hip. 'I haven't sent for all my things yet. A friend is holding them for me. I might stay. I could easily get myself a new position.'

'What exactly is your position?'

'I think you are not usually so forthright, Mr Polkinghorne.'

'No, I'm not, but I'm most curious to know something about a woman who wants her presence in Kilgarthen kept a secret. Indeed, from what I can gather, no one in the village knows of your existence.'

'Good, I'm glad of that.' They were at the doorstep. 'Did you want to see my grandfather? I'm afraid he's taken early to his bed. He got a sudden fierce headache this afternoon and I took his tea up to him.'

Ince was sure he knew what Les's game was. 'Sounds to me like he doesn't want you to leave him. He's got used to having an unpaid servant.'

'Perhaps,' Eve conceded. 'But he is the only living relative I've got.'

'Really?' Ince had thought that was probably the case. 'You were going to tell me about your position.'

'I was not, but I don't mind you knowing. I'm a lady's maid.'

That accounted for her nice way of speaking, this pale-faced lady-like creature. He looked at her hands. They were long-fingered and well cared for, the nails filed short.

'How come you're so good with the goats and pigs? I take it it's you who have been looking after them.'

'I was a Land Army girl during the war but Grandfather has always looked after them well.'

The door was opened and Les peered out, rubbing the sleep from his eyes. 'Oh, 'tis you, boy. I wondered who Eve was talking to.'

'I think Mr Polkinghorne has come trying to catch us out, Grandfather. To see if you had me chained up in my room.'

So she had a sense of humour too.

'Have 'ee come to do some work, Ince?' Les asked blatantly. 'Eve's done a few things for me. Did you notice the gate on your way in? But I could still do with a hand with the heavier work.'

Why don't you do something yourself? Ince wanted to ask, but his curiosity was still not assuaged over this mysterious young woman, so he said good-humouredly, 'I'd be glad to, Les.'

'You can't expect Mr Polkinghorne to start anything now, Grandfather,' Eve said, moving past him with the washing. 'It will be dark soon. He must come inside and have some supper with us.'

'She's good to me but a bit bossy,' Les whispered in an affectionate tone to Ince.

'I'm sure your granddaughter has many interesting facets to her character,' Ince whispered back. And he would be interested to learn about them and all her secrets.

Chapter 13

Kilgarthen had enjoyed fetes and gymkhanas at Hawksmoor House up until the untimely death of Natalie Jeffries seven years ago. When Spencer blamed Felicity for his wife's death and refused to let her have anything to do with her granddaughter, Felicity had shut herself away and all social occasions on her property had ceased. Since Spencer had forgiven her and she had taken her rightful place as Vicki's doting grandmother, she had gradually resumed her role as the lady of the village. This year she was opening the grounds of her house again and was holding a fete and a gymkhana. Many people from all over the locality and most of the villagers flocked there eagerly for the grand opening.

Felicity had persuaded an acquaintance, Sir Ambrose Geach-Ford, to open the fete. He was a middle-aged man well past his prime, whose froggy features told of a life spent wining, dining and womanising. But as he had no distinguished war record, was not attired as expected of a country squire – he was wearing a rumpled suit and a bow tie which didn't quite meet in the middle – and hadn't been divorced in recent years to give the gossips a field day, no one was much interested in him. After two minutes of his blustering nonsensical speech, people were heading off to have a go at the coconut shy, ride on the merry-go-round, try to catch and win the greased piglet, get their mounts ready for the jumps or enjoy the wares of the tea and beer tents.

Laura had arrived early in the morning with Vicki to help with the preparations and they stood beside Felicity who was wearing a stunning dress and hat, satisfied with the array of colourful tents, stalls and bunting on Hawksmoor's huge sweeping lawn. The village brass band and a traction engine powering a fair organ provided the music and the members of the village male voice choir were milling around in their maroon blazers to give a small concert later in the afternoon.

The day had made a wet drizzly start but the sun now shone obligingly on the mid-June afternoon, and utility summer frocks, open-neck shirts, sandals and straw hats were much in evidence. Ada Prisk had to be different. She was wearing a formal grey dress and a green velveteen picture hat heavily decorated with artificial cherries.

'You look lovely, Miss Celeste,' Ada said. Celeste was out to charm in a red silk-chenille suit with a fan-pleated skirt and matching pill-box hat which was trimmed with a black silk bow that was bigger than the hat. Five minutes later Ada pointed her out to a neighbour, Mrs Sparnock. 'Just look at the woman, all done up like a dog's dinner.'

'Ada's on form today,' Laura laughed to Felicity.

'What would village events be like without her?' Felicity said happily, then taking Vicki's hand she went round proudly showing her off to all her guests.

This left Laura with the unwelcome task of showing Sir Ambrose Geach-Ford to the beer tent which was run by Pat and Mike Penhaligon from the pub. Sir Ambrose may have lost his flair for speeches and his dress sense but he retained an eye for a pretty face. Offering his arm to Laura with a flourish, he tried to steer her round the back of the beer tent. After a struggle she managed to get him inside it.

'Have you got a glass of wine for Sir Ambrose please, Mike?' Laura gasped, red-faced, fending Sir Ambrose off while pushing him down on the nearest bench.

'Certainly have, my luvver,' Pat grinned perkily, holding up a bottle of red wine.

Laura continued on a whisper, 'Thanks, and will you make sure he doesn't follow me out?'

'You just leave un t'me!' Mike bellowed jovially, his pale blue eyes twinkling with the prospect of fun in store. 'I know his game. I'll keep un here for a while then get him along to his chauffeur.'

Laura thanked Mike with feeling, glad that Spencer, who had stayed behind on the farm to work and would be arriving later, hadn't seen her predicament; he might have thumped Sir Ambrose soundly and thrown him off the premises, regardless of his being the guest of honour.

Alfie Uren, his younger brothers in tow, was yearning after a wooden model of an aeroplane, a replica of a Hurricane, on the craft stall. All except Alfie had gentian violet to go with moor dirt and sticky jam on their faces. Alfie's also had a bruise and blood streaks which he had got from fighting a bigger boy who'd insulted his family. Alfie's hand reached out towards the aeroplane.

'Don't you dare touch it,' a man with a hooked nose at the stall rebuked him sharply. 'You won't have the one and six to pay for it.'

'I wasn't going to break it,' Alfie retorted, making a rude gesture. ''Tisn't very good anyway. Could do much better meself.'

'Get away with you!' The man waved his arms about.

'Silly old sod!' Alfie shouted. He ran off and his brothers followed him giggling.

Two women on the knitting and crochet stall looked worried for their wares as they ran past, but a motherly fat woman working on the book stall beckoned to them.

'Yes, what is it, missus?' Alfie asked warily.

She held out a bundle of dog-eared magazines tied up with string. 'Would you like these, my handsome? Perhaps your mother would like to look through them.'

Alfie looked at the woman cock-eyed. 'Have they got glamour pictures in them? I collect pictures of Betty Grable and Ginger Rogers.'

'They might have,' the woman chuckled. 'Come back later and I'll see if I can find some comics for you and your brothers.'

Alfie thanked her, then clutching the bundle under his sweaty armpit he looked around for Rachael Farrow who was always guaranteed to give him a lick of her lolly. Then the artful boy saw someone who just might be persuaded to part with some brass.

'Hello, Ince. Don't you look smart today. I'm just taking my brothers off to watch the Punch and Judy show. I was thinking of buying 'em an ice cream but I haven't got—'

'Any money,' Ince finished for him in a light-hearted manner. 'Come with me, all of you, to the ice-cream stall.'

'Wizard!'

Laura was on her way to take her turn at manning the white elephant stall when she saw Ince buying ice-cream cornets for the children. He was standing a little back from them to keep his smart choir blazer clean. Some people were making a wide detour of the little family, muttering uncomplimentary remarks.

'They've as much right to be here as you have,' Ince hissed at a man who'd declared he couldn't understand why Mrs Lean was allowing 'the likes of they' to stay.

'Miserable sod! Hope yer false teeth break in 'alf and choke ya!' Alfie shouted after him, but he didn't seem upset. Insults were water off a duck's back as far as he was concerned. He looked Laura up and down then grinned impishly. 'You're pretty. You were the bride, weren't you?'

'That's right, Alfie. I'm sorry I've been so busy that I haven't had the chance to meet you properly.' Laura would have offered him her hand to shake but apart from dripping ice cream, Alfie's had a thick layer of grime and blood on it.

When Alfie had learned at a much younger age that his uncleanliness, ill-bred habits and cheekiness could shock people, he looked for this reaction. It got him into trouble often but was worth it for the reputation he'd obtained as a fearless rebel-rouser, an heroic figure of sorts to his brothers and other children. He had just the right remark for this beautiful blonde-haired lady.

He screwed up his features, making his pug face. 'You should have married Ince. He'd 'ave made 'ee a much better husband. I 'ear yours is as moody as the moor.'

Laura was shocked but took her cue from Ince who just shook his head wryly. 'Perhaps I should have waited a few years,' she said, 'until you grew up, Alfie, and married you instead.'

Alfie's mouth gaped open in an uneven O; he hadn't expected that and turned his back on her. 'Can we all 'ave some candyfloss as well, Ince?'

'I'll think about it, but only if you say please,' Ince replied. He couldn't get cross at the boy's sauce and his brothers' hopeful little faces. Heaven knew they had little enough in life. A chorus of delight drowned out the fair organ for a moment as he placed some coins in Alfie's hand.

'Mind your brothers aren't sick,' Ince warned lightly.

Alfie's thanks expired on his thin, cracked lips. He could hear his mother quarrelling shrilly with Ada Prisk and he dashed off, weaving in and out of the throng, to see what the fuss was about. His brothers followed in his wake like ducklings swimming after their mother.

'He's a good child really,' Ince said, referring to Alfie, gazing fondly and sadly after them.

'It's a pity they've had such a poor start in life,' Laura said, thinking about the difference between their lives and Vicki's and Joy Miller's children. 'They are so dreadfully neglected. Celeste has told me about her plans to help the Urens. I must ask Spencer if we could have them over on the farm one day. They'd probably enjoy that.'

'Rosemerryn is your home,' Ince said darkly. 'Why not just invite them over?'

Laura had not missed the note of antagonism in Ince's voice and the shadow that crept across his rugged features. Ince was going out of his way to be his usual kindly, patient self but Spencer's moments of unreasonable jealousy had done some damage. Ince adored Vicki but he took less interest in her these days. Spencer hadn't seemed to notice it but Laura knew Ince was no longer happy at the farm.

'I want Spencer and me to talk everything over, that's why,' she explained gently. 'Ince, I know things haven't been easy for you since we got married but I—'

'Good Lord! Well, I never.'

'What is it? You look quite shocked.' Laura followed the direction of Ince's wide dark eyes. A lot of people were milling about but she could see who he was staring at. Dressed up in his old badly fitting suit and tie, a broad smile on his raddled face, Les Tremorrow was strolling in a dignified manner with a young woman on his arm. Laura glanced at Ince and saw it was the woman who was claiming the greater part of his attention. She was an imposing figure. Her clothes were good quality, a simple narrow-waisted dress cut perfectly to her graceful form, concealing here, showing off a gentle curve there. A small hat sat at just the right angle on her immaculate short dark hair, a white clutch bag held in her gloved hand. People were giving her more than a second look.

'Who on earth is that?' another male voice breathed down Laura's neck and startled her out of her unabashed scrutiny. 'Not the most beautiful woman I've seen,' Harry went on, 'but she's really something.'

'I don't know who she is,' Laura whispered back, although Les and the young woman couldn't possibly hear her. 'I think Ince does though.'

Harry slapped a hand on Ince's shoulder, bringing him out of the mesmerised state he'd slipped into. 'Introduce me to her, will you, Polkinghorne? I don't care if you saw her first,' Harry straightened his tie and murmured to himself, 'I've simply got to get to know her.'

Ince rubbed the place where Harry had slapped him but he seemed to have forgotten he was in Laura's company. He walked away, leaving her and Harry dumbfounded.

'You've come out into the open then?' Ince said, standing directly in Les and Eve's way.

'Let me introduce you to my granddaughter, Ince,' Les replied, looking deeply into Ince's eyes as if pleading for understanding. 'I'm glad you're the first one to meet her. This is Miss Eve Pascoe.'

'Pascoe?'

Eve put out her hand and because Ince was mesmerised again and his hand hung at his side, she took it and shook it. He imprisoned her fingers. 'So you're still keeping secrets, are you?' he said gruffly. Although he knew it was really none of his business, he was greatly irritated, and more than that he felt rejected, betrayed. He had thought the Tremorrows considered him a friend. It irked him that first he had been asked to keep Eve Tremorrow's existence a secret, and now he had to go along with a lie about her real name.

'If you please, Ince,' she replied in coolly modulated tones, meeting his vexed stare boldly.

He sighed heavily, as if some of Spencer's belligerent character had rubbed off on him. 'I hope you enjoy the fete, Miss *Pascoe*,' he muttered ungraciously. He stalked off and bumped literally into Laura who had followed on his heels.

Rather than introduce her to the other young woman, Ince grabbed her arm and dragged her away.

'But I wanted to meet her,' Laura protested as Ince kept his strong hands on her arms to stop her going after the Tremorrows. 'Who is she? Why haven't you told me you've met her before, Ince?'

'She's nobody special,' Ince grunted. 'She's Les's granddaughter.'

'Granddaughter? I didn't know Les had one. I don't think anyone did. How long has she been at Carrick Cross? I take it that's where you met her before. She's very attractive.' Laura thought the possible cause of Ince's incongruous behaviour was that she had refused to go out with him. 'Don't you think?'

'I don't know anything about her.'

'But you must do. Why are you being so grouchy? Come on, you can tell me. We're friends.'

Laura was suddenly yanked away from Ince. 'What are you two doing?' Spencer asked heatedly. 'You're making a spectacle of yourselves, standing in the middle of the lawn, holding on to one another for everyone to see. What the hell's going on?'

Ince was in no mood for Spencer's possessiveness. 'Nothing's bloody going on,' he snapped. 'What's the matter with you these days?' Then he stalked off, his shoulder brushing Spencer's and spinning him round.

Laura clutched her husband tightly to stop him going after Ince. 'We were only talking, Spencer. You seem to read something that isn't there every time I speak to Ince.'

'Are you sure nothing is there, Laura?' he uttered between his teeth, and then he, too, strode off, in a different direction to Ince.

Laura was furious with him. She looked about to see if anyone had witnessed Ince and Spencer's discontent, and was dismayed to see that at least Harry had.

'I was the only man he allowed to talk to Natalie,' Harry remarked, his eyes on Spencer's retreating back. 'Well, never mind him. Who's the mystery woman?'

'Les Tremorrow's granddaughter,' Laura said dolefully. The fete was quite ruined for her now. Spencer would be quiet for hours when they got home. Well, she wasn't prepared to wait until then, she'd have it out with him now, once and for all, before he lost Ince's friendship for good and her respect. What sort of marriage would they have then? Not one that would be good for Vicki, that was certain. 'Oh, go and find out all about her yourself, Harry.'

Harry would have done just that but he saw a more important quarry close at hand, and needing some assistance. Tressa was struggling to get a pram wheel loose from the rope of a tent peg. He ran up to her.

'Keep the pram still, Tressa,' he ordered in a kindly voice, 'or you'll have the hoopla stall over.'

Tressa wasn't at all pleased to be given help by this man but she had no choice but to do as he said. As he unwound the rope from the pram wheel, she looked down on his thick black hair and Dolores' warning ran uncomfortably through her mind.

'There you are,' he said, straightening up a few moments later. 'You're free to carry on your way.'

Tressa waited for him to try to detain her, but he stepped back. Was he trying to fool her? Or had he lost interest in her at last and moved on to new pastures? Tressa was one of the many people who had noticed the attractive stranger with old Les Tremorrow, but unlike all the others whose eyes had only been on the woman, Tressa had seen Harry ogling her. It seemed silly to believe in the fortune-teller's warning in the broad light of a sunny day when she was surrounded by so many people, her husband, father and aunt not far away. What could Harry do to harm her here anyway?

'Thank you very much,' she said, then added before making to walk on, 'Your gardens are splendid this year. I've never seen so many butterflies about.'

'Thank you. My mother's very proud of the azaleas.' Harry replied. He turned to walk in the other direction but then saw a marvellous opportunity. 'Oh, look, it's those poor little children from the village. Ada Prisk is shouting at their mother and they look terribly upset.'

Tressa left her baby and stood beside Harry. He stole secret glances at her pretty little face while she watched in horror as Ada Prisk got stuck in to Dolores Uren in full venom. They had been quarrelling for some time and now their voices were raised, echoing clearly across the dip of Hawksmoor's gardens that stretched out to the moor. An audience, many of whom were enjoying the spectacle, had gathered round them. Alfie and his brothers weren't in fact the least bit upset; their mother wouldn't back down under any circumstances and would probably win the day. Some kind soul had bought the children candyfloss and they were munching their way into a further sticky mess.

'Evil, that's what it is, and there's no getting away from it,' Ada shrieked.

Dolores, her baby dressed in some of the clothes Tressa had passed on to her and tied with a shawl to her hip, pointed a long finger at the old woman. 'You've a right to your views but there's no need to speak to me like the dirt beneath your feet, woman. I won't have it, do you hear?'

'Do something, Harry,' Tressa implored him.

Harry had quite forgotten he was the host here and it was his responsibility to deal with any unpleasantness. Reluctantly, he left Tressa and approached the two warring women. 'Now, now, ladies. This is a happy occasion. I suggest you part and go your separate ways.'

'Oh, Mr Lean,' Ada appealed to him. 'This woman was going round making money by telling fortunes. I put a stop to it and she didn't like it.'

Harry couldn't see that Dolores Uren had done anything wrong. She could hardly be blamed for trying to make a shilling or two for her large brood of children; her lazy husband didn't do anything to provide for them. He turned to Dolores to hear her side of the story.

'I was going to give half the proceeds to the fund to provide the village children with a play park,' she said, indignation making white spots appear on her rouged cheeks. ''Tis for my kids' benefit too. What business is it of hers anyway? If someone doesn't want their fortune told, they don't have to have it. I wasn't forcing anyone.'

This seemed satisfactory to Harry. 'Well, we'll leave it at that then.'

'Benefit she took her children home and gave 'em all a good wash instead of bothering decent folk like we,' someone in the crowd mumbled.

Ada grunted self-righteously. 'See, Mr Lean. We don't want her sort here.'

Tressa had lifted Guy out of his pram and pushed her way to the front of the crowd. 'I don't think that was charitable of you, Mrs Prisk.'

Harry could see a big row brewing involving a lot of people and for his mother's sake he didn't want the fete ruined. She was beside him now with Vicki, clutching his arm somewhat fearfully; she was no good at calming troubled waters. But Harry couldn't miss the opportunity of agreeing with Tressa and getting into her good books. 'I agree with Mrs Macarthur there, Mrs Prisk. That remark was uncalled for.'

Andrew had come looking for his wife and he pulled her gently towards him. 'Keep out of this, darling. It's none of our business.'

'If you call yourselves a community then it's all your business.' Celeste's tone was crisp and full of disgust. 'Few of you have tried to be kind to the Urens, to get to know them for themselves. Because they have a different lifestyle you've allowed your prejudices to take precedence over your Christian values.'

'It's all right for you to talk but I lost my two sons during the war while her husband shirks his national service.' This offering came from Jacka Davey who rarely gave an opinion in public. He moved to where he could be seen by all. 'It's not only prejudice here, Miss Cunningham, although there are those, particularly you, Mrs Prisk, who are against the family just because they're a big one and they'm poor want locking up. Like Mrs Uren said, if you don't approve of fortune-telling you don't have to have it done. Folk can follow their own conscience. But you, Mrs Uren,' Jacka turned gravely to Dolores, 'should be ashamed of yourself for the neglect of your little children. A bar of soap costs very little and while it doesn't hurt to let them get grubby out playing, for the most part they should be kept clean. Good food should go into their stomachs instead of beer going down your man's gullet. If people resent you for the way you're bringing your children up then you can hardly be surprised if you provoke bad feelings wherever you live.'

Jacka had finished. He left the gathering, silent now, and went off to the tea tent to wet his parched throat. Ada Prisk and Dolores Uren couldn't look one another in the eye and many a face was directed uncomfortably at the ground.

Kinsley Farrow had heard the end of the altercation and had kept his counsel during Jacka's reproach. Now he told the crowd, 'Well, I think Mr Davey has put his case over very well. I suggest we all take on board what he said and go about the business of enjoying ourselves.'

The crowd duly broke up and scattered into small groups to mull over the afternoon's happenings. Ada went back like a lamb to the cake stall. Dolores gathered her brood and left the grounds of Hawksmoor House. She was nearly in tears. She had received a lot of insults in her life and hadn't cared at all, but faced with Jacka Davey's calmly spoken accusations, in full hearing of her children, she was cut to the quick.

Celeste caught her up as they herded out of the wrought–iron gates. 'Mrs Uren, may I talk to you, please?'

Dolores hesitated but this was the one person who had spoken up for her. 'You take your brothers on home, Alfie,' she told her eldest son who was abnormally subdued. When the children were out of earshot, she eyed Celeste. 'What do you want with me, Miss Cunningham?'

'I want to help you. Will you let me? I've worked with families in your circumstances before. I won't patronise you, I promise.'

Dolores shrugged her shoulders. 'I might. I know why you're concerned for Alfie and my others. I know why you're here. I can see it in your face. I'm going home now. I have things to do. Call on me tomorrow if you want to.'

'I hope you won't be offended but I'd like to give you this.' Celeste held out a five pound note.

Taking a mighty gulp, as if she was giving up all her pride, Dolores took the money and pushed it down the top of her dress. 'Thank you.'

'There's no need for that. I hope it helps.'

Celeste returned to the fete with a smile on her face. Dear Ada Prisk and Jacka Davey. Because of her big, spiteful mouth and his gentle, truthful nature, Celeste thought her hopes for the Uren children might be quickly realised. She could not stay here much longer but with any luck she would see her plans come to fruition before she left.

'Does that sort of thing happen every time you have an event in the village, Mother?' Bruce Tambyln chuckled. He and Daisy had left the little shop stall to listen in on the proceedings. He was feeling cocky because he had tried to harass Harry Lean but Harry had ignored him. Bruce thought Harry wasn't as brave as he had sounded at the time of the car incident in the lane, but Harry was keeping on his best behaviour today and he felt the brute would keep.

'Well, there's always a bit of gossip and sometimes the odd tiff but we've had nothing like that before,' Daisy tut-tutted, sorry she had missed the beginning of the row. 'Good for Jacka though, it was about time somebody said something like that. Oh, look, here comes Joy and her family. Doesn't she look nice today? Joy seems to be getting younger these days. Must be having regular money in her purse with both her and Bert working.'

'Yes, that must be it.' Bruce picked up a packet of Spangles from a box on the trestle top. 'I'll pay for these, Mum. They're for Joy's kids.'

'You are good to them, Bruce.'

'I've only met the children a couple of times and they seem such a lovely family. Makes me realise what I'm missing out on. Look, Mum, why don't you go and have a look around the stalls, get yourself a cup of tea or something, have a chat to Laura. I can manage here.'

'Right then,' Daisy said gratefully. 'I'd like to meet Les Tremorrow's granddaughter. I must say Les looks delighted. Angela must have done well for herself. Eve Pascoe is very well turned out.' It was so good having Bruce with her. He more than made up for the loss of her late friend Bunty. Picking up her purse, Daisy went off to find someone who could fill her in on all the details of the row.

The Millers arrived at the stall and Joy, giving Bruce a secret look, introduced him to her husband. 'You haven't met Bert before. This is Mrs Tamblyn's son, Bruce, Bert.'

Bruce wanted to laugh at the sight of Bert Miller. He was wearing his demob suit, a massive paunch stuck out like a ridiculous molehill through his jacket front and over the tight waistband of his trousers. His almost bald head shone like a beacon in shades of nut brown. The flesh on his trusting face looked as if it had given up the fight with the forces of gravity, his jowls hanging down like a bulldog's. He had big trusting eyes like a puppy's. He was short and he was ugly, his hands were stained with the earth he worked on and his nails were broken and dirty. He looked as boring as Joy said he was. And he looked stupid, as though he would find it impossible to string two coherent thoughts together. Bruce knew he himself was no great catch but it was no wonder Joy had turned to him, he thought scathingly.

Bert let go of the hand of a nine-year-old girl who resembled Joy in every fine detail and shook Bruce's hand shyly. 'Pleased to meet you at last, Mr Tamblyn. We were just on our way to the merry-go-round. We'd best get on, the children hate being kept waiting.'

So you're intimidated by me, Bruce thought with pleasure. You'll be a walkover if my affair with your wife ever gets out.

Joy lingered to talk to her lover. 'He's going to a Buff's meeting tonight and Mrs Grean, my neighbour, will sit with the kids while I take a little walk at seven o'clock. And he's working at Tregorlan tomorrow afternoon. They get very busy at this time of the year. The kids are spending the day with their grandparents. I'll be taking a little stroll to our usual place, about three o'clock.'

There was now a mother and child waiting to buy sweets. Bruce handed Joy the Spangles, squeezing her hand as he did so. 'I agree with you, Mrs Miller.' He left it at that; Joy knew what he meant.

Chapter 14

Laura had not heard the fierce quarrel between Ada and Dolores or witnessed its consequences. She had gone off in search of her husband and tracked Spencer down inside the house. He was standing in the elegant drawing room, his hands in his trouser pockets, gazing wistfully at a wedding photograph of himself and Natalie. It was normal for Spencer to seek a quiet corner away from a gathering but Laura knew he wasn't here because of his dislike of crowds.

'What are you doing in here?' She closed the door behind her with an unfriendly thrust.

He turned and faced her, his posture, his sullen expression showing he was, like her, in a confrontational mood. 'Is Vicki asking for me?'

'No,' she replied gruffly, 'she's quite happy with her grandmother. I asked you a question, Spencer.'

His face closed over. Slowly, he took his hands out of his pockets and clenched his fists at his side. 'I wanted some peace and quiet.'

'Why? You've only just arrived. Your habitual shyness of public occasions is a bit extreme today, isn't it?'

'If you've got something to say, Laura, then for goodness sake spit it out.'

'Very well, I will,' she retorted, lifting her chin defiantly. 'I want you to know that I think your treatment of Ince is unfair. It's gone far beyond a joke now. Ince and I are close, I won't deny that, but for some reason you will insist on reading more into our friendship than is there. We had a romance once, now we're good friends, and it's time you accepted that without question. We're no friendlier than we were before you and I got married. Why are you so jealous? I just don't understand it.'

He came closer to her. 'I never had a stake in your life until we were married. You could do as you pleased before. But now I baulk at the sight of you and my best friend being constantly all over each other.'

Laura had been steadily getting angrier since Spencer had snapped at her and Ince and stormed off. What amounted to an accusation little short of infidelity threw her into a rage. 'We are not! Ince and I live and work on the same farm, for goodness sake. It's inevitable that we sometimes share a joke or have a cosy chat. He's my friend too, damn you.'

'Andrew Macarthur's also your friend, a very close friend from way back, but I never see you touching him or fussing over him.' He was sneering now. 'Perhaps your friendship with him didn't go as far as it did with Ince. Just how close did you and Ince become when you had your romance?'

'That's none of your business.' Laura was getting nervous as to where his questions were leading. 'It's all in the past and I'm only concerned with the future. Why can't you be like that too?'

Spencer strode across the room and stood right in front of her. He looked as if he wanted to shake the soul out of her. 'Look me in the face and tell me exactly what Ince meant to you. Tell me the truth!'

Laura stepped backwards but he came at her step for step. His hot breath scorched her skin. He had her trapped and the truth would have to come out. He had obviously thought this through at length. How long had these thoughts been going through his wretched mind? She tried to muster some dignity. 'Get away from me. How dare you treat me like this.'

'If nothing happened between you then why don't you just say so? It's all I want to hear.'

Laura's face was burning. She couldn't answer him. Spencer let out a demented howl as if he had been kicked in the bowels. 'You went to bed with him, didn't you? You were lovers.'

'What if we were? What's that got to do with us now and our marriage and Vicki?'

He grabbed her by the arms. 'How do you think I feel? Knowing that the one man I would have trusted with my life, who sleeps under my roof and sits at my table, had my wife before I did and you've both kept quiet about it? How did it happen? You were newly widowed and he's very religious, the bloody hypocrite.'

Laura became wild at his outrage which to her was unjustifiable. Wrenching herself away from him, she cried, 'I may have been newly widowed but I'd been starved of love for five years, remember? And Ince is not a hypocrite. We made love once, the circumstances of which I shall maintain till my dying day are none of your business, and we decided not to carry on with an affair. Ince is religious but he doesn't pretend to be perfect. None of us are, especially not you, Spencer Jeffries.'

They were out of control now. Laura couldn't tolerate his unreasonableness. Spencer couldn't come to terms with the truth of his suspicions.

'How can I be sure you only did it once?' he hurled at her. 'I think you're in love, that you only married me because you wanted Vicki. And it suited you because it put you under the same roof as your lover. You're probably carrying on your affair right under my nose.' Laura smacked Spencer hard across the face, the sound rapping round the large room and echoing frighteningly in her ears. 'You're mad, you're insane with jealousy. If you think you're living in the shadow of mine and Ince's old relationship, what about yours and Natalie's? I've never thrown that up in your face. What did you want to come in here for and stare at her photograph?'

'My wife wasn't a slut!'

Laura felt as if she'd received a hammer blow to the core of her being. 'You bastard, Spencer Jeffries! I should have followed my instincts on our wedding day. I knew it was a mistake to marry you then. You're no better than Bill Jennings was. In fact you're a hell of a lot worse.' Several emotions and expressions vied for supremacy on Spencer's cold hard face, then he made a choking sound and swept out of the room, slamming the door so violently it made the old house shake. Laura fell down on a settee and burst into tormented sobs.

Spencer pushed his way through the crowds, set on finding Vicki and taking her home.

Ince, on his way to join the male voice choir for their concert in front of the big house, saw his anguished face and hurried up to him. 'What's the matter, Spencer, are you ill?'

Spencer slowed down, letting Ince reach him. Then he struck out with his fist and hit Ince with all his might. Totally unprepared for the sudden onslaught, Ince fell to the ground, blood spurting from his nose and a split lip. He didn't make a sound, he just stared uncomprehendingly at his friend while women screamed and men cried out in shock.

Spencer looked as though he wanted to murder Ince. 'You've got until the end of the day to get your things out of Rosemerryn or I'll burn everything you bloody own. Don't let me ever see you on my property again or I swear I'll shoot you.'

Still Ince said nothing. He knew what Spencer had found out. He couldn't mention it with all these people around them and Spencer wouldn't be reasoned with anyway. He felt dizzy and his vision blurred. A pair of soft arms encircled him and soothing words, which he couldn't make out, were spoken softly in his ear. He wanted to whisper urgently, 'No, Laura, leave me be. It'll make matters worse.' But his muddled brain couldn't form the words.

'What on earth did you do that for?' Felicity demanded angrily of her former son-in-law. 'Have you gone mad?'

Spencer looked at all the shocked faces. He hated them at that moment, the self-righteous, those who would be understanding, those who couldn't wait to gossip about his sudden explosion of violence; he didn't even feel sorry about Vicki's frightened expression, her little heart-shaped face puckered and ready to cry. Throwing back his head, he sneered, 'Let's just say he had it coming to him.'

He took Vicki's hand from Felicity's and marched off with her. 'But I want to watch the gymkhana,' Vicki wailed, struggling to get her hand out of his. 'Where's Mummy? We were going to watch it together.' Spencer picked her up and carried her away protesting.

A crowd was gathering for a second time around the source of unexpected entertainment. Ince heard them talking above him, a hazy loud hum that hurt his head. His mind began to clear and he gave up fighting against the woman holding him and dabbing at the blood streaming down his chin. He smelled violet scent and without opening his eyes he knew the arms round him were Eve Tremorrow's.

Celeste went to the drawing room. She found Laura staring into space, pale and numb, trembling, hair all over the place where she'd been raking her hands through it. Laura had seen Spencer thump Ince from a window and she could hardly believe these terrible events of the afternoon had happened.

Putting her arms round her, Celeste hugged her close. 'I think I know what this is all about, Laura. Were you and Ince lovers? Did Spencer find out?'

'You've got it in one, Celeste Cunningham,' Laura answered, her throat thick with bitterness. 'It only happened once and it was a long time ago. I never told Spencer because I couldn't see what it had to do with him.'

Giving Laura a clean handkerchief, Celeste sighed. 'I was afraid something like this would happen, although I never guessed it would be so vicious. I think Spencer has been suspicious for a long time. I've noticed the way he's looked at you and Ince, the special closeness you share is so obvious. I think Spencer is insecure where women are concerned after Natalie's death. He never dated anyone, not even you, in the years in between. To know that you, his wife, and Ince have been as close as a man and woman can get must have undermined his confidence, especially as Ince is the last man you'd believe would make love unless he married first. Spencer always thought Ince was utterly honourable.'

'Ince is an ordinary young man. Spencer has the habit of putting people on a pedestal. Are you saying I should have told Spencer about me and Ince, Celeste?'

Celeste pulled Laura's head onto her shoulder. 'It might have been wiser, Laura.'

Scalding tears pricked Laura's eyes. 'It didn't seem necessary. My only concern was whether I should marry Spencer or not. I was nervous enough about that. What shall I do now, Celeste? My second marriage is a failure. Spencer called me a slut. He won't want me any more.'

'I'm sure he didn't mean it, Laura. You both must have said a lot of cruel things in the heat of the moment. You'll either have to walk away from Rosemerryn for good or try to patch things up.'

'Oh, Celeste,' she cried freely. 'I wish I was like you, unencumbered, not looking for love in my life.'

This was so ironic Celeste had difficulty curbing her own tears over her fate. 'You wouldn't want to be like me, Laura, believe me. Don't wish that on yourself.' She didn't want Laura to ask questions about her so she changed the subject. 'Would you like me to make you some tea? I'm sure I could find the kitchen.'

'N-no. I just want to sit here and wait for all the villagers to go home. Would you mind? I'd like to be alone for a while. I have a lot of thinking to do.'

Celeste kissed her and left the room. She stopped Harry going in. 'She wants to be alone, Harry.'

'Isn't there something I can do?'

'No, just leave her be, I beg you.'

Harry made a grim face. 'I'll go and find Mother. She's terribly upset. She's worried that Spencer won't let us have anything to do with Vicki again.'

'I don't think he'll do that. What happened has nothing to do with you two, but I should tread carefully for a while.' Celeste recalled Harry's earlier diplomacy. 'Listen, Harry, if you were serious about helping the Urens, there's a meeting at the parsonage on Tuesday evening.'

'Who's going?'

'All the people I mentioned and one or two others.'

Harry stopped the urge to grin. 'You can count me in.'

Laura sat for a long time in the sanctuary of the drawing room. She couldn't face the villagers. The sudden appearance of Eve Pascoe and Ada and Dolores' quarrel had been overshadowed by her husband's act of brutality. Speculation over its cause would be bouncing about like a fierce shower of rain on a moorland pond. Felicity looked in on her, couldn't bring herself to say anything and rushed away in floods of tears. Laura stayed put and cried long and hard again.

Andrew and Tressa came to her. He lowered himself down in front of her and took her trembling hands. 'Do you want to talk about it, Laura? When you didn't appear or leave with Spencer and Vicki, we knew the fight had something to do with you. You know what the obvious rumours are, don't you? Others are saying that it's crazy, with the way old Les's granddaughter went to Ince, and your respectable character.'

She shook her head slowly. 'How's Ince? I saw what Spencer did to him.'

'He's been taken to Johnny Prouse's cottage. He only took one blow but he looks as if he was hit by a tree. He can hardly stand up. Mike and the vicar are going to collect his things from the farm.'

'Would you like to come back to Tregorlan with us, Laura?' Tressa asked gently.

'No, thank you. Will you give me a lift to Rosemerryn, please?'

'Of course,' Andrew replied. 'Are you sure you want to go home right now?'

Laura got up and wiped away her tears. 'My new life is in tatters but I married Spencer for better or worse. I've got to face him again at some time and it might as well be now.'

Chapter 15

Laura left Hawksmoor House as the hired help were dismantling the tents, seating and platforms. It was dusk, chilly winds were blowing off the moor and she shivered in her light summer dress. She did not say goodbye to Felicity. She could hear her crying in her bedroom, and from the apologetic look on Harry's face it seemed his mother was blaming her for ruining the fete. Felicity wasn't a strong-willed woman and was easily upset, partly a legacy of Spencer's recalcitrance over her daughter's death.

'Don't worry about what happened, Laura,' Harry said softly, giving her a reassuring pat on the hand. 'I think the fete-goers enjoyed the drama. Will you be all right?'

'I'll have to be, Harry,' she replied.

She refused his offer to take her home and crunched over the gravel drive, disillusioned, annoyed, not in the mood to receive any act of kindness. It wasn't fair that she should be held responsible for her husband's mean character, his appalling behaviour. She and Ince had done nothing wrong, why should they be punished as if they had? It didn't occur to her that people would be bearing ill will towards Spencer for his outburst.

She squeezed into Andrew's car and no one spoke a word. At Tregorlan Farm, Tressa, Jacka and Joan got out with Guy and said goodbye. Andrew took her on to Rosemerryn Farm.

'I suppose I ought to tell you what this is all about,' she murmured wearily.

'You don't have to, Laura. We know that whatever it is, it's not your or Ince's fault.'

'You don't believe the gossip then?'

'That you and Ince must be having an affair? Of course not. The very idea is ludicrous. Everyone will see that when the fuss dies down. Spencer's got his wires crossed somewhere. He's probably sorry already.'

'He won't be that sorry, Andrew.' Laura flushed, embarrassed, but she thought it better that Andrew know the truth. 'You see, Ince and I were lovers, it only happened once, soon after I settled in Kilgarthen. The time wasn't right for anything permanent to come out of it, but if we hadn't had our romance so soon after Bill's death, and if it wasn't for Vicki, we might well have been married now.'

Andrew raised his fair brows but said nothing.

'I'm very fond of Ince. He's so kind and gentle it would be hard for anyone not to like him. I haven't treated him any differently since Spencer and I got married but Spencer has been jealous of us all along. Ince has changed a little since the wedding. With Spencer sometimes being difficult and unfriendly towards him, he's been quiet and rather offhand. I don't know what this will do to him now. Ohh! I could kill Spencer for what he's done. How can he be so unfair?'

They had reached the track that led up to Rosemerryn Farm. 'Come back with me, Laura. Let him have tonight on his own to cool down.'

'I think I would do that, Andrew, but I'm worried about Vicki. She'll be wondering where I am. She was upset when Spencer suddenly marched her off without an explanation and she needs to be cared for with only Spencer working on the farm.'

'But I shall be worried about you.'

'There's a telephone at Rosemerryn now. I can always call you. I'll ring you tomorrow and let you know how things are.'

Andrew pulled up a few feet away from the yard and Laura hurriedly said goodnight. If Spencer was about, it was likely Andrew would give him a few choice words and she didn't want to risk a scene between the two men.

Barney came bounding up to her. He was in an aggressive mood. He didn't bark or jump up at her but growled long and low and bared his big teeth. Laura skirted round him, her spirits sinking lower, feeling unwelcome in her own home.

It took a lot of courage to go through the back kitchen and into the main kitchen. Vicki and Spencer were sitting glumly at the table, an uneaten meal of scrambled egg on toast before them. Spencer kept his head down over his plate. His breathing was heavy and impatient. Vicki got down from the table and ran to her.

'Where have you been, Mummy? We came home ages ago. Daddy said we had to leave but I don't know why. He said Uncle Ince isn't going to live with us any more or work here. Is that true? Doesn't he love us any more?'

Fearful that Spencer would lose his temper again, Laura gave the explanations she had worked out on the way home in case Vicki asked her some awkward questions. 'Ince is going to live with Mr Prouse, Vicki. Mr Prouse hasn't got any company and it seemed silly for him to be all alone when there are lots of us living here. Uncle Ince has got another job. It's not unusual, Vicki, for someone to change their job and work somewhere else.'

'Daddy won't tell me why he hit Uncle Ince.'

This was more difficult to explain away. When Laura said, 'That was a mistake, Vicki,' Spencer let out an angry sigh of breath.

Vicki wasn't in the least bit comforted. Before Laura had come on the scene, Ince had been the second most important person in her life. 'But Uncle Ince has always worked here. He didn't even say goodbye to me. I'll miss him.'

'Of course you will, darling.' Laura hugged her tearful stepdaughter close. 'Listen, why don't you eat your tea and then you can play with the painting book you won on the tombola at the fete. I brought it home for you.'

Vicki did as Laura suggested, eating a little food then getting out her paint box when Laura cleared the table and fetched a jam jar of water for her. She was only partly placated, her parents weren't speaking, hardly looking at each other, and the atmosphere in the room hung like a heavy cloud. She glanced at them often, feeling anxious and a little afraid. Laura was sitting at the table, encouraging her, but her face looked strangely distorted, she wasn't as beautiful as she usually was, her make-up was smudged. Daddy was standing by the sink, his arms folded grimly, staring straight ahead into space.

Vicki was an intelligent child, she knew parents lied to their children to spare their feelings. Was Laura fed up being her mummy even though she was paying attention to her? Did her daddy not want Laura to be here any more? She'd seen her daddy hit Uncle Ince to the ground as if he hated him. She didn't believe it was a mistake. She had never seen Daddy hit anyone before. Had Uncle Ince done something terribly bad? Daddy had snatched her away from Hawksmoor. Would he stop her from seeing Grandma and Uncle Harry like he did before? Daddy had admitted it was his fault that he'd kept her away from the Leans all that time, so was he being horrible about them again?

She'd painted a few green leaves on a tree in her painting book but she was sniffing. Eventually huge tears rolled down her cheeks.

Spencer hurried to the table and picked her up and hugged her. 'There, there, pipkin. You've had a tiring day. Daddy will give you a wash and help you clean your teeth and put you to bed. Then I'll read you a story. How about *The Gingerbread Man*? It's your favourite.' His voice was tender and melodious, but gilded with the odd clipped tone that gave away his gall.

Vicki nodded mournfully. Laura wanted to kiss her goodnight and try to reassure her but Spencer made no move to bring Vicki to her. When they'd reached the stairs, she said gently, 'Good night, Vicki. I'll come up and kiss you and tuck you in in a little while.'

Laura washed the dishes and made herself some coffee. She made a sandwich but couldn't eat it. She sat and waited for her husband to come downstairs. She hoped they could talk their problems through. He had caused their estrangement, but this was his home, she'd wait for him to speak first and she was determined not to raise her voice for Vicki's sake, no matter what he said, what accusations he hurled at her. She'd spent every moment thinking hard in the drawing room of Hawksmoor House. Her first marriage had been a disaster but she had been married to a cruel, amoral man, nothing she did or could have done would have softened Bill Jennings towards her. Spencer's wrath was inexcusable, yet a tiny part of her understood his reasons.

Celeste had made sense. Spencer probably was vulnerable where women and relationships were concerned. He possessed none of

Harry's raffishness or Andrew's natural confidence. Natalie had been the only love of his life and he had been hurt more than most when he'd lost her.

Laura knew she had been unwise to marry Spencer without a proper courtship. He had loved his wife desperately. She had come to hate Bill with all her heart. A second marriage for either of them should have meant more than convenience or sexual attraction. They should have got to know each other really well first, seen if they were compatible. She would have known then that she should have told him all about herself and Ince. She had tried hard with Bill Jennings, and for Vicki's sake she would try harder with Spencer. It would not be easy to forgive him for his public display of rage, for what he had called her, but she did want her marriage to work. All that remained was to see if he would let her stay.

When Spencer came down, his face like granite, back held stiff and straight, he went straight out to the yard. Laura didn't sit and mope. It looked as if she was staying so she made some plans. Without Ince, Spencer would need manual help on the farm. She could quite ably milk the cows and look after the other livestock. She knew a little about haymaking and tomorrow she would work hard out of doors.

She checked on Vicki and found her sleeping fitfully, then, to get a good start the next day, she did some hand washing, prepared the joint for a roast, peeled vegetables, swept the floor and mats and repaired a big rip in Spencer's work jumper.

It was much later than usual when he finally came back in, smelling of tobacco smoke and whisky from the little bottle he kept in his coat pocket to warm him in bad weather. Laura had made fresh tea and handed him a mugful. She looked him steadily in the eye, willing him to say something.

'So you came back here?' he said sternly, putting the mug, untouched, on the table.

It wasn't easy but she kept up her stare. 'It is my home, isn't it?'

'Yes,' he replied as if he had grit in his throat. 'I knew you'd come back, for Vicki's sake. That's the only reason I'm prepared to tolerate you being here.'

His words were like tiny stinging slaps to her face. She would not allow him to upset her, however. 'Can I get you some supper?'

'Is that all you've got to say, the devil take you, woman!'

She flinched. It was with great difficulty she stopped herself from bursting into tears of hurt and indignation. 'All right. If you want to talk about what happened at the fete then we'll talk. But don't let's shout at each other or we'll wake up Vicki and frighten her.'

Spencer bit back a remark about knowing how to be a good father; he was ashamed that he had behaved badly in front of Vicki at Hawksmoor and he had snapped at her a couple of times on the way home.

'Okay, talk,' he scowled.

She took in an involuntary deep breath. 'First of all I want you to believe that nothing has happened between me and Ince since that one time. I only wish that you and I had got to know each other better before we'd married. I would have seen then that you would have needed to know all about us.'

She waited for him to make a contribution but he kept a stony face.

'We're more like brother and sister now.'

Still he didn't speak. His intransigence was excruciating. Angered, she tossed an accusation at him. 'You were out of order hitting Ince like that.'

His face hardened. 'Maybe I was, but you like him more than me, don't you?'

Did his jealousy go that far? 'That's hardly surprising with the way you behave, wouldn't you say, Spencer?'

'I behaved like a man who was convinced his wife was being unfaithful. We've got to know each other pretty well since our wedding night. You could have told me you'd made love with Ince. If your relationship was so innocent, why didn't you say so? I thought there was a deep affection growing between us, we may even have fallen in love. Huh! That's a laugh.'

'Your jealousy was so obvious I was afraid to tell you.' She stood her ground. 'You should have known us better than to think we were betraying you.'

'I've found out that I didn't know either of you at all.'

'So we're back to that, are we?'

'Yes, we are,' he raised his voice, 'and it'll stick in my craw for the rest of my life.'

'Please be reasonable, Spencer—'

There was a loud knock on the door. Laura jumped and Spencer let out a foul oath. He opened the door to Mike Penhaligon and Kinsley Farrow.

They both pushed past Spencer and approached Laura. There was no doubt where their loyalties lay. 'Are you all right, m'dear?' Mike asked gravely and the vicar repeated the question.

'I'm fine,' she told them firmly.

There was an uneasy silence, then Mike's voice boomed at Spencer, 'You still determined to chuck Ince out on his ear?'

Spencer gazed coldly at Laura for some moments. 'Yes.'

'We'll take the things he'll need for a few days and come back for the rest,' Kinsley said gravely.

Laura directed the two men to Ince's room then appealed to Spencer. 'Please don't do this, not this way. You and Ince have been friends all your lives.'

For once it looked as if it was Spencer who was going to cry. He said quietly, 'Well, he can't stay, not after…'

No, he wouldn't want to, Laura thought with pain tearing at her heart.

When Mike and Kinsley made to leave with a bag and battered old suitcase, Spencer handed them an envelope. 'Give him this. It's his wages. Tell him I'll send him a month's severance pay.'

Kinsley put the envelope inside his breast pocket. 'This is a sorry day for Kilgarthen, I must say. Well, if either of you want me or Roslyn, you know where to find us.'

The moment they had gone, Spencer shot Laura a look so cold and hostile that she knew he was blaming her for coming between him and his best friend.

'You can sleep in his room from now on,' he said in that same accusing tone.

'No! I'm your wife and I'll sleep in your bed.'

'Then I'll sleep in the blasted barn.'

'That's up to you.' She made one more effort. 'Instead of quarrelling, we'd do better to try and make things up.'

But Spencer was in no mood for conciliation tonight. Without another word he went outside and Laura heard him calling Barney. He hadn't reappeared after an hour so she went to bed and cried herself to sleep.

Chapter 16

A sudden heavy shower of rain had broken up and dispersed a low hazy mist, making the air smell strongly of fresh wet earth, leaves, grass, dung, honeysuckle and wild dog roses. Celeste put away the cigarette she was about to light and instead breathed in the mixture of the basic and the romantic offered by the countryside. This would do her much more good.

Having mastered the intricacies of the range in Little Cot, she was fortified by a hearty breakfast and was taking her time walking along Rosemerryn Lane. She felt full and satisfied, didn't mind that she was putting on a little weight, but she wasn't looking forward to arriving at Rosemerryn Farm. She wandered a little way onto the moor, absorbing the sights and sounds and colours, particularly liking the wide sweeps of the various species of heather. She picked a sprig and pinned it to her cardigan with the brooch she was wearing. Dense tussocks of spiky, purple moor grass were in flower, birds trilled and there was the grating and chirping of grasshoppers. How could anyone who lived and worked in such magnificent, peaceful surroundings not fall in with its natural harmony? She wanted to stay here and let it seep into her bones, the deepest fibre of her being, but she had to carry on.

She was in no doubt that Laura needed her company and friendship right now, but she didn't want to see the defeated expression that would be marring Laura's beautiful face this morning, the pain, worry, disbelief that her second marriage had gone so badly wrong so soon, and in public. Celeste wanted to beat Spencer about the head with whatever farm implement was handy. At least the vile Bill Jennings had left Laura with a scrap of pride, keeping his contempt for her well under wraps for appearances' sake. Spencer Jeffries was nothing but a foul-mouthed lout, a bully, a beast like those he bred.

How could Spencer believe Laura and Ince were having an affair? The man must have gone mad! Thanks to Spencer hitting Ince to the ground as if he was Errol Flynn, gossip about them was rife. If he had been suspicious something was going on, why hadn't he done the decent thing and simply confronted them? What did he have to be suspicious of anyway? Men and women may not be so openly friendly in small country environments but didn't he know people of her and Laura's background often kissed and called each other darling? That was what Celeste assumed had caused Spencer's suspicions. Buffoon! Idiot! Barbarian!

She thought of Ince then, lying on the ground, his face bleeding. Her heart had gone out to him but another woman had got to him first to give him succour and press a handkerchief to his wound. The mysterious Eve Pascoe with her quiet dignity, which seemed almost casual but which Celeste could tell was ingrained in her, had caused more speculation and excitement than Celeste's own appearance in the village. There was obviously an interesting story behind her and Celeste pondered on it. No doubt Ada Prisk would soon be calling at the little place where the Pascoe woman lived with her odious-looking grandfather, the place reputed to be haunted by any amount of ghosts and demons; and Ada would pass on whatever she so expertly found out. Celeste picked a long grass swaying in the cool wind from the over-burdened hedgerow and grinned as she slipped it between her neat white teeth. If the art of obtaining tittle-tattle could make one wealthy then Ada would have been a millionairess many years ago.

The church bells echoed up and down the hilly horizons, calling the faithful to worship. Amid interest in the chosen texts, sermons, hymns and prayers, there would be whispers in both church and chapel this morning, the pews packed a little more than usual. The moment the services were over, people would gather among the headstones and behind the chapel walls, which the two ministers could do nothing to stop. Those at the sharp end of the ruminations would not be there. Celeste was sure Spencer wouldn't want to go to church. Laura wouldn't be able to face it. Johnny Prouse had told her that Ince, nursing a splitting headache, would not be attending chapel.

The moment Celeste's feet, in her only pair of flat shoes, stout yet feminine lace-ups, struck a cobblestone on Rosemerryn she knew she had been right. Laura immediately came running to her.

'I'm so glad to see you. I knew you'd come today.' She was dressed in her boots, old trousers and one of Spencer's work shirts. A scarf pulled her hair back severely from her pale face. She looked only partly a farmer's wife in her shapeless clothes suited to hard work, no make-up or fancy hairstyle, but her haggard looks let her down; no rosy face bursting with health and vigour here.

They hugged and exchanged kisses and Celeste held on to her friend to examine her face.

'Just as I thought. You've cried all through the night, haven't you? Look at your poor eyes and your hair's gone all dry and dull. Where's that swine you call your husband?' She glared fiercely round the farmyard, paying attention to dark corners and the slightly opened barn door as if she suspected Spencer was hiding from her. 'I'm going to give him a piece of my mind.'

Laura had sat up in bed hoping Spencer would join her but her hopes had been fruitless. The scene of him felling Ince had replayed itself relentlessly over and over in her mind, as had all his angry words, his unforgiving attitude. She had tortured herself thinking about how this must be affecting Vicki. The little girl wouldn't know if she was coming or going, as Daisy often said over dilemmas. In the past, Laura and Spencer had had vicious rows, one of them inadvertently in front of Vicki. Spencer had banned Laura from the farm, from even speaking to his daughter; now he had done the same to Ince. It was a nasty quirk in his character, one Laura had hoped was gone when she married him. Spencer had soon come round after banning her that time, but the grudge he had against her and Ince now was far worse. What if he never came round? She couldn't bear the thought of how that would make Vicki suffer. Laura had heard her cry out in her sleep and had gone in to her twice to stroke her hot brow and soothe her… And if she and Spencer were never reconciled, how would she ever have that longed-for baby?

To combat her wretchedness Laura had hardened her resolve to make her marriage work. She'd panicked when she'd realised that her plan to help Spencer with the manual work meant she'd need someone to stay at the farm and look after Vicki. Then common sense told her that although the wish not to embarrass her or interfere might keep some people away, at least Celeste would turn up the next day. Now she was relieved to see her friend but frightened of Celeste's indignant tongue.

Drawing on the reserves of her wilting strength, Laura made Celeste promise not to fire off and make things worse. 'Anyway, Spencer's out haymaking. If you haven't come to help me, Celeste, then I'd rather you went home.' She told Celeste about her plans to make her marriage work.

'What? You mean you've forgiven him? You aren't going to drub him for humiliating you like that? I'd kill the swine if I was married to him. I suppose all this is for Vicki's sake as usual. But what about you, Laura? When are you going to think about yourself?'

Laura gazed a moment over the top of the farm buildings and the few wind-bent trees in the direction of the field where Spencer would be working. When she'd heard him moving about in the kitchen in the small hours, getting himself something to eat and preparing for the day's work, emitting the odd grumble and pushing things angrily out of his way, she'd wanted to run downstairs to him, fling herself into his arms and beg him not to despise her, to forget his jealousy, suspicions, to hold her like he had done before on warm and loving occasions.

In a wistful voice, she murmured, 'It is for me.'

Celeste tossed her mane of red hair disbelievingly and groaned. 'Oh, don't tell me you've fallen in love with him? You couldn't have. Laura, the man's... well, he's despicable.'

'It's my life, Celeste. I have very strong feelings for him. If you've come to help me then come into the kitchen.' Laura turned on her heel and stalked away.

'So you want me to play house-mother while you go off after his lordship and play skivvy?' Celeste said drolly after Laura had filled her in on her plans for the day. 'I hope you can cope, my girl.'

'I'm quite tough and strong.'

'I meant cope with Spencer's rebuffs. If he hasn't climbed down off his high horse yet then he's not likely to make things easy for you.'

'Yes, I know.' Laura was packing lots of food in the crib bag – Spencer had left without it. She was feeling weak, trembly and vulnerable and wasn't at all sure she would be able to cope with another straffing from his tongue. 'But I still want to put things right with him as soon as possible. I'll fetch Vicki from the garden and tell her what's happening.'

'Well, do what you think you must, but I still think you're mad. Have you considered how Vicki's going to feel with you leaving her with me?'

Laura ignored the sinking feeling in her stomach. It would be a wrench leaving Vicki and the little girl had made no bones about disliking Celeste.

'But you're my mummy,' Vicki had whispered at breakfast when Laura had brought up the possibility that Celeste might look after her today. She dropped her toast on her plate. 'I want you to stay with me.'

Laura had hugged her close. 'I know, darling. But you remember Mummy and Daddy had cross words yesterday? And Daddy was cross with Uncle Ince?'

A disheartened nod of the head.

'Well, Daddy has been left very unhappy and Mummy wants to go to him and try to make him happy again. Then we'll all be happy. I won't be away all day, I promise you that. Celeste is a nice lady when you get to know her properly. Will you let Mummy go and be a good girl for Celeste?'

Vicki nodded mournfully, looking about to cry, but she was sparky enough to use the situation to her advantage. 'Can Celeste bring Alfie over to play with me one day? She's friends with him and he makes me laugh.'

Laura wasn't sure that Spencer would like the mucky child playing with his precious daughter but she readily agreed. Vicki had brightened and run off to make her playhouse more fit for her hero.

'Vicki doesn't like the idea of me going off to the fields but I'm sure she'll co-operate with you,' Laura said. Having regained a little confidence since her friend's arrival, she put on some make-up. 'She understands that it's important her father and I make up the quarrel. Harry and Tressa have rung this morning. Harry would have come over but he feels obliged to stay with Felicity. I told them both I've got everything under control. Daisy will either ring or come over but I'm not expecting anyone else.' Worry creased her brow suddenly and she hesitated at the door. 'Are sure you'll be able to cope, Celeste?'

She was holding up two aprons, one floral, the other a paisley design, deciding which was the less drab to wear to protect her clothes. 'Oh, you go off and don't worry about us. I quite like the idea of having children round me these days.'

'Looks like Jacka's words hit home yesterday,' Joy Miller's neighbour of two doors away, a woman in her mid-sixties with small close-set eyes in a wide face, said over Joy's privet hedge. She was patting the hat she had put on for church.

'What was that, Mrs Grean?' Joy asked absent-mindedly. She had come outside for some peace from her four children's noisy squabbles, and because these days she couldn't stand the sight of the ungainly Bert. She had been thinking over the time she had spent with Bruce last night and ahead to her assignation with him this afternoon and didn't appreciate being interrupted.

'Her in between us – Dolores Uren. She's got washing out on the line, on a Sunday too. Didn't you see her throwing out all that rubbish last night? Made a huge bonfire, on a fine summer's evening when me and my Len wanted to sit out in the garden. Stank the place out, she did. I heard her asking that lazy husband of hers, if he is her husband. Did I tell you that my cousin, Vi, who lives at Liskeard near where they last lived, reckons they're not even married? Vi said he's much too young for her too. She was married to somebody else apparently, he was killed in the war, but they've always been a dirty family. Then she took up with this other fellow. No wonder that madam can't face the vicar and refuses to have her children, poor little souls, baptised. Well, anyway, she was talking loudly, asking her husband to get off his backside for once and come and give her a hand, but Gerald, whatever his name is, must have refused to budge as usual because there was no sign of he all evening. Do you realise, Joy, that no one in the village has set eyes on that man? I was beginning to wonder if he really existed.' Mrs Grean twisted her face, making it appear to shrivel up. 'Still, things are looking up round here, it seems. With a bit of luck she'll tidy up the mess in her garden, the back and the front. My Len said if she does, he'll offer to give her a hand, be worth it to see the place looking respectable again.'

Mrs Grean made to go back inside and fetch her Len who would be sitting in the kitchen listening to his wireless until she collected him. Reminded of where they were to go, she added with a twinge of guilt, 'Mind you, you have to feel sorry for the woman, don't you? Can't be easy having all they children to care for. It's all right for me to speak but then I only had one, my Bernard, and I found he handful enough. I baked some nice currant buns yesterday. Do you think she'll be offended if I offered some for their tea?'

Joy had slipped into shamefaced silence at talk of Dolores Uren's sins; she couldn't condemn the woman while she herself was having an affair and was mightily relieved when Mrs Grean changed tack. 'I think she would be delighted, specially if she's turning over a new leaf. I'll have a turnout of my cupboards and pass on the clothes my lot have grown out of. Wonder I didn't think of it before. I shouldn't think Mrs Uren will mind, she's accepted some baby's clothes from Tressa Macarthur. I've always been glad of a few hand-me-downs for my lot.'

Mrs Grean came very close to the hedge to whisper, 'The vicar's getting a committee together, I hear, with that Miss Cunningham to help the family. You know anything about it?'

Joy did, she had been roped in on it, but until now she hadn't given it a single thought. She resolved she'd work hard finding ways to help out to report to the committee on Tuesday evening. It went some way to salve her conscience at the betrayal of her own children and their boring father. It helped her look Mrs Grean in the eye and tell a lie as to why she wasn't going to church this morning. She couldn't face the inevitable gossip about an affair between Laura and Ince, a dreadful misconception as far as Joy was concerned, when she herself was indulging in the very same thing. In case Mrs Grean brought up the subject, she beat a hasty retreat indoors.

—

'I'm fed up being stuck in bed like this, Alfie,' five-year-old Maurice wailed again. All the boys were lying in their beds, two sheetless, thin, lumpy mattresses on the bare floor, their only covering a rough blanket to hide their nakedness.

'There's nothing I can do about it, Maurice,' Alfie hissed back, exasperated. His face was as red as his hair with indignation at having to stay in the bed he shared with Colin, the next eldest. The other three boys were crammed on the other mattress – Rodney, the youngest, top to tail with Maurice and Graham. 'I've told you before, you little runt, that Mum said she would whip us if we dared put our noses round the door. This time she meant it.' Alfie already had two weals on his legs for his disobedience.

'What's she done with our clothes?' Colin asked, taking his finger out of the hole he was making through the striped ticking so he could pull out balls of the rough stuffing. He was the most patient of the Uren boys, not even complaining at the brutal scrubbing their mother had subjected them to in the old tin bath from which she had tossed out their toy boats and water snails and fetched in from the garden. 'Why have we got to stay naked like this and not get dirty? She's not taking us to church or chapel, is she? Gerald'll go mad.'

'She's not takin' us anywhere – yet,' Alfie replied frostily. 'It's got something to do with what that old fart of a farmer said to her yesterday. Now she's gone bleddy bleedin' mad cleaning us and the house up. The reason why we gotta stay 'ere like soddin' freaks is because she's thrown away all our play clothes and turned out what she calls our best ones, and we can't wear them because they need to be soddin' well washed first! The rate she's goin' on she'll probably iron the bleddy things too! She'll make us polish our shoes next. She'll have us lookin' like a right lot of soddin' ponces. I don't know how I'll dare show my face round the village then.'

'We got some nice grub last night though,' ventured seven-year-old Graham, impressed with the amount of swear words his brother had thrown into his tirade.

'Nice eggy,' added little Rodney, smacking his purple-stained cracked lips at the memory of the one substantial tea he'd had in his young life.

'What?' Alfie snarled at his traitorous brothers, and Rodney ducked his head under the blanket. The boys weren't afraid of Gerald who was too lazy even to work up a temper, but they were sometimes afraid of their big brother who was always the best fighter wherever they lived and had a specially cruel way of twisting the flesh on their arms and making it burn. Alfie wasn't grateful to Celeste for giving their mother some money yesterday or Daisy Tamblyn who had allowed her into the shop today to spend it. Because she rarely had much money to spend on food she had a lot of food coupons saved up and had come back with supplies to last a whole week. She had made them eat cheese and salad and drink a whole mugful of milk. Alfie had an aversion to anything he was told was 'good for him' and although he had ravenously eaten the food, he had tried rebelliously, and unsuccessfully, to make himself vomit.

Dolores could be heard downstairs now, throwing away rubbish, sweeping and scrubbing and tidying as best she could with no proper cleaning implements. But she hadn't started cleaning upstairs yet. Alfie took his hands out from under the blanket (he had been digging the scabs off a small boil on his stomach and one on his bottom). Sitting up, he rubbed the flats of his big rough hands in the thick dust on the floorboards then pressed the grime all over his chest and down his arms and legs.

'Alfie,' Colin cautioned. He had never seen their mother in a more determined mood; Alfie would get a severe stramming for doing that.

'Shut your bloody mouth up!' Alfie ordered, feeling in command of his heroic, daring image again. 'Right, who's for spit 'n' duck?'

There was a loud chorus of, 'Me!'

All the boys loved this unhygienic game which Alfie had devised and was very proud of, and Mum would never know they had played it.

They all lay on their backs and pulled the blankets over their heads. Then ripping the blankets down, revealing most of their naked bodies, they all spat heavily into the air and whipped the blankets over their heads again just before the balls of saliva hit their cheeky faces. They would do this over and over again, giggling uncontrollably.

Dolores had stopped her mammoth cleaning task long enough to feed her daughter and change her nappy. Kissing Emily's soft clean cheek and smoothing the frilled skirt of one of the dresses Tressa had passed on to her, she sighed and looked up at the ceiling. 'Listen to them. I wonder what those monkeys are up to. I'll whip Alfie if he's getting them up to mischief.'

Putting the sleepy baby down in her crib, Dolores took a broom, which consisted more of handle than head and bristles, and banged on the ceiling. 'Shut up, up there, and behave yourselves, the lot of you. 'Tis a fine drying day and you won't have to stay there much longer.' As expected, the boys ignored her banging and shouting and she went off to tackle the other male in the family.

The stairs usually being too much for his habitually drunken head and legs, Gerald Uren slept in the sitting room on what could be loosely termed a settee. He was sleeping now. His hand clutched an empty bottle of beer. Dolores looked down on him fondly and took the bottle away. He did not stir. She pulled back the ragged curtains and opened the windows wide. Warmth and light flooded in showing that although the room was ill-furnished and drab, there was not a speck of dust or cobweb anywhere. Gerald had complained profusely when she'd cleaned the room around him last night.

Returning to the settee, she knelt down and shook Gerald's shoulder gently. 'Gerry, Gerry, wake up. I want to speak to you.'

Gerald slept on, looking as if it would take a force ten gale or several hours of exposure in freezing hail on the moor to wake him. Dolores traced a long fingertip over his lips.

Mrs Grean had been right, no one in the village had actually seen Gerald Uren, and if they had, given his reputation as a terminally lazy, hard drinker, they would have received a shock. He was little more than a youth. His eyes were small and set too close together, his nose was long and thin, his mouth a dull pink slash in a pale narrow face, his hair a ragged mousy mop. But there was something innocent, almost pure about him. Dolores had adored him when she had first set eyes on him as a sixteen-year-old boy. Recently widowed, lonely but not bereft, she had just had to have him.

Gerald had been born bone idle. His family, honest, hard-working people, had counted his beauty as nothing, and Dolores had soon enticed him into her home and bed. Scandalised, his family had driven them out of Callington and they had moved to the outskirts of Liskeard. Dolores loved Gerald uncompromisingly. She had taught him the arts of love. She slaved for him willingly. Pandered to his every whim. Supplied him with the drink he craved. She was content as long as he did not leave her. But yesterday Jacka Davey had shamed her with the neglect of her children, two of them Gerald's. Now she hoped he could be persuaded to think differently, at least about Rodney, Emily and the coming baby.

She caressed his unnaturally flushed cheek and kissed his lips. 'Darling... wake up. Come on, Gerry, wake up for me, please.'

A little shake and still he did not stir or moan his way back into the world of wakefulness. So Dolores shook him with all the strength required to bring him out of his deep, intemperate slumber.

His lips parted slightly, furred tongue slipped out. He licked his dry lips, gave a violent shudder, opened his eyes and groaned. 'Mmmm, leave me alone, Dorry, go away.' And he turned over on his side, away from her.

Dolores swung his body back to her and brought him round again. 'Darling, you must wake up. I want an important word with you.'

Fully awake now, his mouth stretched wide in a yawn letting out foul breath, Gerald sat up grumpily, leaning his slight weight on the crooked upholstered arm. 'Not now.' He pushed Dolores away from him, pulling up the single crocheted cover to conceal his naked body; Dolores couldn't get enough of him, one reason why he was always so tired and the boys were sent outside to play for the greater part of each day.

174

'It's not that, darling. Do you remember what I told you yesterday about what that farmer said to me? About me not looking after the children properly.'

'Yeh.' Gerald reached for his cigarettes, lit one, throwing the spent match on the floor. 'What of it? Who cares what the nosy old bastard said?'

'He made me feel ashamed, Gerry, that's what. I want things to change a little.'

'What?'

'I think it's time we settled down, as a family, I mean. Try to get a few nice pieces of furniture together, make sure the kids are well fed and clothed. I want my kids to have a future. I don't want these people talking about us unless they've got something good to say. I'd like you to help me. I can't do it all on my own. I thought I could get your breakfast and then you could go and tidy up the garden a bit. I burnt some things last night but there's still some more that needs seeing to. Also, Gerry, there's a farm near here called Rosemerryn. I've heard the farmer fell out with his farmhand yesterday. I thought you could go over there and ask for his job, before someone else gets there first. Failing that, you could try the local quarry. What do you say, darling?'

Gerald drew in deeply on his cigarette and blew out smoke rings. He smiled. 'You want my answer now?' She nodded eagerly.

'Did you look into your crystal ball this morning?'

'Eh? What do you mean? You know I haven't got a crystal ball.'

'Pity, then you would have seen this coming.'

He brought his arm back in a wide arc, thrust it forward, and smashed his fist across her face.

Chapter 17

Spencer had been cutting grass since five o'clock in the morning, before the sun came up, when it was cooler and the grass was easier to turn. Coming along after him, turning the grass with the hay kicker to air it and keep it dry would have been Ince's job but he would have to do that himself now. It was hard work and he did not relish the extra sweaty labour, but he was eager to get his haymaking finished while the grass was young and sweet, making better hay for the cattle. He prayed that the ominous rattling coming from the tractor's engine wouldn't mean the wretched thing was going to pack up on him.

To add to his already bad mood, the previous poor winter of swirling winds and heavy rains had flattened much of the grass and in many places it was impossible to achieve a clean cut. Spencer turned himself round at intervals and cursed the finger beam grass machine with its half-diamond jagged blades for not doing the job properly.

On the last occasion when he turned back he saw Laura heading towards him, her blonde hair bouncing as she took long athletic strides. In normal circumstances he would have admired her tall stately form. Now his bold features tightened with displeasure and he swore softly under his breath. Then he saw she had his crib bag. He was glad of that. He'd forgotten it and he couldn't work on pride and anger alone all day and evening. Turning off the engine he jumped down from the tractor and waited, gloomy-faced, for her to reach him.

She was smiling self-consciously at him and before she could speak he said tersely, in a manner of dismissal, 'You needn't have bothered bringing that. I've managed without before. I can drink from the stream.'

'I haven't just come with the crib,' Laura replied, quickly handing him the bag then sweeping her eyes up and down the two and a half acres of enclosed field. She added, deliberately loudly, 'I've come to help you.'

'Don't be ridiculous!' he scoffed, flinging the crib bag over his shoulder and making to climb up on the tractor.

Laura pulled him back, making him stumble and press his heavy boot on her feet. She winced but made no sound. 'I meant it, Spencer. You can't work here alone all day.'

'Why not? What do you know about it?'

'There's no need for you to be so hostile.'

'There's no need for you to be here.'

'Well, I am, and I'm staying whether you like it or not. What do you want me to do?'

'Nothing if you haven't brought Brindle with you. A true farmhand would have known he'd need her to pull the kicker. Anyway, as I'm working alone I'll do it later.' His face rearranged itself from irritation to fear. 'I take it you've left someone with Vicki?'

Laura forced herself to answer calmly. 'Of course I have. Vicki is quite happy being with Celeste.'

'Her?' Spencer boomed scathingly. 'What does that woman know about children?'

'Enough to keep Vicki safe and well and occupied. Now, what do you want me to do for you? You won't shake me off, Spencer.'

'I don't need your help. You'll only get in my way. I can manage on my own today and tomorrow I'm going to see about taking on a new man.'

'That's tomorrow. Today I'll help you.'

'You're impossible.' And with that Spencer got back on the little grey tractor, started it up after some difficulty and Laura had to spring back to avoid the five-foot arm of the grass machine knocking her off her feet as he drove on.

She was left standing in the middle of the field in the two-foot high green grass. So as not to be in Spencer's way when he turned the tractor round and came back, she moved to where the grass was cut, its texture like a saggy carpet, moulded together like fleece off a sheep. The grass smelled sweet, its syrupy strength seeping up her nostrils and threatening to make her head ache, she was so tense. She knew it was the kicker's job to turn over and separate the grass so it could dry out, and there was a high hot sun for that today, but even if she had brought Brindle with her, she would have had difficulty attaching the kicker to the horse's harness and controlling the mare.

Standing there, left abandoned, fields all about her, the outer reaches of the moor boasting their silent dramatic tors, she felt small and helpless. She picked nervously at the cloth of the old shirt she was wearing. Washed many, many times, it smelled of the moor, animals and Spencer. There was a patch on the shoulder, a small tear at the back she had not seen to yet. There was a huge tear in her marriage. By remaining here, could she repair it, patch it up, or was she risking destroying it for good? Spencer did not tolerate anything interfering with his wishes.

The tractor was coming towards her. She felt like running home to the farm and taking over from Celeste, but she was rooted to the spot and felt it would take the grass machine itself to remove her from it. Spencer was sure to leave her standing there like an idiot, a scarecrow with its arms clamped rigidly to its sides. He'd drive straight past, not looking at her, his face set like granite, angry, resentful.

A fieldmouse scuttled just in front of the tractor's front wheels. Laura gave a warning shout but it was too late. The little brown creature disappeared in a small bloody splash and she screamed in horror, feeling wholly responsible for the fieldmouse's death.

Spencer jumped down and grabbed her arms. 'What is it? What's frightened you?'

The words wouldn't come, she could only point at the red stain on the ground.

He followed her staring eyes and taut finger but could not make out what had alarmed her. He felt frightened. 'Laura, for goodness sake, tell me what's wrong.'

Tears rolled down her cheeks, streaking the make-up she had put on for him. At that moment she couldn't have been more distraught if she'd witnessed a child being killed. That innocent little field-mouse would still be alive if she hadn't come here and insisted on staying. Spencer wouldn't have stopped the tractor to talk to her. He would have been somewhere else in the field now and the tractor wouldn't have run over the fieldmouse. It mattered; like everything that happened when one was distraught and almost past reason, it mattered terribly.

'It's all my fault,' she sobbed.

Lost and bewildered, Spencer pulled her into his arms. He had pondered on her reason for being here, why she was so keen to help him, be in his company, but if it was an attempt at a reconciliation, presumably so Vicki wouldn't suffer, she hardly seemed to notice she was now in his arms.

'What's your fault, Laura?' he breathed softly.

'The fieldmouse. It was killed by the tractor's wheel. If I hadn't come it wouldn't have happened.'

For a moment Spencer didn't know whether to laugh, hug her tightly, or order her back home for being a fool. Not the latter; because of her distress over the death of a little insignificant creature he had just lost a bit of his heart to her. He shook his head and let her go, but stroked her arm.

'Small animals are killed every time a field is cut. If not a fieldmouse then perhaps a rabbit. It's nobody's fault, Laura, it just happens.'

'Why is life so cruel?' she sobbed, turning away from him. Expecting a sarcastic answer, and not wanting to hear it, she started the walk home, quite defeated.

Spencer grabbed her by the shoulders. 'If you really want to help, there's a fork over by the gate. You can scrape the bits all along the hedges, where the kicker can't reach, and in the ruts where the cattle have left hoof prints which the kicker can't reach into. Would you like to do that? It's laborious and sweaty work but a very valuable job.'

Laura looked across at the gate, at the fork leaning against it, then at her husband uncertainly, rather suspiciously.

'We'll work for an hour,' he said briskly. 'Then have some crib in the shelter of the hedge by the gate. Me and... I always eat there. It will be cool after the hot work.' He gave a gentle parting shot. 'Don't overdo it, mind. You're not used to this sort of work.'

From the gate, set about halfway along the hedge, Laura had worked nearly to the first corner of the field when she realised the cranky drone of the tractor's engine had stopped. During that long hour she had not looked across at Spencer once, it was enough that he was letting her stay, had given her a job. She hadn't had much time for thought, only to hope that Vicki was getting along with Celeste. An ugly thought, that Vicki might not forgive her for leaving her with a woman she didn't care for, she cut off as sharply and brutally as the fieldmouse had lost its life.

Leaning the heavy fork against the hedge, she walked over to Spencer where he was laying out the crib. She flopped down next to him on the hard ground and gratefully took the mug of tea he was holding out to her. 'Thanks, my throat's never felt so parched.'

'Haymaking's thirsty work,' he muttered.

And then her hands were filled with hot stinging needles, sharp searing pains. She put the mug down on a large stone and looked at her palms. They were bumped all over with blisters, up every finger and both thumbs, a big fat one at the bottom of her wedding ring. Before she could hide them, Spencer took her hands in his.

'You'd better call it a day.'

'Ooh...'

Her sound of disappointment was so like one that Vicki made, his heart did a strange flip. He had never thought of Laura as childlike before, but she was twelve years younger than he was and, as her husband, he had promised to care for all her needs. It occurred to him then, and it was an uncomfortable thought, that his behaviour towards her contained a strong element of childishness.

'I didn't feel them forming.' She frowned, holding her hands up close to her face. She had considered bringing gloves with her but had felt they wouldn't give her the authentic look of a farmer's wife.

'You can't carry on like that, Laura,' he said softly. 'You'll be in agony. I'm grateful for your help but why don't you go back to Vicki now?' He formed a smile, and it had warmth in it. 'She must be missing you.'

Responding, she admitted, 'I quite enjoyed working out here but I am missing her.'

'There you are then. I'll see you this evening. I hope Celeste can cook a good roast, you'll need her help with those blisters. I'll be ravenously hungry when I get back.'

Gingerly holding the mug, two Spam sandwiches and a slice of seed cake, Laura consumed her share of the crib silently. She had won a small victory by receiving Spencer's sympathy and didn't want to force a conversation that might annoy him. It was only now she realised how closely he had held her after the fieldmouse's death and she regretted that she hadn't made the most of the situation.

'Food never tastes better than out of doors when you've been working hard, does it?' she said conversationally, brushing crumbs off her trousers and getting up to go. 'I've packed lots of food and some Mason's herb beer for you. Don't forget to wear your hat, the sun's extremely hot.'

Spencer made a wry face. They parted amicably.

—

Laura rushed home, hot, perspiring and dust-streaked, happier than when she had left, anxious to know if her absence had bothered Vicki. Celeste reported that she had been polite and well behaved and had kept mainly out of her way in the playhouse. Vicki waited for Laura to take a bath and change her clothes then clung to her for the rest of the day. Daisy had turned up that morning and helped Celeste to get everything at the farmhouse under control. Seeing how tired Laura and Vicki were after their restless night, Celeste suggested they take a nap, and cuddling up together, they slept all afternoon.

Tressa came over in the evening, and with bandages over her blisters, Laura helped her do the milking. Vicki went with them, never more than a few inches away from her stepmother. Spencer was surprised to find them in the shippen, finishing the work by putting the milk churns in the granite trough of cold water to keep cool overnight.

'We're just finished here, Spencer,' Tressa said. She kept her voice light but there was a touch of contempt in it for him.

'Thanks for coming over, Tressa,' he said. He held his hand out to Vicki but she shook her head and held on to Laura's white coat.

'I'm always glad to help my friends,' Tressa replied, looking him tartly in the eye. 'Now I must get home. It'll soon be time for Guy's next feed.'

When Tressa had left, Spencer asked Laura how her hands were.

'They feel much better, thank you,' she said, his concern giving her hope that he was over the worst of his wrath with her. Still being cautious with him, she added, 'Well, I must go upstairs and change. Celeste has cooked us a lovely meal. We might as well make an occasion of it.'

Vicki finally kissed her father but she was unwilling to let Laura out of her sight and went with her.

Celeste had waited all day for an opportunity to berate Spencer, and the moment he came inside she left the gravy she was stirring on top of the range and went straight in on the attack.

'You owe Laura and Ince an apology.'

'Mind your own business.'

'Don't be ridiculous, Spencer. Are you a man or a lemming? Why are you so set on self-destruction and of those around you too? Why are you behaving like an utter bastard? Do you feel so guilty about wanting to be happy again after Natalie's death? Is that it? Does it frighten you so much? If Ince and Laura's old relationship hadn't been the excuse to cause a rift then you would have picked on something else – Laura's cooking perhaps. You just want to crawl back into your shell of woe and self-pity again, don't you? Are you so used to being in the slough of despond that you want to stay in it for ever?'

Spencer was listening to her as he buttoned up his clean shirt. If he hadn't come to some of the same conclusions himself during the lonely afternoon's work he would have been so furious with Celeste he would have thrown her out of his house by the scruff of her neck.

He held up his hands in submission. 'I don't need all this, Celeste.'

'Oh yes you do!' Celeste was very angry. 'All one hears on this farm is Vicki this and Vicki that! Vicki is very important of course and if this present trouble is upsetting you and Laura, then think what it's doing to her! And for goodness sake stop and really think about Laura in all this stupidity of yours. You are the most arrogant and selfish man I've ever known, and yes, I admit it, I've known a good deal! Don't let your marriage slip away from you, Spencer, over your damnable jealousy. Laura is kind and patient, but do you want to risk reaching a point where she may not be able to forgive you? I had a chance of real happiness once, not so long ago, and I threw it all away. Why can't you realise just how lucky you are? You had one happy marriage and tragically your wife died. Now you have something most people rarely get, a second chance, and you're hell bent on destroying it.'

Blistering hot tears were streaming down her face and she wiped them away with her sleeve. Spencer handed her a towel and she buried her face in it. To stop her trembling he put an arm round her shoulders and led her to sit down.

'Have you got it all out of your system now?' he asked gently, brushing back a tress of red hair that had fallen in front of her eyes.

She was astounded. 'You're not angry with me?'

'No. I've been thinking along similar lines all afternoon or I would have given you short shrift. And I got the feeling you were scolding yourself some of the time. I wouldn't advise you to get het up like that too often. It's not good for the baby.'

Celeste's mouth fell open. 'You know I'm pregnant? Does it show? With my full figure I thought I'd succeeded in concealing it.'

'No, it's not obvious. You're about five months, I'd guess. I can't explain it, there's something about you that I recognise from when Natalie was carrying Vicki. How do you feel about it?'

A look of tenderness filled Celeste's splendid face. 'I was devastated at first but now I couldn't be more pleased. In fact I'm thrilled. I can't wait to hold him or her. No one knows but you and me, and perhaps Dolores Uren, she muttered something along these lines the other day. I came down to Cornwall to consider what to do. I'd never intended to keep the baby, but something stopped me from getting rid of it. I thought I'd go away somewhere, give birth and put it up for adoption. At least it would make a childless couple happy. But since coming to Kilgarthen something has made me cling to the child just as it's clinging now inside me. Seeing Laura mothering Vicki and getting involved with Alfie has helped.'

'Does the father know?'

A sprinkling of tears again. 'That's the irony of it. I met David at a New Year's party. We hit it off straight away. I liked him a lot. We're the same age, we share the same interests, his people have a large estate in Buckinghamshire which I enjoyed staying at, we were compatible in every way. Then he asked me to marry him and everything was ruined. It was all my fault. You see, I panicked. I was too used to a mad social whirl, having different partners, no ties, no commitments. I was beastly to him. I sent him away. I missed him terribly and soon realised I'd made a dreadful mistake. I was going to go to him, beg him to give me another chance. Knowing David, I was sure he would.' Using the towel she mopped her face.

'Why didn't you go to him?'

The words came out in a sort of wail. 'I discovered I was pregnant.'

'But David would have stood by you. He obviously loved you.'

'I was afraid he'd think I only wanted him back because I was pregnant. I couldn't have borne him marrying me out of a sense of duty. I wanted his love or nothing, and too late I let my chance of happiness slip away from me. At least I will always have a part of him with me for the rest of my life. I'm going to have to leave here soon. I'd love to stay here and bring up my baby in the country, near Laura and the friends I've made, but the village will be scandalised if I stayed on here as an unmarried mother. I've got a little property in the Lake District. I shall go there, pretend I'm a widow or something.'

Laura and Vicki came into the room and Laura rushed to her friend. 'What is it, Celeste? I thought I heard raised voices. Oh, Spencer, what have you done to upset her?'

Spencer moved aside for his wife. He could hardly protest at receiving the undeserved blame, his past behaviour merited it.

Celeste laughed through her tears. 'Spencer has just been comforting me, Laura. You see, we've been talking about the baby I'm expecting.'

'Baby?' Laura gasped. Celeste had always said she'd hate to have children. Then Laura felt a surge of excitement. 'Why didn't you say so before, silly? You shouldn't have let my worries stop you from confiding in me. When's it due?'

Spencer and Vicki were left to dish out the roast while the two women talked animatedly. With Vicki sworn to secrecy about what she'd heard, the news making her forget that things weren't quite right between Mummy and Daddy, the forthcoming child was the main topic of conversation until Celeste said it was time for her to go. Worried about her walking back along the darkening lanes alone, Laura persuaded Celeste to stay the night in Ince's bed.

Celeste lay awake, caressing her slightly swollen tummy, looking forward to her future. Strange, was her last thought before falling into restful sleep, Ince had been a possible chosen candidate as an ally to turn to over her pregnancy, not the irascible Spencer Jeffries.

When Spencer had done his last rounds he climbed the stairs and got into bed beside Laura. They didn't speak, and feeling shy and uncertain of each other, lay on their sides facing away.

The day had been full of realisation, revelation, resolved hurts, and coming to terms with home truths. Laura went to sleep quickly. Spencer had been civil and, she sensed, somewhat apologetic with her throughout the evening. She knew she had gained ground she was unlikely to lose.

Things were more difficult for Spencer. He had said and done some terrible things to Laura and Ince. Things he knew he couldn't simply just say sorry for and expect life to go on as it had before.

Chapter 18

It was Johnny Prouse who saved both Laura and Ince's reputations and put the blame for the sudden violent outburst at the fete firmly at Spencer's feet. Johnny spread his opinion faster round the village than Ada Prisk could have done.

'Spencer Jeffries is a funny bugger, we all know that, don't we? And which one of us has ever had reason not to trust Ince or Laura? Whatever the reason for that scene at the fete, it's none of our business but it's bound be something daft going on inside Spencer's head.'

The fact that Spencer, having left his work early on Monday morning, turned up at Johnny's cottage asking, in a humble manner, to see Ince helped to prove Johnny's point.

Ince had spent the entire time in his room since entering Johnny's home, nursing a thumping headache and remaining in a dark, contemplative mood. He refused to talk to Spencer, asking Johnny to tell his old boss that he would go over to the farm when he felt like it.

Johnny managed to pin Spencer down on the doorstep for a few minutes. 'Come to ask him to take his job back, have 'ee?'

Sighing impatiently, eager to be on his way now his approach had been rejected, Spencer said he had, adding, 'And to say I'm sorry and ask him to forgive me.'

'I should think so too. You must have gone ruddy mazed to do something like that to the poor boy. Borried a trick from the Devil, did 'ee?'

Spencer left believing Ince must have overheard the conversation; Johnny had spoken loudly and he hadn't kept his voice down. He hoped it would help put things right. He hated the thought of working with someone else.

He went into the churchyard and stood awhile over Natalie's grave. 'How did I bring myself to this?' he asked her memory.

He'd had to step down off his pride to go to Ince this morning, but saying sorry and asking for forgiveness, although not to Ince's face, had been easier than he had anticipated. Somehow it was different with Laura. Now he was talking to her without biting her head off, sleeping in their bed again, all seemingly well on the surface, she appeared to have lost some of her eagerness of yesterday to get back into his good books. While she lavished every care and attention on Vicki, she seemed cool towards him. Given his suspicions, thumping Ince had almost been an honourable thing to do, but he had called Laura a slut, a terrible thing to accuse a decent woman of, and his distrust of his new wife was more unforgivable than his distrust of his friend.

Natalie couldn't give him advice. He would have to work out how to win Laura over completely himself. He knew now that the reason he had lashed out so violently was because he had fallen in love with her.

So convincing had been Johnny Prouse's counterattack to the scandalmongers that the incident wasn't mentioned at all in the vicarage when those concerned for the Urens' welfare gathered there on Tuesday evening. As far as Kilgarthen was concerned, all that remained was for Ince, after a suitable period of cooling off, to return to work at Rosemerryn.

Harry, pursuing a devious campaign, sat on the other side of the room to Tressa. He looked and smiled at her only occasionally. Actually, Harry was glad he had taken this seat on the clumpy furniture. Tressa was wearing a thin summer dress and when she moved, he got the chance to drink in her shapely legs. Trim ankles, perfect silky calves, knees no doubt superb and dainty. Thighs—

'Sherry, Mr Lean?'

'Eh? Oh, yes, thank you, Mrs Farrow.'

Roslyn was bending forward slightly in front of him and Harry got the unexpected bonus of a view of her firm cleavage. Harry took the sherry glass off the silver tray and mischievously waved his hand in front of his face. 'It's very hot tonight.'

'Y-yes, yes, it is,' Roslyn stammered, her full cheeks going pink. She'd had very few dealings with Harry Lean who never came to church unless it was to a wedding, baptism or funeral and seemed to leave the vicinity afterwards very quickly. As he fastened his dark eyes on hers, stretched a smile full of wicked charm, she felt very disconcerted by him. Pray God he never called at the vicarage when she was alone. She hadn't felt this sort of excitement in her tummy since her courting days with Kinsley.

Well, well, Harry digested her reaction to him. The vicar's wife? Now she would make a pleasing distraction. She was an attractive lady, comely in the old-fashioned sense. He sipped his sherry. Frowned. Ugh, horrible cheap stuff. I thought clergymen were proud of the contents of their wine cellars. Roslyn was pouring out another drink. She had forgotten one for herself. Her hand was shaking. Harry grinned, just stopping himself from laughing out loud. Steady on, Harry boy, one woman at a time. And he languished in his chair and for the thousandth time imagined how Tressa would feel, naked in his arms.

Celeste took a notepad and fountain pen out of her handbag and put on her glasses. With black sweeping frames enhancing her clear green-flecked eyes she smiled round the room at the company, all clearly in view now, noting the fragile, breathtaking beauty that was natural to Tressa. The young wife and mother would stay beautiful all her life. Tressa would never have to resort to powder, paint and high fashion; she was so unaware of her looks and charisma it wouldn't even occur to her.

Also there was Mr and Mrs Farrow, Daisy Tamblyn, the Reverend Brian Endean, Harry, Pat Penhaligon, Joy Miller and the quiet little Mrs Sparnock. A one hundred per cent turn-out. Celeste would have invited Ada Prisk to join them but her persistent tongue, peppered with unwelcome sarcasm, would have kept them here all night.

'We might as well begin. First, let me thank you all for coming. I'm sure you're all aware that Mrs Uren appears to have taken to heart what Tressa's father said to her on Saturday so I don't think we'll have any difficulty in persuading her to accept our help. All we need to do tonight is to pool our suggestions and decide, if we all agree each has a good idea, who will put them into action. I'm sure it goes without saying that we must be very careful not to offend the family. And we must think of the children's feelings in this – young Alfie has a very fierce sense of pride. Now, Tressa, I might as well start with you. The baby's clothes you passed on to Mrs Uren were well received and I've heard she has gladly accepted some from you, Mrs Miller, for the boys.' Joy nodded. 'Have you any ideas you'd like to share with us, Tressa?'

Unused to and not liking individual attention, Tressa shifted about uncomfortably and colour crept up the pale ivory column of her neck, prettily pinking her small face. She cleared her throat.

Harry restrained the urge to lean forward as she spoke but he listened to every word intently.

'It was embarrassing after what my father said to Mrs Uren but I took some milk and eggs to the house yesterday. Andrew, Dad, Aunty Joan and I would be glad to send over something each week, perhaps a chicken occasionally. It's nice to see the children looking cleaner and not dressed in rags. Alfie took the milk and eggs from me at the gate. He said his mother was too poorly to come to the door. He said she had a tummy upset. I think we ought to keep an eye on the children in case it's something catching and they need a doctor.'

'I'll do that,' Mrs Sparnock said shyly, then appeared to shrink half in size in her chair. The others knew she wouldn't want to contribute anything more for the evening so she was thanked and left in peace after that.

'Good, good, that's excellent. You're accumulating a number of things for us, aren't you, Daisy?'

'I'm keeping a large box at the back of the shop,' Daisy duly replied, her kindly face displaying the itch to impart her glad tidings. 'Laura's given me a lot of things and I've put in several items of old stock and bits and pieces people have handed in to me. I've got a couple of nice blankets they can have and Mrs Lean is going to contribute some more bedding. Bruce has one or two items of clothing that will do for Mr Uren. He's waiting to carry the box down as soon as he gets the word and has offered to do any more lifting and carrying.'

The Reverend Endean spoke next. Resting his small white hands on his slight paunch he spoke each word precisely, as in his manner from the pulpit. 'I've asked my congregation for help and the first offer came from Mr and Mrs Penhaligon. Mr Penhaligon's mother, who lived in a little cottage at St Day, died a month ago and has left her son several items of good furniture and there are some nice pieces not required at the pub. Perhaps Mr and Mrs Uren would be glad of them. Also some other folk have come up with oddments, curtains, tablecloths, a cot, a mangle, a um…' He raised his beetling eyebrows at Pat to come to the aid of his failing memory.

'And a piece of wool carpet and some kitchen mats. A rocking horse for the little children, a bike that would suit Alfie, and some board games,' Pat finished for her minister proudly.

'Goodness,' Celeste exclaimed, writing it all down. 'Alfie will be thrilled at receiving a bike.' She could imagine the boy whizzing along the lanes on it and was sure the resourcefulness in his character would mean he'd find a way of using it to make some money for the family. 'While I have Alfie in mind, I have a friend who owns his own private airfield. He has promised to look into the possibility of giving Alfie an apprenticeship when he's the right age.'

There were murmurs of how pleased the gathering was at that.

'I'll pop into the pub later and thank Mike, and I must go to chapel on Sunday to thank your congregation, Mr Endean,' Celeste went on, then rapidly added, after a piqued frown from Kinsley, 'And church too, Vicar. I already know what your flock has come up with and I'll detail that later. In fact, as I shall be leaving Kilgarthen soon, it will give me the chance to say goodbye to lots of people at the same time.'

There were murmurs of disappointment and one or two direct questions but Celeste warded them off. She turned to Harry. She was sure he hadn't come up with anything to help. She knew there was only one reason why he was here.

'What about you, Harry? We're doing ever so well. Have you got anything to add to round off the evening?'

He looked directly at Tressa for a split second then he turned to Celeste with a hard stare. 'I've given the plight of those dear little blighters a great deal of thought and concluded that they would benefit from a good day out. We could get some cars and adults together and take them for a picnic on the beach, Polzeath perhaps, it's the nearest. Other children, like my niece Vicki for example, could be invited too so the Urens won't look on the outing as charity. We could play cricket with them, take them paddling, build sandcastles, buy them ice creams, indulge them to the full. Give them a day out they'll remember all their lives.'

The others were so impressed, a spontaneous applause broke out. If she had voiced her derisory thoughts out loud, Celeste would have been happy to eat the words. She expressed her heartfelt thanks to the good-looking cad.

'A Sunday afternoon would be best,' Kinsley said enthusiastically. 'We can forgo our traditional roast and pack up a feast to share instead. Our three children would love to go, wouldn't they, Roslyn?'

'Yes, dear,' Roslyn agreed, smiling admiringly at Harry. 'What an excellent idea, Mr Lean. I confess I had only thought of the usual kind of help. I'm sure the Urens will be overwhelmed with what they'll be given. If they accept everything on offer they'll be quite self-sufficient which, of course, is our main aim.'

As she had nothing else to add, not wanting to blow her own trumpet by mentioning her gifts of clothes and another note of hard cash, Celeste brought the proceedings to a swift and satisfactory end. All declined the offer of tea, and moments later Kinsley and Roslyn were standing on their doorstep watching their guests depart for their homes – all except Joy who had mentioned going for a breath of fresh air and strolled down the hill. The Reverend Endean cycled ably uphill to his home on the other side of Lewannick. Mrs Sparnock and Daisy crossed the road and after a brief good night went into their respective houses. Celeste and Harry went into the pub. Tressa didn't accept Celeste's invitation to join her for a drink and carried on up the hill, daydreaming as she was apt to do, and Harry gazed after her until she had disappeared round the bend for home.

Harry stayed drinking for a few minutes, long enough to down a brandy and bask in Mike and the regulars' approval of his splendid idea to show kindness to the newest family in the village. Then he bid a hasty good night, got into his car, and followed the way Tressa had taken.

In a tiny chink of time he had caught her up, stopped his car, and wound down the window. 'I'm on my way to North Hill, to friends for supper. Want a lift the rest of the way home?'

His tone was casual, almost uninterested, but Tressa glared at him suspiciously. She threw down the stalk of wild grass she'd been threading through her fingers. 'You're always driving somewhere, Harry Lean. You must be getting your petrol off the black market.' But it wasn't his underhanded deals she was worried about. Did he really have friends to see at the next village or was he trying to get his hands on her again?

Harry retaliated with a huge grin. 'I can always help your husband out with a little extra juice, he only has to ask. Are you going to carry on walking or get in, Tressa?'

Used to walking long distances, climbing rugged tors and doing heavy farmwork without getting out of breath, it seemed ludicrous to get into a car for a two-minute journey. But in the light of his earlier apparent uninterest in her, and her own secret scorn of Dolores Uren's warning, it felt ridiculous to refuse. She would keep on her guard though, ready to fend him off if he did try anything.

'You can drop me off at the end of the farm's track,' she said firmly, not appearing or sounding in the least bit grateful. Before he could spring out of the car and see her into the front passenger seat in his best gentlemanly fashion, she moved round the car and got in beside him. It was a hot, breezeless evening but she put on the cardigan she was carrying.

Harry's dark eyes twinkled. He started up the engine and drove very slowly. He wanted to savour these few moments of close proximity with her. He kept his hand on the gear stick, well aware that Tressa was keeping her leg as far away as possible.

'Andrew wouldn't like you accepting a lift from me,' he commented.

'No, he wouldn't. He hates you.'

'I know. I don't care for him either.' Harry changed his mind about asking her if she still hated him; she had told him so often enough before and after the time she had reciprocated Andrew's adoration. Tressa was bound to say yes and that would put the old barrier up between them. He glanced at the stony profile of her delectable little face, and didn't mind if it took him forty years to achieve his lecherous aim.

His aftershave was strong and overpowering in the confined space. Added to the brandy lingering on his full smooth lips, expensive tobacco ingrained in his fine clothes, it was a totally masculine smell. It didn't have quite the same sensuous quality that drew Tressa time and time again to Andrew, but she tried to ignore the fact that she found Harry's combined male scent pleasing.

All too soon for Harry, creeping round the bends and tickling the stretches of straight lane he usually crashed along, destroying anything overhanging from the hedges, choking the area immediately behind the sedan with dust, the journey was over. He pulled in at the bottom of Tregorlan's track.

'There you are, Tressa.'

'Thank you.' Turning her back on him she put her hand on the door handle.

'Will you be taking your little boy on the beach outing?'

Was he trying to detain her? Without turning round, she answered, 'Why do you ask?'

'Just wondering if he was too young for that sort of thing, that's all.'

'He'll be fine as long as he's not exposed to the sun.'

'Do you know, I often think it's about time I got married, had a family. After all, I'll be thirty-two this year. Have you heard from Laura today? I hope she's all right. I don't like my niece having such a bad-tempered brickbrain for a father.'

A feeling of dread was filling the inner reaches of Tressa's stomach. He was only chatting conversationally to her but there seemed to be a ring of evil intent about it. *Be afraid of him, Tressa. Be very afraid of him. The danger will come in an unexpected way.*

'L-look, Harry, I really must go.'

'Of course. Good night, Tressa.'

Tressa pushed down on the door handle. It didn't move. She pushed harder but it was stuck fast. She yanked it upwards, thinking that she was trying the wrong direction. The door handle wouldn't budge. She panicked. Pumping the handle up and down she pushed and shoved and then pounded on the door with her fists. She was trapped. 'Let me out! Let me out of here!'

Harry jumped out and ran round to the door on the outside, wrenching it open. 'It's all right, Tressa. It's open. What's the matter? Are you claustrophobic or something?' He seemed genuinely surprised at her distress. 'I pranged the hedge on the way home from Launceston this afternoon. There's a dent in the door. That's what made it stick.'

Tressa was standing beside him now, on shaky legs, feeling very foolish. She was panting, chest heaving. Perspiration was dripping down her back. In the quietness of the evening she realised the engine was still running. If he had intended to trap and ravish her he would at least have turned the car's engine off.

'I'm sorry, Harry.' How could she explain? The man was a rat and a louse but he didn't deserve her assumption that he was a rapist. 'I... I thought, I...'

A dark look passed over Harry's face like a rain-filled cloud. 'I hope you will remember in future, Tressa, that I would never, never hurt you. You're shaking. Can I walk you up the track?'

'No. I'll be fine. Thank you for the lift, Harry.'

'Any time, Tressa. I'll do anything for you, any time.'

He drove off like a fiend, sending the car screeching round bends, decapitating cow parsley and swaying foxgloves. A few yards away from the turning to Tregorlan Farm he ran over and killed a badger.

Tressa turned tail, running up the track to escape from his dust storm. She saw Andrew sauntering towards her, relaxed, whistling, hands in his pockets. He had come to meet her. She ran straight into his arms.

Not realising her anguish he was overwhelmed that she had missed him so much after such a short parting. She clung to him, burrowing her face against his familiar body, touching him, kissing him, reassuring herself that she was safe whenever they were together. He was her love, her life, her very essence. Aroused by her intensity, Andrew took her onto the moor and laying her down gently on the soft turf made love to her with the same abandon she had greeted him with. When their passion was spent, he held her clamped to him and stroked her hair and hot tender flesh. With love like this to share there was no need for words.

The sounds and smells of the moor filled his senses, as Tressa's desperate need, and his, had a short time ago. Black earth, pungent ferns, timeless stones, wild flowers, chattering stream, buzzing insects, the dome of hazy darkening sky streaked with fiery colours all around them. Andrew loved these things of Nature, but he loved the woman in his arms to the depths of his soul. He would suffer Hellfire for her if events ever demanded it of him.

At that moment he understood the terrible, aching loneliness Spencer Jeffries must have suffered when his wife had died. Fear made Andrew pull Tressa closer and closer to him. If he ever lost her his life would be an endless unendurable void.

Chapter 19

Two weeks went by, and still hoping that Ince would come to the farm and retake his job, Spencer had not looked for anyone to take his place. He managed with Laura and Harry's help and the time Bert Miller put in to earn extra money. Now rain had stopped work in the fields, and although he was cross about it, Spencer sought the opportunity to mend his marriage properly. He hoped he would find Laura alone with Vicki. There had been a constant friendly stream of villagers visiting the farm – friendly to Laura – to show they believed in her innocence. Spencer wasn't worried about their lukewarm attitude to him, he just wanted his family to himself.

He had killed a chicken and left it hanging up in a corner of the yard, to drain its blood. When he went to take it down off the hook it had disappeared. Thinking there was a thief about, he hastened away to tell Laura. He was surprised to find she had the chicken in the back kitchen. It was immersed in hot water in the old tin bath to make the feathers easier to pluck. Sitting on a low stool, her face full of grim determination, sleeves rolled up above her elbows, Laura was plucking it.

'I was going to do that,' he said carefully. He was going out of his way not to upset her these days.

'It's time I learned,' she replied simply, hiding the distaste she felt at the pungent smell and the feel of warm, wet feathers.

'Who told you what to do?'

'No one. I've watched you several times.' She pushed off the wet feathers which were climbing up her wrists. 'It isn't very easy to get a grip.'

'You'll soon get the knack. Try a little twist to the wrist with a good hard tug. You might find it easier.'

Laura followed his advice and gave a little squeal of delight when the next feather came out on one quick pull rather than a tug and struggle. 'I did it. It took me five minutes to get the first feather out.' She looked at him solemnly for some moments. 'Did you want me for something?'

'No. No, I, um, like I said, I was going to pluck the chicken. Can I get you a cup of tea? For when you've finished?'

He was so desperate not to sound patronising, Laura's heart was warmed through. She had watched him control his rancour over the wet weather, careful not to make angry remarks. He was kind and polite but since their row he had not called her by any terms of endearment. For her part, she was careful to give him space, staying quiet for longish periods so as not to annoy him with chatter that might sound forced. They had a lot of fences to mend, there were still many things they could not discuss, like money or future events that involved them both. Ince's name was never brought up. But Laura felt they had just made a little more headway.

'I'd love some tea. Would you mind taking some milk and biscuits out to Vicki and Benjy? They're in the playhouse.'

'Right, fine. Be ready in fifteen minutes then.'

Spencer poured out the tea when Laura came through with the plucked chicken. She laid it on the draining board with its giblets and gazed at her handiwork. 'It looks so small now it's bare,' she said, washing her hands.

He came to see. 'You've gutted it too. I am impressed.' Then he rested a hand on her shoulder. 'I am proud of you, Laura.'

Laura was gladdened by his praise. 'It's not a pleasant task but someone has to do it. I'll skin and gut a rabbit the next time we have one.'

She dried her hands and turned round. Spencer had not moved away and they were very close. Then they were looking into each other's eyes. Laura was sure he was going to kiss her and she closed her eyes. The best chance for their marriage to work was for their physical relationship to resume. She had thought to make the first advances but Spencer was old-fashioned where women were concerned, and after what he had called her at Hawksmoor House, she feared he would think her too forward.

Spencer was longing to make love to Laura again. Here was the chance to make the first approach and the resulting closeness would help to resolve many of their knotty problems. He would be able to hold her and say sorry convincingly. He raised his arms to hold her close.

And then Vicki ran into the room, her little face indignant, her golden hair damp.

Laura moved past Spencer. 'Oh, Vicki, darling, mind the clean kitchen floor. Remember to take your boots off when you come indoors in wet weather.'

'Sorry, Mummy. But Daddy didn't bring our biscuits.'

Laura bent to kiss her daughter's peeved face. 'I'll get them for you.' She put four plain biscuits into a sandwich box so they wouldn't get wet on the journey back to the playhouse and pulled up Vicki's hood, tucking in her hair.

'Thanks, Mummy. Are you going to join us? We could have a tea party.' Vicki tugged on her hand. 'Say you will. You can be the grand duchess in our game.'

Laura glanced at her watch. 'All right, darling. I can spare twenty minutes.'

'But Laura, I've poured you a cup of tea,' Spencer said, his heart dipping.

'That's all right. I'll put it in a flask.'

In two minutes Laura had put on her mackintosh and boots, and with the flask in her pocket she was dashing across the yard in the rain holding Vicki's hand and the pair were laughing and giggling.

Spencer sat down gloomily and picked up his mug of tea, feeling superfluous. If only Laura could love him as much as she loved Vicki.

Joy Miller ticked off items on Felicity Lean's weekly grocery order as she placed each one into a cardboard box.

'Can you pass me a packet of baking powder please, Bruce?'

'Certainly, honey.' He came up behind her where she was leaning over the counter, put the baking powder down beside the shopping list, and covertly ran a hand up her leg.

Joy closed her eyes to enjoy the caress. Bruce was so good at this sort of thing. Her skin crept deliciously every day in anticipation of these moments. Instinct made her open her eyes and stand up straight, momentarily frightened that they had been caught out. 'Quick, darling, I see a customer coming. Oh, it's Dolores Uren.'

Joy's sudden movements back to respectability obliged Bruce to disentangle his thick hand from her suspender. He rolled his eyes, making his heavy features look shifty, sniffed like a ruttish dog and ran his nicotine-stained fingers through his hair.

'Hell, I'm horny today. Roll on dinnertime, then I can take you upstairs and give it to you real good.' Thanks to Daisy's almost daily jaunts to Rosemerryn – to make sure for herself that Spencer was treating Laura right – their visits upstairs to Bruce's neat little room were frequent. Even when not on duty his mistress often found an excuse to be in the shop around dinnertime. 'We haven't seen the Uren woman for ages. She usually sends that eldest boy of hers in for shopping, all done up like a dog's dinner these days, poor little sod. He asked Mother if she wanted a delivery boy now he's got a bike. She said she'd think about it.'

'That would be very useful for those who are infirm or busy. Mrs Prisk was only saying yesterday that no one's seen Mrs Uren about for nearly two weeks. Not even us, her closest neighbours. We were beginning to think she was getting as elusive as her husband. She's been too busy putting her house to rights.' There was kindness and admiration in Joy's voice. 'There's been curtains going up, furniture and things going inside in a steady stream. She had washing out again on the line last night, long after the dryth had gone out of it. There's so much sound of cleaning and scrubbing coming from her house, I should think you could eat off her floors by now.'

'She's well dressed today,' Bruce remarked, going to the door to open it for Dolores. He liked to pay his mother's customers these little courtesies and it had paid off, for there had been a small rise in the takings. 'Quite an attractive woman. I see someone's given her a pram.'

'That was me,' Joy said, crossing her fingers that her infidelity wouldn't give rise to her needing it again. She was always careful with Bert, and spurned his occasional approaches vigorously, usually with success, but in the heat of the moment with Bruce…

Dolores rewarded Bruce with a small smile as she passed through the open doorway with baby Emily held on her wide hip. Joy noticed with a start that the woman was pregnant again. It was all too easy to get that way.

Dolores placed her book of food coupons on the counter. 'I'd like a bag of sugar and a box of porridge oats please, Mrs Miller. And a bottle of disinfectant.'

'Three Hands or Maxi-Clene?' Joy asked, reaching round to the nearest shelf.

'What? Oh, I don't care what brand the disinfectant is. Give me the cheapest.' Dolores paid for her goods and picked them up.

Then she looked Joy full in the face and for one horrible moment Joy felt that she could see right into her mind, that Dolores knew of her unfaithfulness to Bert. And Joy's sense of shame was growing, a different sort of shame, over something which Bruce hadn't noticed. Kilgarthen had been inhabited by a wife-beater before. The vile schoolmaster whose filthy ways had been responsible for the burning down of the village school. Only Laura Jeffries, Jennings as she was then, had been brave enough to do something about it. Now there was another wife-beater in Kilgarthen. Joy had heard the sounds and seen the signs next door to her, but her desire to mind her own business and her preoccupation with Bruce had made her ignore them. Dolores Uren's face showed the signs of a once savage beating, the fading yellowing marks of bruises, a swelling not quite vanished, a cut on her cheekbone barely healed, and dark circles of fear and lack of sleep under her eyes. Joy wanted to say something, ease the other woman's burden by offering a haven of safety in her own home if it was ever needed. But dark gypsy eyes, harbouring a hundred secrets belonging to others, made the words stick in her throat.

Dolores had something to say, brief and succinct. 'I want to thank you for the clothes and pram you sent round. Everybody in the village has been very kind to us. Working here you see more of the people than I do. Please pass on my thanks, will you?'

'I'd be glad to,' Joy murmured.

Dolores left without another word and Bruce didn't notice that his paramour's mood had taken a swing into guilt-filled quietness. Later, when he tried to lead the way upstairs, Joy resisted, pulling back on his hand, looking as if she was about to cry.

'What's up with you?' he demanded, impatience replacing his exuberant anticipation. He hated the sudden changes of mood women were susceptible to.

'I don't feel like it right now, Bruce. Can we just sit down and talk?'

'Talk? What the hell for? Why spend time talking when we can enjoy ourselves.' Bruce hated the very thought. Talking? Carol had been a great talker, she had even talked while he'd availed himself of his conjugal rights. She had talked because she'd hated sex and it had been one ploy to turn him off her. It had sent him into the beds of numerous other women before and during the war. When the war had ended, Carol had been even more reluctant to receive his loving. She and the children had settled into a cosy life without him, routines and habits which he did not fit into. Carol had become fat, middle-aged and as comfortable as a parlour cat in the war. Life with her had been stupefying. Bruce had resented it. Never a level-headed man, he had got into fights, at work and the local bars, with cuckolded husbands and outraged fathers, one of a girl under age.

At work one day, after a night of drinking and brooding, he'd got into a fight with another logger and fists had flown. The other man had died from the beating he had received. Bruce had slipped off, packing his bags and getting out of town, before the police could pick him up. He had travelled around Canada and then the world, living off favours from former army buddies. Only the sudden longing to come home and see the county of his origins had been true in the tale he had given his mother. He planned to make a final run to South America. He'd have to move on soon. It was only a matter of time before the Canadian police approached his mother in this insignificant little Cornish village.

While living here Bruce had been happy to keep his sexual encounters exclusively to Joy. She had been leading a boring life and he had provided the exciting outlet she'd wanted. He'd taken it for granted that she knew it wasn't a permanent arrangement. That she'd enjoy it while it lasted, be grateful for their time together, leaving her free to live on pleasant memories or look for another lover. Why the hell was she ruining things now?

With a sliding heart, Joy knew that Bruce would never understand her feelings. It had taken eight weeks for the shame of her betrayal of her husband and children to catch up on her. Bert had always been a hard worker. The family had been hard up until recently but Joy had never gone without money in her purse, her children had never gone without clothes on their backs, food in their tummies. Bert loved her. He was not the best-looking man in the world, he wasn't clever, perceptive or sophisticated, but he was honest, kind and loyal.

Joy didn't see Bruce as quite the thrusting Romeo of her dreams now. The air of refinement she'd thought she'd seen in him had chipped away into sordid little cracks. But for all that she was afraid to lose him and took the short journey up Daisy's stairs with him. It was no good though, things had been spoiled. The excitement of their affair had disintegrated for her. For the first time she was worried that they would be caught, that Daisy would come home early, or one of the children would be sent home poorly from school, or Bert would have an accident at Tregorlan Farm and be forced to come home and send someone looking for her. She was tense and unresponsive.

Bruce did not enjoy their union either. That evening he was in a dank and bitter mood.

'I was wondering, Mum,' he said, trying to sound casual as he helped Daisy clear the tea table. He was putting the condiments back in the larder so he wouldn't have to look at her. 'Could you lend me a few quid until my savings in Canada have been transferred over here? I'll let you have it back straight away then.'

'Of course, Bruce. I'll fetch my purse. How much do you want?' Daisy never missed the opportunity to be generous to Bruce, to make up for the years she had thought herself a poor mother, the reason why all her children had left home early. She paid him two pounds a week for working in the shop, a very generous sum, and he had free board and took as many cigarettes from the shop as he liked.

'I was thinking of a bit more than that,' Bruce replied, shuffling his feet in a nervous little dance as he folded up the tablecloth and put it back in its drawer. 'I want to get some new clothes and a pair of shoes and I was thinking of buying a present each for the kids and sending it to them.'

'Oh, I see.' Daisy was glad he wanted to do something for the children he rarely mentioned but she couldn't see why he wanted to add to his wardrobe; it wasn't vast but he had everything he needed. 'How much do you want then?'

Bruce reddened and his stance showed he was on the defensive. His voice came out gruffer than usual. 'I, um, was thinking of about one hundred pounds.'

'One hundred pounds! I haven't got that sort of money.' Daisy had more than that, but she was careful where money was concerned.

'You must have something stashed away,' Bruce asserted aggressively. His mind had been busy making calculations from the day he had got here. 'You must have made a tidy sum over the years with the shop. You could draw some out of the bank.'

Daisy was annoyed at his insistence. There was no pleading in his angry countenance. He was motivated by plain greed and was using bullying tactics. Although she enjoyed his company she knew she had been right not to trust him too deeply.

She said tartly, 'I'm not as well off as you think, my son. For a start, all the income from the shop doesn't come to me alone and I haven't got the sort of big savings you think I have. Just a little bit put by for my retirement.'

'What do you mean, all the income doesn't come to you? Have you been sending some to Susan or Alison?'

'No, I have not. I never hear a word from your sisters so I'm not in the habit of handing my money over to them. I've worked hard for what I've got and I intend to hang on to it.'

'Who is getting your money then?' It was an angry demand.

Daisy saw red but she hoped a partial explanation would soften him. She didn't want to fall out with him. 'Laura owns half the shop so she has half the takings.'

'How come?' Bruce hissed in exasperation.

Daisy couldn't admit the truth, that many years ago she had tricked her sister, Bill Jennings' mother, out of her lawful half of the shop. Laura had discovered the truth and realised that the sister's half should have gone to Bill Jennings and then, as his widow, to her. Because Daisy had been so good to her since her arrival in the village, Laura had made peace with her, and Daisy had given Laura half her savings and half of the shop as recompense.

Bruce looked so twisted and hateful he no longer resembled her son. Daisy was becoming nervous of him. 'I was going through hard times and she bought into it,' she told him.

'Okay, fair enough. But even so, surely you can lend me a hundred pounds.'

Daisy could but he didn't deserve it and she doubted if she would ever get it back. Her silence made him explode.

'I don't want you to give it to me, Mother. I only want a bloody loan. You'll get it back, every damned penny. Hell and damnation! You help out a bloody gypsy and her filthy brats but you won't help your own son.'

Daisy was feeling afraid now, but she wagged a finger at him. She felt she must stay in control or he would never stop browbeating her. 'I won't be spoken to like that, Bruce. I might not have been the best mother in the world to you after your father ran out on us, but you can't come back into my life and order me about. I won't lend you any money, not now, not ever after this. If you don't like it, well, you know where the door is.'

Snatching up his jacket, he strode across the room. 'Don't worry, you rotten old cow. I'll be walking out through it for good soon enough.'

Daisy cried for a few minutes after he'd slammed the door then wiped her eyes and washed and dried the tea dishes. She knew Bruce wouldn't have stayed with her for ever, there was too much restlessness in his dark spirit. She sat down in her armchair at the side of the range and got comfortable, picking up her knitting. She'd quickly get used to life on her own again, she had lived alone for years and felt she was missing nothing. It wasn't what she wished but perhaps the sooner Bruce went, the better, hopefully before he dragged the Millers' marriage through the mud.

Chapter 20

Ada Prisk had waited a long time; three weeks was an achingly long time to have so much scouting and scouring go unrewarded. She had been looking out for Eve Pascoe. But except for two attendances at chapel with Les, which Ada, being in church, had missed, there had been no other appearances in the village by Miss Pascoe. The young lady hadn't been seen anywhere else either. Ada had skulked about Johnny Prouse's cottage in the hope that Eve would call on Ince Polkinghorne to continue offering him her comfort. No one knew much about her, except Ince apparently, and he wasn't saying anything about anyone to anybody at the moment. So Ada baked an apple crumble and took it to Carrick Cross.

Mindful of the smallholding's hauntings, Ada had another worry as she squeezed her big feet, one in front of the other, along the narrow grassy track. She was terrified of snakes and slowworms and prayed none were slithering about in the thick growth, ready to bite her ankles.

As she closed in on the smallholding, Ada's thoughts returned to her mission and centred on the questions she would thrust on Eve Pascoe. She excused her blatant curiosity by telling herself that as one of the oldest inhabitants of the village it was her duty to welcome newcomers. Fear of the ghost of Tholly Tremorrow rearing up to show her his 'ferrets' had kept Ada away from Carrick Cross before today, and after the rumours of its dilapidation she was amazed at how orderly the place was. She admired the painted plaque on the gate.

To her relief, she found Eve outside with Les. She had been afraid she would find the place deserted and tempt its spirits to torment her, and because of her age and arthritis she was in pain and wilting fast under the blazing hot sun. Les was snoozing in a shaky-looking deckchair, a newspaper over his head and chest, a loose hand coming up every now and then to flick away a troublesome fly. Eve was sitting at a little round table, painting a small piece of flat wood. She was wearing a straw sunhat and a neat dress covered with an apron. An umbrella kept the sun off her. She got up at once to greet Ada.

'Good afternoon, Miss Pascoe,' Ada said with all the graciousness of a true high-born lady. 'I'm Mrs Ada Prisk. We said hello at the Hawksmoor fete but I'm afraid we didn't have time to get to know each other then so I thought I'd come and introduce myself properly. I've brought this for you and Mr Tremorrow.'

'That's very kind of you, Mrs Prisk,' Eve replied, taking the proffered dish of apple crumble and peeping under the red and white checked tea towel.

Woken by their voices, Les lifted the newspaper, saw who had come to disturb the peace, grunted in unfriendly fashion at Ada, then settled back again under his paper hideaway.

'Good afternoon, Mr Tremorrow.' Ada hoped he would stay asleep, she hadn't come here, on unhallowed ground, to see him.

'I'll just take this inside, Mrs Prisk. It will go nicely with our evening meal,' Eve said. 'Can I get you a cup of tea or a cold drink?'

'A cup of tea, not too strong, would be very nice,' Ada replied, gazing all around.

'Do take my seat, Mrs Prisk. I shall fetch out another chair.'

Ada wasn't fast enough to take a peek inside the house before Eve closed the front door. She sat at the table, grateful for the shade given by the umbrella. She looked at Eve's handiwork and was impressed by the picture of a badger, a fieldmouse and a thrush amid a border of campion, bluebells and buttercups. Then she gazed around again, determined to see all there was to see, still a little afraid a ghost or a monster would jump out from behind the boundary walls, the small turf rick, the shed, the water butt, or from either side of the house. Everything was in fine fettle, thanks mainly to Ince's hard work, Ada thought, glaring grimly at the lazy old man beside her.

A few minutes passed and Eve returned with a tray of tea. She had bought a teak tray for just such an occasion, set now with a snowy white lace cloth she had fetched from the sitting room. She poured the tea to Ada's requirements, in her grandmother Ruby's best china, then went back inside to get another chair. When seated on the other side of the table, she poured tea for herself.

'We don't see many visitors here.' Eve raised her neat brows for an explanation, sure that the village gossip would enlighten her on a matter about which her prickly old grandfather would not.

'Well, people don't come this way very often.' Ada stared down into her cup, somewhat embarrassed. She glanced at Les, hoping he wasn't listening, then leaned over the table and whispered, 'It's the ghosts, you see.'

'Ghosts? What ghosts?' The only ghost Eve knew about was the one of her grandmother that Ince had mistaken her for on their first meeting. 'In a peaceful place like this?'

Ada looked at her doubtfully. 'You don't find it… creepy?'

'Not at all.'

'You like it here then?'

'Very much so.'

'It wasn't known hereabouts that Les had a granddaughter. Are you on a long visit or do you live here now?'

'I haven't any definite plans.'

There came a hard set to Eve's chin, a subtle change in her brown eyes. Ada realised she was looking at a closed face; Eve Pascoe would be careful to give nothing away and if Ada asked too many personal questions she would soon find herself ejected, kindly but efficiently, from Carrick Cross.

Never mind, there were other burning issues to be brought up. Watching the young woman very carefully, Ada said, 'You and your grandfather must find Ince very useful about the place.'

'We do, we did. We haven't seen him lately.'

Ada frowned. From the attention Eve had given Ince on the day the village had first seen her she had thought there must be something 'going on' between them. She wasn't the only one who had thought so. Now it didn't seem to be the case. 'Not since the fete, you mean?'

'That's right.'

Eve had seen Ince afterwards but she had no intention of telling the busybody. She had been glad to accompany him to Johnny Prouse's cottage and with Johnny, Mike Penhaligon and the Reverend Farrow she had seen Ince safely ensconced in one of the bedrooms. Johnny had left the room to get clean bed linen, Mike Penhaligon to get a cold compress for Ince's face, the vicar to rush back to the fete to reassure anyone who might have been distressed by the proceedings. Eve and Ince had been alone for a few moments.

Ince had lain on the bare mattress, his arm over his face as if hiding away from the world.

'Can I get you anything, Ince?' she had asked softly.

He put his arm down and shook his head, making himself wince. As well as the physical pain there was an agony deep within him plain to see.

'Do you want to talk about it?'

'No, not now. Perhaps never.' His voice was little more than a murmur.

She sensed he was uncomfortable in her presence. She was a stranger in Kilgarthen. He knew her, but not very well, and he had been extremely annoyed about her assumed name. 'I'd better get back to Grandfather. Goodbye, Ince.'

'Goodbye, Eve.'

And that had been that. Eve had thought their goodbyes had only been farewell. She and Les had expected to see Ince at Carrick Cross soon after that, but he never came, his goodbye had been final. She knew from the mobile baker that Ince hadn't left the village and still lodged at Johnny Prouse's. She wished he would come to the smallholding. She missed him, his gentleness, the solid honesty about him. She missed his fine face, dark curly hair, his rare smile.

Could the rumours about him and his boss's wife be true? No, she had quickly decided, Ince was too honourable a man for that. Les, who usually took delight in being spiteful about others, said the rumours were absolute nonsense. Eve had caught sight of the classically beautiful Laura Jeffries at the fete. She had seen her talking to her handsome, grim-faced husband and there had been an obvious tension between them. But was Ince in love with her? Did he have hopes because of the unhappy marriage? A pity Eve couldn't ask the village oracle, but even without the harsh training instilled in her by her former employer to mind only what concerned her, Eve had never been given to gossip.

'I've always thought Ince to be a rather lonely man,' Ada said, speaking as if she was an authority on Ince's life. 'He confides in me, you know. What he'd really like is to settle down and have a family of his own. I tried to make a match for him with my cousin's daughter but the maid had just started walking out with someone else. That was a shame. There's a dear little cottage up for sale in the village, just right for a man to take a bride to. Ince is a good man, would make someone a good husband.' Ada looked hard at Eve. 'Don't you think, Miss Pascoe?'

'I've given Ince very little thought, Mrs Prisk,' Eve replied, looking directly into the old woman's beady eyes. That same harsh training had taught her never, ever to show her emotions and it stopped her betraying herself although her conscience pricked her for lying. 'Another cup of tea, Mrs Prisk?'

Ada drained her cup to hide her disappointment. She was amazed that Ince, once so keen to take a wife, seemed to have overlooked the somewhat demure but amiable Miss Eve Pascoe. The young woman might seem like someone who belonged to a past age but she would do Ince very nicely, in Ada's view. Ada wasn't wholly convinced Eve wasn't interested in Ince; all unattached women were husband hunters in her opinion.

'Yes, please,' she answered. 'You make a lovely brew, Miss Pascoe.' Ada moved on to her next line of questioning and pointed to the wood painting. 'That's lovely. Are you an artist?'

Eve wasn't above throwing Ada a crumb of information. 'I'm a lady's maid actually.'

That accounts for the air of good breeding about you, Ada thought triumphantly. Eve was obviously out of work now or else she wouldn't be here. 'But you like to paint?'

'Yes, I always have done.'

'I noticed the name plaque on the way through the gate. You're very clever. You could make a good living making that sort of thing for the holiday trade and I'm sure the locals would be interested too.'

'Do you think so?' Eve asked thoughtfully.

'I'm sure about it.' Time to find out something about Angela Tremorrow. 'Do you make things like that for your mother?'

A ring of sadness shrouded Eve's pretty face. 'My mother is dead, Mrs Prisk.'

'Oh, I'm sorry. Recently, was it?'

'Just a few weeks ago.'

'Oh dear. And your father?'

'He was killed during the war.'

'How dreadful. I understand you come from Plymouth. Plymouth man, was he?'

'Yes, he was a docker and I have no brothers and sisters.' Eve hated telling all these lies but it was what her grandfather wanted. After what her mother had done, running away from home and having an illegitimate baby, Eve felt she owed him that much.

'And you decided to look up your grandfather?' Eve didn't deny it so Ada knew she was right on that score. 'I didn't know Angela had married.' Ada thought she might have imagined it, but did Eve Pascoe's rock-solid, prim demeanour slip a little?

Eve began packing up the tea tray, a signal that the question and answer session was over, but she was grateful to Ada, the only person apart from the two ministers who had paid the courtesy of calling on her. Mindful of Ada's anxiety when she had talked of ghosts, she offered, 'It's rather a lonely walk along the track leading here. Would you like me to come with you until you reach the lane?'

'How kind.' The suggestion was very welcome. Ada hadn't forgotten the terrors that could be awaiting her on the narrow path.

There was not enough room to walk side by side on the path so Eve stepped onto the springy moorland turf. They had a noncommittal conversation about the moor, the wildlife, and the coming beach outing for the village children.

'Your help with the little ones would be greatly appreciated if you went along, I'm sure,' Ada said just before they parted on the hot tarmac of the lane. 'I'd go myself but I'm a bit too old to go tearing round with a ball and the sun gets too much for me at the seaside.'

Eve smiled thoughtfully but said nothing. She wasn't sure if she wanted to get involved in the life of Kilgarthen.

Chapter 21

Vicki Jeffries and Benjy Miller ran at full pelt through the farm-yard, making dust sweeps, leaping over the muddy puddles, scattering chickens and ducks, making them squawk and quack in indignant protest. As the children ran either side of the well, Vicki tripped on a granite cobblestone and was sent sprawling. Benjy rushed back to her and pulled her to her feet none too gently; they didn't have a second to spare.

'Come on, Vicki, or he'll catch up with us.'

Resisting the urge to brush down her dress and rub her sore knee, Vicki set her face bravely and ran on, pulled faster and faster by her playmate.

They made the garden, scurried along the narrow cinder path for a few feet then ran straight across the vegetable patch, kicking up the mounded earth between two rows of potatoes, all the while willing Vicki's playhouse to get closer and closer.

'We're nearly there,' Vicki gasped, ignoring her stinging knee and the painful squeeze Benjy had on her hand. 'Quick, quick, or we'll be done for.'

They crashed through the low door of her playhouse. Red-faced and breathless they slammed the door shut and scrambled behind the little makeshift table, pulling the hem of the old piece of curtain that served as a tablecloth over their heads. They clung to each other, just able to make out the panic in each other's eyes. The sound of their deep breathing filled the little wooden building. Vicki clutched a hand to her heaving chest. They waited, fearfully.

In a few minutes the suspense was more than Benjy could bear. Gingerly he rolled up the curtain and peered at the door.

Vicki waited an agonising second then yanked him back down. Under the cover of the curtain, she whispered timidly, 'Did he follow us?'

'Didn't see him. He'll have our guts for garters this time.'

'He'll stram our legs and bums.' Vicki rubbed a hand over her bottom as though it was already sore.

'He might even eat us alive.'

Sensing the added danger of Vicki beginning to wail, Benjy put his hand over her mouth. 'Shush. I can hear him coming.'

The children ducked their heads and clung together tighter. The playhouse door was opened. He came inside. He was touching their things. Vicki's tea set made up of oddments Laura and Felicity had given her chinked as he moved it about. He was picking up toys scattered on the floor. If he got hold of Benjy's toy bow and arrows, made from hazel stems and a strong piece of elastic, he might use it on them. Benjy's big brother had sharpened the ends of the arrows with the penknife he'd got for his birthday. 'Sharp enough for pig-sticking,' Tony had proudly declared. Sharp enough for Benjy and Vicki to get stuck like a wild pig.

He was coming closer. He only had to look over the tabletop, see the shape of their bodies scrunched up under the curtain and their numbers were well and truly up.

There was a long intake of breath followed by a little triumphant laugh. The curtain was pulled off. 'Out you come.'

Vicki and Benjy scuttled back against the playhouse wall and broke into a simultaneous fit of screaming and pleading for their lives.

'Vicki! Benjy! Whatever has frightened you like this?' Laura was most alarmed.

'Oh, it's you, Mummy,' and Vicki ran to her to be comforted. Benjy forgot he was a 'big boy' and clung to Laura's apron.

'Who on earth did you think I was?' Laura crouched down and took Vicki on her knee, keeping an arm round Benjy's trembling waist. 'Out with it, the pair of you. Anyone would think you were about to be murdered.'

'We were,' Vicki whimpered, shuddering as she leaned against Laura's bosom and wiped away a tear.

'By whom? What have you been up to? Vicki? Benjy?'

Feeling braver, and rather stupid now, Benjy owned up, 'We were playing.'

'Yes, but what were you playing?' Laura demanded, caressing Vicki's feverish cheek then retying the red ribbon on the crown of her head. 'I can't approve of you playing games that are scaring the wits out of you both. You must tell me or I won't allow Benjy to come to the farm for a few days to play and I'll tell his mother.'

'He was coming to get us,' Vicki whispered dolefully, her chin wobbling as she imagined the terrible fate she'd been convinced had awaited her and Benjy.

Laura felt her alarm growing again. 'Who was? Have you been making up stories about moor spirits coming out of the marsh again? Or imps and goblins coming to steal you away?'

'No, it was Pawley.'

Laura gazed at her stepdaughter and shook her head. She'd been afraid Vicki was going to say that. She would have to talk to Spencer about this. Vicki and Benjy's colourful imaginations had been getting out of hand and could be the cause of a lot of hurt and embarrassment. It was also extremely unkind of them and she would not tolerate it.

'You can play indoors for the rest of the day where I can keep an eye on the pair of you,' she said sternly, shooing them outside.

'Ohh,' both children protested. 'We were going to play Robin Hood.'

'I won't have any arguments. In you go. I came to fetch you for your milk and biscuits anyway, and after that I'm going to explain something to you.' Laura picked up Benjy's cache of arrows on the way out of the playhouse. 'And I shall blunt the ends of these. Don't let me catch you playing with them like this again, they're quite dangerous. I saw you running through the yard. If you trip and fall on one of these you could be very badly hurt.'

'I did trip, Mummy,' Vicki said, mournfully sticking out her bony knee and displaying her graze, hoping Laura would be more lenient with them because of it.

But fifteen minutes later, chastened and grumpy, Vicki with a plaster on her knee, the children were sent to Vicki's bedroom to play there until lunchtime.

'I don't want to play with dolls,' Benjy muttered, his small squat face turned down in mulish disgust as he flopped down on the bed. 'There's nothing but girls' toys in this room. We can't even jump up and down on the bed because your mum will hear us.'

'I know where there are some boys' toys,' Vicki said mysteriously, wanting to impress her friend.

'Where? Something your father had as a boy?' Benjy said hopefully.

'Come with me.' Vicki poked her head round her bedroom door and listened. She could hear Laura singing and the sound seemed to be coming from the back kitchen. They had time to nip in and out of the spare room.

'Who sleeps in here?' Benjy inquired, gazing round the bare surroundings.

'Nobody, silly. Can't you see the bed isn't made up? This was my Uncle Ince's room when he used to live with us,' she added wistfully.

Vicki often came into this room and sat and moped on the single bed, wondering why Ince hadn't come back to see her. He had been nearly as close to her as her father was and she missed him dreadfully. Her hopes that things would return to normal had been crushed when Mike Penhaligon and the vicar had arrived and taken the rest of his belongings away. The little room was a sad and lonely place now. Gone was the blue and yellow counterpane that had once belonged to Ince's mother and had covered the bed. Gone were his Bible, the adventure books he had read, war and cowboy stories, the photographs of his late parents, the one of him as a beaming curly-headed schoolboy, and the old wind-up gramophone and records he had proudly brought home one day. She had been three years old and she remembered his delight that the contraption actually worked and how she had run to his lap, disturbed by the deep scratchy voice of a singer called Paul Robeson. His hairbrush, comb, the jar of Brylcreem he had used on special occasions, a ship in a bottle, a framed school certificate for excelling at cross-country running – they had all gone, no longer a part of her life. Uncle Ince seemed to have been gone for ever.

Sometimes she was very cross with her daddy. He had got Laura as her new mummy and then got rid of her beloved uncle. Because he had hurt Uncle Ince, Uncle Ince didn't love her any more. He was never mentioned at the farm and Vicki was perceptive enough to know she must not bring up his name or ask questions about him. But last night, as she'd lain in bed thinking about Uncle Ince and how she was missing him, she had an idea. Next time she saw Uncle Harry she would ask him if he would take her to see Ince. She knew from careful listening outside church that he was still in the village. She was sure Uncle Harry would do it for her.

Quickly, before she and Benjy were caught at their mischief, she pulled a big tin box out from under the bed. Benjy got down on his knees beside her.

'I found this here the other day,' Vicki whispered. 'When Mr Penhaligon and the vicar came for Uncle Ince's things they missed this box. It's got all sorts of things inside it, toy cars, farm animals and a tractor, a magnet, peashooter, compass, a broken watch, all sorts of lovely things made out of nutshells. It must be Uncle Ince's secret treasure trove. I can't give it to him yet and I know he wouldn't mind me looking inside and taking things out if I'm careful. You can too, but only if you promise to be careful.'

'I promise,' Benjy said, suitably awestruck and full of anticipation.

'Cross your heart and hope to die?'

Benjy made dramatic lines over his narrow chest with a finger. 'Cross my heart and hope to die. You have my word on it.'

Scampering like two kittens they carried the box to Vicki's room and sat on the mat on the other side of the bed, ready to push the box of delights under the bed if they heard Laura coming up the stairs.

'Why doesn't Pawley sleep in your Uncle Ince's room?' Benjy asked at length while studying a brass nut and bolt on the palm of his hand and wondering what they had come from.

'He doesn't want to,' Vicki shivered. 'He's got a tent pitched in the top field. You can see it from my mummy and daddy's room. He asked me if I'd like to see inside it but I said no, of course.'

'Do you think your mum was right about what she said about him?'

Vicki added the figure of a tiny painted horse to go with the farmyard animals she was laying out in a line on the mat. 'I suppose so. No more games like this morning though. Agreed?'

'Agreed. But wouldn't you like to see what Pawley's got inside his tent? All grown-ups might have boxes like this one, full of goodies to play with.'

'I'd like to see inside it, but not with him there.'

'We'll have to sneak up there some time, take a quick look inside.'

Vicki nodded, but both children knew they'd never summon up the courage.

With no disgruntled sounds coming from upstairs, Laura hoped the reason had something to do with the strict chiding she had given the children. All was quiet, with only the noise of the fire hissing and crackling and the bubblings of a large ham simmering on top of it. She hoped Vicki and Benjy had understood all she had said to them.

Pawley Skewes had turned up at the farm a week ago. Laura had answered the sharp knocking on the back door.

'Evenin', missus. Is your man at home, the man who farms this place, that is?' Pawley Skewes had stood in the twilight, a man aged about forty, Laura guessed, with a soft rich voice. He was of medium height, wide-shouldered, the sleeves of his worn shirt rolled up revealing twisting blue veins as thick as rope on his forearms. He stood with his cap pulled down over one side of his face, slightly turned away from her. A huge haversack, bursting at the seams with what were obviously his worldly possessions, lay at his feet.

Before she could ask him any questions, Pawley Skewes explained his reason for being there. 'I'm looking for work. 'Tis a busy time for farmers right now with the haymaking, but if you're fixed up I'll be happy to take anything. Even a day or two. I'm not looking for much pay. Just somewhere to pitch my tent and access to a stream for water.'

Laura knew Spencer could not struggle on alone every day. He was becoming bone-tired and she feared it could eventually lead to an outbreak of bad temper. They were getting on quite well but she felt it wouldn't take much for them to have a quarrel – there was a lot of unresolved hurt to be dealt with yet. She invited Pawley Skewes inside, and it occurred to her then that Barney hadn't barked to alert them of the approach of the stranger. The dog was watching him, lying flat on his stomach, his long pink tongue hanging out, as if he was waiting for something.

Wearily eating his supper, Spencer didn't bother to get up for the stranger. He put down his knife and fork and hoped the man's business wouldn't take long – probably a holidaymaker come asking permission to set up camp.

'This is Pawley Skewes, Spencer,' Laura said. 'He's looking for work.'

'Take a seat,' Spencer said, pulling out a chair. 'You've heard I'm looking for someone?'

'No, I'm just here on the off chance.' Pawley Skewes kept his face half turned away.

'Can I get you a cup of tea, Mr Skewes?' Laura asked. Spencer hadn't said anything but she knew he had given up hope that Ince would come back and had put the word around that there was a vacancy for a farmhand on Rosemerryn Farm. Pawley Skewes could be the answer to one of her prayers.

'Thank you, Mrs...'

'Mrs Jeffries. Laura Jeffries. There's some roast left if you'd care to join my husband.'

'That's very civil of 'ee and I won't refuse, but...'

'But what?' Spencer asked. He had been trying to get a better look of Pawley Skewes' face under his hat.

'You might not want me eating at your table when you see this.' And Pawley swept off his hat.

Laura tried not to gasp but a loud exhale of air escaped her throat and her hands involuntarily made fists. Spencer's eyes flicked closed for a moment, he gulped, then said firmly, 'Sit down. Tell us all about yourself.'

Doing as he was bidden, there was no look of gratitude or anything else on Pawley Skewes' face; he couldn't make expressions. One side of his face, the side he let people see, was white, taut and immobile, the other side was more or less missing. The remnants of red-raw flesh stretched over the bones of his skull from forehead to chin. The eye on the better side was a dull blue, the other eye colourless and bulging. 'You have my thanks, Mr Jeffries. I'm usually sent away.'

'The war?' Spencer inquired grimly.

'Aye, at Dunkirk. The boat I was in, a small fishing boat, was blown up. I was one of the few men who didn't drown.'

'I feel very humble in the presence of men like you. Being in a reserved occupation I didn't get to fight the war in the same manner. I worked hard but in comparative safety. We use first names in this house. You may be in luck, Pawley. My last farmhand… left about three weeks ago. Have you any farming experience?'

Pawley put a hand in his shirt pocket and took out a wad of paper. 'I have references.'

Some minutes later, Spencer said, 'Very impressive. It says you have engineering and mechanic abilities. That would be a godsend with the present state of my tractor. I see you've moved around quite a bit. Why did you leave the last farm?'

'The farmer's son dropped out of college. He couldn't afford to employ the both of us. But you probably won't be surprised that it's usually because a farmer's wife or children object to my face.'

'That's terrible,' Laura said, putting a plate of food and cutlery in front of Pawley.

He looked longingly at the food. 'Thank you, missus.' He ate a few mouthfuls, delicately, slowly, to avoid his hideous injury making it slop over his chin. He looked at both Spencer and Laura, 'If you take me on I'll keep out of the way once my work's done.'

'That's not necessary,' Spencer said.

Pawley went on as if Spencer hadn't spoken. 'I'd like my food to be part of my wages and I'd like to collect it and take it to my tent, if that's all right with you. I like my privacy.'

'Let's give it a try then,' Spencer said. He was pleased when they had worked out all the arrangements. Spencer hadn't liked the thought of someone else using Ince's room.

Laura had tried to prepare Vicki about Pawley's face before taking her by the hand to meet him the following morning after he had mucked out the shippen. She hoped her daughter would be able to accept him without staring or taking fright. They were to find out that Pawley had a marvellous way with animals, he could sense sickness in a beast twenty-four hours before Spencer could, and to introduce his talent he had got the irascible Barney to do tricks. Barney was executing perfect somersaults when they approached them. Vicki laughed and clapped her hands, but the moment she noticed Pawley's disfigurement she went rigid. She didn't scream or say anything nasty or tactless, she went sickly white and looked anywhere rather than at Pawley.

After that, Laura had suspicions that although Vicki didn't mean to be deliberately cruel, she and Benjy were making up monster stories about Pawley, frightening themselves more and more. They had admitted that today they had crept up behind him as he'd been heaving dried bales of hay up to Spencer to make a new rick, and when Pawley had turned round to say hello, they had run away, scared witless.

That night in bed Laura put down the book she was reading and turned to Spencer. He had been in the house all evening, going over his account books, but there was another reason why she had waited till now to discuss the problem of Vicki's reaction to Pawley. It was getting on for four weeks since she and Spencer had made love. Apart from wanting this for their marriage's sake, she was very attracted to him, and it was frustrating not to get that close to him. She was sure he wanted their lovemaking to resume too but was worried she might rebuff him. He was a proud man. She was certain he had been about to kiss her in the kitchen the other day and she had allowed Vicki to spoil the moment. If it had left him feeling rejected, he would need some sort of encouragement.

'Spencer?'

He was just settling down and was lying on his back. He usually didn't turn away from her until she put the light out. 'Mmmmm.' It was an indistinct sound.

'Have you realised that Vicki has been frightening herself by making up scary stories with Benjy about Pawley's face?'

'No.' He sat up in bed beside her. 'The horrid little monkeys. Does Pawley know?'

'I'm not sure. I hope not. She does speak to him, but only when I'm around, but I've got the feeling the children have been making up a sort of silent "What's the Time, Mr Wolf" game.' She told Spencer how she had found the children whimpering in fear in Vicki's playhouse.

Spencer was very cross. 'The little horrors. Have you spoken to them?'

'Yes and I punished them and threatened I'd tell Joy. I don't think they will do it again. I explained that Pawley got his injury because he was very brave during the war, and all for their sake. I reminded Vicki about the white-tailed calf, how despite it being born deformed she'd loved it, that she wouldn't have dreamt of being cruel to it. I hope she'll come round to Pawley. I know he says he likes his own company but I think he's lonely. I'm sure he'd appreciate the occasional meal with us in the house. Do you think I did the right thing with Vicki?'

'Yes, but if she does something like that again I'll punish her quite strongly.'

He said no more and Laura made an attempt to keep the talk going. 'You get on well with Pawley, don't you?'

'He's a good bloke, a hard worker. I've got no complaints.'

Laura didn't need to ask, she knew well enough by the slight bitter inflection in his voice that he was missing Ince's friendship. She wished she could look deeper into his mind, to know how much he regretted thumping Ince, if he would ever forgive himself for it, what his true feelings were for her.

Without putting out the light, she lay down beside him, hoping it would provoke a reaction from him. She lay still. He lay still. Her body was hot and damp and it heightened the smell of the musky perfume she had dabbed on just before he'd come up the stairs. The clock on his bedside table seemed to tick more loudly than usual. A sudden gust of wind pressed against the window. Barney barked at a small creature that scuttled through the yard. They lay still.

Vicki cried out in her sleep and Spencer got out of bed and went to the door. Laura half sat up. There were no further sounds from the little girl and Spencer closed the door and came back to the bed. Laura lay down. She had left the buttons of her nightie undone and he stared down at the smooth swells of her breasts.

The next moment he was running his hands through his hair and crying out, 'Bloody hell, Laura, I can't go on like this!'

'You mean you want us to finish?' All her hopes and dreams disappeared in one terrible flash.

Flopping on the bed, he looked down on her. 'No, I mean not being able to... I want to... Damn and blast it, woman, we are married. Can't we... ?'

Laura's heart did so many twists and leaps she couldn't breathe for a moment. She ventured, 'Make love?'

He nodded. She swore she saw tears in his eyes but he swiped his hand across his face. 'Sleeping alone is one thing. Lying next to you every night, feeling you there beside me, warm and alive, is sheer bloody torture.' After her moment of fear, to know he wanted her so much filled Laura with a desire that made her body tremble. She held out her arms to him. 'I want the same thing too, Spencer.'

His sigh of relief threatened to blow out the lantern. Pulling off his pyjama bottoms he got back into bed and they greedily assuaged much of their hurt and frustration.

Chapter 22

Celeste was completely satisfied with the transformation of Dolores Uren's house even though she had not lifted a finger to help with any of the cleaning. When the front door was opened now a visitor was greeted either with the fresh odours of disinfectant or polish, or the homely smells of baking. The walls throughout the house had been scrubbed, some newly painted. Each room had basic furniture, curtains at the windows and some form of floor covering. Bedsteads had been added to the children's mattresses. Outside, the front and back gardens, thanks mainly to neighbours Len and Biddy Grean, were more than acceptable, planted with flowers and vegetables, the lawn mown and all the rubbish burnt or discarded.

The rub was that Alfie and his brothers didn't seem to be any happier and their baby sister, who Joy Miller had told Celeste had rarely cried, was always fractious these days. Celeste had hardly known Dolores before giving her the money at the fete, but she was sure she had been more cheerful then. Celeste was worried her efforts would turn out to be ill-judged interfering. She never saw Gerald Uren to find out what he thought about the villagers' acts of kindness. Dolores had been unsuccessful in moving him upstairs to the big bedroom she used and she always kept the sitting room door tightly closed when she had visitors.

'I'm afraid this visit must serve as a goodbye today,' Celeste said as they sat at a proper wooden table on sturdy varnished chairs, drinking coffee from clean cups in the kitchen. 'Unless you come to the farewell drink I'm giving in the pub tonight.'

'I don't expect I'll come,' Dolores said, spoon-feeding Emily with rusks and milk at the highchair someone had provided. She would

224

like to have gone and she was sure she could get someone to mind the younger children for an hour, but she was reluctant to face a mass of villagers all in one go, and she had to keep an eye on Gerald. Since he had beaten her in a rage over her pleading that he get a job he was always in a foul mood, demanding more and more drink and getting drunk earlier in the day. 'It's a shame you're going, Celeste. I shall miss you. But it is time for you to move on.'

Dolores obviously knew Celeste was pregnant and although the two women had talked all round her condition they had never mentioned it openly before. Celeste did now; Dolores was her friend and friends confided in each other. 'I hope my baby is as sweet as Emily.'

'I'm sure it will be.' Dolores eyed Celeste's face for some time. 'I hope you're wanting a little boy.'

'You think it's going to be a boy, do you? I can't wait to hold my baby.'

'I'm not usually wrong, but if you want to take some girls' clothes with you, I've got plenty to spare.'

'I'd be delighted to.'

Dolores was pleased that a woman as wealthy and classy as Celeste would even consider accepting passed-on clothes for her child. She was curious about the lack of a father for the child but felt she had no right to know all the details.

'Dolores?' To hide a flush of embarrassment, Celeste toyed with a cigarette but didn't light it in the baby's presence. 'I hope I've done the right thing by you.'

'How do you mean?'

'Well, you don't seem as happy as you ought to be. I hope no one, especially me, has made you feel patronised. I've only ever wanted to help you. I hope you don't feel I've interfered unnecessarily in your lives.'

'Not at all,' and Dolores smiled warmly. 'Others talked behind our backs or were sarcastic to our faces. They may have followed your example, but you were the only one who actually did something for us and Jacka Davey was the only one who had the guts to say exactly what was on his mind. I'm grateful to everyone who's been kind to us but especially to you two. If the kids aren't happy it's because they aren't used to being well dressed and having to keep themselves clean and tidy.'

This had occurred to Celeste. She had seen Alfie pulling at his shirt collar, scowling at his polished shoes, messing up his shiny cropped red hair, heard him swearing at being 'done up like a bleddy ponce'.

If she had been looking at Dolores at that moment instead of putting the cigarette back in its case she would have seen the other woman was going to say something else but changed her mind. If she told Celeste that Gerald was beating her it might cause more trouble.

'If you don't mind some blunt speaking, is it necessary to keep the boys so spotless all the time? It's important for school and if they go to church or a special occasion, of course, but can't they play more like they used to? Even the vicar's three children wear old clothes and get grubby playing at times.'

Dolores looked as if a great truth was dawning on her. 'I suppose I have got carried away with the idea of cleanliness, haven't I? Alfie in particular hates being all dressed up. Poor love. He hasn't made much fuss for my sake. He's realised how important it is to me to have people think well of us. I don't want to have to move again because the neighbours are hostile.'

'If we lead a normal life then people should either take us as we are or they aren't worth knowing, Dolores.'

Dolores stuck her head outside the back door. 'Alfie!'

'What?' He was never far away these days, forgoing the pleasure of racing round on his bike, worried that his mother would receive another beating, ready to keep his younger brothers from wandering into the sitting room and risking Gerald's cruelty.

'Come here a minute.'

'Why?' He retained a touch of cheek.

'Never mind why. Just you come in here.'

Alfie came and the other boys trooped in after him, all afraid they were going to be told to wash their faces or scrub their knees; Alfie afraid he'd have to run an errand in full view of the village while dressed like a soppy young lord.

226

'You know those clothes I put on your bed this morning?' Dolores said to her eldest son.

'Yeah,' he replied cagily.

'Well, I haven't finished sorting 'em out yet but they're old clothes, clothes you can play in. Take your brothers upstairs and you can all put something on. I don't mind you getting a bit grubby out playing but mind you keep your shoes on. I don't want people thinking you haven't got none.'

'Wowwee! Thank goodness for that. I was getting afraid we were going to have to dress up like ponces for our day out on the beach.'

There was a clatter and a good deal of whooping as the five boys raced upstairs.

Dolores carefully wiped Emily's face clean and fed her a bottle of goat's milk, a supply she was obtaining, via Alfie's willing feet – he was scornful of all talk about hauntings – from Carrick Cross. 'So, when are you leaving, Celeste?'

'Tomorrow, Sunday.'

'But that means you won't be here for the beach outing next week.'

'Never mind,' Celeste replied, looking as if she was putting on a brave face. 'Laura will write to me and tell me all about it.' Wiping sticky, sandy, little faces wasn't for Celeste and as Dolores had said, it really was time she left. Ada Prisk's eagle eyes wouldn't miss the significance of her swelling middle much longer.

'I'd like to see your baby.'

'I'll send you a photograph.'

'Thanks, that'll be nice. I'll try to get one of my new baby for you. We're due about the same time. Wonder which of us will deliver first. Make sure you take plenty of exercise and try to walk around when you're in labour, it makes the birth easier.'

They talked about babies and childbirth then Celeste's thoughts turned to Alfie. Aware of how much Dolores relied on him, Celeste reckoned he deserved a little break from his responsibilities.

'Could you manage without Alfie around for a little while? I'd like to take him over to Rosemerryn with me this afternoon. I'll give him lunch too. Laura would have invited all the boys over to play with

Vicki but, well, you must have heard about the quarrel her husband had with Ince, his farmhand. Things are a bit difficult there.'

'Ada Prisk stopped me one day and told me all about it. I was grateful to them for giving people something else to talk about. Yes, you can take Alfie with you. I think I'll pack up some food and take the rest of the kids for a picnic on the moor. I could do with a bit of fresh air myself.'

When Alfie came back downstairs, he was looking his old lovable scallywag self, the saucy swagger back in his step, chin raised in cheeky defiance. He was thrilled when told of his coming treat. He left with Celeste, leaving a bundle of jealous little brothers miserable on the doorstep.

Dolores had got herself into a routine, and today being Saturday, she fried egg and chips for dinner and when her four remaining sons had eaten theirs and were outside playing, she cooked Gerald's meal. He was awake when she took in his tray, his face dark and blotchy from drink and marked with discontent. A pungent offensive smell reeked from his body. Dolores was taken aback to notice a slight sagging to his jawline and realised his lifestyle, something she was partly responsible for when she had corrupted the boy, was turning the man into a repulsive slob.

'About bloody time,' he snarled. 'I'm bloody starving.' He pitted the rank air with foul oaths as she put the tray over his lap. 'What's this? Sodding tea? Get me a decent drink.'

'There isn't any money left for beer,' she said firmly. She had lost her adoration for Gerald when he had persisted in using his fists on her and then had started to slap the children about. He had even brutalised his own son. Rodney had a big ugly bruise on his back where Gerald had kicked him viciously out of the room. Going to the window, Dolores pulled back the curtains and opened the top pane, letting in the cool fresh air. 'I'd rather spend it on food for the kids.'

'Bitch! Bugger those little bastards! Get me some beer or I'll smack you one again. And don't open the bloody curtains!'

Dolores was trembling but she turned round and placed her hands on her hips. 'I realised the other day, Gerald, that you have two children and you've rarely set eyes on them. It's about time you got off that damned settee and did something for them.'

'Like what?' he scoffed, ramming a forkful of chips into his mouth.

'Like getting a job to support them and the one you've got on the way.'

Gerald waved the fork at her stomach. 'That's your sodding fault. If you always want to romp, you should be more careful. Speaking of which, after I've eaten this, you can come and join me over here.'

'I've got too much work to do.' She left the room.

Ten minutes later Gerald came through to the kitchen. He threw the tray, the empty plate and mug, knife and fork across the room, then grabbed hold of Dolores. Beating her down to the floor in front of a screaming Emily, he raped her.

Outside weeding in her garden, Joy Miller closed her mind to the slapping and crying she could hear.

—

'I could do with a few things from the shop, Ince,' Johnny said slyly, shuffling through from the kitchen with a straw bag and some money in his hand. 'Your legs are younger than mine.'

Ince had just come down from his room and edged back towards the stairs, looking as if he wanted to make a retreat. 'You brought a bagful back with you yesterday, Johnny.'

'I forgot to get margarine and salt.'

'Can't it wait?'

'What, until you feel like facing the world again?' Johnny demanded stubbornly. 'Like sometime next year perhaps? You can't hide away all your life, Ince.'

Sighing impatiently, Ince waited for the daily barrage he got from Johnny on how he was wasting his life and it was time he pulled himself together. He put up his usual protest. 'I don't intend to hide away all my life, Johnny. I just want some peace and quiet until I sort myself out, that's all.'

'Understandable for a few days but it's over three weeks since your face saw the light of day. It won't do 'ee any good to sit and mope any longer. 'Tis time you got yourself over to Rosemerryn and saw Spencer and sorted things out with un. He come here to say he was sorry. If you can't accept that,' Johnny wagged his finger as he did every day, 'and it's not like you to be so unforgiving, then punch the living daylights out of him if it'll make you feel better! Look him in the face and say what's on your mind. And you ought to see Laura again. I don't think things will be put right between they properly until you and Spencer air your feelings. You say you don't want your job back, fair enough. Spencer's taken on someone else anyway, a war veteran. He can't afford to let time stand still. You ought to do the same. You've got a permanent home here with me, all you've got to do is get yourself a new job and start over again.'

Ince had heard it all before and he wasn't listening properly. 'You needn't worry about my keep, Johnny. I've got savings—'

'Did I mention keep?' the old man bellowed, getting angry. 'You can live here for bleddy nothing for all I care! But isn't that a stupid thing to be doing anyway? Spending your savings like this? If you pull yourself together and go looking again you might find yourself a nice young woman to marry and you'll need your savings then. And through all your disillusion and self-pity there's one person you're forgetting and I think it's pretty rum of you.'

'Who?' Ince snapped. He snapped at Johnny a lot. He didn't mean to hurt his feelings but Ince was in the grip of a depression and harsh words spilled from his mouth before he knew he had said them.

'Young Vicki. Have you forgotten her? You mean a lot to that dear little maid, you helped rear her and you seem to have forgotten your obligations to her. She must be missing you a lot. What do you think all this staying away is doing to her?'

Ince looked down guiltily at the floor and moved the passage runner around with his toe. He missed Vicki too, more than Johnny could ever know. It was because of her that he had set out three times on the short journey to Rosemerryn, but Spencer's sudden outburst of fury had played through his mind, the unfairness of the situation, his public humiliation; the closer he'd got to the farm, the slower had been his steps. The last time, he'd seen Pawley Skewes driving the tractor, cutting the hay that Ince had taken for granted only three weeks before would be his job. While he was glad the unemployed man had found work, it had seared his soul to see another taking his place. He had not been able to go on. Vicki might be suffering but he couldn't bear to set foot in his old home yet.

'I'll get the shopping,' he said meekly, and he took the bag and half a crown from Johnny before he started off again about the glowing attributes of Eve Tremorrow.

With some relief Ince made the short journey round the corner and up the hill without seeing another soul and he was the only customer in the shop. He was served by a whey-faced Bruce Tamblyn. Bruce seemed to have lost his friendly manner and plonked the two items Johnny required on the counter in stony silence. Ince asked for some sweets, paid for his shopping and then walked back briskly down the hill, praying he wouldn't be assailed by Ada Prisk. He heard someone calling his name and when he looked behind him he didn't mind that it was Alfie. Alfie ran up to him, head up, face clean, hair brushed, hands plunged confidently in his pockets.

'You're a stranger,' Alfie said cheerfully.

'Hello, Alfie. You look like you're off somewhere.'

'Aye, I am in a minute. Miss Celeste is goin' over to Rosemerryn this afternoon. She's takin' me with her to see the animals and play with Vicki.'

It was typical of Alfie, vivacious and benevolent, not to mind playing with a girl much younger than himself. Ince was reminded that until recently he had been of a similar disposition to the boy, but his cosy, familiar world had been rocked to its foundations. He had tried hard, and the Reverend Endean had urged him to come back to chapel and let the Lord do His healing work on him, but Ince needed more time to be alone before he could face starting a brand new phase of his life.

He took a small paper bag out of the shopping bag. 'Will you take these to Vicki for me, please? It's two sherbet dips. I'm sure she'll share them with you.'

'Right-o, thanks.' Alfie kept abreast of all the gossip and knew he would find himself on dangerous ground if he mentioned Mr and Mrs

Jeffries to Ince, but he wasn't above making playful mischief. 'You been over to Carrick Cross lately? Me mum sends me there to get goat's milk for me baby sister. There's a pretty lady livin' there now. But you know that, don't you? You used to go over there to help out, didn't you? But not these days. I know because Miss Eve talks about you all the time.'

'Does she now?' Ince replied nonchalantly, but his stomach churned to hear Eve was apparently taking an interest in him. He had thought she might have called at Johnny's cottage to inquire about him. He'd hoped she would. It had been an agreeable experience to have Eve fussing over him, holding his head against her soft bosom, gently dabbing his face with a handkerchief. He had been touched by her thoughtfulness in accompanying him to Johnny's cottage. When he had said he didn't want to talk about the unleashing of Spencer's fury on him, he hadn't meant he didn't want to speak to her again. So why hadn't she come to see him? He knew he had been short with her at the fete when Les had introduced her as Eve Pascoe but he'd thought they had parted friends. He had felt hurt by her abandonment of him and had fallen deeper into his melancholy, telling himself he couldn't care less about Eve Tremorrow.

Alfie blew his cheeks out like a hamster then made a quizzical face. 'I reckon she's got a fancy for you. If you don't get over there soon I reckon you'll miss your chance.'

'Don't be silly, Alfie,' Ince said crossly and he stalked off.

'I didn't mean anythin',' Alfie shouted after him, then he shrugged his scrawny shoulders and went back up the hill to see if Celeste was ready.

Dumping the shopping in the kitchen, Ince tossed the change on the dresser, ran upstairs to his room at the back of the cottage, flopped down on the bed and closed his eyes to think about what Alfie had said about Eve Tremorrow. He was pulled up sharp to hear her talking to Johnny in the garden. He sprang off the bed and went to the window. There she was, as large as life, neat and elegant in a fitted dress, small straw hat and white gloves, her clutch bag tucked under her arm. The window was open and he could hear every word.

'I congratulate you on your bantam hens, Mr Prouse. They're fine, healthy stock.'

'Call me Johnny, m'dear.' Johnny looked at Eve pointedly. 'They were all the company I had until Ince came to live with me. He's a fine young man.'

'He was very good to my grandfather. I'm grateful to him for putting things in order at Carrick Cross. We'd like him to come and do some work for us. Grandfather can't manage the place like he used to. I know people think Grandfather is lazy but he really is quite frail and he gets these terrible headaches. We can only afford to pay Ince for a few hours a week but I understand he hasn't taken another job yet, it might help tide him over until he does. I hope he won't be offended at my asking him.'

'Not at all,' and Ince could see the glee spreading over Johnny's wrinkly face. 'Come inside for a cup of tea. He should be back from the shop by now.'

Ince stayed stubbornly in his room. A few weeks ago he wouldn't have believed he could behave like this. He had first helped Les Tremorrow out of the kindness of his heart but he baulked at his granddaughter making arrangements for his life – which was how he viewed it.

Johnny saw the shopping bag and called up the stairs to him. 'Ince! Miss Pascoe is here wanting a word with you.'

Ince stayed put and did not reply.

'Ince! Did you hear me?'

He kept his mouth clamped shut and didn't move a muscle.

'Ince!'

Grumbling under his breath, Johnny began the slow struggle up the stairs. Ince sighed in submission. He couldn't let Johnny shift his old bones on the unnecessary climb.

'I'm coming!'

'About time too,' Johnny uttered when he reached the bottom of the stairs. 'What do you think you're playing at?'

'Where is she?' Ince asked, not altogether contritely.

'In the sitting room. Get in there and keep her company. I'll bring in some tea by and by.'

To show he wasn't particularly pleased at seeing Eve, Ince entered the room with his hands deep in his pockets. '*Miss Pascoe*,' he said coolly.

Eve had a small ornament of an eighteenth-century lady playing a lute in her hands and she took her time admiring it. After putting it back in its exact place she observed Ince for several moments, weighing him up, until the annoyance dropped off his face to be replaced by shame. Ince knew she had overheard how long it had taken Johnny to get him down the stairs.

'I heard you were still in low spirits.'

He took his hands out of his pockets. His next words, although challenging, were a mite friendlier. 'What if I am?'

'I'm sorry about what happened with your friend.'

'You've heard the rumours as to why it was supposed to have happened?'

She nodded briefly. 'Mr Jeffries must have been out of his mind.' She made a small movement, a slight tensing of her body, and Ince knew she wouldn't pry. 'I've come on Grandfather's behalf to offer you a little work.'

'I know. I overheard you talking to Johnny.'

'You look as if you're offended by that. I'm sorry. Do you want the work?'

He shrugged his shoulders. 'If I say no, Johnny will never let me hear the last of it. I wouldn't like to see all my hard work go to waste. I suppose it will be good to be useful again.'

Eve smiled at him. 'Shall we expect you on Monday then? You can work out the hours and pay with Grandfather then.'

Ince couldn't bring himself actually to smile back but he felt his tense facial muscles slackening. Eve Tremorrow wasn't a patronising busybody. She was a gentle, modest woman and she had a quieting effect on him. He found he was looking forward to being at Carrick Cross again. 'I'll be there bright and early.'

Johnny came in with the tea and Ince took the tray from him and set out the cups and saucers. Ince was amused to see Johnny eyeing him and Eve to ascertain how they had been getting on. Ince put him out of his misery.

'I'm going to work at Carrick Cross on Monday, Johnny.'

'Oh, really? That'll do 'ee good, boy. Out in the fresh air, getting your hands in good clean earth again. That's what you need.' Johnny winked slyly at Eve and nodded in delight. 'How do you like Kilgarthen then, Eve?'

'I haven't seen much of it yet nor met many people, Johnny.'

'Easy answer to that,' Johnny said artfully, looking at Ince then Eve. 'Come to the pub tonight. There's a little farewell do for Miss Cunningham. She told me all about it. She's laying on some nice grub. Be free drinks all round. You won't have the chance to get to know she but you will some of the other folk. There'll be music, maybe even some dancing. Everybody's going. The Reverend Endean's going, told me himself. Why don't you come as well, Ince?'

Ince's immediate reaction was to say no but he stayed silent, waiting for Eve's reaction. She appeared to be thinking, then she looked at him.

'You're not a teetotaller, are you?' Johnny prompted her.

'No, but I rarely take a drink,' Eve said, dropping her eyes demurely to her cup of tea.

Johnny got up from his chair and fussed with the tray, pouring tea into an already full cup. 'Ince,' he hissed through the side of his mouth. 'Ask her out.'

Ince choked on a mouthful of tea. He thought Johnny would break a blood vessel, he was so eager. Entering a pub full of noisy people was the last thing Ince desired. He would be gawped at, talked about, given all manner of advice and consolation and receive a certain amount of scorn, but it would stop a few mouths in mid-track if he walked into the Tremewan Arms with the enigmatic Miss Eve Tremorrow/Pascoe, who was nearly as elusive as he was in the village nowadays. Ince liked the idea of that. Suddenly he didn't want to hide away any more.

'Would you like to go, Eve?' he asked boldly. 'You could make your second debut and I could re-emerge into the social life of the village.'

Both men waited with bated breath for her answer and in the main both found it satisfactory.

Sipping her tea, she looked straight ahead at nothing in particular. 'Grandfather could do with an evening out. We'll meet you and Johnny there.'

Chapter 23

Laura was baking bread. Celeste declined to grease the bread tins for her and sat back and filed her nails.

'You may be looking forward to motherhood but I don't suppose we shall ever see you become the slightest bit domesticated,' Laura smiled at her friend.

'Mmmm,' Celeste replied thoughtfully. 'Judging by the satisfied look on your face I should say you'll soon be joining me and Dolores Uren with a stomach out here.' She made an arc in front of her. 'I take it all is well in the bedroom again with you and Spencer?'

'Yes, thank you,' Laura replied breezily, still feeling warm and deliciously alive after last night's loving.

The moment their passion had been spent Spencer had held her in his arms and apologised over and over again for calling her a slut and not trusting her. She told him she forgave him and took the plunge and brought up Ince's name. Spencer had poured out his heart about his feelings for his friend, how much he regretted hurting Ince physically and what he had accused him of. Spencer had said he was going to try to repair their friendship the first chance he got.

'And you're happy and content again?' asked Celeste.

'I'll settle for what I've got and hopefully soon a baby of my own.'

'Well, you can have plenty of fun making up for lost time, darling. And don't we unattached women all envy you your gorgeous man. You'll soon be bouncing chubby blonde babies on your knee. There could be quite a few of us in the same boat. Tressa Macarthur wants another baby, so I've heard.' Celeste studied her nails and chuckled wickedly. 'And then there's Joy Miller.'

'Oh, Joy doesn't want any more. She's told me so herself.'

236

'Then she ought to be more careful.'

Laura stopped kneading the dough and used the side of her arm to wipe flour off her nose. 'What do you mean? Do you know something I don't?'

Celeste gave Laura an even more wicked look. 'The trouble with you, darling, is you've been so caught up with your own problems that you must be the only one in the village who doesn't know, apart from her poor faithful dog of a husband of course. Joy Miller is having an affair with Bruce Tamblyn.'

'What?' Laura's eyes shot wide open. 'Are you sure?'

'Of course I am or I wouldn't have said so. Joy is often in the shop alone with him during the lunchtime closing when she should be elsewhere, or they slip out on the moor or one or two other little places when Bert is at his Buffalo meetings in town. When Benjy plays here with Vicki, the other three children are packed off to their grandmother's, leaving Joy free to enjoy herself.'

'Good grief! So Kilgarthen has a real life affair after all. I never expected it of Joy, though, she's always seemed so sensible. I'd never have thought she'd do this to her family. I'll have to have a talk with her.'

'Why? The wisest thing is to keep out of it.' Celeste was using the tone of the wise and elderly now. 'With the way talk is flying round the village I should think her husband will find out soon and all hell might break loose. You don't want to be involved in anything nasty.'

'I wouldn't say a word normally but Joy works in the shop in my place. Bruce is Daisy's son and she's going to be terribly upset if there's ever a big scene in the shop.'

'Well, you have a point but I would still keep out of it, Laura. It's not your responsibility. Spencer might not be happy if you got caught up in someone else's scandal.'

Laura had not thought of it from that angle. She didn't want anything to undermine her new happiness. 'I'll think about it then,' she promised. The echo of a sudden whoop of delight came from outside. 'Sounds like Alfie's enjoying himself.'

'Vicki's showing him the animals. His little face was beaming when I came indoors. He really likes the farm. I'll miss that boy when I leave

237

here. You will keep an eye on him for me, won't you, Laura? And let me know what's happening with the Urens? There's the added worry of Gerald beating Dolores and I don't want the children hurt.'

'Is that happening?' Laura said guiltily as she put two loaves in the oven. 'Since I married I seem to have lost touch with what's going on in the village.'

Celeste took her purse out of her handbag and put a few pound notes on the table. 'You just look after your own family, my girl,' she said sternly. 'I said observe, not get involved. I don't want to be worrying about you from the Lake District.'

'What's that for?' Laura asked, pointing at the money.

'Rent for Little Cot. You can stop making that face, Laura, I insist. I suppose you'll be renting it out again,' then Celeste's face unfolded in a wry expression, 'or will you be keeping it empty as a haven away from Spencer and his moods?'

They laughed but with Celeste's departure so close they fell into a sad silence. Then Laura said, 'Why don't you get in touch with David, Celeste? It's got to be worth a try.'

'You know the story, Laura. I left things too late, and anyway he probably has someone else by now. I shall always love David but now I'm going to look forward and do the best for our baby.'

His face sticky from the sherbet dip, Alfie looked critically at a large pink and dark grey pig slumbering half in and half out of the sty. Bending his neck, he whispered in Vicki's ear, 'Be careful what you say. That's really Goering, the Reich's master spy.'

Vicki, her face also sticky, shivered as his warm breath tickled her skin and she clapped a hand to her ear. 'Eh? What are you—'

Then she remembered that everything she had shown Alfie so far had become part of his playful imagination. The hens had been a scouting party of Navaho Indians. Alfie had let out a bloodcurdling cry as they stood amidst them and the hens had scattered squawking in fright in all directions. Alfie had thought that hilarious. The ducks on and about the duck pond were dangerous crocodiles that only he,

Alfie, could deal with as Tarzan of the Apes. Alfie had greatly admired Button, the two-day-old calf, although he had rudely declared her name, chosen by Vicki, as 'ruddy stupid'. Then Button had turned into Dr Franklinson, a mad scientist who cooked children's brains to steal their intelligence. Five minutes ago Alfie had terrified Vicki by declaring he was going to pull back the cover of the well, leap up on the wall and dance a jig all the way round it, to show the Sheriff of Nottingham that he, Robin Hood, wasn't the least bit afraid of him. Vicki had taken in all his high jinks in the spirit of the hero-worship that the boy acquired as readily as dirt and bruises. Now they had to be careful not to give away vital secrets to the Nazis.

'I know,' she whispered back gleefully. 'Careless talk costs lives.' She'd heard that in the school playground.

Putting his strong rough hands on her narrow shoulders, Alfie gently pushed Vicki behind him. 'Goering is a murderous swine,' he hissed back to her, 'but you're quite safe now. When I give the sign we'll make a break for it over to that bombed-out building.'

The old trap house had been pulled down and there was some rubble left on its site. Vicki thought he must mean there. She tapped his back. 'What's the sign?'

Alfie was about to say something but decided that scratching his bum would be a bit too disgusting for a small girl to follow. 'When I raise my hand and drop it suddenly. Got that?'

'Yes,' she replied dutifully.

Vicki waited with bated breath. She took her eyes off the pig, who would never seem quite so friendly and snuffly to her again, and stared at Alfie's hand. Up it came on the end of his long spindly arm which was covered with stiff ginger hairs. Down the hand came and she sped off, racing so fast she reached safety in front of her leader's longer legs.

Always one to give honour where it was due, Alfie patted her shoulder. 'Not bad for a girl.' He spat on the palm of his hand. 'Put it there.'

'Put what there?' she asked, looking at the proffered flesh dubiously.

'Cor, you have been brought up soft. Your hand, of course, and you have to spit on it first. We'll shake on it and you'll be my friend for life.'

'Really?' To Vicki this was one of the highest honours she had ever received.

'Come on,' Alfie mouthed impatiently.

Vicki spat on her small hand and put it on his and he clasped his fingers round it tightly and shook it hard. It hurt but she bravely made no fuss. Alfie tossed her hand aside, and on an afterthought muttered cautiously, 'That doesn't mean that I want to marry you when we grow up, mind.'

'Course not.' Vicki shook her golden hair indignantly. 'I'm not going to marry anyone. I'm going to go to agri-something college. My daddy wants me to and so do I and I'm going to have the biggest farm in the world.'

'I'm going to be a test pilot,' Alfie boasted, puffing out his scrawny chest. 'If you get big enough fields then I'll come and land in them.'

'Wizard!' she shouted, copying a word from Celeste.

Alfie had been scanning Rosemerryn's fields as he'd spoken. 'Whose tent is that up in that field? A holidaymaker's?'

'No, that belongs to Pawley who works for my dad.'

'The man with half a face? I've heard about 'e in the village. I'd like to meet 'im.'

Half an hour ago Pawley had driven the tractor into the yard and was fitting a part to it that Spencer had ordered. Before Alfie demanded they talk to the disfigured farmhand, Vicki suggested they take a look at Brindle and led the way to the paddock. They sat on the wall and stroked the old mare when she trotted up to them.

'What's she then?' Vicki asked, to get the first word in before Alfie's adventurous nature took over.

He looked at her. 'A horse, stupid. I'd have thought even you'd have known that.'

'You're the one who's stupid. Is she a spy or something? That's what I meant.'

'Oh, I see.' Alfie combed Brindle's rough grey mane with his fingers and thought about it. 'She's Rainbow, the steed of Richard the Lionheart and the bravest horse in the Crusades.'

'What's the Crusades?'

'They were holy wars in the olden days. You'll learn about it at school when you're as old as me.'

'You are clever to remember all those brave tales, Alfie.'

'Of course I am. Can I ride the horse?'

'Better not. I'm only allowed to ride her when there's a grown-up around.'

Alfie was off the wall in a trice, tearing a button off his shirt. 'Let's go and find one then.' He helped Vicki down, none too carefully, and earth and ferns marked her dress.

On the way through the yard, Alfie looked inside the barn, shippen and outhouses, all the while spouting more adventures and making up colourful stories. Vicki was very impressed by him and thought him much more fun to play with than Benjy. When they came across Pawley, who was bending over the tractor engine, Alfie ran up to him. Vicki hung back.

'Can I have a ride, mister, when you've finished doin' that?' Alfie blurted out in his usual cheeky energetic manner.

Pawley turned his head slightly and Alfie strained to get a good look at his face. 'I'll have to think about it, boy. Who are you?'

'Alfie Uren, only me proper name's Alfie Roscrow really. It's a good little tractor. You fixin' that awful noise it was makin' just now?'

'I'm doing my best, Alfie,' Pawley said, busy with a wrench.

Alfie stood beside the farmhand and stuck his nose under the bonnet. 'Mmmm, it's got a lot of bits and pieces, ain't it? I'm goin' to be a pilot when I grow up and I want to learn all about aeroplane engines.'

'Good for you.' Pawley sounded friendly. He always did, Vicki reflected, and with Alfie there she plucked up the courage to move in close to him.

'Hello, Vicki,' Pawley said, peeping down at her. 'You here too?'

'Hello, Pawley. We aren't getting in your way, are we?'

'No, not at all. Anyway, I've nearly finished here. The engine should be as right as rain then.'

'You're clever,' she said, making ready to duck her eyes but wanting to impress Alfie into believing Pawley was a special friend of hers.

Hoping to make up for her behaviour with Benjy towards him, she added, 'Daddy could never get it to go properly.'

Pawley was finished and he wiped his tools carefully on a rag. Then slowly, as if he was reluctant to face the children, he straightened up and turned about.

'Wow! What a beauty of a scar!' Alfie exclaimed, quick as a flash. 'Did you get it in the war? Were you a fighter pilot, Pawley? Did your crate get shot down over enemy territory?'

'No, Alfie,' Pawley answered patiently. 'I was a footslogger, in the infantry, and I copped this at Dunkirk.'

'Wow, you were some bloody brave. What happened? A mine? Huge piece of shrapnel? Where did you land? Did many of your mates get killed?'

Alfie was the first child who hadn't run away from Pawley in horror or shouted abuse at him. Pawley light-heartedly chided him about his language and told him some of his story. 'The boat bringing me back to Blighty was shelled and sunk. I lost my younger brother, Ernie, and as far as I know most of my mates. I was unconscious for days.'

As the boy continued to ply Pawley with questions about his war experiences, the revulsion and fear Vicki had felt slipped away and she listened as keenly as Alfie who was now sitting up on the tractor seat, pretending he was driving a tank.

When Pawley looked at her fully, she blinked. Then she smiled, and although Pawley couldn't smile back she knew he was pleased. She asked him a question, something she'd always wondered about him.

'Where do you come from, Pawley?'

'Well, Vicki, I was born in Perranporth but lived for most of my life in Shortlanesend, a little village not far from Truro. After the war I travelled around with my tent and found my way onto Bodmin Moor where I've preferred to stay since.'

'Have you got a family?'

'No one close. I'm all alone in the world really.'

'That's sad. Well, you've got us now.'

Laura had come out into the yard with a mug of tea for Pawley. When she heard what Vicki said she felt a lump rise in her throat.

Pawley looked uncertainly at Vicki for some moments. Vicki moved closer to him. After a few seconds' hesitation he held out his big hand to her. Vicki put her hand in his then gave him a hug. Laura thought she would burst into tears, she was so moved. There seemed to be no moisture in Pawley's one good eye but he rubbed at it with the back of his hand. Alfie carried on mowing down a hundred thousand Jerries, completely oblivious of the poignant scene being played out before his eyes.

The children went indoors long enough to consume a glass of lemonade and a fairy cake, then seeing Laura eyeing the dirt on Vicki's dress Alfie dragged her outside again before she was made to change. In his opinion Mrs Jeffries was beautiful and very nice, but rather prim. He asked Vicki if they could explore some of the fields together and he gradually edged them towards Pawley's tent.

Spencer trotted into the yard on Splendour. He had been looking over his herd of cattle grazing on the common ground. He was delighted when Laura told him that Pawley had got the tractor working in perfect order, then he stayed in the kitchen with the women. Once or twice they looked at him curiously. It wasn't like Spencer to hang about listening to girl talk. He usually made an excuse and disappeared into the yard. He was on his fourth mug of tea when Laura said she had some washing to bring in off the line.

'You look rather pale, Celeste,' he said, gazing down into his mug. 'You could do with some fresh air.'

Celeste glared at him indignantly. 'I was rather thinking that I looked like I was blooming. I'll come with you, Laura, and leave Mr Uncomplimentary to himself.' Outside, she asked Laura, 'What's up with him?'

'I haven't got a clue,' Laura replied.

The moment they had left the kitchen, Spencer sprang up and peeped out of a window until he saw they were safely in the garden. Then he picked up Celeste's handbag and searched inside it.

As the children roamed through the fields, Alfie opened the gates – one of them being a drawbridge to a sorceror's castle, another to a wicked ogre's – and was careful to close them again properly when

Vicki explained importantly that he must, in case livestock was in the fields.

Other times they scrambled over hedges – dangerously high cliffs – Alfie helping Vicki up and down although she could easily do it on her own. 'The trouble with girls,' he said scathingly, 'is you wear dresses. You should have got your mother to let you wear trousers or shorts.' Vicki's dress was liberally covered in grass stains and a bramble had pulled down the hem. 'Watch out for that dragon!' Vicki saw a slowworm slink away under a stone.

They jumped down into the top field where a narrow stream tinkled its way down and where Pawley had pitched his tent. It was a small white affair, gone a dirty grey with age and exposure, but it looked strong and sturdy. A fireplace was set up outside and some interesting-looking things lay about the vicinity.

'Right, let's go and have a look in the tent,' Alfie said, scanning it from the bottom of the field as though he was looking through binoculars.

'No, it wouldn't be right, it's Pawley's home.' Vicki wasn't frightened of Pawley any more but she was concerned about trespassing in his home.

'Don't be a sissy!' Alfie said scornfully. 'We won't take anything from it, just have a quick look inside it. We'll pretend it's an enemy camp.'

Alfie pulled off his shoes and socks, stuffed the socks inside his shoes, tied the shoelaces together and slung the pair round his neck. 'Come on, we'll wade upstream but we'll have to be very careful if we don't want our blocks shot off.'

Not wanting to be a sissy, Vicki took off her sandals and thought Alfie most gallant when he stuffed them in his pockets for her. He led the way, treading over the shifting stones on the bed of the stream. Vicki followed, crouched low like her leader. Suddenly Alfie stuck out his arm and pulled her down over the stream's edge. Taken by surprise, Vicki screamed and he clapped his dirty wet hand over her mouth.

'Shush! Do you want to get us killed?'

Wrenching his hand away she yelped, 'What did you do that for?'

He was looking through his 'binoculars'. 'I thought I saw Goering. He gets around everywhere, you know.'

'What's he doing?' Vicki asked, entering the spirit of the game.

'He was pointing a machine-gun at us. Come on, I think it's safe to go now.' Alfie stood up straight and one of Vicki's sandals fell out of his pocket into the stream.

'Oh, Alfie, my mummy will be cross with me.'

'You shouldn't be so soft,' he retorted unrepentantly, shaking water out of the sandal and stuffing it back in his pocket.

Vicki screamed a moment later when he smeared a handful of black mud over her face.

'Shut up, it's for camouflage,' he explained before she could protest. 'We've got to 'ave camouflage. And before you grumble about your mother, we can wash it off before we go back for tea.'

With black faces, necks and arms, the 'Allied forces' crept up courageously on Goering's camp. The leader had declared his plan. They would follow the stream all the way up to the top of the field then crawl along at the bottom of the stone wall on their bellies and launch their attack at the back of the camp.

A wide ditch ran the entire length of the wall. In one place there was a pool of clear, still water surrounded by purple moor grass and the leader was temporarily distracted from the assault.

'What have you stopped for?' Vicki whispered, getting up from her belly.

'There's heaps of water bugs and plankton in here, and look, baby frogs.'

The children lay still and watched the wildlife and tadpoles swimming about. Alfie stirred the weeds and water boatmen, recognisable by their habit of swimming upside down, used their long spread-out legs to swim about rapidly.

'Mind they don't bite you,' Vicki said. 'My Uncle Ince got bitten by one once and he said it was very painful.'

'I know,' Alfie spouted; there was nothing this little girl could tell him he didn't already know. 'After all, 'tis the poison they use to paralyse and kill their victims with. See that? That's a leatherjacket, the larva of a daddy-longlegs.'

Vicki brushed a fly away from her face and, not to be outdone, pointed at the water. 'And that silvery creature is a water spider.'

Alfie looked at her with pursed lips. Then he did another of his sudden stunts and she found herself pushed down flat on her back. 'Keep your head down. There's a bandit at three o'clock.'

Knowing the jargon used when an enemy bomber was spotted during the war, Vicki looked up. There was no aeroplane in sight in the white-clouded blue sky, but just over her head a creature with a bright blue segment on its abdomen flew gracefully past. Her father had once said its blue matched the colour of her eyes. 'Isn't it beautiful?' she said.

'It's only a dragonfly,' Alfie returned sharply, greatly irritated that his second-in-command could be so soppy.

'No, it isn't.' Vicki stuck out her tongue, hurt by his caustic tone. 'It's a damselfly. Dragonflies are much bigger.'

With a rude grunt Alfie took out his slingshot which he'd wedged in the back of his waistband. 'Come on, we've got Germans to get rid of.'

A shadow fell over them and the children scrambled to their feet. Pawley looked from one to the other. 'Well, you two've got yourselves into a fine mucky mess. You'd better come with me and clean yourselves up a bit before you have your tea, which incidentally can't be too far off.'

Alfie was disappointed he couldn't attack the enemy camp but he was pleased to get a lawful chance to look inside Pawley's tent and he detected a delicious smell. 'Mmmm, what's cooking?'

'Sausages,' Pawley answered, leading the way to his home. 'The missus gave them to me. I like to cook and eat out of doors.'

'Got enough for us?' Alfie cheeped.

Vicki dug him in the back. 'Mind your manners, Alfie.'

Pawley couldn't smile but he could laugh and he laughed heartily. 'My, if you aren't the cheekiest little toerag I've ever come across. You can have half a sausage each or the missus will be a touch mazed with me if you don't eat the nice tea she'll put on for you.'

As the sausages sizzled and browned, Pawley showed the children his home. There was a camp bed, sleeping bag and two blankets. Lamps were strung up safely and a dark suit and a couple of shirts hung from coathangers. A small table with foldaway legs held some of Pawley's few possessions. He showed them the photograph of his parents and although he admitted to having service medals he refused to show them to them.

The half-sausage they were allowed was delicious and ravenously consumed, then Pawley suggested they ought to be getting back. They thanked him and waved goodbye from the bottom of the field.

'He's a nice man,' Vicki declared, wondering why she had ever been afraid of Pawley.

'A nice bloke,' Alfie confirmed, rubbing a very dirty hand over his tummy at the memory of the delicious sausage. 'You're a lucky maid,' he said a trifle wistfully, comparing their lives for a moment. Then he was bawling at the top of his voice, 'Race you back!' And he tore off like a hare.

'You're bound to win,' Vicki puffed out, trying to keep up with him. 'Your legs are longer than mine.'

They were running through the paddock when Alfie tripped and went sprawling over the rough grass and thistles. When Vicki reached him she roared with laughter to see he had fallen on a heap of horse droppings. Alfie got up and picked up two handfuls of the mess.

'I hate to see neat and tidy and clean little girls,' he threatened playfully.

Vicki ran on, screaming in fun. Alfie grabbed her and she shrieked and giggled as he ran his dirty hands up and down her arms and down the front of her dress, adding to the mess she was already in. Her hair in disarray, dress ripped and wet, every visible bit of skin splashed or dirty, blood here and there from scratches she'd received, Vicki thought she had never had so much fun in her life. She thought Alfie was brave and clever and told him so.

'Yah,' he muttered bashfully, wiping his hands on his trousers. 'I've got brains I haven't used yet.'

'Vicki! Alfie! It's teatime!' Laura's voice echoed.

Despite their recent sustenance, the children were ravenously hungry. They raced on again, slowing down only to pick their way carefully over the cobbled yard in their bare feet.

247

They entered the kitchen together and at the sight of them Spencer dropped the sugar bowl he was carrying to the table and stared at them with his mouth wide open. Laura heard the crash, witnessed sugar spraying over the lino then seeing her husband's shocked face whirled round to view her daughter and guest. Her hands flew to her face.

'Vicki! Alfie! However did you get into such a filthy state?'

Celeste grinned mischievously from her seat at the table, much amused by Laura's horror. 'Well, I'm pleased to see that you two have obviously had an absolutely marvellous time.'

That night the Tremewan Arms was packed early with villagers wanting to say goodbye to Celeste and wish her well. Even Ada Prisk climbed down off her usual moral pedestal and popped in for an hour. Bert Miller brought along his accordion and, fortified with the occasional glass of beer, stood beside the bar and played anything that was requested.

'Is Joy here?' Ada asked him darkly when he paused after a rendering of 'Roll Out the Barrel' to which many of the party-goers had sung along. She looked at him fiercely through the waves of cigarette and pipe smoke.

'She's about somewhere,' Bert answered amiably, sipping his beer. 'Over talking to Mrs Tamblyn, I believe.'

'Talking to her son, more like,' Ada muttered, peering through the crush of people. Her shrewd eyes located Joy, but although the Tamblyns were there, she was disappointed to find Joy chatting innocently to a group of women.

Glad that Bert had not heard the old woman and eager to avoid possible trouble, Pat Penhaligon steered Ada out of the public bar and into the snug where the food tables were laid out. Ada went willingly, certain that she was being singled out for something important or confidential. Pat made a big show of asking her what she thought about the refreshments. Ada said they were all right, she supposed, and set about rearranging all the plates and trays. Pat sneaked out and left her to it.

Vicki was staying the night at Hawksmoor House – Felicity wouldn't show her face at such a gathering – and Laura was enjoying the night out. Spencer was in a very good mood and had made it plain that she was in for an exciting night when they got home. With Tressa and Andrew, they were standing round Celeste who was wearing a fan-pleated cocktail dress and enjoying playing hostess to the full.

'I hope you'll make your way down to Cornwall to see us again,' Andrew said, his arm tight about Tressa's tiny waist.

Celeste's large dangling earrings swung as she nodded her head enthusiastically. 'I'm sure I will some day. I've made many friends in Kilgarthen.' Her eyes dancing, she turned to Tressa. 'Perhaps when I see you again there will be another little Macarthur for me to coo over.'

Celeste had never once cooed over Guy but Tressa went a little pink when she admitted there would be a new arrival at Tregorlan Farm next year. 'It's just been confirmed.'

'Congratulations,' Laura interrupted, hugging Andrew and Tressa and feeling more than a little jealous. She could hardly wait to get home and do something about conceiving a child of her own.

'It will be nice if it's a girl next time,' Tressa said, smiling proudly, and she squeaked when Andrew squeezed her fondly.

'Come on, Spencer,' Andrew grinned manfully, taking his glass from him to get a refill. 'We're waiting on you and Laura to catch us up.'

The rest of the company held their breath; Spencer wasn't known for having a sense of humour and the remark could be misconstrued as a jibe at his virility, but he slipped his arm round Laura's graceful shoulders and chuckled. 'I'm doing me ruddy best, Andrew.'

They all laughed. The door opened to let in the umpteenth well-wisher and they looked to see who it was. Harry came in, his roguish face abeam, and he joined them. Andrew put Tressa on the other side of him, away from Harry.

Harry pretended he hadn't noticed. He kissed Celeste's cheek and gave her a bunch of flowers from Hawksmoor's gardens. 'I'll be sorry to see you go,' he said with all the graciousness of his mother. 'You've given the village a certain something.'

'Thank you, Harry,' Celeste replied demurely, sniffing the bouquet. 'How sweet of you. I hope your idea of taking the Uren children to the beach will be a resounding success next week.'

Harry had left all the arrangements to the Farrows and the Reverend Endean but he was looking forward to the outing. 'Pity you'll miss it, Celeste,' he said, then after saying hello to Laura he ignored Spencer and the Macarthurs and took himself off to the bar.

'Harry seems to have gone much quieter these days,' Laura remarked. 'He's quite the reformed character.'

'I wouldn't bet on it,' Celeste said, looking deeply at Tressa and making her glance down at the floor.

Ince and Johnny were waiting outside the pub for Les and Eve Tremorrow. It was a warm evening with the sun making the sky glow as it drifted slowly towards the horizon. Ince shuffled from one foot to the other. He looked relaxed in shirt sleeves and casual trousers, but he felt rather nervous, like a young man dragged along on a blind date.

'She'll be here in a minute,' Johnny said, checking again in his little purse at how much money he had brought with him. 'Eve's a woman of her word.'

Ince returned Johnny's words of comfort with an impatient sigh. 'I'm not bothered if she doesn't come at all.'

'Don't be like that, Ince. She's quite a little lady, just your sort, if you ask me. And if you're not bothered, why have you put all that aftershave on? You smell like a tart's handbag.'

Whipping out his clean handkerchief, Ince wiped hastily at his face and neck. He had gone a violent red and a look of near panic shone out of his brown eyes. He wasn't sure what he felt for Eve Tremorrow but he didn't want her to think he was trying to be a gigolo.

Johnny smacked his hand. 'Stop that, you idiot, I was only joking with 'ee. You want to be well turned out for her, don't you?'

'I haven't been seen out and about for a while so I want to look my best anyway,' Ince retorted grumpily, rubbing his hand as if it hurt.

Johnny was peering down the hill. 'Here they come now. Stand up straight and put a smile on your blooming face, boy. You won't get nowhere with her if you carry on looking so damned miserable.'

'Why must you insist on putting me and Eve on a romantic footing?' Ince hissed from the side of his mouth. 'She's my new boss's granddaughter. I only want to be on good speaking terms with her.'

'Bah.' Johnny kneaded his fist in Ince's side. 'Sometimes you get on my ruddy nerves. I wish I was forty year younger. I would leave you standing in my dust.'

Eve approached on Les's arm. They were walking slowly on account of Les's age and her high heels. 'The walk seemed much longer tonight,' she said apologetically. 'I hope we haven't kept you waiting.'

Ince said nothing. He was staring into Eve's face. She had put on a little powder and a dark pink lipstick and there was something different about her eyes. They stood out large and beautiful over her high cheekbones. She was wearing a pearl necklace and matching clip-on earrings. Her hair, sleek and glossy, framed her face to perfection. Ince was swept with a feeling of possessiveness for her.

'We didn't mind waiting, did we, Johnny?' he said in his old familiar, friendly voice.

Johnny lifted his cap to Eve. 'You look lovely, m'dear.' Then he pulled Les away from her and before the crotchety old man could complain he said, 'I'll buy you a drink, Les.'

'Good,' Les muttered ungratefully. 'My throat's as parched as a desert and me head's aching something awful. Make it a double.'

Ince ushered Eve through the bar door. He stood beside her as they faced the gathering. As each group saw them, voices stopped and folk nudged one another. Ince was back in circulation and here he was with the elusive granddaughter of old Les Tremorrow, the last woman they had expected to see tonight. The bar fell into silence and when the singing stopped, Bert Miller stilled his nimble fingers on the accordion keys. Eyes flicked from Ince to Spencer. Spencer must be feeling a fool. Here was firm evidence that his suspicions had been totally wrong.

Ince glanced at Eve. She didn't seem the slightest bit fazed by their reception.

Les and Johnny came in after them. There was not much room in the bar and they had to squeeze past Ince and Eve. Les screwed up his scaly face, bristling his eyebrows. Staring at the array of stunned faces, he declared on a hearty grumble, 'What a damned miserable party. Wouldn't have bothered to stir me bones and come out if I'd known it was going to be like this.'

Celeste came up to the four newcomers, her face wreathed in smiles, both hands extended. 'You're very welcome. How lovely to see you again, Ince. I was afraid I'd miss saying goodbye to you. Now, what can I get you all to drink?'

Ada had come out of the snug to see why it had gone quiet. 'Oh, Miss Pascoe,' she said loudly and as though Eve was a very important guest. Playing lady of the manor, Ada swept up to her. 'I didn't know you were coming tonight.'

'Good evening, Mrs Prisk. I want to get to know the villagers better,' Eve said simply, more to the crowd than to the old lady.

Pockets of conversation broke out and Ince and Spencer's eyes met over the tops of people's heads. Spencer inclined his head and offered a small friendly smile. Ince did not reciprocate but held his gaze for several moments then looked at Laura. Laura thought it would be best if she took the first step towards mending the men's broken friendship. Knowing many eyes would be on her, she left her group and went to him.

'Hello, Ince. I haven't met Miss Pascoe. Perhaps you'd like to introduce us.'

Ince wasn't pleased to be the centre of so much attention, but sounding as normal as he could, he said politely, 'Hello, Laura. Eve, this is Laura Jeffries.'

Eve put her handbag under her other arm and the two women shook hands and exchanged the usual pleasantries.

'Do come over to Rosemerryn Farm at any time,' Laura said, hoping that Spencer would join her and take this opportunity to make amends with Ince. She couldn't believe that Ince bore a grudge and would snub him. But Spencer, probably unsure of the situation, stayed put beside Tressa and Andrew. Although Eve chatted to her happily enough, Laura felt there was a reticence in the other young woman. Laura had heard how Eve had gone to Ince after Spencer had punched him. What feelings for Ince were running under that prim exterior?

After some moments, the usual polite conversation had been exhausted and Laura gave up and returned to Spencer. 'Why didn't you come with me?' she asked, under the cover of sipping her gin and tonic. 'You could have got talking to Ince.'

253

'I'll talk to him when he's alone, not with an audience watching and listening,' he replied, his tone guarded.

'What do you make of Eve Pascoe?'

'So that's Les's granddaughter, is it? I've never noticed her before. She looks interesting.'

'Nothing more?'

Spencer knocked back the last drop of beer in his glass, his eyes on the slim, dark-haired woman. 'Well, if I was looking around for someone, I don't supposed would pass her over.'

Ince went to the bar with Celeste to fetch the drinks. After she'd given Mike the order, she challenged Ince pertly, 'So, it looks like you'll be settling down, Ince. Congratulations. She seems charming.'

Ince was worried at this jumping to the wrong conclusion. 'There's nothing between me and Eve, we're only friends,' he retorted in a churlish voice. 'I'm starting work for Les on Monday. Johnny and I met them at the door and we came in together.'

'Who are you trying to fool, Ince Polkinghorne?' Celeste persisted, determined to wring his feelings out of him. It might even be something he needed doing for him. 'From your manner the meeting was obviously prearranged. I don't know Eve at all but she's quite unlike anyone else I've met around here. I think that you think so too.' She perused Eve's neat form with female deliberation. 'And I must say you seem right together somehow.'

Ince didn't answer as he picked up the tray of drinks. Most people in the bar were on their feet but Eve, Les and Johnny had sat down in a quiet corner. Ince sat down beside Les and passed round the drinks, giving Eve a particular smile when he put a glass of port and lemon in front of her.

Les leaned towards him and hissed into his ear, 'I don't know what your bleddy game is, matey, but you can keep your eyes off she! I've only just got my granddaughter after all these years and I don't intend to lose her already.' The words thudded into Ince's heart like a sledgehammer.

At eight thirty Pat banged a tablespoon on a table to gain attention and announced that the buffet was ready and people were to help themselves. A little later, Mike made sure everyone's glasses were replenished and he banged his fist on the bar top for silence, then called on Celeste to give a speech. Celeste, who had never known a shy moment in her life, obliged, standing in front of the bar next to Bert Miller, where most people could see her.

'I won't make this long,' she smiled all round the pub. 'I'm sure you'd rather get on with the business of eating and drinking.' Roars of approval went up and Mike banged once more. Celeste continued, feeling unexpectedly sentimental, 'I'd just like to say that I'm so glad that Laura came down to Cornwall and settled here, giving me the opportunity to meet you all and make friends with you. I shall miss you but I will keep in touch with Laura and she can tell you what I'm up to, and as I love the village so much I'm sure this won't be the last you see of me.'

There was a thunderous round of applause and Laura hugged Celeste and Bert played 'For He's a Jolly Good Fellow' which was sung with abandon.

Les's sharp remarks had taken more than the spring out of Ince's step. He felt totally demoralised. Although Johnny kept prompting him, he didn't have much to say, particularly to Eve. If he was going to work for the wretched old man, he didn't want to do it under a cloud. The job would do for now, but he would look for something full-time and permanent. Perhaps even away from Kilgarthen. He downed his beer quickly and went to the bar and lingered there. Spencer was suddenly beside him.

'Can I buy you a drink, Ince?'

Ince looked him in the eye. For a few moments, after Les had dragged him down again, he had felt all the old resentment against Spencer that he'd spent so much time fighting. But he knew rejecting Spencer's approach would not bring him any joy, and he was desperate to find peace again. He didn't hesitate before answering, 'I'll have another pint, please.'

Mike was in front of them on the other side of the bar the moment he saw Spencer arrive at Ince's side, a stern look on his whiskery face. 'Two pints, is it, gents?'

'That's right, Mike,' Spencer replied, pushing their empty glasses forward. His grouchy character had caused him to clash with people in the pub before.

When Mike moved out of earshot to pull the pints, Spencer said in the humblest tone he could find, 'If you're drinking with me, does that mean you've forgiven me?'

Both men were embarrassed and wished they could be having this conversation somewhere else alone. Ince felt like a silly schoolboy. 'Of course I've forgiven you, Spencer.'

Spencer wasn't an earnest man but he spoke intently. 'I'm really sorry for what I did, for what I was thinking. I was jealous of you and I was totally out of order. I was sorry the moment I got home but it took a while to come down off my pride. I kept your job open as long as I could. I was hoping you'd come back and work on the farm.'

'Before today I wouldn't have been able to face the farm.'

Spencer sighed, long and hard. 'I'm sorry I hurt you so deeply, Ince. In case you're wondering, Laura's forgiven me. I've been making it up to her ever since.'

'I'm glad to hear it. How's Vicki?'

'Missing you like hell. Why have you stayed away from her for so long? Did you think I wouldn't let you see her?'

'No, nothing like that.'

Mike put the two glasses of beer down in front of them and refused to take Spencer's money. 'On the house,' he roared cheerily. ''Twould be worth a barrelful to see you two friends again.'

'It was all my fault,' Spencer admitted. 'I can be a bloody-minded so and so.'

'You can say that again,' the landlord bellowed so loud he stopped the singing for a moment because Bert thought he was complaining about the choice of song. Mike waved to him to carry on playing then left the two friends to it.

'Laura's changing me,' Spencer grinned at Ince. 'I think you'd approve of my slightly better temperament these days. She watches me like a hawk to make sure I keep it up. You were going to tell me why you haven't seen Vicki.'

'I can hardly explain it. I fell into a sort of depression. I was envious of you and Laura. I was no longer in love with her but I thought highly of her and would have given anything to change places with you. I wanted so badly to have what you had. A wife, a child, the chance to have more children. And I wanted a home to call my own. It wasn't your fault but I felt out of place living at the farm.'

'It was my fault, Ince. You were my closest friend and almost as much a father to Vicki as I am. I made you feel unwelcome in your own home, deliberately at times, I'm ashamed to admit.'

'I'd made up my mind to move in with Johnny before the fete. I was hoping that if I just worked at the farm things would get better. But it wasn't just our difficulties that were making me unhappy. Les and Eve were having a sobering effect on me too. But after a struggle and a lot of barracking from Johnny I've put all that behind me now.'

'So, can we be friends again?'

Laura watched as Spencer held out his hand to Ince. Ince shook it, and not caring if they were being watched, the two men embraced. She went over to them and joined in the hug. 'Oh, thank goodness. I was so afraid you wouldn't make it up. Where do you both go from here?'

'I was just about to invite Ince over to the farm to see Vicki tomorrow,' Spencer said, kissing the tip of her nose.

'Will you come, Ince?' Laura asked, willing him to say yes.

'Try keeping me away,' he replied happily.

'That's wonderful.' She danced about excitedly. 'Come all day, as soon as chapel's over, and bring Johnny with you. We'll make it a special day for Vicki.'

All the serious and emotional talk had made Spencer thirsty. He emptied half his glass then turned to Ince. 'Now we're mates again, would you mind telling me what sort of effect Eve Pascoe has on you now?'

'Yes,' Laura said enthusiastically. 'I want to hear all about her. Bring her over to the farm one day.'

Ince looked across the room at Eve. She was watching them, her face expressionless. When their eyes met she looked away.

'There's not much to tell,' Ince said. 'I can't fathom her out at all.'

Ada had helped clear away the plates and was putting her coat on to go. She tapped Celeste on the shoulder and asked her to accompany her to the door. Outside in the freshening air, Ada produced a little parcel from her pocket.

'I have a little something for you, dear,' she said shyly.

'Oh, how sweet of you. You shouldn't have, Ada.' Celeste took the parcel and kissed Ada on the cheek. She untied the thin ribbon wrapped round the parcel but Ada caught her hand.

'Not here, dear,' she whispered and there were gentle tears in her eyes. 'Wait until you're back in the cottage. It's a little matinee jacket. I knitted it myself. You will let me know whether you have a little boy or a maid?'

'Oh, Ada,' Celeste sniffed, giving the old lady an affectionate hug. 'I should have known I couldn't keep it a secret from you. I'll make sure Laura tells you the moment I've let her know.'

'I hope it will all work out right for you, dear.' Then putting a quick kiss on Celeste's cheek, Ada marched off down the hill for home.

Inside the pub, Joy Miller had found her way to Bruce's side and he was including her in the round of drinks he was buying. 'Your mother doesn't look very happy tonight,' she said, tugging on his arm. 'When I spoke to her just now she was quite sharp with me. She hasn't found out about us, has she?'

'No, I don't think so. She's teasy because I asked her to lend me a few pounds. I want to set up a little business of my own.' Bruce wished he had thought of that lie when he'd tried to tap Daisy for money. 'You'd think she'd want me to settle down locally. I don't suppose you could lend me something to help get me started, eh, Joy?'

His last sentence had been said in jest to stop himself getting worked up into a rage, but he nearly took Joy into his arms and kissed her there and then when she answered, 'I've got an insurance policy I could draw out. We could talk to Bert about it. He might fancy the idea of going into business with you.'

Just like that? Bruce thought smugly. The woman had begun to feel pangs of guilt about their affair but she was still besotted with him. 'What does Bert drink? It's about time I got to know him better.'

Harry was slouching against the bar, deciding whether to go on ignoring Tressa or to make a subtle overture to her, or perhaps to go and chat up the elegant Eve Pascoe. He'd glanced at Eve often throughout the evening. He had caught her eye only once. He had smiled at her and she had looked straight through him. He decided to wait for the beach outing to further his plan with Tressa and his dark eyes returned to Eve. She was talking to the Methodist minister, her face turned up, emphasising the smooth angle of her jaw. Almost certainly a virgin, he mused. Rather too moral to succumb without a wedding ring and too clever to be someone's mistress. What would you be like with all those layers of respectability peeled away? One by one, very slowly? I would savour each mo—

'Mr Lean, I was talking to you.'

Harry gulped. While those lecherous thoughts were going through his mind Kinsley Farrow had been trying to attract his attention. Harry hastily rearranged his features, in case they gave him away. 'Sorry, Vicar,' he smiled with all his charm. 'I was miles away. I was thinking about next week's outing for the kiddies.'

'The very thing I wanted to talk to you about,' Kinsley said, rubbing his hands in satisfaction. 'I thought I'd just confirm that you are taking the five Uren boys in your car. My wife and I are taking baby Emily. I'm afraid I couldn't talk Dolores into coming, but it will give her a welcome opportunity to put her feet up.' Kinsley hesitated, but he felt he had to say it. 'I, um, hope you will drive a little slower than you usually do.'

'You can depend on me, Vicar, to get them to the beach and back home safely.'

Bert was having a break and Bruce was holding out a glass of his favourite tipple to him, a tot of rum. Witnessing this, Kinsley caught his breath and Harry looked round his rangy frame. 'Something wrong?'

'No, no,' Kinsley said rapidly. 'Now, what was I saying?'

'I think we dealt with it, Vicar,' Harry said, wanting to get back to his sensual thoughts.

Then he remembered the gossip that Mrs Biddley, his mother's daily help, had imparted to Felicity recently about the two men on the other side of the vicar. Bruce Tamblyn was knocking off the other man's wife. Harry hoped the farewell party would be livened up with some sport. He'd start it off himself, would be pleased to see the brute who had harangued him over his driving getting thumped by a jealous husband, but Tressa was present. He looked at her. Her nitwit of a husband wasn't with her for once, probably gone to the toilet. She was laughing at something some old dear had just said to her. She was looking gorgeous in a simple beige dress with a little white lace collar, her long brown hair lying on her delicate shoulders. She was delectable and so very desirable. If she was his, he wouldn't leave her alone for a minute – in more ways than one. He hoped she would wear a swimsuit on the beach.

Biddy Grean, the Millers' neighbour, grabbed Laura by the arm and pointed at Bert and Bruce. 'Did you see that, Mrs Jeffries? That poor man has just taken a drink off that terrible Tamblyn creature, and he carrying on with his wife! Can't you do something about it? His mother is your aunty by your first marriage. We don't like that sort of thing going on in the village.'

'Shush, Mrs Grean,' Laura said vehemently. 'If Bert overhears you it will cause a row.'

'Well, something ought to be done about it.' Mrs Grean moved her head about like a rancorous turkey. 'It's disgusting. And look at the vicar there. Practically standing beside them and not saying a word.'

'It's hardly the time or the place,' Laura returned crossly, trying to free her arm from the woman's tightening grip. 'Now please keep quiet about it.'

'I was only saying—'

Mrs Grean was cut short by Daisy. Bruce and Joy were doing wrong but she'd had enough of the tittle-tattle that had been going on behind their backs. 'Only trying to cause trouble, that's what you're up to, Biddy Grean. Now shut your mouth as Laura said and sit down and enjoy the party. That's what we're here for, not to go moralising.'

'Well, really,' Mrs Grean snapped, feeling very much an injured party. She had only been passing a comment about something that was common knowledge, something low and underhand that everybody else seemed happy to have going on under their noses without doing a thing about it. She'd had no intention of causing trouble, had never done so in all her life. A person only had to ask her Len to confirm that. And Daisy Tamblyn was the last woman who had the right to speak to her like that. Her temper rising, she raised her voice. 'How dare you, Daisy Tamblyn? It's your son who's committing adultery and it's time he was stopped!'

Silence was brought quicker to the Tremewan Arms than by Ince and Eve's arrival. Hands jerked and drink was spilled, jaws dropped and eyes grew round. Everyone had heard every word. Joy let out a shriek and dashed her hands to her face. Daisy gasped and looked at her son and then his mistress, as much guilt written over her plump face as Joy's.

If Bert Miller could not add up two and two from Biddy Grean's outburst, the sudden silence and his wife's subsequent shriek, he would have been considered the stupidest man who had ever lived in Kilgarthen.

But although Bert was quiet and ordinary and perhaps boring, he wasn't stupid.

He had just thanked Bruce for the rum and now he dashed it in his face. He tore his accordion off his stocky body and had his hands round Bruce's throat in a split second. He squeezed with all his might and the usually mild-mannered man was using the foulest language he had picked up in the army. Women screamed in fear and fright. Men gathered their wits and tried to pull Bert off. Kinsley pleaded for good sense. Mike shouted for order. Pat ran to the telephone, prepared to ring the police. Joy cried for someone to do something before Bert killed Bruce. Celeste stopped her from launching herself at Bert's back.

Spencer and Ince got hold of Bert's arms and wrenched his hands away from Bruce's neck. Bert's fury had given him superhuman strength and he shook them off as easily as if they were young boys. Then he punched Bruce with all the strength his distress was giving him. Bruce was sent hurtling backwards and ploughed into Tressa, taking her with him. The screaming reached fever pitch and Biddy Grean started to sob in her Len's arms. Harry beat Laura and Eve to

Tressa's aid, throwing his arm round her waist and dragging her out of the way before she got trampled.

The party-goers scattered to the edges and corners of the bar. Bruce was on his feet, ready to fight back. His face was ugly, purple and bleeding. 'I'm going to kill you for that, you useless bastard!'

'Give him what he deserves, Bert,' Les called out, mightily enjoying the skirmish, waving his arms about, shadow boxing. 'Kick him where it hurts.'

Bert wiped sweat off his top lip, his eyes boring into the object of his hatred. 'I'm going to kill him,' he raged.

Catcalls followed and Mike rang the bell and bellowed threats to try to break up the fight. They were in vain. Bert didn't hear a sound. Every sense and feeling in his mind and body wanted only revenge. He had always been a kind, loving and true husband, and in one vile moment he had learned that this big-headed wretch had been making a fool of him, and apparently he was the last to know about it. He had killed a German with his bare hands during the war and he'd make short work of this evil swine. He wanted Bruce's blood to run and he didn't care if he swung for it afterwards. He pounced on Bruce and with one punch broke his nose. As blood spurted down Bruce's shirt, Bert drove his fist into the fleshy part of Bruce's stomach, once, twice, three times. Bruce howled and groaned and hit the floor, sending tables and chairs flying in all directions. Bert laid into him with his feet, lashing out at his head, back, legs, anywhere.

Mike had got round the bar and pitched in, grabbing Bert's arm. The other hand flailed about, clawing to get at Bruce, and Spencer and Ince grabbed it together. Then with Kinsley, Brian Endean and several other men, Johnny taking a foot, they got Bert on the floor and held him down.

'That's enough, Bert!' Mike boomed. 'Or I'll have to knock 'ee out.' He looked about for Daisy. She was shaking and crying into her hanky. Laura had her arms round her and Eve was standing beside them, frowning at her grandfather who was still grinning and muttering, 'Spoilsports.'

'I'll get some of the men to take your son home, Daisy,' Mike said. 'You'd better call the doctor and tell him he's had a little accident. Pat, did you call the police?'

'No, Mike,' she answered firmly.

'I don't think anyone else is going to either. There's been no fight here tonight.' Mike looked at the younger men present. 'Get him out of here,' he said in disgust. Then he glared at Joy. 'And you go too. We'll keep Bert here for the night, poor sod.'

Spencer and Ince were among those who carried the semi-conscious body of Bruce Tamblyn across the road to the shop. Laura led Daisy, who was crying uncontrollably, and Eve took her other arm and went with them. Joy fled on her own. Bert was crying now, sobbing in great distress. Mike lifted him up like a baby and carried him upstairs.

Pat looked at Celeste. 'I'm sorry about this.'

'No matter,' Celeste said philosophically. 'It had to happen some time. It was nothing to do with my party really. Let's get the drinks going again, shall we?' Celeste looked sombre but she was pleased to have witnessed the fight rather than be told about it in a letter from Laura.

All the while, Harry had cradled Tressa in his arms, having crept behind an upturned table with her where they wouldn't be noticed. She had been stunned and took several moments to come to her senses.

'What happened? Oh, I'm aching all over.'

'It's all right, Tressa. Don't move. There was a fight. One of the men knocked into you. Are you hurt?'

She struggled to sit up and he helped her to an upright position, keeping his arms firmly about her. 'My arm hurts and my back where I fell,' she groaned, pushing her hair away from her face.

'Just stay here quietly,' he murmured soothingly. He looked at her lips, slightly parted, red and full, and was tempted to kiss them. A wave of nausea came over her and she rested her face against his chest. Harry caressed her hair. 'It's all right, darling. I'll look after you,' he whispered tenderly.

The combatants had been taken from the bar and Harry knew he must remind the others of Tressa's plight. Her wretched husband would come back at any moment and if he saw him holding Tressa, he would be the next man to have his lights punched out by a furious husband. Harry wasn't afraid of Andrew but Tressa would never trust him again no matter how much he schemed. He sat Tressa up and got behind her in a more innocent position, just supporting her, and pushed the table away from them.

'Could someone give me a hand with Tressa?' he called. 'She nearly got crushed by those men.'

Pat came running, so did Celeste and half the people in the pub. Harry let them take over and when Andrew came back from the toilet, Harry was just another bystander.

'Good heavens! Tressa! What happened to her?' He pushed people out of the way until he was holding her and she was clinging to him. 'I heard some shouting but I thought it was just the party getting noisy. What on earth's been going on?'

Chapter 25

'I hope the fight in the pub the night before last hasn't given you a bad impression of the village, Eve,' Ince said, putting down the wheelbarrow he was pushing and looking down on her as she tended a sick goat. They were in the goathouse where he had come to remove the manure from the night before and she was administering Epsom salts dissolved in warm water to a nanny which had eaten something that hadn't agreed with her.

'Not at all,' she replied over her shoulder, expertly getting the purge into the goat without much spillage. 'I'd hate to be that woman, Joy Miller. How will she ever dare to show her face in the village now? Goodness knows what her husband has said to her, the poor man.'

Eve had enjoyed the night out and she liked having Ince about again. She was in higher spirits than was normal for her. She changed her tone to one that was designed to entertain him. 'Actually, I've been close to fights before, Ince. Mrs Howard-Armstrong, whom I worked for, had a very rebellious son. Mr Clarence was a bit of a wag and he hated his mother's set and the hypocritical high moral stand they took. He used to insult them every chance he got. Sometimes one of the gentlemen would take exception and once or twice it ended in fisticuffs. Mrs Howard-Armstrong would take to her boudoir for days and recline on her chaise longue with the vapours. She would shiver and shake and wail. She would swear she was going into a decline. You wouldn't believe the amount of pills and tonic water she got through and how many times she made the doctor call on her.'

Having arrived at Carrick Cross an hour earlier than the time agreed with Les in the pub, eight o'clock, Ince felt it was in order for him to pause and chat for a while. He had no idea where he stood with Eve, and he couldn't make up his mind what footing he wanted their relationship to be on, but now she was opening up at last he wanted to ply her with questions. 'Did you work for anyone else apart from this Mrs Howard-Armstrong?'

'No, only her, apart from my stint in the Land Army. She was most put out when I left her employ for a year. I went into service the moment I left school and when Mrs Howard-Armstrong's maid, Maud, retired I was elevated to that position. I had worked as kitchen maid for two years when one night Maud was taken violently ill. Mrs Howard-Armstrong was throwing a large dinner party that night and a duke was coming, and Madam, as we called her, became nearly hysterical about who was going to dress her and do her hair. I used to do the servants' hair to save them money. The cook told the butler and he told Madam and in desperation she allowed me to help her get ready for dinner. I was very nervous but she was so impressed at what I did she promised me that if I trained under Maud in my spare time I'd get the job when Maud retired.'

Ince made an ironic noise. 'So you did your training unpaid and in your own time? Typical of that sort. Did she lead you a hell of a life?'

'I suppose you could say that. Mrs Howard-Armstrong was meticulous in her demands and very temperamental. Everything had to be just so or there was the devil to pay. She could be utterly scathing and I had always to mind my place, but she paid me a little better than most women in my position and she gave me good-quality clothing for Christmas and my birthday. I usually received her handbags and scarves when she'd finished with them, and she was so happy on the night of Mr Clarence's engagement party that she gave me a single string pearl necklace that she hardly wore. I thought myself fortunate that I had a job in a good household and it was much better than skivvying for a living. The best part was the travelling. I've been to some lovely places.'

'You must find living here very dull,' he commented.

'Not after Saturday night,' she laughed. Putting aside the jug of purge, she looked at Ince while stroking the goat's head and giving it an occasional soothing word.

Goats liked human companionship as well as their own kind but Ince had noticed that the three nannies particularly sought out Eve who looked perfectly at home in this situation.

'Was your mother proud of you?' he asked. He was curious about Angela Tremorrow.

Eve turned her head away but not before Ince saw a dark shadow mar her pale skin. She answered him sharply. 'I didn't see much of her after I left home. She moved about a lot.'

Sensing he had made her clam up, Ince reached for the handles of the wheelbarrow. 'Well, I'd better get on with this or I'll have Les after me.' He stopped in front of the raised platform that the goats, as natural climbers, had been provided with to jump up on, and took off the top. He scraped the dry pellets into the wheelbarrow. He cleaned all round the area and laid down some fresh hay and topped up the water buckets.

Eve had left the sick goat and gone outside, probably, Ince thought, to avoid further questions. He would have to be careful what he asked her in future, her mother was obviously a no-go area. He trundled the wheelbarrow past her and tipped the manure on the heap that would be used to dress the garden.

Eve would tend to the rest of the needs of the goats but Ince had more to say before he went off to draw potatoes. He wanted to ask her out to the cinema or for a meal but first he had a message to pass on to her. He went up to her as she made to go back into the goathouse and stood very close.

'I went over to Rosemerryn yesterday. Laura asked me to pass on another invitation to you. She said you're very welcome there at any time.'

'I'm glad everything is settled between you and her husband.' She added offhandedly, though her eyes were staring at him, 'Will you be going back there to work?'

Ince thought back to yesterday. The best part had been when he'd walked into the yard and Vicki had seen him. Laura and Spencer had told her he was coming and she had been looking out for him. Her face had lit up like the sun coming out from behind the clouds and she had run to him, shouting excitedly, 'Uncle Ince! Uncle Ince! Uncle Ince!' He had gathered her up into his arms and she had smothered his face with joyful kisses. 'Uncle Ince, you've come back. I waited and waited for you and you didn't come. If you didn't come today I was going to get Uncle Harry to take me to see you.' Vicki had stayed at his side all afternoon and had taken him to see Pawley in his tent. He had been loath to leave her when he'd said goodbye after tea, promising he wouldn't stay away again.

Ince was so wrapped up in the memory it took him a few moments before he realised Eve had sidestepped Laura's invitation. This woman could open up then shut people out as quickly as others blinked.

'Don't you like her?' he challenged Eve, determined to force a way into her secretiveness.

'Mrs Jeffries? Why shouldn't I?'

'Well, you don't seem to want to go to Rosemerryn.'

'I didn't say I didn't want to go there,' she said defensively.

Eve didn't want to go to Rosemerryn Farm. Laura had been kindness and hospitality itself at the shop when they had taken Daisy home but somehow Eve hadn't been able to respond. If Laura's name had not been linked with Ince's, Eve would have quickly formed a friendship with her. And if she had been more used to the ways of the world and adult relationships instead of witnessing them mainly in unreal circumstances in a class that was not hers, she would have realised that what she was feeling was good old-fashioned jealousy.

'Then why didn't you answer me just now?' Ince persisted.

Eve's calmness vanished and she made an impatient sound. She pouted and looked like a defiant schoolgirl, and seeing her like this for the first time, Ince's heart gave a little jerk.

'I've got nothing against Laura Jeffries. I will make my way to Rosemerryn sooner or later but in my own good time. I won't be interrogated, Ince, or pushed into doing something before I'm ready to.' For the first time in her life Eve was going to make a dramatic withdrawal but instead she cried, 'Ow!' and dashed a hand to her face.

'What's the matter?'

'An insect's flown into my eye.'

'Let me see.' Ince's hand hovered over hers.

'Please be quick. It's really hurting.' She took a clean hanky out of her skirt pocket and gave it to him.

'Right, close your other eye and turn to the light.'

She obeyed his instructions, and because she had to lean her head back to give him access to her eye, she reached out and held on to him for balance. Very gently he pulled down her lower lid. Using a corner of the hanky he removed a tiny black winged insect. Eve blinked and her eye watered and he stared into her face, his only a breath away.

'Is that better?' he asked softly.

'Yes, thank you, Ince.'

'And are you angry with me for being nosy?'

'No, I'm sorry if I sounded cross with you.'

He smiled at her. 'You've got lovely eyes, Eve.'

'Thank you.' She smiled back. Her natural reserve meant she had received few compliments of this kind.

Realising she was still touching him, Ince put his hands on her waist and moved in closer. He had never been forward with women but now he was going to kiss Eve. It seemed the natural thing to do and he wasn't going to let this perfect opportunity slip by.

Eve gasped when she realised what his intention was but she let her body yield to his and closed her eyes to receive the kiss.

'What the bleddy hell do you two think you're doing of?' Les bellowed, tearing round the side of the house at them. He was in an absolute fury and was waving his clenched fists. His threadbare slippers were slopping off his feet and his braces were hanging down round his waist and he was in danger of losing his shabby trousers. 'Good job I was watching you from a window. I was about to ask you why you weren't doing no work and then I saw why with me own bleddy eyes. You're supposed to be working for me, you ruddy Casanova, Ince Polkinghorne, not seducing my granddaughter. I trusted you. Maybe there was something between you and that Jeffries woman after all, eh?'

'For goodness sake, Grandfather!' Eve shouted angrily. She had leapt far away from Ince in fright, anger and shock. Her face was crimson. 'Ince was taking an insect out of my eye. It was very painful and I couldn't do it myself. You have no right to talk to him like that. There was no need to jump to that conclusion.' Her voice shook.

'Huh! What do you take me for? For all your ladylike ways and posh speaking you could be just like your rotten mother, for all I know,' Les sneered with a bitter edge to his voice. The old man had worked himself up into a lather and spittle ran down his chin. 'Get on with your work, Ince. I'm not paying you good money to have you standing round doing bleddy nothing.' And with that Les stomped off.

Eve moved several more paces away from Ince. 'I apologise for my grandfather's lack of good manners and his bad mind,' she said tightly.

'I thought I was going to be sacked again,' Ince said wryly, hoping to shrug off the incident with a little humour. He had not been offended by Les's outrage and, after all, he had been about to kiss Eve, but she was very upset. 'You've no need to apologise, Eve.'

Her face was burning and she looked as if she had been shaken by a bomb blast. She turned away. 'I – I must get on, Ince. I suggest you do the same.'

But Ince couldn't leave her like this. He felt responsible. 'What he said about your mother. That was spiteful, wasn't it? What did he mean?'

Ince put his hands on her shoulders but she shook them off vehemently. Les had made her feel ashamed. 'I'd rather not say, Ince. Please, I have work to do.'

Ince did as she asked, feeling he could happily take Les by the scrawny shoulders and shake out his few remaining teeth.

Eve stormed indoors after the old man. He had just got himself comfortable in his chair and gave a start when she wrenched open the door. She banged it shut behind her and presented herself in front of him like a determined schoolmarm. Her mother had treated her shoddily all her life. Mrs Howard-Armstrong had been wont to put her down with ruthless precision. She would not take that sort of treatment from anyone again and she would leave her grandfather in no doubt about it. She stood straight and stiff, lifted her chin up high and with eyes afire, let rip.

'How dare you mention my mother like that in front of Ince? Whatever must he be thinking? I know her character left a lot to be desired but there's no need to tar me with the same brush. And although I wasn't proud of her either, I won't have her insulted now she's in her grave. It's time you forgave her for falling pregnant with me. It's not that unusual these days, I'll have you know.'

Les leaned back in his chair as if the strength of a whirlwind was blowing over him, but he had plenty of fight and a good deal of moral indignation left in him. 'It wasn't just that, Eve,' he said sternly. 'Your mother was a lot worse than what you knew her as.'

'She couldn't have been!' Eve snapped. Angela had led the sort of life that Eve would never confess to Les.

'Take it from me that she was.'

There was a threat of tears in Eve's eyes. 'I'm not like her.'

'She gave you a temptress's name, didn't she?'

'What's that got to do with anything, you old fool?' She shouted so loudly that Ince threw down his fork in the potato patch and considered going indoors to find out what was happening.

Eve was crying softly and Les was sorry. Her wrath had knocked the wind out of his sails but despite his frailty he got quickly out of the chair. He was afraid that his own cruel character would make him lose her rather than a budding romance with Ince whom he really did trust.

He hadn't held anyone in his thin raddled arms for years and he stretched them out uncertainly towards her. 'Don't take on like that, my handsome. I know you're a good girl or else I wouldn't have had you here. 'Twas a bit of a shock to see you so close like that to Ince, that's all. It took me by surprise. I haven't had you with me for long and if you find yourself a young man and go off and get married I'll lose you again. I didn't mean to be cruel.'

'Well, you were, Grandfather,' she sniffed, forcing her tears to stop and dabbing her eyes with her hanky. 'Cruel and unfeeling.'

'I'm sorry, Eve.' Les put on his best appealing face and looked like a hideous hobgoblin. 'Come on,' he patted her arm. 'Sit yourself down and I'll make 'ee a nice cup of tea.'

'I don't want one. I've got the goat to see to. She needs me.'

She went to the door and as she opened it, Les said, 'Do you like Ince in that way?'

Throughout her childhood Eve had reached out to her mother for love and affection and as an unwanted child she had been spurned every time. When she had told Angela her hopes and dreams, she had scoffed at her. As a servant she had been a nobody, not expected to have feelings and emotions. To prevent hurt and rejection she had learned to keep all her thoughts and feelings to herself. Les was utterly selfish; her mother had inherited all his bad traits. He would never understand the things she cherished or show proper sympathy to her hopes and wishes. She would tell him nothing of that nature, in particular her feelings for Ince.

She gave the answer that would best satisfy the old man. 'It hasn't even crossed my mind.'

She was mortified to see that she had been overheard. Ince had come round the front of the house, ready to intervene in the quarrel and come to her aid if necessary. He stared at her for a moment then, dropping his dark eyes, turned on his heel and went back to his work.

Chapter 26

Celeste was up in one of the double bedrooms of her house in the Lake District, planning the new decor which would turn it into a nursery. Lakeside House was a warm and friendly dwelling, built on a hillside with a breathtaking view of Derwent Water, rolling hills and lush green fells. The ideal place to give a baby a good start.

Celeste had turned out all the pieces of furniture that she could lift, the pictures, ornaments and dressing table items, putting them out on the long landing. Dressed in comfortable slacks and a loose, short-sleeved lacy jumper, she was kneeling down, rolling up the thick pink, blue and cream Chinese rug that lay in front of the fireplace, when a woman popped her head round the door and smiled down at her.

'Good morning, Miss Cunningham. I hope you aren't overdoing it,' the woman said kindly, walking into the room and eyeing the things Celeste had moved about. 'You've been on the go ever since you arrived from Cornwall four days ago and that was a long journey, remember. You should wait for me and Ian to arrive and we can lift things about for you.'

'I've never felt more energetic, Marnie,' Celeste said, her face automatically breaking out into a grin in response to her daily help's smile. 'I thought I heard Ian out in the garden just now.'

Marnie Smith was a short, plump, middle-aged, slow-moving woman, with dark, grey-streaked hair coiled in a neat bun and good skin which shone as if it had butter rubbed on it. Her perpetual smile made people feel instantly relaxed and welcome. Celeste was very fond of her domestic help and her spindly, six-foot husband Ian who worked part-time as the gardener. He had been invalided out of the Royal Navy when a torpedo had sunk his ship in 1942, leaving his mind in a childlike state. He would give sudden shakes of his head as he whistled merrily and lovingly tended the garden, talking gibberish, his only language now, to the plants and shrubs. The Smiths kept the house and its small acreage in tiptop condition for Celeste.

This would be a good moment, Celeste thought, getting to her feet, to tell Marnie she was going to turn this room into a nursery. Celeste had known Marnie long enough to know she would not be overly shocked or outraged because she was unmarried. Marnie loved children, and although childless herself owing to her husband's condition, she would probably look forward to having a baby in the house.

'I've got plans for this room, Marnie,' she began on a tentative note. She felt embarrassed and to hide it she made much of tidying her hair.

'I gathered that,' Marnie chuckled brightly at the chaos. 'Are you having someone to stay?'

'No. It's one of the lightest, airiest rooms in the house and perfect for something special. You see—'

There was a knock at the door. 'I'll answer that,' Marnie said cheerily. 'Probably someone calling to say hello to you. It will give you the perfect excuse to stop and have a cup of tea.'

Celeste was peeved at the interruption. 'Oh, blow. I'm not ready to receive visitors yet, Marnie. Tell whoever it is that I'm not at home. Hopefully it will be someone wanting to see you or Ian. I'll stay up here until they've gone.'

'I'll make you a pot of tea, all the same,' Marnie said, moving unhurriedly out of the room.

Celeste had rubbed shoulders with a few people in the locality but had not informed any of them that she was in residence at Lakeside House, wanting to get herself and the house sorted out first. She had to work out her 'story'. Would she be a widow who had lost her husband in a tragic accident and had come here to make a fresh start for the coming baby? Had she left her husband because she had found out he was unfaithful to her? Or had she married a diplomat who'd had to go abroad but she had stayed here in England to have her baby in the best surroundings? She would rather tell everyone the truth and live with the consequences but it wouldn't be fair on the baby. He or she would have to face the world with the stigma of being illegitimate, it would be shunned, unable to make the good start she desired for it. The baby's future and feelings must come before her wishes.

Marnie came back, her face so full of energy it looked as if it would crack. She had climbed the stairs unusually quickly for her. ''Tis a gentleman to see you, Miss Cunningham. He's acting really strange. He said he knows you're here and he's not going until he's seen you. He was most insistent. Said if you don't come out of hiding he'll search the house until he finds you. I shut the door in his face and left him on the doorstep.' Marnie had gone to the window as she blurted out these details and looked down on her husband where he was whistling as he tended the rock garden. Ian may be what was called simple-minded but he was strong and brave and capable of seeing off trouble. 'Shall I shout for Ian or telephone the police?'

Celeste rarely backed down on anything and she was furious that someone had invaded her peace and frightened her domestic. 'I'll see to him myself, Marnie,' she said, picking up the poker by the fireplace and brandishing it in the air. 'Follow me. I'll soon send him packing.'

She marched down the stairs with Marnie creeping timidly behind her. As an extra precaution before she flung open the door, Celeste looked out the side of the bay window. When she saw who was waiting there, impatiently pacing the gravel drive, dressed in driving clothes, his hat and gloves in his hand and looking every inch the determined invader, she crumpled and clutched the doorknob.

Marnie squealed, thinking she was going to faint. 'Who is it? Shall I get the police? You look as if you've seen a ghost.'

Clutching the poker, Celeste backed away from the door and on wobbly legs made her way to a chair in the hall. 'It's David,' she breathed, hardly able to get the words out.

Marnie snatched an embroidered runner off a dresser and flapped it in front of Celeste's face. 'Are you all right, Miss Cunningham? Does he mean you harm? Oh dear, what's going on?'

The doorbell was rung again, persistently, and Marnie wailed, 'I'm going to run and get help.'

275

'No, no,' Celeste gasped out. 'You can let him in, Marnie. He's a friend of mine.'

Marnie wasn't convinced she should do any such thing but the young man at the door would break the bellpush in a minute, and in some trepidation she obeyed her employer.

Before Marnie could speak, the man called David pushed his head through the space she had made and shouted, 'Celeste! I know you're in there and I'm coming in now!'

And he did. Within a few moments he was kneeling in front of Celeste and had taken the poker out of her hand while Marnie rushed off to make some tea to revive her.

'Oh, darling, I'm sorry for giving you such a fright. I was afraid that if I told you I was coming you'd leave and I'd have to come after you again.'

In odd moments of fantasy Celeste, like a romantic young girl, had dreamed of her lover turning up out of the blue and rescuing her from a future as an unmarried mother. To help her believe he was really here, she wanted to reach out and touch his strong wide face, feel his familiar dark-shadowed chin, but her hands stayed rigidly clasped on her lap. How she had yearned to look into his humorous light blue eyes again. Now that she was, she had forgotten all the things she would have said to him. She felt shy, unsure of herself for the first time in her life.

'Wh-why are you here, David?'

He unclasped her hands and would have none of it when she tried to pull them free. 'A mutual friend got in touch with me. I might as well tell you, darling, the game is up. I know all about the baby and why you didn't tell me about it.'

The old spirit returned to Celeste and her colour came flooding back in one rapid surge. 'Laura!' Ripping her hands out of David's grasp, she was on her feet in a fighting mood. 'The cunning little cow! I'll kill her for this. She's the only one who knew I was coming here.'

'It wasn't a woman, old thing. It was a man. A Cornish farmer called Spencer Jeffries. He telephoned me at home two days ago, after he'd given you time to settle in here, and spilled the beans. He wasn't sure of your address and it took me a couple of days to track you down. Oh, Celeste, you silly girl, why didn't you tell me I'd put you in the family way? I'm sorry about that, by the way, it was very careless of me. Didn't you believe that I'd stand by you, do the decent thing?'

She was stopped in her tracks. 'I – I – I…'

Marnie came through from the kitchen with the tray of tea and this gave Celeste time to gather her wits. She was too stunned at Spencer's audacity to think straight. It was so unlike him to do a thing like this. Marnie led the way into the sitting room and Celeste followed with David fast on her heels.

'Would you mind pouring the tea, Marnie, please?' Celeste said, smiling to reassure her, then giving David a tart look; she had just gone through another swift change of mood and was full of indignation. She would not talk to David alone.

'I won't have my life ruled for me in this way. How dare Spencer interfere with my life! What gave him the right? And you can't just turn up here like this, David, and think you can throw your weight around.'

Marnie thought she shouldn't be hearing this but she couldn't leave while she was pouring out the tea. Miss Cunningham had been different on this visit to her holiday home, quieter and subdued, not given to so much outrageous laughter. She had not drunk any wine or smoked any cigarettes. She had talked about fresh air and wholesome food and took delight in simple everyday things that she hadn't seemed to notice before. Could this smart amiable-looking gentleman have anything to do with the changes? Probably not if Miss Cunningham's first reaction and her attitude towards him now were anything to go by. However, Marnie pinned back her ears; there was something very interesting going on here.

Knowing how stubborn and strong-willed Celeste could be, David included Marnie in his next statement, drawing on her presence for moral support. There was only one thing to do – plunge in. 'I came here to tell you that I love you, Celeste.'

Marnie made a little sucking noise and blushed while handing David his tea. She lowered her gaze as she held the sugar bowl for him and he fixed his eyes on Celeste as he used the little tongs to put two lumps in his tea.

Celeste sat down again. If what David had so blatantly declared was true, it was the most wonderful thing she could possibly hear. But she knew David was a man of honour. She didn't want to be another woman who had merely had the decent thing done by her.

'You don't have to commit yourself... because of... because I'm...'

'You mean more to me than that, darling,' he said quickly.

Marnie had seen too many modern films to be left in any doubt about what exactly was going on now. So that was why Miss Cunningham had put on so much weight. The couple had jumped the gun a bit and he had turned up to put things right. It was all very romantic. Her chubby features broke into their habitual smile and she said, 'Well, I think it's time I got on with the luncheon.' She raised a conspiratorial eyebrow at the visitor. 'You will be staying to eat, Mr David?'

'You may depend upon it,' he replied stoutly.

'You may not, Marnie!' Celeste snapped. She was desperate to stay in control of the situation.

'You may, Marnie,' David said, and he stuck out his hand to the bemused woman. 'I'm David Millington, by the way. Miss Cunningham's fiancé.' He added on a whisper, 'Although I might have a bit of persuading to do yet.'

'I'm pleased to meet you, sir.' Marnie left the room tittering.

Celeste folded her arms, muttering archly, 'You have more to do than a little persuading, David Millington.'

'Don't be like that, darling,' he said breezily. He walked around the room, drinking his tea, gazing at the glorious panorama out of the window. 'I can see why you came here. It's a perfect place to give birth to our baby. I hope you haven't decided on any names yet. I'd rather like to have a say. Something traditional would be nice. Elizabeth or Edward perhaps.'

The only response he got was a stiff-faced silence. But beneath her starched demeanour Celeste's heart was thumping.

Draining his cup, David placed it on the tray. Then he couldn't keep up his forced cheerfulness any longer. He knew that convincing

278

Celeste that he really did love her might be harder than attempting a safe landing after a heavy wartime night of flak from a flight over Germany. He would argue with everything he could dredge up and play on her every emotion.

'Damn it, Celeste, when you sent me packing I thought you'd had enough of me. I wanted to come after you but you were so adamant it was all over between us I thought I had no option but to honour your feelings.' He swept his hand through his thick shock of hair and gulped loudly. 'You left me utterly miserable. You didn't know that, did you? I sank myself into the family estate and rarely set foot off it. I'd assumed you were doing the season as usual. It wasn't until Spencer Jeffries rang me that I truly knew how the land lay. Then I could have kicked myself for not coming after you. I hope you'll forgive me for that.'

A little devious distress turned into pleading. 'Celeste, darling, I love you. I've loved you for ages. You have to believe me. I want you to marry me. Come back to Buckinghamshire with me and we'll start the next generation of Millingtons. I've told Mother all about us and she is delighted. With three sisters, I'm the only hope for the name to continue.'

Now it was emotional blackmail. 'Look here, if you won't marry me then I'll throw myself into the blessed lake and you'll have my death on your conscience. You wouldn't want that, would you? What would you say to our child? Come on, darling, say something. Don't just stare at me with those gorgeous green eyes. Do you believe that I love you or not? Will you marry me or not?'

Celeste could see the love in David's eyes and more. He had all the courage and daring of a warrior and the innocent appeal of a small boy. And somehow she pictured Alfie standing behind him, peering round his side with a flying helmet on his head and his cheekiest expression on his freckled face.

She said, with emotion, 'David, I know someone whom I would very much like you to meet.'

Twenty minutes later Celeste was on the telephone to Cornwall.

'Laura. Hello, darling, how are you and the family?'

'We're fine, thank, you, Celeste. You sound jolly. You've settled in all right then?'

'I have. Guess what?'

'What?' Laura sensed something momentous had happened. 'Don't keep me on tenterhooks.'

'By the end of the week I shall be on my honeymoon. David turned up here a short while ago and proposed. We're getting a special licence and we're off to the Riviera and then we're going to settle down on his family estate.'

'Oh, that's wonderful news! I'm so excited. So you had second thoughts and got in touch with him? You must be so thrilled. Celeste? Celeste? Are you still there?'

'Sorry, darling. David was kissing me. Listen, I must say cheerio now. I've got heaps to do, not least rushing out and buying a wedding dress. Hope you have a wonderful day at Polzeath on Sunday. Write to me, tell me all about it. Oh, and if you want to know all about me and David, ask Spencer. 'Bye, Laura, 'bye.'

Laura was in Ince's old room, mentally planning what changes she would make if she could copy Celeste's labour of love and turn it into a nursery. She heard a familiar tread on the stairs and she ran from the room and threw her arms round Spencer's neck.

'Well, what have I done to deserve this?' he asked, looking hungrily at her lips and pulling her intimately close against him.

'I had a phone call from Celeste this morning. She was on cloud nine.' Laura put a peck on his lips. 'You can probably guess what it was about.'

He grinned smugly. 'So David came up trumps, did he?'

'Yes, he did. They're getting married by special licence. Why didn't you tell me you'd got in touch with David?'

'And risk you telling Celeste and ruining things? Besides,' he whispered huskily, 'I would have missed out on this.'

He ran his lips down her neck, finding the special places that made her tingle with pleasure.

'Fancy you doing a thing like that. I didn't realise you could be so kind and sensitive,' she murmured, deliciously aware that he was loosening her clothes. She nuzzled the base of his neck. That drove him wild.

'Well, I thought it was a shame to let things drift on with them both being unhappy when they obviously loved each other.' He pulled her gently and firmly towards their bedroom door. 'Vicki's with Pawley. We're not expecting anyone. Why don't we go in here for a while so I can practise again at making that baby?'

Bert Miller was out on the moor. He had no idea how long he had been trudging across it. He wasn't sure where he was right now, there was no familiar tor or rock formation in sight. He didn't care. He didn't care about anything. Nothing at all.

For five days he had existed on rage and disbelief and a turbulent desire to kill Bruce Tamblyn that became so strong it bordered on madness. Emotion had surged and convulsed through him every tormented waking moment, filling him with savage and desperate thoughts. He didn't care about the circumstances in which he'd heard the news about him being cuckolded, that practically all the village had heard and it would be the juiciest piece of gossip for a long time to come. He didn't care that he was probably the last one to find out about it. As a man who had loved and adored his wife, all that mattered was that Joy had been unfaithful to him, that she had behaved like a whore and placed so little importance on him and their children.

When Mike Penhaligon had escorted him home the day after the fight, he had found that Joy had packed the four children off to stay with her mother. Pale as ashes, red and puffy-eyed from constant crying, she had jabbered at him the moment he'd got inside the door, hoping to get a few words in before he stormed at her or threw her out of their home.

'P-please, Bert,' she sobbed, 'I want to talk. I'm so ashamed. I don't know what came over me.'

'What do you bleddy mean, you don't know what came over you?' he roared, forcing her to scurry back against the kitchen cupboards. 'You knew full well what you were doing all right. You knew it was wrong. I can see it all now. The minute that bloke set foot in the village you were getting yourself all dolled up. I wasn't stupid enough to think it was for me. I thought you wanted to look nice like Laura and Celeste Cunningham. I thought you wanted to show the kids that it was good to look after your appearance and make something of yourself, that you wanted your poor wretched family to be proud of you. But all the time you were thirsting after that big-headed bastard like a bitch on heat!' He raised his hand. 'You filthy bitch. I could beat your brains out.'

Joy flinched and ducked her head. Tears ran down her face. She whimpered, 'G-go on then, Bert. If it makes you feel any better. I deserve it.'

Instead, Bert smashed his fist on the table, making the dishes on it jump about. Frightened, Joy screamed. He said harshly, 'You know I'm not that sort of man. I've never raised a hand to you in my life. I've rarely smacked the kids.' Then all his bitterness came pouring out like the froth that gathers and runs on top of a cesspit. 'It would make you feel better, not me, you heartless Jezebel! You'd like that, wouldn't you? Going round the village showing off a black eye, getting people's sympathy, hoping they'd say, well, she's learned her lesson, had her punishment, now 'tis all best forgotten and put in the past. You want to be a bloody heroine, don't you? Go round in sackcloth and ashes. You want people to say Tamblyn dazzled you, and no wonder. Look at that shambling fat sod of a husband she's got. He's got no skills, no money, no posh ways. He looks like a pathetic great ox, he's ugly and boring and stupid.'

As he let off steam, he banged his fists on the table, louder, harder, fiercer. The dishes danced about crazily. One slid onto the floor and broke, the pieces scattering. He banged harder. Another dish fell, broke into smithereens, then a cup, then a jug. He pushed off a plate and watched it smash on the lino. Next, the salt cellar, then the pepper pot. He swiped at the rest, sending them flying in all directions, littering the floor with broken crockery, until the table was covered only with its new floral oilcloth, bought with Joy's wages. Sweating, breathing heavily, Bert picked up the oilcloth and ripped and tore at it, shredding it. When the last scrap hit the floor, he broke down in a fit of demented crying.

'Y-you've ruined my life. I've nothing left. I hate you, hate you, hate you.' The words were almost unintelligible.

'There's still the kids, Bert. Think of them,' Joy pleaded.

But Bert's heartache was too much for him to bear. He couldn't stand the sight of his wife a moment longer. After picking up a cushion he hurled it at her with a cry of anguish, then he ran upstairs and barricaded himself into their bedroom.

For two days Joy had tried to coax Bert out of their room. She had talked for hours on the landing but got no reply. Sometimes he hurled something at the door and she retreated. She left food and drink outside the door but he did not take the tray inside. She tried to get him to come out by telling him Andrew Macarthur and the vicar were there, wanting a word with him. But Bert didn't want to speak to his boss or spiritual comforter.

Finally admitting defeat, believing he would never come out of his self-made prison, that there could be no chance of repairing their marriage while she stayed in the house, she put on her coat and left. She couldn't get at her clothes with Bert refusing to let her in the bedroom, so with just the little money in her purse, she caught the bus and went to join the children at her mother's. All she could hope was that Bert would come round on his own, read the letter she had left him on the kitchen table, and one day soon come and fetch her.

There was no thought of reconciliation and forgiveness in Bert's mind. It was another day before he realised that the house had gone quiet and Joy had left. He didn't feel hungry but thirst drove him downstairs. He drank a pint of water. Dirty, sweaty, unshaven, he ambled round the house, numb with grief, not fully comprehending why he was in this state. Then he saw Joy's letter and it brought all his heartbreak back, hammering and thundering into his foggy brain. He didn't want her apologies, her pleas for understanding. She had gone and he never wanted to see her again. She mentioned the children. They seemed distant and unreal to him now. He felt he hardly knew them.

Suddenly he could take the pain and despair no longer. He went to the cupboards and took out two items. Stuffing them in the pockets of his coat, weak from lack of food and sleep, he stumbled outside. He hardly took in that people were speaking to him as he shambled through the village. One person tried to take his arm and lead him somewhere but he pushed the well-wisher away. He didn't know who it was. He had not recognised anyone.

He could not recall how and when he had got onto the moor. He could not tell what the weather was like, whether he was hot or cold. He did not hear or feel the cold wind tugging at his clothes, buffeting his face. It did not register if it was night or day. He had stumbled many times, tripped over boulders and grassy tussocks, fallen into brambles. This time he slid all the way down a steep incline. When he hit the bottom, he had no breath left. He lay on his back, stared at the colourless sky, unaware of the gurglings of a stream nearby. When he could breathe a little easier, he sat up.

He had no feelings, no emotions, just one overwhelming desire. He wanted to be alone, for ever. To get away from everyone and everything, to never know another sensation.

He sat up. He pulled a half bottle of whisky and a full bottle of aspirins out of his pockets. He swallowed the contents of both bottles. Then he lay down again and waited for the darkness.

Chapter 27

A convoy of vehicles, four cars, two motorbikes, one with a sidecar, and two horse and carts left Kilgarthen for Polzeath beach the following Sunday afternoon. The horse and carts had left a good time before the motorised vehicles and Harry's sedan overtook them as they neared the beach. Alfie and his four brothers waved excitedly out of the windows to their fellow beach-goers, including Laura, Spencer and Vicki, Ince and Johnny.

'That was brilliant, Mr Lean,' Alfie enthused as Harry brought the car to a swerving stop close to the green in front of the beach. 'Can we go faster on the way home?'

''Fraid not, old son,' Harry laughed, taking off his sunglasses, adding in a mock sombre tone that made the boys squeal with glee, 'I promised the old fuddy-duddies I'd drive like an old maid with you lot in the car.'

Nevertheless, Harry had driven reasonably fast on the stretches of open road to show off the car's speed. He had enjoyed Alfie's outrageous banter on the journey and had promised the boy he would find him a job in the stables so he could earn a few bob. As he waited for the rest of the party to catch up, Harry unloaded the overflowing picnic hamper Mrs Biddley had packed for him and allowed the older boys to wander off the short distance to the beach and take off their shoes and socks and play in the sand. With Rodney needing more supervision, being only two years old, and because he was limp and droopy from being car sick, Harry held him in his arms and the forlorn little boy watched from Harry's shoulder as his brothers marked out shapes with sticks. Harry had picked Rodney up gingerly but the boy smelled clean and fresh.

'You have to ask him often if he wants a wee,' Alfie said, his red hair mischievously lifted by the strong breeze, squinting in the sun.

Harry's insides recoiled in horror. He was about to say Alfie could take charge of his brother's toilet habits, but seeing the older boy in carefree mood and remembering that this was what the excursion was all about, he made a submissive expression. 'All right, but he won't do it while I'm holding him, will he?'

'Probably not,' Alfie said in the serious tone of an adult, then he got back to drawing a wigwam.

'When are the others coming?' Colin asked Harry. Because Alfie trusted the man, he did also. 'I want to go in the sea.'

Harry looked past the few shops. Andrew Macarthur's car had just come into sight and behind it the Reverend Farrow's was pulling out to pass the first horse and cart. 'We're in business, boys. Go get your buckets and spades.'

'We ain't got none,' Alfie shouted back. Used to improvising, and very good at it, his large brown eyes had been sweeping over sand, rocks and bank seeking suitable objects as substitutes.

'I've brought some for you.'

'For all of us?'

'That's right. They're in the boot of my car. You can fetch them, Alfie.'

'Brilliant!' Alfie shrieked. 'Thanks. You're a nice man. Can't see why people don't like you.'

Harry made a wry face. There was only one person in Kilgarthen that he cared about liking him and she was walking their way, wearing a straw sunhat, sleeveless blouse, thin cotton skirt and sandals, holding her chubby baby on her slender hip.

Playing his cat and mouse game, Harry merely smiled at Tressa then gave his attention to Rodney, moving him to his other arm and stroking his head.

'Is he all right?' Tressa asked. 'Can you manage?'

'Poor little chap was car sick, weren't you, Rodney? We had to stop for him twice.'

Rodney was enjoying the unaccustomed closeness of being ensconced in a pair of big arms. He was feeling better already but

286

some of Alfie's artfulness had rubbed off on him and he reckoned he could get a big ice cream if he played his cards right. He looked at Tressa mournfully out of big blue eyes.

'Never mind, Rodney.' Tressa rubbed his back and Harry breathed in her gentle perfume. 'The sea air will soon buck you up.'

'I hope you're looking after that child properly,' Andrew said curtly, hurrying up to them.

'I'm perfectly at home with children, Macarthur,' Harry said, keeping his voice light. It amused him how the other man worried about his wife's welfare when he was around. 'Shall we lead the way to the beach? There are a few people about but there's a nice spot just there by the stream,' he inclined his dark head. 'The children can paddle safely where we can keep an eye on them.'

The rest of the party joined them in small groups. After a short trudge across the sand, there was a prolonged bustle as rugs were laid on the fine sand, hampers and bags of food and towels were put in the shade of two umbrellas, deckchairs were set up.

The women helped the children into their bathing suits and insisted that those who had sunhats must keep them on. Ice cream was promised to those who were well-behaved. The Reverend Endean's wife had brought a first aid kit in the event of grazed knees and insect stings. There were twenty-two adults in all, and while some supervised the children's play, others took the opportunity of having a flask cup of tea.

Kinsley Farrow announced a programme which the 'committee' had agreed upon. First there would be a sandcastle building competition which his friend, the vicar of St Enodoc who had joined the party, would judge and award prizes for. Then the picnic would be eaten. After a period long enough for tummies to settle, the children would be taken down to the shoreline to paddle and splash in the sea; swimming was banned because the sea was running high. Finally there would be a cricket match.

Laura was sitting on a rug between Tressa, Guy and Ince. She passed Ince a cup of tea and made a comment that had been on her mind since they'd set out. 'I rather thought that Eve Pascoe would have come today. You did ask her if she'd like to, didn't you, Ince?'

'I don't think it's her sort of thing,' Ince muttered, scanning the rolling waves that could thunder inland on this north coast of Cornwall with great ferocity.

Tressa hadn't missed the moody note in his voice and looked round Laura curiously at him. 'You must bring her over to Tregorlan some time, Ince.'

Ignoring Tressa, Ince sipped the tea then put the cup back in Laura's hand. 'Thanks. I think I'll go and play with Vicki.'

Tressa and Laura had discussed the possibility of a romance between Ince and Eve. They were disappointed that nothing seemed to be progressing along those lines.

'What can we do to help?' Tressa said after Ince had gone, both women watching him pad across the sand with his head down until he reached Vicki who was building a sandcastle with Rachael Farrow.

'I don't think we'd better do anything,' Laura replied cautiously. 'Ince has changed since Spencer and I married. I don't think he would appreciate what he would see as interference. Anyway, we could stir up something that Ince might come to regret. Eve Pascoe is a mysterious woman. Sometimes I wonder if she could be married.'

'Really? I hadn't thought about anything like that. Pity there aren't more young women about. You can see how much Ince would like a family.'

'I'm beginning to wonder if Harry would like the same thing. Look how he's getting on with the Uren boys.'

Tressa only grunted at that suggestion. Her eyes had been following Andrew as he'd gone round organising two sides of men and children for the cricket match, but every now and then they had strayed to Harry's tall, dark, striking frame. While most of the men were casually dressed but smart, Harry wore his clothes with his own devil-may-care flair. When he laughed his teeth showed neat and white between his wide mouth.

In the pub last week Tressa had been forced to stay in his arms for her safety and because she'd felt sick, but she had been aware that he'd nearly kissed her. She regretted deeply that she had been unable to move away from him. She had not told Andrew it had been Harry who had saved her from possible further injury. Now she felt she had been disloyal to Andrew and had the uneasy feeling that Harry could threaten her marriage. Given the right opportunity, she intended to talk to him, to tell him that she was sure he was still out to seduce her despite his apparent disregard. If he thought she would always be on her guard perhaps he would give up his lecherous campaign.

Alfie won the sandcastle competition for the best overall work of art. Loosely interpreting the rules, he had built an aeroplane complete with cockpit that he could sit in. He had worked on his creation for over a sweaty hour on his own, refusing to let any of his brothers help him. Sculpting, piling, patting, pressing, smoothing, fetching water, his artistry impressed all the gathering and he blushed proudly at the round of applause. He remembered to say thank you when he received his prize, a large stick of rock and an illustrated pocket-sized book about the sea and its creatures. Vicki and Rachael, their joint effort being a traditional sandcastle complete with moat and flags, shared the second prize of a quarter pound of lemon suckers.

After the picnic, in which heaps of sandwiches, splits, yeast buns and lemonade were consumed, the party relaxed in the sun. Roslyn Farrow was enjoying caring for baby Emily who, away from the strained atmosphere at home, was bright and content. Roslyn laid her down with the other very small children to doze under makeshift shades of tea towels and cardigans. Johnny Prouse, who had come for the change of scene and sea air, snoozed contentedly in a deckchair under his ancient straw hat. To the amusement of their wives, Andrew got together with Kinsley to discuss tactics for the cricket match. It was only a friendly game, with most of the team members being children, but Andrew was leading a team against Harry and he was taking it very seriously. Ince sat back from those left in the group, sifting sand through his hands, his knees drawn up, head bent over.

'You don't look very happy,' Spencer said, crouching beside him and lighting a cigarette. 'Anything I can do? I hope you know you can turn to me like you did before I went off half-cocked at you.'

Ince held out his palm and let a pile of sand gather on it. 'Outings like this remind me that I haven't got my own family, that's all.'

'I, um, thought perhaps you and Eve Pascoe had something going.'

'You must be joking! I can't make head or tail of that woman.'

'Do you like her? I mean have you got feelings for her?'

'No,' Ince said sharply. 'Anyway,' he laughed sourly, 'Les is so frightened I'll whisk her away from him he doesn't let her out of his sight.'

Blowing out smoke, Spencer looked at Ince sympathetically. 'You've had a bloody rough time this year, thanks to me and a few others.'

'I don't bear you any grudges, Spencer, so you can get that out of your head. I was even pleased for a while that you thumped me. I thought it would help me get somewhere with Eve.'

'So you have tried then?'

'I almost got to kiss her!' Ince exploded, then quietened down when a few curious faces turned his way. 'But Les saw us and went wild.'

'Sounds like you shouldn't give up hope, mate. Why don't you ask her out again?'

'I don't think she's much interested in me,' Ince told him. She had become rather aloof and seemed preoccupied with her own thoughts. Occasionally he caught her looking at him with what might have been a wistful expression, but she soon looked away again.

'Well, she won't be interested if you go around with a miserable face like you've got now,' Spencer counselled, putting a hand on his shoulder. 'Anyone would think you were me.'

Spencer had never been given to making fun of himself and Ince stared at him. Spencer was grinning. 'Come on, cheer up. I could have lost Laura by dragging my heels so long over our wedding date. Eve looks a determined sort of woman to me. If she wants to go out with you, then she'll find a way. You've got nothing to lose by asking her out for a drink, have you? Surely you can find a moment when old Les isn't around.'

A smile formed at last on Ince's gentle features. 'You're right. I'll do it. It isn't as if she's under twenty-one and has to answer to Les for everything.' He was quite spry now. 'Thanks for the pep talk, mate.'

Spencer looked fondly at Laura. She was cuddling Guy who was sleeping in her arms. He wanted Ince to know the comfort and affection of a woman which he was experiencing for the second time. He always kept a careful check on Laura's dates and he knew she was two days late and his hopes were as high as hers that soon it would be their baby clasped lovingly in her arms.

Wanting to monopolise Guy a bit longer, Laura suggested to Tressa that she take a walk along the beach. Being somewhat of a loner by nature, Tressa welcomed the break. She paddled the length of the shoreline, walking in the direction of Pentire Point, a headland that rose up a glorious three hundred feet of rugged granite. She let the tips of the waves lick her bare feet and she pulled the scarf out of her hair to let her long brown hair spill free in the wind. Putting her hands over her flat tummy, she thought about her coming child, considering names with a sea flavour for it, Robert after the shanty Bobby Shaftoe, Helen after Helen of Troy whose beauty had launched a thousand ships. Out in the bay was a stretch of treacherous sand called Doom Bar; she hoped her children would sail easily through their lives and not come a cropper like so many sailing ships had on the Bar.

The tide was steadily coming in up the beach and she was too cautious to carry on to the base of the cliff. She turned about and retraced her steps. The tide was quickly consuming the sand and she had to keep moving inland to avoid getting her skirt wet, but there was still a wide expanse of the beautiful lichen-covered, purple and green-streaked rocks of Trebetherick Point to be explored. She had been a little girl, the same age as Vicki, when she had last jumped over the rocks here and looked for shore wildlife in the pools of water.

She was out of sight of the others, dipping her toes amongst the seaweed in a rock pool when Harry came up to her. He was smoking a cigarette with his usual reckless grin.

'I'm surprised your husband has let you out of his sight with me around.'

Tressa had been half hoping Harry would seek her out. For once she had plenty to say to him. 'I've been wanting to speak to you alone.'

One eyebrow rose very slowly. 'I am honoured; Go on.'

Putting her small, rough hands on her narrow hips, Tressa said as sternly as she could, 'You took liberties with me in the pub that night.'

'I did?' he said as though amazed, touching a hand to his chest in a gesture of innocence. 'I rather thought I'd saved you from being trampled to death.'

'I'm grateful for your quick actions in saving me from being hurt, but you know what I'm talking about. You held me closer and longer than was necessary. There was no need for you to take me behind that table. I hate to think what you would have done to me if we'd been alone.'

Harry laughed dangerously, then he moved nearer to her and placed a hand on her shoulder. He'd had enough of playing silly games with her. 'I don't exactly remember you struggling to get out of my arms, sweetheart.'

She swiped his hand away from her. 'How could I? I was nearly unconscious!'

'So you say.'

'It's the truth. How could you think I'd want to be that close to you by choice?'

'You make a lot of self-righteous noises, Tressa darling, but I think you may be just the teeniest bit excited and flattered by my attention. I don't think you want me to stop chasing you. You didn't tell your husband that it was me who came to your aid that night, did you?'

'O-only because he w-wouldn't have liked it,' Tressa stammered. A panic rose inside her, clamping the edges of her heart, and she backed away from him. 'What are you trying to say?'

'Let me put it this way, Tressa. I want to make love to you. I always have. I could have just about any woman I like, but there's something about you that keeps me in a state of constant arousal.'

'You're disgusting!' she shrieked, edging further away. She was now knee-deep in the pool, water creeping up from the hem of her skirt.

'Perhaps I am,' he smirked. 'But it's your fault for being so absolutely delicious. I'll make a deal with you, Tressa. Let me have just one proper kiss and I won't tell your dear boring Andrew that you let me kiss you behind that table.'

Tressa was very frightened but fought to keep her wits. 'You can't blackmail me like that. I won't let you.'

'You mean you'd rather risk your happy marriage for the sake of one little kiss? Come on, darling. Don't be awkward. Who knows, it might even get you out of my system once and for all.'

'I'll tell you what I'm going to do, you wretched swine,' Tressa snarled, wading out of the water and confronting him. 'I'm going to march across the beach and tell Andrew every single thing you've just said. No doubt he'll want to do something about it. We'll see how you like that, shall we?'

'I don't think you ought to do that, sweetheart,' Harry purred evilly.

The threat in his voice made Tressa freeze. She glared at him with fear mounting inside her. 'Wh-what do you mean?'

'I think there's been rather too many fights lately for the good people of Kilgarthen to keep on tolerating, don't you? Spencer nearly ruined the fete by thumping Ince Polkinghorne. Tamblyn and Miller nearly ruined Celeste Cunningham's goodbye party. If you go running to Andrew with that sordid little tale, he wouldn't be able to stop himself from putting a punch on my chin. As a gentleman,' he grinned, 'I'd have no option but to defend myself, and that would certainly ruin the outing for all those dear kiddies. I can see their little faces now. Crying their eyes out because there would probably never be another outing to the beach. And all because some silly young girl kept something from her doting hubby. So, what's it going to be, Tressa? A kiss, or a lot of distraught children and a suspicious husband?'

The danger will come in an unexpected way. Part of Dolores Uren's warning rang in Tressa's ears. But this kind of sordid proposition from Harry Lean was not unexpected or surprising. Tressa was in a terrible dilemma over this, but could Harry do something even worse to harm her and those she loved? If she gave in to his blackmail she knew it would only make things worse. She didn't doubt that Harry would demand she go to bed with him to keep silent that she had agreed to kiss him on the beach, and he wouldn't stop there. She could see all her happiness sweeping away from her in one despicable act. Tears seared her lids. 'Please, Harry, don't do this to me.'

293

'No need to cry, darling, over one little kiss.' His quickness startled her. He placed his hands on her waist and drew her to him,

Tressa felt his breath on her face and his lips seeking hers.

'No!' She wrenched herself away from him, the back of her hand flying to her mouth as if she'd been poisoned. Then she saw something that might save her. Rodney was toddling on his own towards them.

Harry saw him at the same moment and was angry that the boy had been allowed to wander off unsupervised.

'Poor bloody kid!' he snapped, lifting the boy up in his arms. 'Do they want to see him lost or drowned? He may come from a poor family but his mother loves him just as much as any other.'

Rodney put his small arms tightly round his neck. He trusts me, Harry thought. The child trusts a man who has been trying to force another man's wife into his bed. Harry had meant to trap Tressa and then carry on an association with her on a regular basis. He had laughed at Bruce Tamblyn's affair and had never stopped to think what Bert Miller was going through. Bert hadn't been seen for days; he was near to suicide, according to the latest rumour.

Harry looked at Tressa and it was then he really saw her tears and the despair in her tender pale face and had an inkling of how she must be feeling. Small and childlike, fresh and innocent, the qualities that had kept him attracted to her for so long, she looked vulnerable and pathetic with sea water dripping off her skirt. If he had got his way with her it would have wrecked her life and her family's. His lecherous campaign and threats alone had caused her untold distress. He was sickened with himself. For the first time in his life he realised what sort of a man he was. It was a grotesquely ugly sight and he was shaken to the roots of his rotten soul.

And suddenly, he knew it wasn't just her body he had wanted. With despair ripping a path of abject hopelessness inside him, he realised he was in love with her. A devastating state to be in, because he knew he could never, ever have her.

'You probably won't believe this, Tressa,' he said in a choked voice. 'But I'm really sorry for what I've been doing to you. I promise I will never bother you again.'

He walked off, telling Rodney in a gentle voice why he must not wander away from those in charge of him.

Tressa sat down on a rock and cried and cried. She didn't believe Harry's last statement, but he'd had a queer look in his eyes when he'd said it. She pulled herself together quickly, not wanting to have red eyes and to stay away too long.

Most of the party were down at the shore paddling when she got back and she was glad to find that Andrew, Laura and Guy were with them and Harry was nowhere to be seen. She lay down on her front and pretended to sunbathe, hoping the fierce August heat would soon stop her shivering.

Later in the afternoon, after the ministers had left early to prepare for their evening services, Harry came back from the green and said he had twisted his ankle and would not be able to lead his cricket team. He refused to let Mrs Endean look at it when she hurried over with her first aid box; he said he would be happy amusing Rodney and the little ones digging in the sand. He didn't look in Tressa's direction for the rest of the day.

When the party had packed up and left the beach, the convoy drove home, each vehicle travelling at its own pace. With the exception of Tressa and Harry, everyone had enjoyed the day.

Chapter 28

Ada Prisk burst into the village shop with news burning on her tongue. 'Have you heard? The Leans' stable boy was out exercising one of their horses on the moor at daybreak and he came across a body. It was Bert Miller! Looks like he killed himself. The boy said he found empty bottles of whisky and aspirin. Bert must have done away with himself over the affair!'

Daisy was serving the quiet Mrs Sparnock and Pat Penhaligon was waiting her turn. All three women gasped in horror. Daisy's hand flew to her ample breast and she staggered back, ashen-faced, against the shelves behind her.

'Quick!' Pat cried. 'She's going to faint.' Acting with the agility and energetic mind that was typical of her, Pat threw up the counter partition and was on the other side in a trice, her arms out to prevent Daisy toppling to the floor.

'Really, Mrs Prisk!' Mrs Sparnock snapped, quite out of character. 'Fancy telling Mrs Tamblyn like that. You must have known it would upset her especially.' Spurred on by Pat's calmness and efficiency, she picked up the chair provided for the shop's customers, pushed it under Daisy's fat bottom and helped ease her down onto it. Then she began to rub Daisy's wrists.

Ada crept up on them gingerly. 'I'm very sorry, Mrs Tamblyn. I didn't mean to give you a turn. Can I get you a drink of water?'

Daisy was breathing rapidly, gasping for air and trying to speak, her lips colourless and moving like a fish out of water. Pat wiped perspiration off her face. 'I don't like the look of this,' she said quietly. 'Mrs Prisk, go and phone for the doctor.'

Ada rushed through to the sitting room and telephoned the doctor's surgery in Launceston. When she was satisfied that the doctor was coming immediately, she stole a quick peep into the kitchen to see if Bruce was there. He wasn't, but a sound overhead told her he was upstairs. She was about to call to him but changed her mind. Daisy probably wouldn't appreciate having one of the sinners who had been instrumental in causing Bert Miller's suicide around her at this moment.

'I think we ought to get Daisy into the house where she will be more comfortable,' Pat was saying when Ada got back to the shop.

Roslyn Farrow had come in to post a parcel and was watching Daisy's stricken face anxiously. 'Shall I get my husband?' she whispered.

'I don't think she's as bad as that,' Pat whispered back. 'It's women she'll want round her right now.' Pat glowered at Ada. 'Perhaps you'd keep an eye on the shop, Mrs Prisk, while the rest of us get Mrs Tamblyn onto her settee.'

'Of course,' Ada said importantly. This would give her the ideal opportunity to pass on and receive any amount of gossip from the customers. She flinched when Pat added sharply, 'And for goodness sake, keep your trap shut. You've done enough damage for one morning.'

'Oh, um, the doctor's receptionist said not to give Mrs Tamblyn anything to eat or drink until the doctor says so,' Ada said contritely. Daisy was the sickliest colour, she was trembling and emitting the occasional peculiar moan. Ada took off her light summer coat and put on her most stern and righteous face; she was now a stalwart of discretion, not a word about Bert Miller's tragic death would pass her lips, nor would she tolerate one single word spoken about it in the shop while she was in charge of it.

The other three women half carried Daisy into the sitting room and put her down gently on the old lumpy settee. Putting up her feet, they took off her shoes and piled cushions behind her head. Daisy still couldn't form any words and she clung to Roslyn's hand.

'I'll find a flannel and towel to freshen you up, Mrs Tamblyn,' Mrs Sparnock said shyly, and she left the room with tears filling her eyes at the news of Bert's death and Daisy's distress.

Pat spoke slowly and precisely to Daisy. 'Would you like me to phone Laura and ask her to come over, Daisy?'

Daisy nodded feebly and her eyes watered. She wanted two things urgently to happen and one was to have Laura with her. She closed her eyes.

'That's a good idea,' Roslyn said to Pat. 'Laura is the closest person to Daisy and she owns half the shop.' She heard a creaking of ceiling timbers and looked up. 'Whatever he's doing, let's hope he stays up there.'

A short time later, Laura, carrying the big brown harvest kettle and crib basket, was hurrying Vicki to Spencer and Pawley where they were cutting a field sown with mixed oats and barley.

'Something up, love?' Spencer asked worriedly, getting down off the tractor. He studied his wife a lot these days and was receptive to her every mood.

'I've got to get over to the shop straight away, Spencer,' she said breathlessly, putting her burdens into his hands. 'Bert Miller's been found dead on the moor and Aunty Daisy has taken the news very badly. She's collapsed. Pat Penhaligon's called the doctor.' Laura looked uneasy. 'I have to do something about the shop. I – I know Ince isn't at Carrick Cross today and I thought I'd ask him to serve in it. He'd be sympathetic to the customers and I can trust him not to gossip about Aunty Daisy, Bruce and Joy. What do you think?'

'I thought we'd straightened out everything about Ince,' Spencer said quietly. 'It's fine by me.'

Laura went pink-faced at his gentle chastening, but she was not always sure of what went on inside Spencer's head and had felt compelled to get his agreement about Ince. 'I'll leave Vicki with you then. Felicity's shopping in Launceston or I would have asked her to come over.' A fleeting expression of anxiety marked Laura's classic features. 'Make sure Vicki keeps her sunhat on, won't you? And keep an eye on her in case she ends up under the tractor. There's enough food in there for her and some gingerbread men. I expect I'll be back in time to cook supper.'

'Don't worry about Vicki, but you be careful, Laura,' Spencer said sternly. 'You don't want any disappointments.' He paused then added self-consciously, 'Nor do I.'

'You've realised I might be pregnant then?' she said, glancing down shyly at the stubbly ground then into his warm, smoky eyes.

'Yes.' He kissed her cheek. 'If you're not back when we finish here, I'll ring the shop.'

'Thanks, Spencer,' she said, rushing over to Vicki who was chatting to Pawley about how much she missed Benjy.

Laura said goodbye to her, promising she would be back as soon as she could.

Before going to the shop, Laura went to see Ince. He was in Johnny's back garden trimming a privet hedge. He knew immediately something was wrong and was shocked to hear about Bert Miller's death.

'Of course I'll help out in the shop but does Spencer know you're asking me?' he asked warily.

'You're thinking along the same lines as I did,' she said. 'He knows and he says it's fine by him. Can you come at once? I want to get to Aunty Daisy and see if the doctor's been yet.'

'Right,' he said, snapping the shears shut. 'I'll put these away and leave a note for Johnny. He's gone for a stroll.'

Daisy had kept her doors locked since the burglary two years ago, but Laura had a key and let Ince and herself in by the front door. The doctor's car was outside so she took Ince through to the shop first. Ada, rearranging the newspapers and magazines, was surprised to see them and flushed guiltily. She wondered if Laura had been told it was the way she had broken the news of Bert Miller's death that had caused Daisy's collapse.

'I'm just tidying these up,' she said. 'Has the doctor said anything yet?'

'I haven't seen the doctor, Ada,' Laura replied. 'It was very good of you to take over serving in the shop. I've asked Ince to relieve you, so you can go about your own business now.'

'Ince?' Ada was aghast. 'What does Ince know about the retail trade?'

'He knows enough to take money and give the correct change,' Laura said coolly; she had been told about Ada's part in Daisy's distress. 'Good morning, Ada.'

'You will let me know how Mrs Tamblyn is?' Ada blustered as Laura gave her her coat and bundled her out of the door.

'You can be ruthless when you want to be,' Ince grinned as Laura gave him brief instructions on how to work the cash register.

'Sometimes Ada makes my blood boil. If you want to know anything else, just ask, okay? I'll take a risk with you serving stamps but anything else come and get me, I'm licensed for the post office.'

'You don't think Ada will start gossiping about me and you, do you?' Ince asked, dropping the thought delicately. 'After Spencer's previous suspicions – well, an affair is what this is all about.'

'No, the villagers are too busy wondering if you and Eve have a romance going.'

Laura left Ince thinking about Eve. He thought about her a lot, more than he had Laura when he'd fallen in love with her. He had acted upon Spencer's advice the very next day. Seeing Les going into the outdoor lavatory with a newspaper and knowing the old man would stay ensconced in there for ages, he had crept into the goathouse while Eve was milking the goats.

'I want a word with you,' he had declared bluntly before she could fix her eyes absently on something else and give him only half her attention, a habit she had got into since Les had shouted at them. 'Get up off that stool or I'll pull you up.'

Startled by his unaccustomed intensity and the raw crispness in his dark eyes, she looked up with her mouth agape. 'Whatever has got into you, Ince?'

'Come here, Eve, while Les is busy,' he demanded.

'I can't. You know Bella doesn't like me to stop until her udder is empty.'

'All right, if you want to be stubborn, I'll ask you there, but don't blame me if it isn't quite manners.'

'What are you talking about?'

'I would like you to come out with me for a drink in the pub tonight. Or if you prefer, we could go to the pictures or a restaurant. We could even have a meal at Johnny's cottage. I'm a good cook.' He laughed to cover a growing sense of embarrassment and dismay because his intended date was gazing solemnly at the ground. 'I've had to be with me and Spencer living on our own at Rosemerryn for so long. Johnny would be glad to make himself scarce for us. Eve?'

Without looking up, she murmured passively, 'I'm not much of a person for socialising, Ince. And now I'm selling my craftwork, I have orders to complete.'

His hurt pride and frustration he could deal with, but he was so irritated by her dismissiveness that he had an overwhelming desire to dip her proud head into the bucket of milk.

'I understand,' he said letting out a loud exaggerated sigh, his stance stiffening, eyes narrowing. 'To you I'm only a simple labourer.'

She looked up at him then and her neat, pale features held the same pathetic quality as the calves he had taken to market from Rosemerryn Farm. He spun on his heel and strode outside. He didn't hear her say winsomely, 'It's not like that at all, Ince.'

Since then they had kept at a polite distance.

But he was thinking of Eve now as he stared down sightlessly at the baskets of eggs in front of him on the counter. When she suddenly appeared on the other side of the counter – in his preoccupation he had not registered the bell – for a moment he thought he had conjured her up.

'Eve?'

She was just as surprised to find him here. 'Ince?'

'I haven't got another job,' he said in a rush. 'There's been a tragedy and Laura asked me to take over here.'

'Oh, nothing's happened to Mrs Tamblyn, has it?' Keeping an eye out for other customers because he didn't want anyone else but Eve to know all the facts, Ince explained why he was here.

'The poor man. I didn't know him, of course, but he looked so happy playing his accordion in the pub that night. To think his life was to be shattered in just a few hours, and his life ended in just over three weeks.'

'Yes, it's terrible,' Ince said in the soothing voice he would have used on any customer upset over the awful news. Despite her rejection of him, he still studied and admired everything about her. 'Well then, what can I get you?'

She had been gazing at him. 'Oh, yes, I've made out a list.' She handed it to him.

He smiled with the charm a real shopkeeper might use to keep his customers happy. 'Thank you.' Moments later his stab at professionalism vanished as he scanned the shelves and displays looking for the first item on the list. He came round the other side of the counter to continue his search. 'Hair grips, hair grips, hair grips… what are hair grips?'

'I use them in my hair sometimes, to keep it out of my eyes when I'm working,' Eve told him, amused. She put out her hand and picked up a small piece of card on a nearby shelf. 'They're here actually. Perhaps I ought to help you.'

'I'd be glad of that,' then he added quietly, 'I'm afraid I know very little about feminine things.'

'No, of course…' Eve said vaguely.

She turned her back on him because she could not bear to see the slight recrimination in his face. And every time she looked into his rugged dark features with those big gentle brown eyes, she melted inside at the memory of their very near kiss. She would remember the feel of his strong arms about her, the sensitive masculine nearness of him, his fresh male smell… Stop it! she screamed at herself. Don't torture yourself.

She had refused to go out with Ince because of the certainty of Les's disapproval and because of something the old man had said when he had railed against their embrace. She wanted to live in harmony with her grandfather. And she couldn't get it out of her mind that her mother was supposed to have done something much worse than giving birth to an illegitimate child. Could it be worse than the secret Eve had stumbled on at the age of sixteen on a surprise visit to her mother's lodgings? That Angela was a prostitute, always had been. She had even tried to get Eve involved in her twilight life, saying she could earn more money than a maid and enjoy herself into the bargain. Eve had fled in shame and had never come to terms with the discovery.

Eve knew Ince would never look down on her, but with his honesty and deep beliefs she couldn't bear to think of him recoiling at whatever the truth might be. She was desperate to know what it was but Les refused to tell her. Eve wanted more than anything to get closer to Ince and she was sorry she had hurt his feelings when she had declined his invitation. She felt now that she owed it to him to be friendly.

'You'll be over as usual tomorrow, Ince?' she smiled at him as he packed her shopping bag.

'Never fear. I'll be working at Carrick Cross until either I get another job, and then I'll give proper notice, or Les fires me.' He bent his head over the shopping list to reckon up the amount of the goods.

Eve knew a moment of intense panic. 'You're not looking for another job, are you?'

He kept her waiting and worked out her bill.

She couldn't risk him leaving. Eve had a great affection for her grandfather but she could not bear the thought of living there, so remote and lonely, without Ince being there three times a week. She had to do something to make sure he stayed. A favourite phrase of her late employer leapt into her mind: 'When all else fails, resort to subterfuge!' What subterfuge could she use to keep a hold on Ince? Suddenly the answer was so obvious she couldn't understand how she had not thought of it before. She could lie to Les, say she was calling on Ada Prisk or someone else.

'That'll be four and ninepence ha'penny,' Ince said, straightening up from leaning on the counter. 'Why?' he answered her finally, almost insolently. 'If I left would you miss me?'

'Of course I would,' she said miserably. Not keeping strict control of herself for once, she was bobbing about, shuffling from foot to foot. She put a ten shilling note into his hand. 'Ince...'

Ince could see she was agitated and although his hopes were rising, he took a leaf out of Harry Lean's book and prolonged her agony. He

303

rang up the cash and took his time counting out the change into her hand. 'Yes, Eve?'

'L–listen, Ince—'

The shop bell rang shrilly and Alfie and two of his brothers trooped in. Eve pushed the coins into her purse, picked up her shopping and fled.

'What's up with her?' Alfie thumbed over his shoulder. 'Got ants in her pants?'

'Stay here and guard the shop with your life, Alfie,' Ince ordered him dramatically. He sprinted after Eve and because she was walking so fast he did not catch up with her until the bottom of the hill. He clutched her by the shoulders and swung her round.

'Crikey,' Colin Uren announced, peeping round the shop door, making the bell ring persistently until Alfie yanked him back inside. 'He's going to kill her.'

'No, he's not,' Alfie said knowledgeably.

'He was red in the face.'

'Not that sort of red in the face,' Alfie pronounced like a true man of the world.

Eve blinked and stared up at Ince as if she'd been struck stupid.

'What were you going to say just now?' he demanded.

'O–only that if your invitation is – is still open I would like to go out with you.'

Ince had sworn less than half a dozen times in his life and he put his score up to five. 'About bloody time!'

—

The moment Daisy saw Laura, she burst into racking sobs, relieving some of the severe shock Dr Palmer said she was suffering from. Laura hugged her and after ten minutes her terrible trembling ceased.

'I think you're over the worst now, Mrs Tamblyn,' Dr Palmer said kindly when her tears finally stopped. 'What you need is a few days of rest, absolute peace and quiet with no worries. I'm sure Mrs Jeffries and the other ladies will look after you admirably.'

As Laura showed the doctor to the door, he said quietly, 'I don't think she'll have any more problems but if you're worried at all, don't hesitate to call me. Her heart's not as strong as I'd like it to be.'

'Thank you, Doctor. I'll keep a careful watch over her. Would it be all right if I take her to Rosemerryn? I don't like the idea of her being alone here even for a moment. I know she's got her son but I don't think he'd be much use to Aunty Daisy.' Daisy had confided to her all her disillusionment with Bruce since the fight in the pub.

'I think that would be the best thing for her but make sure the journey to the farm is slow, warm and comfortable.'

Laura got back to the sitting room to find Roslyn and Pat had made tea, Mrs Sparnock had gone home and Daisy had found her voice. Daisy beckoned Laura urgently to her.

'What is it, Aunty?' Laura said, kissing her hot brow and holding her hand.

Speaking hoarsely as if she had laryngitis, Daisy whispered, 'I want Bruce out. Tell him to go now.' Then tears flowed down her flushed face and Laura rocked her like a child.

'It'll be my pleasure,' Laura said, and after Daisy's tears had subsided, she turned to Pat. 'Will you come with me? Roslyn can stay with Aunty Daisy.'

Pat could be a fierce little woman, as capable of evicting a troublesome drinker from the pub as her large husband. 'I'll be with you every step of the way, my handsome.'

Leaving Roslyn to coax Daisy to drink some hot, sweet tea, the two women climbed the stairs side by side. Without knocking on the door they walked straight into Bruce's bedroom. He was lying on the bed, his stockinged feet up on the bedstead, his head propped up by an arm on the pillows, reading a magazine, a cigarette dangling from his lips. His nose had been left slightly crooked by the beating he had received. He had kept mostly to his room since that night, not inquiring once about Joy or the family he had helped destroy.

He could see the women were in a confrontational mood and said acidly, 'And to what do I owe the pleasure of this visit, ladies?'

'You probably haven't noticed but your mother has been taken ill and the doctor has just left,' Laura replied sourly.

Bruce looked her coldly in the eye. 'What's the matter with her?'

'She had a shock. She was told that Bert Miller is dead.'

Bruce sat up straight and took the cigarette out of his mouth. 'How?'

'He was found on the moor. It looks like he killed himself.'

Bruce paled but said nothing more.

'Daisy wants you out,' Laura went on bluntly. 'Right now.'

'You bitch.' His lip curled in contempt and he got up off the bed and stood in front of the two women. 'I suppose you put her up to that.'

Laura raised her chin. 'I would have advised her to throw you out weeks ago, but it was entirely Aunty Daisy's decision. It's a pity for her, the Millers and Kilgarthen that you ever came here.'

'We're staying here until you've packed your bags and gone,' Pat said stoutly, folding her arms.

Letting out a string of profane language, Bruce stormed to the wardrobe and tossed out his canvas bag. He stuffed his clothes into it and put on his shoes.

'I haven't got any money,' he snarled. 'So if you want me to go you'll have to give me some and ring for a taxi. I'm not walking anywhere and the bus has gone.'

'Very well, you can stay here until the taxi arrives and then say a brief goodbye to your poor mother. I'll give you ten pounds to send you on your way,' Laura said.

She and Pat made to go but Bruce had more to say. 'I need more than that to make a fresh start!'

'Too bad. That's all you're getting.'

The shop was closed for the lunch break when the taxi driver knocked on the door. Ince stationed himself at the bottom of the stairs with Laura and Pat. Bruce ran the gauntlet of their grim faces and snatched the ten pounds out of Laura's hand. He swept out of the house slamming the door. He did not say goodbye to Daisy.

People were huddled outside their doors talking in stunned whispers about Bert's death when Bruce got into the taxi, the personal car of the local bus company owner. He received jeers and ill wishes, and with a scowl and rude gesture he got into the front seat beside the driver. 'What's going on here?' the taxi driver asked, riddled with curiosity, lifting off his flat cap and gazing at the angry faces. 'You don't seem very popular.'

'Narrow-minded lot of bigots,' Bruce spat. 'Hurry up and drive on. I'll be glad to see the back of this bloody place.'

The taxi driver, a hired worker who lived in Lewannick, raised his thin eyebrows at his fare's venom, but he wanted to chat and find out all Kilgarthen's latest news and started off a friendly conversation with the usual topic, the weather. Bruce lit a cigarette from one of the packets he'd stolen from the shop and kept a tight-lipped silence.

When Kilgarthen was left behind, the driver asked, 'Liskeard railway station, is it, sir?' hoping that if he could get nowhere with friendliness then politeness would earn him a good tip from his well-dressed passenger.

'I'm thinking about it,' Bruce muttered sullenly.

Chapter 29

As dawn broke the next day, there was a sharp nip in the air that threatened to frost the dew although it was the middle of August. Eve was up early. She breathed in this hint of autumn soon to come, then hurried through the chores of milking and feeding the goats and seeing to the pigs.

Back indoors, she skipped up to her room, and although it would risk raising suspicion in her grandfather, she changed into the prettiest of her work dresses, put on a touch of make-up and took more care than usual with her hair. She sometimes wore earrings and clipped on a shiny yellow pair to match her sunny mood. She looked at her reflection in the tarnished dressing table mirror, the same one her mother probably looked into on the night she was conceived, and thought dreamily about the way Ince often studied her. She was sure he would notice her efforts. She wanted to please and encourage him.

This would be the first time she had gone out properly with a man. Mrs Howard-Armstrong had positively discouraged it. During the war, Eve along with other Land Army girls had accepted drinks from groups of servicemen, but her natural reticence and the severe training she'd had drummed into her stopped her from letting any man get to know her better. When she returned to Mrs Howard-Armstrong's employ, all her energies had been used in nursing the old lady who was by then bedridden with rheumatoid arthritis.

Before dashing back into the shop yesterday, Ince had said they would work out the details of their date the moment they knew Les couldn't overhear them. Eve had lain sleepless in her lumpy, narrow bed most of the night working out the lie she had to make up. Her first thought had been to suggest to Ince that they pay a visit to

Rosemerryn and she would say she had spent the evening there, but now wouldn't be the right time to take up Laura's invitation with her being concerned for Daisy Tamblyn. Eve regretted not taking the trouble to get to know more people in Kilgarthen, but she felt she had a good choice in Ada Prisk. She had the feeling the kindly old gossip would like to see something happen romantically between her and Ince, and somehow she felt she could trust Ada, not only to keep their association a secret but actively to assist them. Eve would go over to the village after breakfast and ask Ada if she could say she had invited her to supper.

Eve felt daring and excited, like a young girl. She rubbed hand-cream into her hands and liberally applied her favourite violet scent. After one last look in the mirror, she grinned impishly at herself and tripped downstairs.

Singing softly and gaily, she prepared the breakfast and waited for her grandfather to make his bleary-eyed appearance. It was only after she had a big plate of fried food keeping warm in the oven and toast on the table for him that she realised she had heard none of the usual bad-tempered mutterings and hacking coughs he greeted each morning with. It was broad daylight now and he never stayed in bed after it got light. Perhaps he wasn't feeling well again. He had gone to bed with one of his headaches last night. This one had been particularly painful, and she was going to nag him, if need be, to go and see the doctor at the village surgery tomorrow afternoon.

'Grandfather!' she called up the stairs but got no answer.

She hoped Les wasn't sulking for some reason and felt a stab of conscience that she was intending to deceive him. But she was resolute she would go out with Ince. She was over the age of consent, and as Mrs Howard-Armstrong would have said, 'If you must have a young man one day, Eve, be sure to find one that is suitable.' Ince was more than suitable, he was kind, honest, tender-hearted, strong-minded and very good-looking. And she didn't want to waste any more time. She knew she shouldn't be thinking it in the circumstances, but she was afraid that Andrew Macarthur would offer Ince Bert Miller's job and she would not see so much of him.

Eve called again, louder, then again at the top of her voice. But all stayed silent. After a few moments she went up to Les's room to rouse him before his breakfast dried up.

It was dark and gloomy inside the bedroom with the thick curtains pulled across and there was an unpleasant sweaty, mossy smell added to the usual stink of stale urine. Eve had not had any luck getting Les to use the lavatory at night but she insisted that he wash himself more often. With a resigned sigh, she drew back the curtains and opened the top window before going to the bed.

'Grandfather, wake up, your—'

Les was lying absolutely still. His scrawny body was twisted in a strange S-bend shape, his head lunged to the side, mouth wide open, white-furred tongue protruding. His pallor was like clay, his eyes rolled back in his head.

Eve knew deep down he was dead, but struggling to keep her panic in check, she shook his shoulder violently. 'Granddad. Wake up. Please wake up!' His shoulder was cold and stiff and she gulped and backed away from his body.

She shook her head, eyes wide with shock. 'Oh no, you can't be dead, not so soon after I've come here to be with you.' Then she fled from the room.

'What to do? What to do?' she muttered as she ran down the stairs.

She didn't stop when she reached the kitchen. Her chest felt tight and she could hardly breathe. Running out into the yard, stopping by the well, she clutched the battered handle and gasped in lungfuls of air. Her resolve and reason had left her, her mind would not work and she was at a loss to know what to do. But one thing she did know, she could not go back inside the house with her grandfather dead inside it. This was supposed to have been a morning of hope, a new beginning, but it had turned into death, despair, the end of a life. Her future was uncertain again.

Somewhere through the fog that glazed her mind like a sudden change in weather filtered a glimmer of comfort. Ince would be walking to work by now, he wouldn't be too far away. Suddenly she was desperate to see him. He would know exactly what must be done.

All at once a gust of wind whistled round her head and plastered her skirt to her legs. It shook the shrubby little trees and moaned through their branches, whistled through the gaps in the moorstone walls, scattered dust and grit, rustled the hawthorn hedges. The gate which she was sure had been shut banged and whined on its hinges. The atmosphere became heavy and ominous, the sky seemed a deep and angry grey with heavy black clouds sweeping across it. The goats shifted about in their yard and bleated complainingly, the pigs snorted and snuffled. Eve shivered violently and the bubble of panic that had been gathering into a tight knot inside her burst, replaced immediately by dread and a wave of fear.

With a hand to her mouth to stifle a cry of despair, she rushed away from the smallholding and onto the lonely narrow track, pounding along in her slippers, her fraught nerves rubbing their edges sickeningly raw inside her. She had not believed the stories about Carrick Cross being haunted, she had never been prey to fears and fancies, but she felt something was taunting her, hunting her.

She tore along the track, the wind whooshing in her ears, stinging her face, wailing all around her. She imagined a hundred crazed demons and demented souls were chasing hot on her heels, including the recently released tormented spirit of her grandfather, out to get her for planning to go against his express wishes.

The track was straight and she could see a long way ahead – open moor, stark granite rock shapes, heavy bleak sky. Where was Ince? Dear God, don't say he wasn't coming this morning. Had Laura Jeffries, damn her, got him to work in the shop instead? Ince! her mind screamed, but the words refused to come from her lips. She could hear her heart thundering in her ears, her breath bursting ragged and laboured.

The moment she saw Ince she thrust her arms out to him like a sleepwalker and increased her speed. He had been striding along jauntily, thinking about the evening ahead, hardly able to wait till then. He couldn't take Eve to the Tremewan Arms because Les would soon find out, but he thought they could risk going on to the pub in North Hill, the next village. His chirpiness vanished when he saw Eve tearing up to him as if all the terrors of Hades were after her.

There were several yards of ground to cover before their paths met. He ran towards her, calling out to reassure her, and even from a distance he could see she was staring at him from huge, desperate eyes. The instant her outstretched fingers touched him she fell in a heap into his arms, clenching his shirt with clawed hands, pushing her face like a little burrowing mole into his chest.

'What is it, Eve?' he asked, appalled at her frenzy, trying to hold her away from him so he could look into her stricken face.

She didn't want to speak, she didn't want to think, she just wanted to get as far away as possible from Carrick Cross.

Realising she was out of breath and wouldn't be able to speak until the violent shivers coursing through her abated, he held her close and stroked her back. 'It's all right, princess. I'm here now. Whatever it is I won't let anything hurt you.'

Very slowly her rasping breaths gentled and some of her natural calm returned to her. She loosened her stranglehold grip on Ince and rested lightly against him, waiting for her trembling to cease. Now he was here her reason returned and she felt foolish at what her mind had fabricated. When she was sure she was in control, she pulled away from Ince, then wiped her hands across her burning cheeks and smoothed at her hair. He kept his hands out, an inch away from her, in case she became wobbly.

She coughed and cleared her throat. 'I'm sorry, Ince. I've had such a shock. I – I went upstairs to get Grandfather up for breakfast and… and found him dead.'

'Good heavens, are you sure?'

She nodded, pulling on all her reserves of willpower to keep a rush of tears at bay. 'You can't mistake that look on someone's face, and anyway he's… it must have happened in the night.' A tickle of panic filled her stomach as she found she couldn't think clearly again. 'Wh-what do I do, Ince? What do I do now?'

'You don't have to do anything alone, Eve. I'll call the doctor and inform the police – it has to be done in a sudden death. Then I'll get in touch with the Reverend Endean.'

Eve felt numb, but with Ince to help and comfort her she became more confident. 'Yes, of course.' She looked up at the sky. The black clouds had been blown out of sight but the wind was cold. 'I'd better go back and get a cardigan and my handbag and do something about my hair and face.'

Windswept and flushed, young and vulnerable, she looked lovely to Ince, but he knew she would feel better keeping up her usual immaculate appearance when they went on to the village.

They walked side by side, Eve with her back perfectly straight but her body more yielding than normally.

'Was Les feeling ill last night at all?' Ince asked her gently.

'He complained of a headache and went to bed early.'

'Could have had something to do with that, I suppose.'

'Oh no,' Eve gasped, wringing her hands. 'I should have insisted he saw the doctor before. I knew it couldn't be right for him to be having so many headaches. They didn't seem like migraine attacks.'

'It's not your fault, Eve. You mustn't think that. Les was too stubborn to go anywhere he didn't want to, and whatever happened to him it was probably inevitable.'

'Yes, I expect you're right. It's such a comfort having you here, Ince.'

'Good, I'm glad of that.' He stopped walking and she, too, came to a standstill, gazing up at him uncertainly. He held out his arm and she went to him. They walked on and eventually she put her arm round his waist.

When they got to the house, Eve froze. 'I – I don't want to go in there again. Not with…'

'You stay here.' Ince gave her a soft hug. 'I'll fetch your cardigan and bag.'

'Thank you, you'll find them in my bedroom.'

Just to be sure that Eve hadn't been mistaken, Ince looked in on Les. The old man didn't look much more gruesome in death than he had when alive but there was a look of agony frozen into his face. Shaking his head sadly, Ince said a prayer then pulled the bedcover up over Les's head.

He went into Eve's bedroom and noticed the small disarray on the dressing table. He smiled. He was sure Eve was fastidiously tidy with her personal things yet the stopper had not been put back into the perfume bottle, a brush and comb were askew and a small jewellery box was left open. He had breathed in that wonderful violet scent when he'd held her. It had been stronger than usual, she must have applied more. Was it for his benefit? He couldn't see that it was for any other reason. He picked up a cardigan from the back of a chair and her handbag from on the foot of the bed.

Eve was pacing the yard when he got back to her. She searched his face when he passed her things to her. 'Did… you see for yourself?'

'Yes, I did.' He took her gently by the arms. 'I'm very sorry, Eve.' And he softly kissed her cheek. It was at that point that the tears she had been holding back burst like a dam and he gathered her to him. She sobbed wretchedly for some time. When she became quiet she stirred and he let her go.

Taking a handkerchief out of her handbag she dried her eyes then used a comb and mirror to tidy her hair. Ince looked away discreetly. She tapped his arm. 'I'm ready now. I've seen to the animals so nothing needs to be done here really until this evening.'

'I'll see to them then.' He liked to touch her and it was a natural thing to do in the circumstances. He rested his hand on her shoulder. 'Listen, Eve, after we've made the necessary phone calls, why don't you stay with Mrs Prisk until Les has been taken away before coming back here? She'll be glad to have you.'

'Yes, I would like to do that.' It hurt that she would be turning to Ada for a different reason today. 'Oh, Ince, I only knew I had a grandfather a few months ago and I've lost him already. I've got no one now.'

'You've got me, Eve. You know that, don't you?' He looked at her lowered lashes. 'Don't you?'

She raised her face and gave him a watery smile. 'Yes, Ince.'

Putting his arm round her, he walked her to the village.

–

After arranging with the post office for a part-time assistant to work in the shop until Daisy had recovered, Laura shut up the premises and went down the hill to Ada Prisk's house. She wasn't worried about losing custom for an hour. She felt she couldn't face any more gossip and speculation and would have closed the shop for the whole day but that would have been too much of an inconvenience for the villagers.

'I've heard the terrible news from Mrs Farrow,' Laura said in hushed tones to Ada at the doorstep. 'Could I see Eve? Just for a few moments to pass on my condolences?'

'Shocking, isn't it?' Ada replied, beckoning her to come in. 'That's two deaths in two days – well, two come to light. Apparently poor Bert had been dead for at least a few days. There'll be a third, mark my words. These things always run in threes. I'm sure Eve'll be glad to see you, Laura. It'll show her that we care round here even though she is a newcomer. And it'll take her mind off it too, poor little soul.' The old lady made a wry face as she led the way to her spotless sitting room. 'I'm running out of things to say to her. She's a strange little thing. Doesn't really talk much and soon clams up.'

'I wish I knew her better,' Laura said, unsure of the reception she would get. Eve didn't seem keen to form a friendship with her; in fact Laura had felt traces of hostility from her. 'Is Ince with her?'

'He's out making arrangements at the moment. He should be back soon. Good job it was a day he worked there. I think he's just what Eve needs, don't you? You can tell he thinks the world of her.'

'What about her? Does she show any signs of liking him in the same way?'

'Mmmm, judging by the way she looked when he had to leave, I think there is a hope of something there.'

Eve was sitting in a fireside chair wrapped in Ada's shawl. Ada had lit the fire for her and the room was warm and cosy. She stood up when Ada brought Laura into the room.

'Laura's come to see you, dear. I'll make some fresh tea.' Ada left for the kitchen.

Eve gave Laura a half-smile. 'Mrs Prisk's been very kind. I've drunk gallons of tea since I arrived here.'

'Ada's got a heart of gold. She saved my life once,' Laura added to make conversation. The atmosphere was stiff and formal and Laura was

315

finding this difficult. 'I was very sorry to hear about your grandfather's death, Eve. If there's anything I can do…'

'Thank you.' Eve moved to her chair. 'I suppose we might as well sit down.'

They sat down, shifting about to get comfortable, smoothing skirts. The clock on the mantelpiece chimed the eleventh hour on a long, mournful note. They waited for it to finish before speaking, both ill at ease.

'How is Mrs Tamblyn?' Eve asked formally.

'She's a lot better today but she'll need several days of rest and quiet.'

'And… Mrs Miller?'

'I haven't heard anything about her.'

'It was a terrible thing to have happened.'

'Yes.'

They looked at the door, willing Ada to hurry up and come in with the tea. She could be heard talking to someone at the door.

'Sounds like the butcher,' Laura said half to herself.

'Yes. How's your little girl?'

'Oh, Vicki's fine, thank you.' Laura looked at Eve to see if her visit here was welcome. It was hard to tell. Laura thought it would not hurt to confide something that might ease the strain. 'I can't be absolutely sure yet, but I think I'm expecting a baby.'

Laura's obvious joy and radiance melted the tiny bit of hardness Eve harboured in her heart for her. If she had a loving relationship with her husband and was so looking forward to having his baby, then Laura couldn't be interested in Ince in that way.

'That's wonderful,' Eve enthused, brightening. 'Would you like a boy or a girl?'

'I don't mind. I'd just like it to be happy and healthy. I suppose Spencer would like a boy to carry on his name. I don't think Vicki will mind either way. If all is well, she'll be ever so excited when we tell her. She often talks about wanting a little brother or sister.'

Now they were getting friendly, Eve said, 'I was thinking of accepting your invitation to come to Rosemerryn tonight but I knew you had Mrs Tamblyn to consider. Now, of course…'

'Do feel free to come at any time. There's plenty of room for everyone.' Laura thought she would test the water. 'You and Ince could come together.'

'We might just do that,' Eve said, making it sound as if they were a close courting couple.

Ada brought in the tea tray and Laura asked Eve the question both of them were dying to know. 'Are you and Ince going out together, Eve?'

Under the avid scrutiny of Laura's beautiful blue eyes and Ada's hawk-like features, Eve replied confidently in a rather ladylike voice, 'Yes, we are actually.'

—

The rest of the hour Laura spent there was quite pleasant. As she was leaving, a man in working clothes called, asking to see the lady from Carrick Cross.

Late in the afternoon the local bobby PC Reginald Geach, middle-aged, stocky, always looking for a cup of tea to recover from the physical exhaustion of his bicycle ride, was shown into Ada's sitting room. Ince was there and he and Ada stood protectively either side of Eve's chair.

'Phew,' the constable began, his well-fleshed chest heaving and blowing as he endeavoured to impart the information he had come with. 'I've had a telephone call from the hospital, Miss Tremorrow.'

'Miss Pascoe,' Ada corrected him.

PC Geach frowned over his notepad and gazed down on the small neat woman sitting so attentively. 'You are Miss Eve Tremorrow, aren't you, miss?'

'Yes,' Eve admitted, blushing as Ada's mouth gaped. 'Well, Miss Tremorrow. The preliminary report on the post mortem at the hospital on your grandfather, Mr Leslie Ernest Tremorrow of Carrick Cross et cetera, et cetera, is that he died of a brain haemorrhage. The pathologist stressed that your grandfather would have died despite anything you could have done for him. I hope that will be a comfort to you.'

Eve shed a few fresh tears and assured the constable that it was. Ada offered the puffing constable a cup of tea but ushered him to the kitchen to drink it, to leave Eve alone with Ince. Tonight she was going to cook a meal for three.

Ince lowered himself down in front of Eve. Smiling, he asked gently, 'Are you ready to go home yet, Eve? I shall be leaving soon to see to the animals.'

'I'm not going back tonight, Ince,' she said, smiling warmly at him. 'I'm staying here with Ada.'

He lifted her hands in his. They were cold and he rubbed them with gentle thumbs. 'I think that's very wise. I'll bring some things back for you.'

'It's not necessary for you to do that tonight, Ince. I've made other arrangements for the animals and Ada will lend me a nightdress.'

Ince's heart sank to his feet. Les hadn't been dead twenty-four hours and already Eve did not seem to need him. He felt rejected. He let go of her hands and rose, moving a few feet away from her. 'What arrangements?' he said, careful to keep the hurt out of his voice.

Her small face bright and eager because she was pleased with herself, she got up and went to him. 'A man called while you were out. A Mr Arthur Waller, a goat breeder from Callington. He'd heard the news about Grandfather from Jacka Davey whom he'd met in Bodmin. Apparently Grandfather had been thinking of selling the goats to Mr Waller just before I got in touch with him. They were getting too much for him, Mr Waller said – well, we knew that, didn't we? To save a lot of trouble I agreed to let Mr Waller take them until I know if Grandfather has made a will. He's going to take the goat's milk and the feedstock in return for their keep and he's going to accommodate the pigs as well.'

'Well, you've got it all worked out nicely,' Ince said. 'I take it from that that you won't be staying on in Kilgarthen. I'm sure as Les's next of kin you'll come in for Carrick Cross. Obviously, you've already made up your mind to sell it.'

Eve was puzzled by his curt words. She wanted him to hold her, give her his first full kiss here in this snug little room. She craved his closeness but he seemed to have deserted her, in spirit at least. 'You don't sound at all pleased, Ince. What's wrong?'

'I just thought you could have consulted me before…' Ince made for the door. Some of the depression he had fallen into a few weeks ago had returned to him. 'It doesn't matter. Well, if you'll excuse me, I've got to get home. Johnny will have my tea on the table.'

'But Ada thought you'd eat with us.' It came out in a sort of wail. One reason she had let Arthur Waller take the livestock was the extra time it would give her to be with Ince. Now he was beavering to go.

Ince didn't want to hurt Eve while she mourned but he felt he had suffered one rebuff too many from her. 'I'll come back tomorrow. You know where I am if you want me.'

I want you now. I want you to stay with me, to hold me. But rather than voice the pleadings of her heart, she lifted her chin at his behaviour and looked into his dark eyes coolly. 'Thanks for all your help, Ince.'

Chapter 30

Since their hopes that Laura might be pregnant, Spencer had not sought to make love quite so frequently, secretly afraid that he would hurt her. Ever mindful that Natalie had died giving birth to Vicki, he was constantly exhorting Laura to be careful and take plenty of rest. He wasn't happy that she had taken on the added responsibility of having Daisy at the farm, while at the same time having to work again at the shop, but he kept quiet, knowing that if he appeared to be grumbling it would put more pressure on her.

Although Spencer wasn't so passionate with her, he still left Laura reeling before and after the dizzying moments of their completion. Tonight, she lay sweetly exhausted on the bed, hardly aware of the playful breezes from the open window dancing over her burning skin or the barn owl calling a melancholy tune through the warm night air. Slowly she became aware that Spencer was speaking to her.

'Mmmmm?' She rolled onto her side, pulling the silky rose-patterned bedspread over her damp glistening nakedness, putting a languid arm over the firm muscles of his stomach which was trickling with sweat.

He repeated his question. 'When will you know for sure if you're pregnant?'

'I mentioned it to Dr Palmer when he last saw Aunty Daisy. He said to wait until I'd missed two months then to go and see him. Well, I've done that and I'll be seeing him at the next surgery.' She smiled tenderly into his eyes. 'I suppose he'll want to run tests but I should think it's pretty definite.'

Spencer moved to face her, held her gaze for a moment, then in one gentle movement he brushed aside the bedspread and put his hand carefully and caressingly on her full rounded breast. 'You haven't had any morning sickness but you have the signs here, you're swollen and tender.'

As always, his touch filled Laura with a sweet, fiery ache. She moved closer to him and circled feather-light fingertips over his flesh. He shuddered deliciously, but held back the fresh desire pulsating through him; he wanted to talk – for a while.

'The moment we know for sure we'll tell Vicki first, right?'

'Of course.'

Laura hoped her smudge of guilt wasn't obvious; she had told Eve Tremorrow. One of the things Spencer prized the most was his privacy, particularly family privacy. He was a closed book who would never willingly throw open his pages. Thankfully she hadn't been assailed with hearty congratulations from Ada so it seemed the sombre young woman had kept the confidence to herself. Thinking of Eve reminded Laura of Ince. She did not realise how annoyed Spencer was when she changed the subject.

'Have you seen Ince lately?' She was heated now for a different reason. 'Ohh, he gets me so cross.'

Spencer pulled his hand away from her and lay on his back, staring impatiently at the ceiling. His wife was off again about a matter that greatly niggled her. It was driving him crazy having to hear about it constantly.

'I know I don't know Eve very well but somehow I know she's just perfect for him,' Laura prattled on, resting her chin on his chest and tugging at the strong fair hair there. 'And now she's even more available, with poor old Les dead and laid to rest, for some strange reason Ince has become distant with her. Goodness knows why! She believed they were actually courting. She told me and Ada so.'

Raising her upper body, she leaned on her elbow and looked down on Spencer's rigid face. 'What's the matter with him? Does he think Eve needs some space now that Les is gone? She needs him more, not less! You're his best friend. You ask him what the heck he thinks he's playing at. If I say anything he just shrugs it off and I can't very well say anything to Eve. I haven't had the chance to build a friendship with her. Besides, I'm rushed off my feet these days and haven't got time to keep going down to Ada's.'

She had enough energy to keep on inadvertently annoying her husband, however. 'Les left everything to Eve; she didn't know he had nipped over to Tregorlan and made a will with Andrew's help, but by the look of it she's not planning to stay in Kilgarthen. She's definitely selling Carrick Cross and is probably only staying with Ada until it's all settled. That Arthur Waller is interested in it for his son who's getting married. Eve can pack up and go any time and anywhere she wants to. She won't need to look for a job for a long time, if ever. Les had good savings and a big insurance policy apparently.'

Laura's chin was gradually dropping to his chest and Spencer was hopeful this latest outpouring about Kilgarthen's greatest romantic non-event was coming to an end. But next she was sitting bolt upright, full of vehemence. 'If she does go, Ince will regret it for the rest of his life. You must talk to him, Spencer, you simply must.'

'You're getting as bad as Ada Prisk herself,' Spencer said thinly.

'I just want to see everyone happy, like we are.' Laura had at last said something that he wanted to hear.

He asked in a friendlier tone, 'How do you know so much about Eve Tremorrow anyway?'

'Things I've heard, things I've been told. When will you speak to Ince?'

'I'm not sure that I should, Laura.'

'Why not?'

'Eve Tremorrow's a smashing little thing, in an old-fashioned way, but she wouldn't do for me. Too much haughtiness for my tastes. I don't think she's right for Ince either and as far as I can see that's the reason why he's lost interest in her. He knows she's too much of a madam for him.'

'But Eve is really sweet when you get to know her,' Laura pleaded.

'I just don't think we ought to interfere. Not so long ago you thought the woman might be married. What's changed your mind about that?'

'It was hard for her to admit she is illegitimate. If she had really been Eve Pascoe then Pascoe would have been her husband's name.'

Laura shamelessly attempted to get her own way by caressing him in tender places. 'Please, Spencer, just a few little words to Ince. Don't forget what you did for Celeste.'

Spencer sighed, the sound issuing forth like a low groan. He loved what she was doing but he knew her motives. 'That was different. Celeste was in love with the man and she was carrying his child. Eve Tremorrow is as virginal as a church organ. I bet she thinks all men are dirty anyway.'

Angered, Laura took her hand away and disappointment cut through Spencer. She had picked the best, and the worst, moment to cease her ministrations.

'That was really horrible of you. You haven't got a clue about Eve and Ince. I think they're in love but neither of them will admit it for some reason.'

'If she's in love with Ince then why doesn't she just tell him?' Spencer returned harshly, getting exasperated.

'Because he's made her feel a fool, with her saying that they were courting. Ada's spread it all over the village. Eve hardly dares show her face. She must be feeling more than uncertain of Ince. If we don't do something to help, then she'll leave the village with a broken heart.'

'You've thought this all through, haven't you?' he snapped, desperate to get the matter over with. 'All right, if I get the right moment I'll say something to Ince.'

He looked away. Why couldn't she think about him so deeply? She was good to him, he'd give her that. She was a good farmer's wife, doing a large share of the chores as if she'd been born to it. She was a good housekeeper, the house was spotless and run to precision, he never had to look for a clean shirt. He had a willing companion, nurse, cook, washerwoman. He had no complaints about their love life; hundreds, thousands of men would be grateful, deem themselves blessed, if their women gave themselves as readily as Laura gave herself to him, and she had come to him tonight even though she was very tired. And there were times when she desired him and wasn't too shy to start the proceedings. He was perfectly satisfied in all these respects, but there was something missing. He never had her undivided attention

323

for long. The moment his meal was put in front of him, his crib was packed, a cut or bruise he had suffered attended to, her mind sped off to Vicki, or Ince, or Aunty Daisy, or Tressa, or Pawley, or the bloody lame dog someone had abandoned down Rosemerryn Lane!

He knew he was jealous of all those others. He wanted a part of Laura all to himself, his for keeps. Most of all, he wanted her love, for her to love him as he had grown to love her. He was pinning his hopes on their baby, as the one intimate link between them – before she got big with the pregnancy and thought only of the baby.

Laura knew he had switched off from her and she guessed he was fed up with her going on about Ince and Eve yet again. She sat up and put on her nightdress. 'I wonder when Harry's coming home. Seems ages since he went to London. Vicki's missing him. I think I'll phone him at his flat tomorrow evening so she can have a few words with him. Did I show you Vicki's new dress? The colour suits her so perfectly with her deep blue eyes. She's going to wear it for the harvest festival service. Roslyn Farrow's trained the children to sing "All Things Bright and Beautiful", and then she's going to wear it to little Rodney Uren's third birthday party. It's the first time any of those children have had a party of any kind—'

Thumping his fist so hard on the mattress he made the bed jump, Spencer leapt off it as though it had been torched.

'Can't you forget Harry or Vicki or the Urens and the rest of the bloody world for five minutes and give some of your attention to me!' His words tore through the night air, colder and more damaging than an icy blast of moorland wind.

Shocked by his sudden outburst, Laura cringed on the bed and whimpered, 'But we just made love. How can you say I don't give you my attention?' She did not expect thanks or congratulations for all she did for him, for everything that she was doing for others, but she could not cope with his hostility, his childishness, selfishness. She was getting weary, she didn't enjoy the extra work at the shop, she had no interest in it with so many family concerns.

She crawled between the bedcovers and started to cry softly.

Spencer was filled with remorse. 'I'm sorry, Laura. I've been expecting – hoping – to receive something I've probably no right to.'

He put on his pyjamas and got into bed beside her. Not another word was said.

Laura slept badly and was quiet next morning, but Daisy had a lot to say as they washed and dried the breakfast dishes.

'I've come to a decision, dear,' she said in the thin lifeless voice that had been hers since Laura had brought her to Rosemerryn. 'I can't stay here for ever, for all your reassurances that I'm no trouble to you. On the other hand I can't go back to the way things were before Bruce turned up. I'm not as young as I was and one day soon I'd have had to think about retiring anyway. I'm going to sell my share of the shop.'

'Are you sure about that, Aunty Daisy? You've lived there for so long. Where are you thinking about going? Hopefully not out of Kilgarthen.'

'I couldn't do that, Laura. I don't know anyone anywhere else and I'd be terribly lonely. You say talk about Bruce and the Millers has died down, and in any case gossip only follows you. People round here know it wasn't my fault what Bruce did, and with Bert Miller buried next to his parents in St Enodoc's churchyard, it isn't as if he's been laid to rest in Kilgarthen to serve as a constant reminder.'

Daisy put the last dish away and spread the tea towel over the line above the range to dry. A little spirit emanated from her. 'I thought I might buy the Angrove cottage. It's been up for sale for ages so I should be able to get it at a reasonable price. Shouldn't take too much work to have it done up fit enough to live in. Until it's ready, now that I'm feeling so much better, I could do a few jobs here, take the workload off you. I can see how tired you've been getting.'

'I can't say I wouldn't be grateful for that, Aunty. I think you've made the right decision. The Angrove cottage should suit you very nicely. Harry's away but I'll get in touch with his office and tell them you're interested in it.'

'What will you do about the shop, Laura? Take on a new partner?'

'I don't have to think about it. I'll sell too. It will be easier to attract a buyer as a whole concern. It won't mean Ince being out of work again, they want him at Tregorlan, but even if they didn't I can't solve all the problems of the world.'

'Oh, I am sorry, Laura.' Daisy looked guiltily at Laura's pale, slack face. 'You've got enough to do and all these weeks I've been an added burden to you.'

'No, you haven't, Aunty.' Laura went to her and pressed firm hands on her shoulders. 'I haven't had the worry of who to leave Vicki with while you've been here. Life will be so much easier without the shop to worry about. Let's hope we get a buyer soon. Now, it's half-day closing today so I think I'll put my feet up when I get back from the shop. There's some beef in the cold cupboard. Do you think you could manage to make some pasties for lunch? I'd really have something to look forward to.'

Daisy beamed happily. 'I'll need something to do when I've properly retired. Think of yourself as having a willing head cook and bottle-washer from now on.'

Laura felt like going straight to the shop without bidding Spencer goodbye, but his outburst last night had been preying on her mind. Perhaps she did neglect him a bit.

With Vicki and Barney trotting along beside her, she went up to Spencer in the yard. He put down the buckets of water he was carrying to the animal pens. She told him about her and Daisy's decision.

'It might be for the best, Laura,' he said noncommittally.

'Well, I wanted you to be the first to know.'

'Thanks.'

Vicki tugged on her hand. 'It's my day for sweets, don't forget, Mummy.'

Laura didn't turn at once to hug her stepdaughter as she usually did. She kept her eyes on Spencer's stern face. 'Is there anything you'd like me to bring you back from the shop, Spencer?'

In an instant his face relaxed. He kissed her lips. 'Just yourself.'

Not having the energy to ride her bicycle all the way to the village, Laura got off and pushed it along slowly most of the way, deliberately taking her time. The shop felt like a millstone round her neck and she wished she could get it off her hands today. She had given Ince a key so she knew the shop would be open in time for even the earliest customer.

Not unexpectedly he was a little worried about her because she was late and noticing her drawn face he slipped out of the shop to make her a cup of tea. During a quiet moment, as they sipped from their mugs, she told him the shop was to be sold.

'I didn't think you could go on the way you have been much longer,' he said thoughtfully. 'You look exhausted. Not a good thing for a woman in your condition,' he ended, lowering his voice demurely.

'So Eve told you?' she asked, somewhat surprised. 'How does she know? No, I guessed. You've been careful not to lift anything heavy.'

'You haven't mentioned it to anyone else?'

'No, of course not. Congratulations. Spencer must be cock-a-hoop with happiness.'

Laura didn't want to talk about Spencer. She realised she must make a bigger effort to include him in things, but she was still irked that he couldn't have talked it over sensibly instead of snarling at her. 'I've still got to get it confirmed with the doctor.'

'How come Eve knows?' Ince said, pretending to be absorbed in packing a shelf with washing soda. 'Did she guess too?'

'No,' Laura replied. 'I told her I might be pregnant on the day Les died. I thought some good news might cheer her up.'

'Even Charlie Chaplin and half of ENSA couldn't cheer her up,' Ince remarked. Laura had noticed that a number of his comments about Eve lately had been sarcastic or sneering.

'Get into the back of the shop,' she stormed.

'Eh?'

'You heard. Into the damned storeroom this minute.'

Ince glanced out of the window, hoping to see an approaching customer but the road and doorstep were empty. Laura looked as though she was about to blow a gasket and he hastily complied with her order. He didn't get the chance to ask her what was wrong; she breathed it all over him like a fiery dragon.

'I thought I had married the most stubborn and difficult man in the world in Spencer, but you, Ince Polkinghorne, beat him by a full

Grand National! There is no reason for you to be acting like this with Eve, coy, cool, offhand. It's obvious you love her and she loves you, but now that she really needs you, all you do is behave like a damned stupid fool. I don't know why you're shunning her but I bet the reason isn't a good one. Well, is it?'

He felt silly, like a schoolboy offering a lame excuse to a head-teacher. 'I thought I was getting somewhere with her but the moment Les died she proved she didn't need me.'

'Oh, did she now? And how was that, pray tell me?'

He described the way she had given over Carrick Cross's goats and pigs to Arthur Waller. 'Now can you see what I mean?'

Laura picked up a ball of string and threw it at him. In her agitation her aim was poor but it cuffed his upper arm.

He looked at his arm, thunderstruck. 'Steady on, Laura, you'll make yourself ill.'

'I see it all right. Stupid male pride again! That's what this is all about. While the little woman is clinging to you and crying her eyes out all over your manly chest, all is well. The moment she makes an adult, commonsense decision all on her little own, the likes of you can't cope with it. Eve is used to having to look after herself, remember? She's a thoroughly reliable, capable young woman. But she's got feelings, you know, and you must have hurt hers terribly. It'll serve you right if she never forgives you and leaves Kilgarthen for good and wipes away the memory of you with the dust from her feet!'

There was a chair in the storeroom and although Laura, shaking and red-faced in her rage, needed it more than he did, Ince sank down on it. 'I never thought of it like that.'

'Since when does a man think?' Laura snapped.

'What you said, about Eve being in love with me. Did she tell you that?'

'She told me and Ada that you were going out together.'

'She did?'

'That's right.' Ada's voice suddenly boomed through the stacked shelves. 'You made her look a right fool. I came through to see what all the raised voices were about. 'Tis about time someone put you

328

right, young man. Get off that chair at once. Can't you see Laura's looking faint?'

Ince jumped up and apologised. Ada took Laura by the arm and sat her down. 'There now, dear. What you need is a good lie down.'

Ince wasn't oblivious of Laura's needs but he had something more pressing on his mind. 'I must go and speak to Eve immediately. Is it all right if I pop down the road for a few minutes, Laura?'

'It wouldn't be a few minutes,' Ada said, her hawk-like features contracting. 'You won't find Eve in my house.' Ince knew the worst moment of panic in his life. 'Has she caught a train? Where's she gone? Give me her new address and I'll follow her.'

'Hold your wild horses. She's gone over to Carrick Cross to sort through the last of Les's things,' Ada said. 'I'll take your place in the shop. Laura looks as if she's had enough of you for one day, and if you haven't promised to put a ring on that maid's finger when you get back, we'll both have something to say to you.'

Ince ripped off the apron he wore and flew out of the storeroom.

Laura felt weak for a few more moments. She was grateful to Ada for taking over. But with Ince seeing sense at last, her energies soon rallied. 'I was beginning to think we'd never see that happen,' she said, shaking her head at the foolishness and blindness of the male of the species.

'I know,' Ada replied as if she had trouble believing it even now, raising her eyes to the ceiling. 'Waiting for those two to get together is as tedious as watching paint dry.'

Chapter 31

Standing in front of the black painted gate at Carrick Cross, Eve felt small and insignificant. Since she had signed the papers Andrew Macarthur had brought to Ada Prisk's house yesterday evening, the little ramshackle place no longer belonged to her. She had not wanted to retain ownership of her grandparents' smallholding. It had no child-hood memories or ties for her to cling to. It was too far off the beaten track for her to want to live here alone. She had nothing. She had no one. She had nowhere in particular to go to either, but very soon she would leave Kilgarthen behind her.

The sun was high and bright today, only playful little breezes stirred the heath and open spaces, but there was no attraction for her here. The place seemed as if it had been deserted for years; the livestock was gone, the flowers she had tended had nearly all died off, the beds looked cold and cheerless. She would go through the contents of the house and take away the personal things, leaving the rest for Arthur Waller's son and his bride. Just for a little while, she had allowed herself the dream of living here as a bride herself.

Steeling her emotions, she opened the gate and headed for the battered low door. It wasn't locked. She had never seen a key about the place and Ada had assured her she wouldn't need one, saying no one would dream of taking a thing out of the house. Eve thought the ghostly rumours would provide enough security anyway. Something about the vegetable patch made her go and take a look at it.

Ince had dug up or cut everything ready for the market trader during the first week after Les's death, then Eve had agreed to let Arthur Waller help himself. He seemed to have made a terrible mess. Where vegetables had been pulled up, earth lay heaped about and over

330

the paths. Rather than cutting the cabbages, they had been yanked out by their roots and the stumps and outer leaves strewn about. Eve shrugged her shoulders. It was no concern of hers what the Wallers did. A pity, though, to treat Ince's hard work in this way. She told herself, as she did a hundred times a day, that she would not think of Ince.

She went inside and was puzzled to see the door to the food cupboard open. A prickle of apprehension lifted her scalp. When she was last here, a week ago with Ada, they had made sure that everything was closed firmly. They had taken away most of the food, stale bread and crackers, some cake and biscuits, butter, ham, cheese and a pheasant that had been hanging, but the non-perishable goods they had left were now gone. Not a jar of jam, marmalade, pickles or chutney was left; even the salt and pepper pot were gone. Eve felt the fine hairs on the back of her neck stand up and she shivered. The Wallers had promised not to set foot inside the house until after she had informed them that she had cleared the house. She trusted them. Someone else had been here.

Putting the box and two bags she had brought with her on the table, she edged warily towards the foot of the stairs. She listened hard, but heard nothing. Feeling a little afraid, she went up the steps, taking each one gingerly, straining to hear sudden noises. Her nerves were jarred with every creak she made. She peeped into her bedroom first, glad that she had left the curtains open so the room wasn't dark. Something else chilled her to the bone. She and Ada had taken away the bed linen to launder it, but now the blankets and bedspread were missing, as were the pillows. Grasping her throat so she wouldn't cry out in alarm, she turned and fled down the stairs.

As she reached the bottom step, a man suddenly loomed up in front of her. He gripped her arms and she screamed, beating him off with her fists.

'Eve! Eve! For goodness sake, it's only me.'

Her hands fell to her sides. 'Ince! You terrified me,' she gasped accusingly.

331

'So I can see,' he returned, his big hands hovering about her, wanting to gather her in to him, not just to comfort her, but to feel her soft body against his. 'Who did you think I was?'

'An intruder. Someone's been here, taking things. Did you notice the garden?'

'No, I was looking for you.'

Eve eyed him warily, then brushing past him pointed to the food cupboard. 'Jars of food have been taken. I don't know about valuables. I haven't had time to look. Who do you think it was?'

'A tramp probably. If you'd been living here he would have knocked and asked you for something, but as the place is obviously empty he no doubt thought it would be all right to help himself. Don't worry. I've never known them to hurt anyone, they're not called gentlemen of the road for nothing.'

As he spoke his dark eyes swept up and down her slender form. She was looking very lovely today, wearing a red and yellow floral summer dress and dainty sandals, her sleek hair tucked neatly behind her small ears. How could he have let this woman slip away from him again? She wasn't bold or brassy; she possessed a unique understated beauty that appealed to the innermost reaches of his soul.

'Aren't you curious as to why I'm here?' he asked, arching his strong brows.

'Not really,' she said offhandedly, looking slightly uncomfortable now her fright had died down. She brushed her dress down unnecessarily with tremulous hands. 'I assume you've forgotten something that belongs to you.'

'Something like that,' he said smoothly, moving in close and putting his hands on her waist. 'You.'

'What do you think you're doing, Ince?'

'I'm romancing you.' He smiled into her eyes. 'For a while I stupidly forgot that I love you.' He pulled her as near to him as he could, bent his head and closed his eyes to kiss her lips.

Eve struggled. This was beyond the wildest dreams she had invented through the long lonely nights since he had so mysteriously gone cold on her, but she wanted an explanation. 'Have you gone mad? I'd expect this sort of behaviour from that man Lean, but not you. Let me go this instant, Ince.'

He put his hand behind her head and eased her face to his. 'It was pride that kept me away from you, Eve, because you made a deal with Arthur Waller without telling me. Don't let pride come between us now.'

Her movements against him were not violent, her protest only half-hearted. Her ladylike resistance was merely token. Her heart stopped beating and started again, faster. Ince's warm breath was fanning her cheek, then his lips were covering hers, pressing, gently exploring, sweetly singing the song of love he had just declared to her. Eve felt that she would die of bliss. When finally he ended the kiss, she rested in his arms, her face against his warm neck.

'I thought you would put up more of a fight than that,' he murmured dreamily into her fragrant hair.

'Ada said this would happen but I didn't believe her,' she breathed back. 'She kept saying that you wouldn't let me go but would come to me and sweep me off my feet. She made it sound like a fairytale ending and I thought she was just being a silly old lady. I swore to myself that I would only ever be polite to you.'

Lifting her chin, he gazed into her eyes. 'I hurt you. I'm sorry, Eve, darling. Forgive me?'

'Yes.' She hugged him. 'What happened to make you come here?'

'I was feeling sorry for myself. It got Laura hopping mad. She tore a strip off me and then Ada said you weren't at her house and I panicked. I thought you'd left Kilgarthen. I would have followed you to the ends of the earth. I love you, Eve. Will you marry me?'

It was a good, old-fashioned proposal, one Mrs Howard-Armstrong would have approved of but one the sour old lady had said Eve would never receive.

Eve answered him in a similar vein. 'I will be honoured to be your wife, Ince.'

They sat side by side on the stairs and kissed, long and passionately. Then holding her close, Ince looked at her very seriously. 'I know it would have been a devil of a job to get old Les to agree to us getting married, but it's a shame he's not around. I think he would have changed his mind eventually and been glad to see us happy.'

'Yes, I think so too.'

'We have to think about somewhere to live, princess, but I've already got an idea. Laura and Daisy Tamblyn are selling the shop, and the house goes with it. How about us buying it together? I've got a hundred and fifty pounds in savings and I know you like to be independent, so if you don't want me to approach the bank for the rest, you could put it up. I know it's different to your old life, but could you fancy running a shop with me? I find it very different to farming and I miss being outdoors but I like meeting the people, serving the community.' Ince had formulated this plan on the way here. His only worry was that Eve might not want to mix with the villagers. He looked at her anxiously.

She kissed his chin and snuggled into him. 'I couldn't think of anything better for us. The house has got three bedrooms, hasn't it? Plenty of room for children.'

'Lots of children.' He pecked the tip of her nose and winked. 'And we can always build on an extension.'

They stayed on the stairs kissing and cuddling for several moments. Then went upstairs to Les's bedroom so Eve could sort through his personal papers, both eager to get back to the village and tell Laura and Ada they were officially engaged, yet happy to stay here so they could be alone.

Eve pulled an old biscuit tin out of the bottom of the wardrobe. She tipped the contents onto the bed. There were dog-eared photographs of Les and Ruby whom Eve resembled a little, and a small girl, presumably Angela, on the smallholding. Others were of Les in army uniform during the Great War. Legal documents included birth, marriage and death certificates, invoices and receipts, and a certificate stating that Les, as a private in the army, had passed some exams.

'This is my mother's birth certificate,' Eve said excitedly, waving a document at Ince.

He sat behind her and with his arms round her waist looked over her shoulder as she read it. He felt Eve freeze against him and he read the reason why. 'Dear Lord, he wasn't her father,' she murmured thickly. 'Grandfather wasn't my mother's father. The name on this is William Lean. Who was he? His address is given as Hawksmoor House. That's where Felicity and Harry Lean live.'

'Harry's father was called William,' Ince said softly, caressing her shoulders and holding her close.

'So it's possible Harry could be my uncle?' Eve groaned. 'Grandfather left me three hundred and twenty-five pounds. I wondered how he had amassed that amount. You don't think he could have blackmailed this William Lean to keep quiet about him fathering my mother, do you?'

'Let's not jump to conclusions, darling.'

Eve dissolved into tears and clung to Ince. 'Just when I thought everything was working out smoothly I come across this.'

Ince moved and held her face between his hands. 'Don't get upset. As long as you don't turn out to be my sister it doesn't matter who you're really related to, does it?' He smiled and the depth of his love and concern took her breath away.

She twitched her nose and sniffed back tears. When she'd dried her eyes, she said, 'You're right, perhaps I shouldn't look through any more of this.'

'I should find out all there is to know, then you can start a new life with me with it all behind you.'

The next thing Eve picked up was a long buff envelope, addressed to her, sealed with red wax. She looked at Ince nervously. 'Grandfather could only have written this recently. I'm afraid of what it might contain.'

'There's no need to be afraid. I'm here with you.'

She opened the envelope with trembling fingers and took out two sheets of white writing paper. They had been taken out of her own pad. She glanced at Ince uneasily then read the scratchy writing out loud.

> *Dear Eve,*
>   *When you read this I should be dead. God bless you, child. I want you to know I love you. You'll find out that I weren't your*

real grandfather but let me tell you that he that was, William Lean, weren't no good, anyone in Kilgarthen will tell you that, if you care to ask them. You asked me about your mother, why we hated each other, and I couldn't bring myself to tell you. I think you have the right to know so I'm writing this although it causes me pain. Ruby, your grandmother, worked at Hawskmoor House and was seduced by William Lean's glamorous ways. She told me the child she was expecting weren't mine.

It hurt me because it was after we was married. After that I couldn't go near Ruby or any other woman again.

Me and Angela never got on. I tried to love her but couldn't, not because she was another man's child but she was evil. When she got pregnant at sixteen she told Ruby that I was—

Eve made a terrible choking sound and tears flowed down her pale face. Ince gently prised the paper out of her fingers. He continued reading.

—she told Ruby that I was the father, that I'd raped her, but it was all lies. I was glad when she up and left but Ruby never forgave me. I don't know who your father was, Eve. If I did I swear I would tell you. All I know is that I bless the day I agreed to meet you. You comforted a lonely old man in his last days on earth. I hope one day you will find the love and happiness you deserve, hopefully with a man like Ince. He's a good man. Don't feel you have to stay on here. Do what you like with the place and the money.

Your loving 'grandfather',
Les Tremorrow

P.S. I won the pools backalong. You'll find the official letter in this tin.

Eve was sobbing wretchedly in Ince's arms. He put the letter down and cradled her to him.

Some time later, he whispered to her, 'Well, that leaves out all the blackmail theories, darling. Do you feel better now?'

She nodded against his shirt, soaked with her crying. 'Th-that sweet old man.'

'Yes.' Ince ran his fingers through her hair. 'Les wasn't a bad old stick. I enjoyed working for him even though he was a bit of a slave-driver. And if it wasn't for him I would never have met you.'

Eve was quiet for a while then, bitterly, she made an uncharacteristic statement: 'My mother was a right bloody bitch.'

'Forgive her, Eve. Without her we wouldn't be here like this.'

'Yes, you're right.'

Once more she mopped her face then kissed Ince with all the tenderness and emotion she had dampened down inside her for most of her life. 'And now we have a wonderful future to look forward to. Let's pack up the things I want to keep and start by going to the shop and asking Laura if she'd like to have us at Rosemerryn for supper.'

Chapter 32

Laura's pregnancy was confirmed. Ince and Eve announced their engagement. The sale of the shop and premises went through to them like clockwork. Daisy bought the old Angrove cottage, the renovations and decorating were finished and she moved in. New tenants, a young, childless couple called Barry and Alison Hoskins, moved into the Millers' house. Laura decided not to rent Little Cot until the following summer. Guy Macarthur was baptised and Laura passed him to Kinsley Farrow with the added joy of looking forward to having her own baby baptised next year.

For six weeks there were no dramas of any kind in Kilgarthen and it settled down to its old sleepy pattern. Autumn had come, sweeping its beautiful unique hues of gold, brown, red and russet over moorland, plantations and hedges, bringing with it a few frosty mornings and fresher winds and darker evenings. Fallen leaves scurried about, congregating in the church porch, heaping up against verges and doorsteps, choking the ditches and floating away to pastures new down the streams and the Withy Brook. Creatures were not seen so often as they prepared to batten down the hatches for the next season.

The village was, however, still half expectantly waiting for the 'third death' to occur. So it came as no astonishment when the postwoman, delivering a rare letter to Ma Noon, discovered the fat old woman dead on the stout wooden settle in her kitchen.

'Horrible, it was,' she recounted to Ince and Eve after she had made a dash back to the sub-post office on her bicycle. Being a stalwart woman with a severe perm who, she claimed, 'had seen it all', she passed on the details a trifle gleefully. As luck would have it, it was pension day and the shop was heaving with customers out for their weekly chat. Having dislodged 'question time' on Ince and Eve's wedding plans and the furnishings they were choosing for the house, the postwoman played like a prima donna to the eager audience that crowded round her.

'I felt something was wrong, you see – you know how you get a sixth sense about this sort of thing? So I knocked on the front door to put the letter straight into her hand and ask if everything was all right. Well, you like to, don't you? Mrs Noon has always been far from friendly, a bit of an enigma really, but you like to think all is well with her.'

Everybody nodded.

'Well, there was no answer so I went round the back, and although there was no sign of her little pony, the jingle was there. Odd, I thought, perhaps her pony had died or been taken away by the farrier for re-shoeing or something. Anyway, all was quiet, strangely quiet, and the back kitchen door was slightly ajar.' The postwoman paused, raised her hands and spread them out dramatically. All eyes followed them. '"Mrs Noon," I called out. Of course I got no answer. Matilda, I said to myself, there's something strange going on here.'

Matilda lowered her voice to barely above a whisper. 'I crept forward, like you do.' She made the actions. 'I peeped in the kitchen window and got the fright of my life.' A gasp, tilt of the head, hand to the heart. 'And there she was, on the settle, as dead as a doorknob.' Matilda shuddered exaggeratedly. 'I can tell you there was no way I was going in there. I could see she had been dead for ages. Ugh!'

With the sorry tale finished, instead of an outbreak of chatter and speculation, a pin could have been heard dropping to the floor. Without exception, all were feeling a measure of guilt. Excuses and reasons would be given later, but for now each individual knew full well that Ma Noon had not been seen out and about for several weeks and no one had bothered to go to her home to see why.

'The poor woman,' murmured Eve, feeling the least guilty because she had never known Ma Noon, only heard about her. 'If we weren't so new here we would have wondered why she hadn't come in for her pension.' This stirred sad memories of Les and she went to Ince for comfort.

339

'There's nothing we can do,' Ince said quietly, putting his arm protectively round Eve's waist, 'but wait for the doctor and Constable Geach to arrive.'

It was several hours before Ma Noon's body was removed from her dilapidated dwelling, during which time her death was chewed over and digested in the village.

'Well, that's the third. Better she than one of the young'uns.'

'If she'd been a bit more forthcoming somebody might have gone over to see her now and then. She hated people setting foot on her property without she inviting them.'

'She never really was one of us.'

'A shame really.'

'Awful to die alone, but there's been so much going on round here lately, how were any of us to know?'

'S'pose she'll be buried on top of her husband in the churchyard.'

If Kilgarthen had been aware of the circumstances of this latest death, it would have braced itself. Suddenly it found itself aswarm with policemen and an incident room was set up in the residents' lounge of the pub. Soon after the law arrived, a few newspaper reporters started buzzing around like hungry bees.

'Murdered? Who'd want to murder an old woman like she?' Mike Penhaligon shook his great bushy head disbelievingly as he relinquished part of his premises to a tall, thin, plainclothes officer with a jolly air about him.

'That's what we're here to find out, Mr Penhaligon,' Chief Inspector Lionel Whitehead informed the landlord brightly. He had a West Country accent but it was hard to define from which region. He parked his small buttocks on the deep window ledge and with an expression that spoke of time and patience, watched the movements of a young fresh-faced constable as he placed papers, pens and pencils on the writing table.

'I hope you've got a map of the area, Constable,' Whitehead said briskly, rubbing at his nostrils with the back of his hand, something he did with gusto at regular intervals.

'Yes, sir. Of course, sir.'

'Three bags full, sir.' Whitehead grinned impishly at Mike as the constable scampered out of the room. 'Can't do enough for you when they're new like him. A few years into the job you're lucky if you can get the bleeders off their backsides to get you a cup of tea.'

'Would you like a cup of tea now, Inspector?' Pat said politely. She had just rushed downstairs after changing into her best white blouse. A plainclothes sergeant in crumpled trousers and a tight-fitting, dog-toothed jacket let a box of papers thud onto the magazine table and she found herself staring at him. He had a mass of interesting spots on a pockmarked face. Pat thought that if she took a pen and joined the spots together on one cheek she could make a map of the British Isles.

'Chief Inspector, Mrs Penhaligon,' Whitehead corrected her airily, tossing his trilby aside and revealing thinning grey hair. 'I'd be obliged if you could keep the tea coming, strong, sweet and often. Making inquiries is thirsty work.' He winked at Mike and Mike tapped his big nose in understanding.

'Wheel in the postwoman in five minutes, Sergeant,' he bellowed in a voice not dissimilar to Mike's. 'She found the body. But first I'll have a few words with the landlord and his good lady. You two must hear all the gossip. What was Mrs Ariadne Lavinia Noon, widow of nearly half a century of the late Wilfred John Noon, like?'

As he spoke, the chief inspector had been making faces as if he had an invisible toothbrush inside his mouth cleaning his wide-gapped, yellow teeth. Both Mike and Pat had been avidly following these contortions and took a moment to answer. The reason for the yellow teeth appeared when Whitehead took a cigarette out of a new packet and offered them round.

Pat declined, Mike took one for later. As Pat marvelled at what she thought were Ma Noon's romantic first names, Mike, bemused, rubbing his thatched chin, making loud scratching noises, said, 'We haven't been in the village more'n twelve year and didn't know her at all really. No one did. She were an unfriendly soul, kept herself to herself, inclined to be cantankerous. Only saw her passing through the village on her jingle. 'Twas rumoured she were mad and the mothers wouldn't let their kids go near her. Some said she hated her husband

and was glad when he died, sudden from all accounts, of pneumonia. She never visited his grave in the churchyard down the road, to my knowledge.'

Mike found himself at the receiving end of a dark, shrewd gaze. He felt that this police officer would recognise a lie from the most qualified of conmen. 'And what else was said about her?'

'That she were rich, very rich,' Pat took up the theme. 'Come from a good family somewhere and married beneath her. Supposed to have had a home like a palace, although she only ever had the smallholding, and in later years only her pension, as far as we know.'

'Family?' rapped out the policeman, contemplating his cigarette smoke.

'No children, no one at all as far as we know,' Mike answered. 'Very sad when you look at it. How did she die, Chief Inspector?'

'Preliminary reports suggest she was asphyxiated, Mr Penhaligon.'

Two days later Lionel Whitehead and his sergeant were sitting down to one each of Pat's huge pasties and steaming mugs of tea. They ate their meal for privacy in the kitchen, and as they did so they chewed over the evidence gathered so far.

'We don't have much to go on yet, Sergeant. The old lady was choked to death by the shawl she was wearing, fibres of wool were found in a cut on her throat. After you with the salt and pepper. It must have taken a lot of strength to kill her because evidence shows she put up a desperate fight, borne out by the bruising on her hands and a broken finger, and she was strong for her age, according to the state of her heart. Motive appears to be theft. A cameo brooch people have mentioned she always wore is missing. Her pension, of course, hadn't been drawn for several weeks and there was no money in her purse, but we can't be absolutely certain which day of the week she was murdered. Money might have been stolen or she may have been broke from the week before. As she had no family, friends or visitors, hadn't even seen the doctor in years, we don't know if any other valuables have been taken. This pasty is good.'

'Nearly as good as my mother's, Chief.'

'The letter which led to the discovery of her body has been of no help, just a quarterly bill for foodstuff for her pony. The pony has turned up, identified by a farmer, Spencer Jeffries, who found it browsing with his moorland stock.

'Our best piece of information comes from Miss Tremorrow of the shop. After her grandfather's sudden death — not in suspicious circumstances, I hasten to add, he could have dropped dead at any time apparently — she noticed things were missing when packing up his house. The young couple who took over the place, a Mr and Mrs Tom Waller, newlyweds, have stated that an apple and cinnamon pie went missing mysteriously while cooling on a windowsill, that vegetables have continued to disappear from the garden, but being somewhat wrapped up in each other they had put it down to the ghosts which are supposed to haunt the place. Other villagers have reported minor things like washing missing off clothes lines, milk stolen off doorsteps, a feeling that someone is watching them about the lanes and on the moor. A few people, like Ince Polkinghorne, the fiancé of the aforementioned Miss Tremorrow, have voiced the belief that there is a light-fingered tramp in the vicinity.'

'Can I have the salt back, please, guv? This tramp could have been thieving from Mrs Noon and she could have surprised him.'

'I don't think so. If you had sneaked into someone's house to steal from them and she caught you at it, would you make her sit down before killing her in a panic? No, Sergeant. There's no evidence to suggest Chummy broke into the front of the house. Unlike most people round here, Mrs Noon kept her front door locked and bolted. There isn't a key to her back door, just one bolt which hadn't been forced. I believe Mrs Noon was already sitting down or her assailant made her sit down. Either way suggests premeditation. We've got men and locals out combing the moor. Let's hope they come up with something. Pat says there's a rice pudding in the oven. Dish it out, will you? I'm going down the road to see a Mrs Daisy Tamblyn after this. She had the shop before the engaged couple. We've been told her son was having an affair with a married woman and was involved

343

in a punch-up with the cheated husband in the bar not so long ago. The husband killed himself by taking an overdose out on the moor and is now, of course, reputed to be haunting it. Mrs Tamblyn threw her son out. It was soon after Mrs Noon last drew her pension. I want to know where he's been since then. I want a word with him.'

Alfie and his brothers were thrilled at having a murder so close to home and having police and reporters about the village. They made pests of themselves, hanging about and making up misleading stories, until PC Geach threatened, 'I'll lock you all up in a cell for the night and what would your poor mother do then?' Alfie told his brothers the constable was only joking, but from then on he stopped them and himself from being a nuisance.

That afternoon there wasn't a small Uren in sight in the village; they were having a rare treat, Rodney's birthday party.

Not having any idea how to go about a child's party, Dolores had enlisted Tressa and Roslyn to help her with the food and games and Laura had offered to make the cake and party hats. Careful to keep away from the sitting room where Gerald was sleeping in a drunken stupor, the women put Woody, the old dog, in the shed for his own sake, then decorated the kitchen and laid the table. With Dolores heavily pregnant, Tressa just beginning to show, and Laura in the delicate early stages, Roslyn climbed about putting up homemade streamers.

'I had these left over from Rachael's party,' Roslyn said, pushing in the last drawing pin with a determined thumb. 'She feels she's getting a big girl now and said she didn't want so much fuss this year.' She viewed the other three women wryly when she got down off the chair. 'Look at you. Three happy mothers-to-be. I hope it isn't catching.' She took Guy from Tressa's arms. 'And aren't you getting to be a fine young man, the weight of you. What's your mother feeding you on? Iron nails and spinach?'

As she was the only one who had not given birth before, Laura was bombarded with all sorts of useful advice. 'No need to tell me about the birth,' Laura protested in sport, wondering how she was going to remember everything. 'I delivered Guy, don't forget.'

'That might come in useful,' Dolores laughed, patting her huge bump. 'Mine's due any time now.'

'You're not having pains, are you?' Tressa asked, getting the urge to rub Dolores' back for her.

'No, I think I'll get this party over with before I add to the family.'

The birthday party was a happy fun-filled occasion which Alfie, despite his more grown-up eleven years and attendance now at the senior school, enjoyed as much as Rodney. Laura had made a square sponge cake, sandwiched it with jam and buttercream and iced the top. It had piped rosettes decorating it and tiny, hard, silver sugar balls spelling Rodney's name. Roslyn had produced three miniature candle-holders and white candles and Rodney was fit to burst with pride and happiness when he blew them out.

When the tea was over, sticky hands and faces were washed and the pregnant women sat drinking tea while Roslyn, organising the children in a circle on the floor, sang popular songs to provide the music for a game of Pass the Parcel.

'I'll give a party for Guy's first birthday and they can all come over to Tregorlan,' Tressa said, watching the newspaper parcel being passed eagerly from hand to hand.

'I don't think Alfie will go to that,' Dolores smiled, proud of her eldest son's support and loyalty. She could rely on Alfie, whereas the lazy wretch in the other room was, nothing more than a burden to her now. There was a tender area on her stomach where Gerald had kneed her the day before. 'What does Vicki think about your baby?' she asked Laura.

'She can't wait,' Laura replied, seeing again her stepdaughter's delight when she and Spencer had told her about the baby. 'Aunty Daisy taught her how to knit while she was staying with us and she's knitting a blanket for it and is making all sorts of plans. She wants to choose the baby's names though. I'm trying to get her to drop Jasper after a rabbit in one of her story books or Ophelia after she'd heard the name mentioned in connection with Shakespeare's play on the wireless.'

'Jasper's not too bad,' Tressa said doubtfully. 'Have you chosen your baby's names yet, Dolores?'

'I haven't really thought of any boy's names because I'm hoping for another girl. I like Grace, after Gracie Fields – I've always liked her singing.'

'That's lovely,' Laura said. 'Spencer would like a boy and wants to call him after himself. What? I said. Can the world bear two Spencer Jeffries?'

The women giggled, then clapped their hands as Rachael won the prize of a long liquorice whirl in a little brown bag. She broke off tiny bits and gave some to each child, saving the biggest bit, much to Vicki's chagrin, for Alfie. Everyone joined in for Blind Man's Buff and Winking. Alfie refused to play Postman's Knock, raising his voice and making the other children squeal with mirth at declaring that kissing of any sort was only for sissies.

There was a sudden urgent banging on the other side of the kitchen wall. Dolores became anxious; Gerald was complaining about the noise. Quick as a flash Alfie suggested Hide and Seek outside and, always ready to comply with their hero, all the children ran obediently outside.

'Now, ladies,' Roslyn smiled cheerfully to mask the awkward moment. 'Where's my cup of tea?'

Daisy peeped round the front door. A huge smile was lighting up her face from ear to ear.

'The chief inspector didn't arrest you then?' Laura joked, relieved at seeing Daisy in such good spirits. She had called in on her just before coming here and Daisy, in the middle of the questioning, had looked fearful and guilty, as if the policeman was about to lock her up for the rest of her life.

'Like I told him, I've no idea where Bruce is and I don't care. I gave him Bruce's address in Canada in case he's gone home to Carol. Anyway, that's enough about him.'

Daisy's hand shot into sight and the others saw a bottle of champagne in it. 'This has just been delivered to Rosemerryn with a telegram. Spencer was bringing it over but when he saw me he asked

346

me to pass it on, what with just women being here. There's wonderful news. Early this morning Celeste gave birth to a seven pound, five ounce baby girl, Elizabeth Helen Rose.'

There were cheers and whoops of joy. Laura burst into tears. Tressa and Roslyn hadn't even known Celeste was pregnant, and Daisy told them she was now respectably married. Mindful of Gerald, the women calmed down quickly. The champagne cork was popped and the pale golden liquid poured into cups and mugs.

'That's fantastic,' Dolores exclaimed. 'Celeste's baby sharing the same birthday as one of my children.' She frowned. 'I was sure she was having a boy.'

'There's still plenty of time to have your next one before midnight,' Daisy pointed out.

'Celeste was having the baby at home,' Laura said, wiping her eyes. 'I can't wait to phone her, hear how everything went.'

Daisy tapped Laura on the arm. 'Spencer said to tell you not to get too excited.'

'Oh, isn't it lovely how they fuss over you?' Spencer had insisted on carrying a bundle of towels upstairs for her this morning.

'Tell me about it,' Tressa grinned. Andrew had brought home a box of chocolates last night, 'Just in case you're feeling weepy and need cheering up, darling.'

'Wait until you've had the third one,' Roslyn grunted with the air of an old hand at the game. 'He'll hardly give you a second thought.'

Some men never care at all, Dolores thought for one sad, bitter moment.

When the party guests had gone and Alfie, being wise, had taken his brothers off to play outside, Dolores settled Emily down for a nap and put her feet up. The other women had insisted on washing the dishes and clearing up the crumbs and the kitchen was clean and tidy. It was quiet and peaceful. After a few minutes her eyelids drooped and she fell asleep.

A hard slap on the head woke her up. 'I've run out of b-booze,' Gerald slurred on rocky feet. 'Get up to the pub and knock up the landlord.'

Dolores gave a despairing sigh. 'He won't let me have any. I keep telling you, Gerry. Mike said he won't serve me out of hours any more.'

'Do as you're bloody told!' Gerald snarled, gripping her by the throat and hauling her out of the chair. 'You rotten bitch! I want a drink and I want it now.'

'I haven't got enough money,' Dolores pleaded. 'I've had Rodney's birthday present and party this week.'

Gerald smashed her across the face. She screamed and shied away.

'You'd no need to give the bleddy kid a party. Bringing a bunch of stuck-up interfering bitches in here. Making so much bleddy noise I couldn't sleep.'

Before when he had beaten her Dolores had shouted at him but she had learned that the more she said, the more brutal he became. So she had clamped her mouth tightly shut in a disapproving line, but this had driven him wild with fury too and he'd struck her for it. The last few times she had hung her head and waited for him to stop abusing her. Today her hangdog demeanour infuriated him.

'Say something, you fat, useless bitch. Don't you dare keep ignoring me.' He laid into her, slapping, punching, kicking, paying no heed to her cries and pleas.

Biddy Grean was outside her door listening. The new tenants in the Millers' house came outside and stood on their back doorstep.

'Is he at it again?' Barry Hoskins called across to his neighbour.

'Started the minute the children and their mothers left the party,' Biddy informed him, neck bent forward, a hand to her ear.

'We've only been here a week,' said Alison Hoskins, her temper rising, 'and that's the third time I've heard that swine beating her up. Do something, Barry.'

Barry, built like a brick wall, his head like a block of wood, flexed his mammoth hands and ran them through his Brylcreemed hair. 'Right, I will. No one keeps hitting a woman when I'm around.' He cocked his tree stump leg over the dividing fence then changed his mind. 'I've got a better idea. The village is full of coppers. Let one of they catch him red-handed. They can lock the bastard up and throw away the key.'

Having given up peeing in the ditches because he felt it set his brothers a bad example, Alfie had popped home to use the lavatory. On hearing his mother's screams, he leaped over the back garden wall. His heart was beating wildly in fear for his mother and hatred for Gerald. The two negative emotions turned into hard resolve. He wasn't going to let his lazy good-for-nothing stepfather hurt his mother any more.

'Wait, Alfie,' Biddy called to him, appalled by his fierce expression; his intention was plain. 'Barry's gone for help. You'll only make things worse if you try to interfere.'

Alfie ignored both her and Alison who also begged him not to go inside. He thrust open the back door and saw his mother down on the floor, Gerald was kicking her; he wasn't wearing shoes but he was still doing a lot of damage.

'Leave her alone! Get away from her!'

'Sod off!' Gerald snapped, looking over his shoulder. 'Your old lady's asked for this.'

With a cry like a banshee and a mighty lunge Alfie launched himself at Gerald's back. He pummelled and pounded, trying to get Gerald off-balance and down on the floor. It was easily done with the man drink-sodden and hungover, but as they hit the floor it was Alfie who was pinned underneath. They were near the sink. Sitting astride the boy, Gerald pushed aside the piece of curtain hanging from the draining board and grabbed a handbrush. He bashed the wooden handle down on Alfie's forehead. Alfie howled and struggled to push the man off him. Gerald hit him again and again and again.

Dolores reached them, crawling on all fours, her heavy stomach hanging grotesquely beneath her. 'Stop it! Leave my son alone. We're finished, Gerald! Get out of my house and leave us alone.'

Flinging out his hand, Gerald hit her face cruelly hard, sending her toppling onto her back. Alfie was stunned, his head spun, the pain thumped unbearably. Weakly, he put up his hands to fend off further violence. Gerald brought the handbrush down on his temple and all went black. Dolores screamed in terror for her son.

'Got you, you little bastard.' Gerald wiped sweat and spittle off his chin. 'Now for your mother.'

Dolores screamed again. She couldn't get up out of his reach. She couldn't move a muscle. She was petrified for herself and for Emily.

'Oh no you don't!'

Gerald was knocked senseless by a woman wielding a saucepan. He crashed to the floor unconscious.

Alison Hoskins put the saucepan down and glanced at Biddy Grean cowering behind her, hands clutched to her face. 'We've been ruddy fools,' she said scornfully. 'We should have been the ones to run for the coppers and Barry should have stopped this from happening.' She shook Biddy. 'Pull yourself together, you silly cow, and run and phone for an ambulance.'

Alison made to go to Dolores but she pointed agitatedly to Alfie. 'Is... is he all right?'

Kneeling beside the boy, Alison pressed her fingers on his neck, feeling for a pulse. 'He's breathing. Let's hope he's not too badly hurt.' A row of coats hung on hooks on the back of the door and she laid a couple of them over Alfie. Looking dispassionately at Gerald and seeing his chest heaving as it rose and fell, she stepped over him and crouched down beside Dolores.

'I heard you order your man to get out. I hope you meant it. Can you move? Do you think you've got any broken bones?'

'I'm just aching all over. Thank God Emily was really tired because of the party and slept all the way through it. Will you help me up?'

Alison helped Dolores to a sitting position then linked her arms round her from behind. She didn't have to struggle to get Dolores into a chair. Barry was suddenly there helping her. With him was Chief Inspector Whitehead and the sergeant.

'Looks like we nearly had another murder here, maybe two,' Whitehead said, crouching over Alfie and dabbing at the blood spattered thickly on his ginger hair.

'I hit Gerald Uren with a saucepan, officer,' Alison spoke up defiantly. 'I had to, or he would have murdered Alfie, Mrs Uren and maybe even the little girl too. I don't regret it and I'd do it again if I have to.'

'I've heard all about Uren's brutality,' Whitehead said, shaking his head. 'You can tell the villagers are close, but it always seems to take a newcomer to do something about a situation like this. Go with Uren to the hospital, Sergeant. When he comes round, charge him with assault and attempted murder.'

Dolores looked down at her lover. 'I'll stand in court and testify against him. After that I never want to see him again.' For good measure she muttered a curse on Gerald.

Chapter 33

Tressa was walking back home from the village. She had been to see Dolores, to ask after Alfie and to see if she could be of any help. Dolores had been grateful to have someone to chat to for a few minutes while she rested in bed, but the district nurse was calling twice a day, Alison Hoskins was looking after the house and Roslyn was caring for Rodney and Emily at the vicarage. With Alfie recovering from concussion and a fractured skull in hospital, Colin had ably taken over as 'head of the household'.

Tressa felt a queer sort of disappointment at not being needed. Much as she loved being a mother and was looking forward to the new baby, she was feeling at a loss, being used to long hours of hard manual work. Now Tregorlan had lost Bert Miller, it was frustrating watching the new farm boy making mistakes and needing instruction, and she not able to throw herself into the task wholeheartedly, but she realised the sense of not risking a miscarriage.

Usually at this time of the year Tressa took pleasure in the changes the autumn brought to the landscape and hedges. Today, though, she could almost agree with the claims of the soulless that the giant granite boulders and Hawk's Tor looked alarming and aloof, that the ever-present wind bending grass, reeds and bracken made a picture that was bleak and foreboding, even threatening. There had been the occasional shower throughout the morning but Tressa had spurned taking a coat; now the sky was heavy, lowering, clouds darkening. Rain was on the way. She shivered, and not just because she was feeling cold. There had been some grim happenings in the last few weeks, the very air seemed tainted with death and violence, and she couldn't get rid of the uneasy feeling that someone was watching her.

The hedges were high along this part of the lane and she couldn't see the open moor and fields, she felt uncomfortably hemmed in. There was a sudden rustle in the hedge close by and water dripped off a patch of cow parsley, their dead heads nodding as if they had come to life. Tressa gasped and walked faster still. Common sense told her it had only been a little creature scurrying about, but she felt as if she was being stalked. Since Harry Lean had assaulted her with his disgusting proposition she tended to jump like this at the slightest noise and often cried for no reason. She would never forgive him.

Sometimes she had this nightmare about him.

He was the lord of a fairytale castle. Dark arid handsome, in full evening suit and black tie, a cape over his broad shoulders, he stood in the courtyard, smiling with all his sleazy charm, beckoning to her through the sparkling mists that swirled around him.

She was walking towards him, dressed in a Cinderella ballgown, silver slippers on her feet, her hair flowing. She didn't want to go to him but she had no choice. She tried to halt her steps but her feet kept moving, inexorably, towards him. She passed over a drawbridge made of rainbow bubbles, and then there were only three granite slabs of hard ground between them. She stopped here every time.

And he came for her. She could not go back. She heard the drawbridge rising, portcullis being lowered. She was trapped! She opened her mouth to shout at him to stop, to leave her alone, but the words would not come.

He reached for her. She could not run, she could not move. His hands were on her waist, drawing her to him. His face was coming closer and closer. His eyes opened wider and he said, huskily, 'I'm going to have you, Tressa. Make no mistake about that.' And he laughed in triumph.

She struggled to get away. His lips were about to claim hers. She struggled with all her might. She would be crying in her sleep and Andrew would wake her, soothe her and hold her in his arms. The worst feeling when she woke was knowing that Andrew and Guy had not existed in her dream, and although she'd tell herself it wasn't her fault she dreamed like that, she'd feel guilty.

Andrew fussed over her when she was tired and irritable but, like Joan and Jacka, he put it down to her pregnancy. She wasn't enjoying a trouble-free time like she had carrying Guy. The morning sickness showed no sign of easing off and could last all day. Her back and the tops of her legs ached and her belly felt weighed down although she was only four months gone.

A streak of lightning flashed across the sky, illuminating it in an eerie golden colour, and was followed quickly by a loud clap of thunder. Tressa's spine went rigid, she involuntarily swallowed hard and saliva gagged in her throat. She could have screamed in sheer frustration. She had never been nervous during storms before but this sort of terrestrial behaviour was too close to her nightmare for comfort. Once again she cursed the man responsible.

Next moment the rain came down in torrents. Guy started to howl and she stopped to stroke his face and make sure the waterproof covers of the pram were doing their job. 'Please, darling, calm down. Mummy's walking as fast as she can.'

A strange honking noise came from somewhere behind her. Tressa was thoroughly spooked. She broke into a run, making Guy bounce about in the pram and shriek, his chubby little face going tight and crimson. Apart from the talk of ghosts which came with ease to the villagers' lips these days, there definitely was someone hanging about the locality. Only last night milk had been stolen from Tregorlan's cow shed. The thief could be watching her right now.

She ran for several minutes then recognised the mulled sounds of a motorcar being driven slowly over the wet muddied tarmac. It was coming up behind her. The sound she had heard had only been the car's horn, warning other road users it was there as it negotiated a bend. Feeling relieved that someone she probably knew was about, someone she could pass a cheery word with, she slowed down to a comfortable pace. She watched and listened for more lightning and thunder, but as is often the case, there was no storm, just a token protest of temperature clashes up in the heavens. She didn't see the next flash behind the security of the hedge and the thunder was just a soft rumble.

Everything seemed all right now. The rain eased off and soon it would stop altogether. Wondering how she could be so silly, Tressa looked at Guy and began to sing to him. He went quiet and gazed at her curiously with the appealing boss-eyed look given only to babies. Tressa laughed at him and he rewarded her with a happy chuckle. In a few more minutes she would be home. She'd dry her hair and change her clothes. Andrew was leaving the office early today and she could soon snuggle up in his tender arms. He was planning to take her away for the weekend, the location a surprise, and although it would be a wrench leaving Guy for the first time, she was looking forward to having Andrew all to herself.

The car was getting closer. Just up ahead was a gateway. She would have to push the pram into it; there was not enough room in the lane for a big pram and any vehicle. To protect her shoes and the pram wheels she pushed it over the grassy patches, avoiding the deep mud-filled ruts. Cool fresh air flowed over her from the fields, and although it chilled her in her wet condition, she welcomed the sharp tangy breeze. She could hear the car taking the bends very slowly and she hoped she was far enough out of the way not to get splashed.

Her heart fell like a rock when the car came into sight. It was a horribly familiar, red and black Vauxhall sedan and its driver was the last man on earth she wanted to see.

Harry brought the car to a gentle stop and got out. He approached her cautiously but Tressa did not notice. She looked around for something to defend herself with, her eyes alighting on a stout stick in the ditch. She stationed herself on guard in front of the pram.

'Hello, Tressa. Everything all right, is it?' He didn't saunter over to her to get close but stayed a couple of feet away. He was smiling lightly and she was somewhat taken aback to see he had grown a neat moustache. The clothes he was wearing were not his usual flamboyant style; a plain jumper topped an ordinary pair of grey trousers.

'Why shouldn't I be all right?' she confronted him angrily.

'I – I just thought with you being here…'

'I'm here to let you pass,' she retorted, her tone and expression exclaiming, did he think she was stupid? She didn't know what game he was playing this time, but he only had to say one suggestive word and he'd get the stick round his blasted head.

'Yes, of course,' he said, peering round her into the pram. 'Your baby's grown well since I last saw him.' He glanced at her middle but did not mention her new pregnancy.

Tressa eyed him coldly, alert, hostile.

Harry put his hands into his pockets. He knew he wasn't welcome here but wanted to linger. He moved two paces towards his car. He wanted Tressa to see he was no longer a threat to her. 'I was shocked to hear what's been happening in the village since I've been in London. I read about Mrs Noon in the national newspapers. Mother said the police are anxious to trace the whereabouts of Bruce Tamblyn. It seems he brutally killed a man in Canada. I suppose you've had reporters about the place.'

'A few.'

'I'm on my way to see Alfie in hospital. I'm going to fix up a holiday for the whole family when Mrs Uren has had her baby. I've got a friend with a holiday cottage at Sennen Cove. He said they could use it for as long as they like. It will be nice and peaceful at this time of the year. Sea air will help Alfie to recover fully.'

A bitter wind blew through the gateway and Tressa shivered.

'Good Lord, you're wet through,' Harry gasped. 'I didn't notice. Let me lend you my car rug to keep you warm.' He was already on his way to the car.

'I don't want anything from you,' Tressa hurled at his back. 'Just leave me alone, Harry Lean.'

He turned and looked at her sorrowfully. 'I meant what I said on the beach, Tressa. I realised that I was behaving vilely and unacceptably towards you. I can't deny that I'll always find you attractive but I mean you no harm now.'

'And I'll never trust you.' She thrust her chin forward. 'Go back to London and stay there for good!'

Harry did not argue. He drove off, careful not to send mud splattering over Tressa and the pram. He took the next bend with great care. Since the shock of realising what his character really was he saw

356

many things in a different light. He hadn't seen any danger in tearing along the lanes like a mad hound before. But what if he had come across a child – little Rodney perhaps – or a cyclist – Laura – or a woman with a pram – Tressa – and maimed or killed them? What a risk he had been to Mrs Noon and her pony, poor old soul, and what a terrible end she'd had, he thought sadly.

He had told his mother he'd spent the weeks in London working on a piece of lucrative business. In fact he hadn't done anything, just lounged about his flat, reading, listening to the wireless, mostly thinking. He hadn't looked up any of his friends, hadn't had one sexual encounter. He had considered his life, his future. He could never have Tressa, he knew that. If he lived the life of a monk, doing only charitable works, if Macarthur left her or died, she would never want anything to do with him. Harry had thought about getting married himself, producing an heir. Perhaps one day he would, but not now, not while his love for Tressa was so new to him.

He was driving along a straight stretch of road when to his astonishment four bullocks came thundering down the lane heading straight for him. Something had panicked them and nothing was going to stop them. His first thoughts were not for himself or his car. Tressa would have left the gateway and be walking again by now. She wouldn't have time to run back to safety, there was no open moor here and nowhere else to pull in. She and her baby could be stampeded to death.

Putting the car into reverse, he hurtled back along the lane for several yards then eased off on the accelerator, not wanting to plough into Tressa himself. Bringing the car to a halt, at an angle he hoped might stop or slow down the cattle, he ran back down the lane shouting Tressa's name.

'Tressa! Tressa! Get up off the road. You're in danger!'

Seeing him running towards her, waving his arms wildly, made Tressa freeze with fear. What was he up to now? She swung the pram round and ran back the way she had come. If she hadn't already been feeling so nervous and distrustful of Harry, she might have stopped and listened to him, realised there really was a terrible danger. A survival instinct took over, but it was the wrong one, the need to get away as far as possible from Harry Lean.

Harry caught up with her and yanked hard on her shoulder to try to stop her. 'Wait, Tressa! You don't understand.'

Tressa screamed, 'Get away from me, you animal!'

'But you're in terrible danger. Get up the hedge!'

She kept running, trying to beat him off. Harry was desperate. He heard a terrific thud and a bullock bellow in pain and knew it had hit the car. Similar noises meant the other three bullocks had scrambled up the bank on either side of the car and were continuing their crazed run. There was nothing else for it. He pushed Tressa away from the pram and she fell on her backside on the road. She shrieked and threatened him as he pulled back on the pram handle to stop it moving and undid the waterproof cover protecting Guy.

'Leave my baby alone. I'll kill you!' In her desperation she thought Harry was going to use Guy to force her into having sex with him.

The danger will come in an unexpected way. Dolores' warning. This must be it!

She didn't hear the cattle bearing down on them. She got to her feet, and as Harry grabbed Guy by his knitted pram suit and hauled him out, she kicked him violently in the shin. Then she was clawing at Harry to get hold of her baby.

'Tressa! Stop it. For heaven's sake, can't you see?'

She could see nothing but danger to her baby and fought Harry like a lioness. Guy was wailing in terror and struggling and it was a hard task for Harry not to drop him.

The bullocks were only yards away. Harry thrust Tressa away from him and leapt up the bank, hoping that she would follow him and fight for her baby again. But she didn't hurl herself after him; instead she yanked on his legs trying to pull him down.

Harry had no choice. The first bullock was veering towards the bank and it would knock Tressa to the ground, to be trampled by the flailing hooves of the two bullocks careering after it. He threw Guy up to the top of the bank, praying the child would hit a grassy spot and not a stone. A scream ripped from Tressa's throat for her son.

Bending over, Harry grasped Tressa desperately by the collar of her cardigan and lifted her up. She gagged and choked but her fists were still flying. Reaching down, he lifted her legs up out of harm's way and it was then, through the corner of her eye, that she saw the peril they were in. She clawed at him, to hold on to him this time, and with one mighty effort he thrust her further up the bank.

As the terrified beasts hurtled past, Harry began to slip. Seeing what was happening, Tressa clutched his jumper and tried to haul him up beside her. She wasn't strong enough. She managed to keep a grip on his upper body but the first bullock crashed into his legs and the next one ran over his foot.

Stunned, Tressa watched helplessly as the cattle stampeded on, crushing, bending and twisting her pram. Her thoughts returned to Guy. She let go of Harry and he slid down in a heap on the tarmac but she had to put her son first. He wasn't far away, whimpering softly.

'It's all right, darling,' she sobbed. 'Mummy's coming for you.'

Tressa crawled up to reach him. He was lying on a patch of moss, his face pale and shocked. She tried to gain eye contact with him to give him comfort but he gazed, unblinking, over her shoulder. Crying raggedly, making a tremendous effort to keep control, she picked him up very carefully, then holding him close in her trembling arms she swivelled round and slowly eased herself down to the road.

'H-Harry, are you all right?'

He was in a sitting position. She shook as she lowered herself down in front of him, then tucking Guy safely against her, she lifted Harry's drooping head. 'Harry, Harry.'

He opened his eyes groggily. He had been blissfully unconscious for a few moments. 'Oh God. My bloody foot! Oh, my legs. A-are you all right, Tressa? Guy?'

'I – I'm fine. He's a bit quiet, I hope he's not hurt. I've got to get help. I'm s-sorry, Harry. If I'd known what you were trying to do... it's all my fault.'

He moaned and let his head flop back. 'I'd do anything for you, Tressa. Don't worry... my comeuppance... past sins and all that.' He gazed at his left foot. 'Looks like the old foot's bought it.'

'Don't say that.'

'R-rather odd angle, don't you think?'

Her stomach in knots, Tressa looked from his stricken face to his feet. The left one was indeed twisted at a grotesque angle, bone was sticking out and blood was pouring onto the wet road and running in tiny red rivulets. 'Oh God. You're badly hurt. I'll go to get help at once. Try not to move, Harry.'

'Won't have any d–difficulty with that.' He groaned in agony but somehow through the searing pain he managed to smile at her.

Tressa patted his shoulder. 'I'll try not to be long. Ohhhh!'

'What is it? What's the matter?'

'Arrggh!' Tressa doubled over. Unbearable spasms of pain were ripping through her stomach. She fell against Harry, and clung to him.

Chapter 34

Laura knew Tressa had been going to see Dolores. She should be home by now. Laura had run out of spice to make Vicki's favourite gingerbread men, so rather than ring Tressa to find out how Dolores and Alfie were, she decided to go over to Tregorlan Farm and borrow some ginger and ask after the Urens then. She waited for the last heavy shower of rain and the thunder and lightning to end before putting on her mac and boots, tying on a scarf and picking up an umbrella.

She had reached the bottom of Tregorlan's track when she saw the bullock. It was lying in a ditch and had deep, bloodied gashes on its front and side and was lowing pitifully. Laura recognised it as one of Tregorlan's stock. The poor creature was in a bad way and needed to be put out of its misery.

Laura ran all the way to the farm and went straight into the kitchen without taking off her boots. Jacka and Joan were sitting either side of the black range, Jacka puffing on his pipe, Joan knitting a little red jumper for Guy.

'What's up, m'dear?' Jacka said, getting to his feet. Joan put her knitting down on her lap.

'I'm afraid it's one of your bullocks,' Laura explained breathlessly. 'It's badly hurt and needs the vet. If you phone for him I'll get Tressa to come with me and see what we can do for it until he gets here.'

'But Tressa and the baby aren't back yet.' Joan frowned, glancing uneasily at her brother. 'We thought she would have been back ages ago.'

'You get the vet, Joan,' Jacka said hurriedly, reaching for his floppy hat and coat. 'I'll go with Laura and we'll take a look down the lane.'

361

Jacka could hardly bear the beast's distress. He stayed with the bullock and Laura walked on towards the village. She felt a niggle of concern for Tressa and Guy but was sure they must have stayed longer at the Urens'; Tressa had hoped to be made useful there.

It wasn't long before she saw Harry's car. Laura's disquiet grew. Why was it parked at such an odd angle? She ran up to it. There was no sign of Harry. She looked around then shouted his name. She saw blood on the buckled front wing. It must be the bullock's blood. Harry must have collided with it. Everyone said he would cause an accident one day...

She saw that parts of the bank on either side of the car had been brought down, exposing black earth and roots. Foliage was strewn about, leading away from the car on the opposite side. If the bullock had made its way partly back home, what had damaged the bank like this? There was no evidence that the car had done it. Biting her lower lip, her mouth dry, Laura squeezed through a gap between the back of the car and the bank and hurried along the lane.

'Harry! Harry!' she called at short regular intervals but got no reply.

Rounding the next bend she saw the pathetic huddle just up ahead. And she saw the blood on them and the road. Panic gripped her. They were so still she was sure they must all be dead. Running wildly, she threw herself down on her knees beside them.

'Tressa. Harry. Oh, my God, what's happened?'

'Ohhh,' Tressa moaned. She was bent double.

'L-Laura?' Harry tried to lift his head but it flopped back down.

'It's all right, Harry. Don't worry. I'm here to help.' Laura was horrified at the extent of Harry's injuries and what was happening to Tressa. Both of them were bleeding and it was intermingling on the tarmac. The worst of the panic left her and she felt coolly in charge in the way she had at Guy's birth. Ripping the scarf off her neck, she wound it round Harry's left shin and tied it as tightly as she could. Reaching under Tressa, she put a hand on Guy's face. It was stone cold.

'T-take him,' Harry slurred.

Laura pulled Guy out from between their bodies. The movements made Tressa scream in agony and despair. Harry was fighting to stay conscious and keep hold of her.

Laura didn't waste any time. Clutching Guy tightly to her, she ran like a hare back to Jacka to raise the alarm.

—

Andrew Macarthur was tidying up the last of his papers, about to leave his Bodmin office, when his secretary rang through to tell him there was a lady on the telephone asking to speak to him urgently.

'Tell her I've already left, Mrs Polmere,' he said firmly. He was not going to let anyone stop him leaving early. He had a weekend in the Cotswolds planned for him and Tressa and he was looking forward to every minute they would spend cuddled up together in the cosy little cottage. He had diligently worked all day, now his thoughts were only for his wife and child. He had just put a bottle of Tressa's favourite jasmine scent in his briefcase and a rattle for Guy.

'The caller is very insistent,' Mrs Polmere stressed. 'It's a Mrs Laura Jeffries.'

Frowning, Andrew said in that case he would take the call. Laura was too close a friend to ignore. 'Laura, my dear, what can I do for you? I'm just about to leave here.'

'Andrew,' he knew immediately by her tone that something was very wrong, 'go straight to Launceston Hospital. I'm there now. I'm afraid that Tressa and Guy have been involved in an accident.'

'What?' Andrew fell down on his chair. Something he had always dreaded had just come true. 'Are th–they hurt? What happened?'

'I came across them in the lane, with Harry Lean. His car was all battered.'

'Lean! I'll kill him! I knew he'd cause a smash one day with the way he drives his car. Why did it have to be my family?'

'It's not like that, Andrew. Harry's hurt too, very seriously. Just get to the hospital, as quickly as you can.'

Dropping the receiver, Andrew grabbed his hat and coat, mumbled the details to his secretary and dashed for his car. He would have driven on his wits, as fast as his car would go, but he could not risk getting hurt himself; Tressa and Guy needed him. Tears pricked Andrew's eyes as he imagined what had happened to the two people he loved most in the world. How badly were they hurt? He wished he'd asked Laura what their injuries were.

A moment of sheer black panic almost forced him to stop the car. Pure fear clutched at his bowels. Laura hadn't said if they were alive or dead. Perhaps one or both of them was dying now and he wasn't there to hold them.

Oh, God, if You really exist, spare Tressa and Guy for me and I'll go to church every day of the week if that's what You want. I'll do anything, please, please, please, Lord.

He parked his car in front of the main doors of the hospital, but rather than being able to rush inside he found himself quarrelling with a porter who demanded that he move it elsewhere. Andrew pleaded but the porter pointed out that his family had needed the space themselves a short while ago in the ambulance that had brought them here. Andrew understood and capitulated, but the extra time it took him to park the car seemed like hell.

Laura was waiting for him by the doors when he ran back. He grabbed hold of her. 'How are they? What the bloody hell happened to them?'

Holding his arms, she tried to speak calmly, the shock of the accident telling on her. 'Guy's up on the children's ward. He's in shock and they're keeping him under observation. It's not thought that he's in any danger. He took part of a feed just now.'

'Thank God. And Tressa?'

Laura took a deep breath. 'She's in theatre, Andrew.'

'Why?' He clutched her tighter, hurting her. 'Laura?'

'She's had a miscarriage, Andrew. I'm very sorry.'

'Oh, no.' He let tears flow unashamedly down his face. 'But she will be all right? Tressa won't... Tell me she'll be all right, Laura, I couldn't bear...'

Laura said nothing about the agony Tressa had been in in the ambulance, twisted up and screaming as the ambulance man had delivered

364

the foetus. Laura had sat, numb with grief, holding Guy, listening to her friend. At one point, lying on the other side of the ambulance, also in the greatest pain, Harry had reached out and held Tressa's hand and she had almost crushed his as she'd squeezed it.

'She's in the best place, Andrew. The nurses explained it to me. It's only a procedure to clean her up. She should be out of theatre soon. She'll be wanting to see you the moment she comes round.' For a moment Laura rested her face on Andrew's chest. 'I'm so sorry about the baby, Andrew.'

He was like a small, bewildered child. 'What's happening to us, Laura? Kilgarthen's only a little village, a quiet little backwater, but all these things keep happening to us. Why?'

'I don't know, Andrew. We must just hope and pray that things get better.'

Felicity Lean was in the waiting room, desperate for news of Harry who was in the next operating theatre. She ran to Laura, sobbing, and although she didn't know Andrew very well, needing and wanting to give comfort she put her other arm round him. The three stood in a huddle for some time, the start of a long wait.

After a few minutes Andrew went to the children's ward and was assured by the sister that Guy was sleeping peacefully and they were keeping a watchful eye on him. Someone would come and fetch him if he was needed.

'Have you any idea what happened?' Andrew asked when he got back.

Felicity looked at Laura for an explanation.

'Tressa couldn't speak at all,' Laura said, 'but from what I could gather from Harry, some bullocks stampeded in fright down the lane, heading for the village. Harry saw them first and stopped his car and ran back to warn Tressa. He got her and Guy up the bank but he slipped down just as the cattle ran past. Unfortunately the incident started off labour pains in Tressa. I... I saw the state of the car and pram. Tressa and Guy would probably have been killed if not for Harry.'

'My poor brave boy,' Felicity sobbed.

Andrew found it hard to take in that he had a lot to be grateful to Harry Lean for. 'What are his injuries?' he asked gently.

'It's his legs,' Felicity sniffed, composing herself.

Laura hadn't told Felicity the gravity of Harry's injuries. There was no possibility that he would come out of the theatre with his left foot intact.

Half an hour passed and Laura got up to make two phone calls, one home to keep Spencer in the picture and because she needed the reassurance of his voice. The other to Tregorlan to Jacka and Joan. Jacka had been forced to stay with the bullock until the vet arrived and Joan, who had brought blankets to the scene of the accident, had felt too shaky to go to the hospital. There wasn't much Laura could tell them and she went back to the waiting room with three cups of tea.

Another fifty-five agonising minutes passed before a scrub nurse in theatre garb opened the double doors to one of the operating suites. Andrew rushed out of the waiting room to her. Laura and Felicity followed and stood at a discreet distance.

'Is there any news of my wife?' he demanded anxiously.

'Are you Mr Macarthur?' the nurse asked, glancing at all their drawn faces. Thick glasses sat on her nose, in a round face denoting efficiency and a great capacity for honesty and caring.

'Yes, I am. How is she?' Andrew resisted the urge to grab the nurse's hand and plead with her. He prayed she wouldn't prevaricate as some medical staff were apt to do.

She took off her glasses with a slow smile. 'We've just taken her to the recovery room. The surgeon will come to talk to you in a few minutes, Mr Macarthur.'

Andrew could see she wouldn't tell him anything else but if Tressa was in the recovery room, she must have come through the procedure safely.

There was another wait of ten, long, anguished minutes then the surgeon appeared. Andrew pounced on him and the surgeon, his mask hanging round his long neck, offered his pale smooth hand.

'Sorry to have kept you waiting, Mr Macarthur. I'm sorry, too, that it was too late for us to do anything to save the baby. Please accept my condolences. We had a little trouble stopping your wife's bleeding but

I'm reasonably confident there won't be any further complications. She'll need complete bed rest for a few weeks but she is young and healthy and I don't foresee any long-term problems.'

'Thank God!' Andrew almost collapsed with relief. 'Can I see her now?'

The surgeon carried on as if Andrew had not spoken. 'You're probably wondering if your wife will be able to have any more children. I should say there is a very good chance that she will.'

'I can't thank you enough. Can I go to Tressa now? Please?' All Andrew wanted to do was to see the lovely small face he had fallen in love with the instant he had first seen it.

The surgeon had a gall bladder to remove the moment the operating theatre was cleaned and sterilised and he was just as eager to get away, to eat a meal. 'Wait for a nurse to come and fetch you, Mr Macarthur.' He shook hands with Andrew again and walked away before Felicity could ask him if he happened to know anything about Harry's condition.

Chapter 35

It was three days before Harry felt able to sit up, propped against pillows, in the little room he had to himself. There was the taste of sour plums in his mouth but he ate enough lunch of poached fish to satisfy the rather stern sister of the men's surgical ward. Groggy from medication, still shocked after his ordeal, he could only sip tea from an invalid cup.

A perky young nurse with hazel curls under a severely starched cap entered the room and gave him a smile. 'Have you finished with that, Mr Lean?'

'Yes, thank you, Nurse,' he replied, his voice tired and husky since the accident. 'I can hardly taste it.'

'Never mind, it'll take a few days for your taste buds to recover.' She put the invalid cup on the tray then quickly straightened the bedcovers, draping them again unnecessarily over the cage protecting his broken legs.

'What's going on?' he asked suspiciously. 'It's not time for the consultant's round.'

'You've got a visitor.' She took his comb out of the bedside cabinet and tidied his hair, making little impression on the lacklustre locks.

Harry raised an eyebrow; that hadn't lost its sensuous curve. 'It's too early for visiting time. You've got to be Houdini to get past Sister. I know, my mother has tried and failed.'

'This one's got special permission.'

The nurse left the room and Harry waited, bemused. It must be the vicar, he thought. They let vicars in any time they liked in hospital. The only visitors he had been allowed were his mother and for a few minutes Laura. He had been considered too weak for the multitude of villagers who had flocked to see him now he was something of a hero. His room was filled with their get well cards, flowers, chocolates, books, magazines. Vicki had sent him a picture she had drawn and painted of Charlie Boy, his horse, glued on a stiff piece of cardboard. It took pride of place standing against his water jug on the cabinet. He looked at it often. It was Vicki he would love to see now, her golden hair, sunny smile, sparkling blue eyes. He didn't mind the vicar though, Kinsley Farrow wasn't the sanctimonious sort.

He could hear squeaky wheels coming his way and the nurse was back with someone in a wheelchair.

'Tressa!' Harry tried to sit up. He smoothed at his hair and stroked his moustache. He must look like a scarecrow. 'What a lovely surprise.'

The nurse pushed her closer to the bed and left the room, shutting the door softly. Like him, Tressa had large dark shadows under her eyes and her skin was sallow; but she still looked lovely in a blue and pink dressing gown, her hair tied back with a silk scarf. A blanket was wrapped over her legs and she looked engulfed in it, small, young and so very vulnerable.

'Hello, Harry.' Her voice was quieter too and he knew the effort it took after major surgery just to say a few words. 'How are you?'

He felt shy with her and full of emotion. To mask it he spoke with all the cheerfulness he could muster. 'Oh, not so bad, you know. What about you?'

She looked down the bed, knowing the reason for the cage that kept the blankets off his legs. A slight flush touched her cheeks. She clasped her hands together until they hurt, then looked back at Harry. He really was pleased to see her. She had wondered how he would be feeling about the consequences of her not trusting him. 'I – I'm much better than I was, thank you.'

'And what about little Guy?'

She gave a small smile. 'Oh, he's almost back to his old self. He's going home today. Aunty Joan will look after him. I shall miss him. The nurses have been bringing him to see me. I've got to stay in for ten days. I'm afraid I can't stay here long.' She lowered her eyes. 'It took a lot of persuading for the sister on my ward to allow me to come at all. I – I felt I had to see you, Harry.'

369

'I'm delighted. I never thought the day would come when you would ask to see me.'

Harry's kindness, cheerfulness, was making this difficult for her. He had plagued her in the past, but she had made him pay a terrible penalty for it, one she could see now he had not deserved. Her hands began to shake and she gripped the sides of the wheelchair.

'I w–want to say I'm sorry a–about your foot, about everything that happened.' Andrew had wanted to see Harry and do this for her, but she had felt she must come herself. Andrew had understood.

'Thank you, Tressa.' Harry couldn't keep up his brave front any longer. His eyes misted over and he hoped Tressa would not notice. 'I was sorry to hear you'd lost your new baby. Mother said you should be able to have more in the future.'

'Harry, I feel so responsible… what I've done to you.' Tressa began to cry softly.

'Enough of that now,' he said soothingly. 'If I hadn't been so wicked to you in the past you wouldn't have felt you had to run away from me. I'd sacrifice anything to save you and anyone you love, Tressa. Besides, the way I look at it is that men came back from the war with a lot less. Look at Pawley Skewes at Rosemerryn. And I've got my name in the papers – "Hero saves mum and baby and pays the price". I wasn't a hero or anything, but now I can make a new start in the village as a respected member instead of a despised cad. Don't cry, Tressa. We came out of it alive. That's the main thing.'

'I'll always be grateful to you, Harry.'

'My loss will be worth it if we can be friends from now on. Can we, Tressa?'

She dried her tears and found a smile for him. 'Yes, Harry.'

Hesitantly, he reached out a hand to her.

She clasped it tightly with both of hers.

Chapter 36

Laura tossed and turned once more then admitted defeat. She opened her eyes and stared at the patterns the moon made through the net curtains on the wardrobe mirror. This was going to be another night when she wasn't going to get much sleep.

'Want me to go downstairs and make you a drink?'

'Oh, I'm sorry, Spencer.' She faced him. 'I'm keeping you awake again.'

He turned on his side and put his arm over her, whispering so close to her ear it made her shiver delightfully. 'I can think of another way to make you tired.'

She asked herself if she wanted to make love. The pale silvery light cast exotic shadows over Spencer's bare muscular torso. She allowed her eyes to travel along the sinewy line of his arm, over his shoulder, lingering at one of her favourite places, the part where his throat met his chest. Her lips automatically parted and she put them there. Spencer didn't waste any time. He started to remove her nightdress. Laura sat up and took over from him then smiled down at his handsome face. She liked being close to him at any time, but it struck her then just how irresistible she found her husband.

She bent over him, about to kiss him. A creature on the moor let out a long, haunting shriek. She stopped.

'What's the matter?' Spencer said, pulling her face towards his.

'Just for a moment I thought Vicki cried out in her sleep. I forgot she's staying with Felicity tonight.'

'Forget everyone but me,' he said gruffly, claiming her gently.

Laura slept for an hour but woke again, feeling tense and tearful. She tried not to move about or to sigh; Spencer was so tuned in to

371

her every mood these days. But it wasn't long before he was awake holding her once more.

He caressed her hair away from her brow and kissed it tenderly. 'Is it the accident again?'

She nodded. 'I can't get it out of my mind, even though Tressa and Harry are making good progress.'

'It's understandable, darling. It must have been a terrible thing to come across.'

'I thought they were dead at first. I was terrified, Spencer. I knew it was up to me to get help quickly or they all might die. And with Tressa losing her baby, and me having to run fast with Guy, I was scared I'd lose ours.'

Spencer put his palm gently over her tummy. 'Dr Palmer keeps reassuring you that everything is all right with our baby, darling.'

'I know.' Laura wiped a single tear away. 'He says I just need a little time to get over it. I keep thinking how I'd feel if I found Vicki in similar straits. I love her so much I couldn't bear it.'

Spencer knew it was unkind but he couldn't stop himself from asking, 'And how would you feel if you found me like that?'

Laura shuddered and clung to him as if she was drowning. 'I'd hate it!'

He hugged her. It was just what he had hoped to hear.

After a while she relaxed in the comfort of his arms but feeling it was unfair to keep him awake – he had a very early start and a heavy day's work ahead of him – she eased herself away. Sitting up, she put on her nightdress and slipped out of bed.

'Where are you going?' he yawned.

'Downstairs to make some hot milk. You go back to sleep.' She intended to get a spare blanket and curl up in her chair by the hearth in the kitchen; the embers in the range would have kept the room cosily warm. Putting on her dressing gown she went to the door, then on impulse she went back to the bed and kissed Spencer on the cheek. That little gesture stopped him dropping off to sleep and he lay thinking about what it meant.

Laura plodded carefully downstairs by the light of the lantern. All her movements were slow and exaggerated since Tressa's loss; she was determined to hang on to her baby. She put the lantern on the kitchen table; it would give her enough light to see the milk jug in the cold cupboard in the back kitchen.

Her hand was on the jug when she heard a noise, a low scuffle, but she took no notice, there were always noises in the country, especially on a farm. A fieldmouse trying to gather something before its winter hibernation probably. Laura marvelled that although she had lived most of her life in London she had forgotten how the hustle and bustle of the big city sounded.

The next instant she knew something was wrong. There was someone behind her. More than just the sense of a presence, there was also a horrible unwashed smell and heavy breathing. Dropping the jug, her heart frozen in dread, she spun round. A large black shape reared over her, and before she could scream to alert Spencer, something wet and dirty was clamped over her mouth and she was pulled into the kitchen.

A painful grip was kept on her arm and her assailant warned in threatening tones, 'Don't make a noise. I won't hesitate to hurt you.'

The man had a balaclava pulled down over his face. He was wearing an old Army greatcoat; Jacka Davey had mourned the disappearance of his two weeks ago and Laura recognised some mending on the collar. She didn't know whether to be more or less afraid at having recognised the intruder's throaty drawl.

'Bruce!' She kept her voice low. 'So you were the thief all this time. What are you doing here?'

He pulled off the balaclava. 'Stealing food. I gotta eat, don't I?'

'I thought you'd left the area.'

'That's what you're supposed to think. I hung around to get some money together. When my dear mother threw me out,' he sneered, 'how did she think I was going to make a fresh start? The ten quid you gave me wouldn't have got me far. I need enough to get abroad.'

Laura was terrified. The Canadian police were hot on Bruce's trail for murder and Chief Inspector Whitehead was suspicious he might have had something to do with Mrs Noon's death. Bruce could be a double murderer.

She decided to be helpful, to try and keep him sweet. 'I – I'll get you some food. All that you need.'

Bruce pushed her down on a chair at the table and put a grimy hand round her throat. 'And some money, Laura. Lots of it. You're a rich woman. I don't know why I didn't think of you before.'

'I've got fifteen shillings put aside for the insurance man, about one pound, ten shillings in my purse and I keep ten pounds upstairs for emergencies. I'll fetch it for you.'

'Don't be stupid,' Bruce hissed, looking as if he was going to strike her and she flinched. 'I need a lot more than that. You can go to the bank tomorrow and get me a couple of hundred at least. And if you don't co-operate I'll hurt that bloody little kid you're so fond of.'

'Vicki's not here!' The thought of someone hurting Vicki appalled her.

Bruce slapped her face. 'Keep quiet. I'll see for myself later. Never mind though, I've got you and that standoffish husband of yours. And I've got a little insurance to make sure you do just as I say.' He put his hand inside his coat and produced an Army pistol. He jeered as Laura's eyes grew wide with fear. 'A little souvenir from the war. I know how to use it. I've got nothing to lose. I've killed before.'

'I – I know. The man in Canada.'

'And that old bitch, Ma Noon.'

Laura's breath came in a shallow little gasp. She felt the animosity and hatred emanating from Bruce, it seemed the room was pulsing with it. She broke out in a cold sweat. She had never been in a more desperate situation. Trying to keep a grip on her fright and revulsion, she attempted to play on his natural fear.

'The police have their suspicions that it was you, Bruce. You must get away from here at once. Take the money I offered you. I'll get you some clean clothes. There's some petrol in Spencer's car. I'll give you his coupons. You can get far away from here.'

He sneered, screwing up his bullish features, twisting his once neat beard, now grown rough and wiry. 'Oh, I will, Laura, depend upon it, but I need lots of money and you're going to get it for me. I'll have this gun pointed at Spencer's head while you drive into town and bring it back, and if you bring the cops into this I'll kill him and that disfigured chap who works for you. He's bound to come knocking wondering why his boss isn't working.' Barney hadn't barked to warn them someone was creeping about. Laura was almost too scared to ask. 'What have you done with the dog?'

'Nothing. It wasn't about anywhere.'

Laura sighed with relief, Barney sometimes spent the night in Pawley's tent. 'Where have you been living? By the look of you, out in the open. The police have been searching the moor for days.'

'You forget that I used to live here before. There are many natural hiding places on the moor. I've been moving from one to another, putting my old Army training to use.'

Noises overhead told them that Spencer was getting out of bed. Bruce gazed up at the ceiling. 'Sounds like your old man's coming down to look for you. We'll make a cosy little threesome through the night.' He pointed the gun at Laura's head. 'Don't try warning him.'

Spencer appeared in his pyjama bottoms. 'Laura—'

'Come and join us, Jeffries, and do it nice and easily.'

'Tamblyn!'

Bruce waved the gun at him. 'Sit down next to your wife.'

Spencer raised his hands in the air. 'If you've hurt Laura I'll—'

'Forget the bravado,' Bruce said harshly. 'If you both do as I say I'll be up and out of here by mid-morning.'

Spencer placed a chair beside Laura and sat on it. She clutched his hand.

'How sweet,' Bruce sniggered. 'I'm starving. Make me something hot to eat, Laura, and I want some water so I can have a wash. Don't try any funny business or you'll end up the same way as Ma Noon and I'll finish you off quicker than I did her.'

With fear-swollen eyes Laura looked uncertainly at Spencer and he nodded. 'Better do as he says, darling.'

'Glad you're being sensible, Jeffries.' Bruce pulled some rope out of his coat pocket. 'Put your hands behind your back. I'm going to tie you up as tight as a tart's pursestrings. I'm not risking any trouble from you.'

Laura got up shakily and made her way to the fireplace. She put a log into the range and raked at the embers to encourage a blaze. Spencer was trussed up when she went to the cold cupboard to fetch bacon and eggs. Bruce took Spencer's cigarettes off the dresser, lit one, and sat down in his armchair at the hearth, watching Laura closely as she prepared the meal.

'Mrs Noon's death must have been an accident,' Spencer said, sounding sympathetic; knowing this man would be cruel if antagonised, he was using the same tactics that Laura had.

'I don't think a judge and jury would think so,' Bruce replied, his voice gloating. 'I went to her smallholding the same day you thought I'd left the village. It was always said she was rich, had money stuffed in her mattress. I was in no mood for beating about the bush. Her front door was locked so I went straight round the back. She was in her kitchen, the great fat maggot. Sitting there like the bloody queen holding court even though the place was no better than a pigsty. That didn't put me off. You hear tales of these stinking rich old misers, hoarding their money. The moment she saw me she began cursing and swearing. When I demanded money she laughed at me, said I could search the house and I'd be lucky to find a brass farthing. Then she started calling me names, poking fun at me, saying I was no good and never would be. I'd never heard language from a man like she used, and all in that hoity-toity accent.

'I told her to shut up, but she wouldn't.' He thumped his clenched fist in the palm of his other hand. 'The bitch shook her hand at me, she threw things at me. I'd had enough. I warned her, but she wouldn't stop. I couldn't bear to see that fat red face a second longer so I moved behind her settle, pulled her shawl up round her neck and I strangled her. She fought like a wild animal but she was too fat to get up and do anything to hurt me.'

The kettle whistled to the boil and Laura jumped. To hide her fear, she looked away from Bruce and poured water into the teapot. Her hands were trembling and water splashed and hissed on the range.

Spencer felt helpless and prayed Laura wouldn't lose the baby. Every bit as scared as she was, he gulped and carried on with his ploy. 'You can't blame yourself for that, Bruce. No one likes abuse, even from an old woman.'

'I know what you're trying to do,' Bruce snarled. 'Hurry up with that tea!' he shouted and Laura jolted forward, spilling it over the clean tablecloth. 'I murdered that old bitch and I enjoyed it. And she was telling the truth. I found nothing in that dirty old house! No cash, silver, porcelain. The only piece of jewellery was that cameo brooch she wore and I wouldn't get far on the sale of that.

'I spent the night in a cave on the moor, intending to go and force my cow of a mother to get me some money, lots of it. But you ruined everything.' He threw the cigarette butt violently at the fender. 'You brought her here and by the time she had moved into the Angrove cottage the old woman's body had been found and the village was full of coppers. I decided to stay where I was, wait for the police to come to a dead end and leave. They would never believe I was still around here.'

Laura put a mug of tea down beside Bruce. He grabbed her wrist and she cried out. 'A pity for you that you found me stealing your food, Laura. But now you can be my passport to freedom.'

'I'll d-do anything you say,' she stammered, 'just don't hurt us.'

Bruce wolfed down his meal then stripped to the waist and washed. 'Get me some clean clothes,' he demanded, kicking his dirty ones across the room.

'I'll h-have to go upstairs,' Laura said meekly. She had been sitting next to Spencer, leaning against him, and got up reluctantly.

'Be quick about it.' Bruce aimed the gun at Spencer's forehead. 'And be a good girl if you don't want to see your handsome hubby looking like your farmhand.'

Her legs were wobbling and Laura clutched the banister on the way upstairs. In her bedroom she pulled some of Spencer's clothes out of the wardrobe and chest of drawers. She had no doubt that Bruce was as ruthless as his threats, but through her terror she tried to think of a way of alerting Pawley to run and get help when he entered the yard for the milking at four thirty, in two hours' time. Vicki and Ince's old rooms overlooked the yard; maybe she could open a window and dangle something outside to warn Pawley.

Bruce shouted up the stairs and she was filled with renewed panic. Racing across the landing she paused on the top step to take a deep breath. It punched her lungs and made her choke.

'Hurry up!' Bruce snapped angrily again.

She went down fearfully. He snatched the clothes from her arms before she reached the last step, nearly overbalancing her. 'I'll get dressed then I'll climb those stairs and see for myself if the kid's here or not.'

He didn't smell so bad now but he looked coarse and ugly with his straggly beard, unhealthy flesh and hate-filled eyes. He put on Spencer's shirt and jumper and rammed the gun into the waistband of his trousers. He lit another cigarette then motioned for Laura to go up the stairs in front of him.

She climbed up with him breathing down her neck. She opened the door to Vicki's room and he pushed past her and stared at the little girl's empty bed. He looked under it, then in the wardrobe and behind the curtains. In case Laura was lying, he searched the spare room then the big double bedroom, taking her with him.

'Where is she?'

Laura didn't want to tell him. She said nothing.

Bruce caught hold of her by the hair and yanked her against him. 'You've got no choice but to tell me.'

There was no way Laura would risk her precious daughter. 'Sh-she's staying the night at a schoolfriend's house. They often play together.'

He stroked her face and she turned her head away from him. 'Things will work out well for you if you co-operate with me. You're a beautiful woman, Laura. Cousin Billy thought so and so do I.' He threw her on the bed and she screamed. 'Like I said, it's going to be a long night. We might as well stay up here for a while.'

Spencer had been working to loosen the rope round him. He became frantic when he heard Laura's scream. He knew what Bruce was up to and he had to do something fast. Shouting Laura's name at the top of his voice, he kicked over the chair beside him, then using his feet shunted the heavy table across the room, hoping the commotion would bring Bruce downstairs to investigate. He heard Bruce utter an oath and then his heavy feet, running.

Spencer had an idea. He was near the door that led directly to the staircase, as was common with old farmhouses. With his feet he picked up the fallen chair and, hoping and praying, he waited.

Bruce had ripped open Laura's dressing gown but had left her when he'd heard the noise downstairs. Thumping down the stairs, he pulled out the gun and hurtled through the door.

Spencer was ready. He thrust the chair at Bruce's feet, the effort making his own chair fall over with him tied to it. Taken by surprise, Bruce felt himself falling and he fired the gun.

Laura screamed. 'Spencer!' She scrambled off the bed. Having no thought for anything but Spencer's safety, she hurled herself down the stairs and into the kitchen. He was lying on the floor with blood pouring out of a wound to his head. Bruce was sprawled out in a daze several feet away.

Her first instinct was to run to Spencer but she saw the gun, an inch away from Bruce's hand. She ran, reached out for the gun but his hand shot out and beat her to it. She backed away as he got to his feet and pointed it at her.

'The bastard! I'll make sure I finish him off for that.'

Laura suddenly felt deadly calm. She rasped, 'If you do, you'll have to kill me too and you'll never get your hands on my money.'

He hesitated, then grinned evilly. 'What the hell. I'll kill you both then get the hell out of here. You can go and join Billy. Goodbye, Laura.'

'Wait! Can I at least hold Spencer's hand?'

'You love him, do you? I thought yours was a marriage of convenience for the kid.'

'Yes, I love him. I haven't known it for long. Please, grant me this last wish, Bruce.'

'You've got thirty seconds.'

As she backed away towards Spencer, she saw the kitchen door opening very slowly. She held her throat to stop herself making a noise.

Suddenly Pawley was in the room and Barney came in with him.

'Now!' Pawley commanded.

Barney leapt at Bruce's arm and brought him down. He dropped the gun and Pawley sprinted and grabbed it. Bruce scrabbled to get it

379

back but Pawley lowered himself to his haunches and aimed between his eyes. 'Don't even think about breathing.'

Laura knelt beside Spencer. She turned his head so she could see his face. 'Darling, are you all right? Please don't die on me.' His eyes were open, flickering. They focused on her.

'Mmmmmm, my head aches.'

'Hush now, let me look.' The bleeding was easing and she could see a furrow in his scalp. She cried with relief. 'I don't think it's a bad wound.' She looked gratefully at Pawley. 'Thank God you and Barney arrived.'

'I've suffered from insomnia ever since I was injured,' Pawley said, keeping his sight rooted on Bruce. 'Sometimes Barney comes for a walk with me. Tonight he was very restless so I came down into the yard to check that everything was all right. I heard the gun being fired. You saw the rest for yourself.'

'I shall always bless the day you came here, Pawley.'

Laura had to use a sharp knife to cut through the tight bonds to free Spencer, and then Pawley used the rope to tie up Bruce. Bruce had pulled out the telephone line, and rather than leave him with Laura and Spencer while he ran to knock up Tregorlan Farm where the nearest telephone was, Pawley hauled him outside and locked him in an outhouse, leaving Barney on guard.

—

'It's nearly dawn,' Dr Palmer said, half an hour later, as he put a dressing over the couple of stitches he had made in Spencer's wound. They were up in the bedroom where the doctor had insisted his two shocked patients rest. 'I don't want you working on the farm today. You need at least twenty-four hours in bed. I'll leave some analgesic for the headache.'

'I'll make sure he does as he's told,' Laura asserted wearily. She was sitting on the bed beside Spencer, holding his hand, and she squeezed it affectionately.

Dr Palmer looked grimly across the bedroom at Chief Inspector Whitehead and the sergeant standing patiently beside him. Bruce

Tamblyn had been taken away to Bodmin police station. 'Are you up to being questioned, Spencer? How about you, Laura?'

Spencer answered immediately, with feeling, 'I'll be more than happy to help put Bruce Tamblyn behind bars.'

And Laura echoed the statement.

Laura had been taken away to Bedlam police station. Are you
up to the questions a spy ...ar ... How about you, know...
Spencer answered huskily, with terror. 'I'll be ... then
temp ... here in Broc Laura ... ...
And I attache box, my dream ...

Chapter 37

Vicki ran into her parents' bedroom and found them both asleep. As
she so often did, she jumped on the bed and smothered them with
kisses. They both groaned and Spencer touched his aching head.

Felicity came in. 'I'm so sorry, my dears. She ran inside before I
could stop her. I've just heard from Daisy downstairs about what has
happened. You poor things. Why didn't you ring me? I would have
kept Vicki longer at Hawksmoor. It will be hard for Daisy to come
to terms with what her son has done but she's doing the right thing,
staying here and looking after the pair of you.'

'Alfie's got a baby sister,' Vicki blurted out, happily bouncing on
the bed, blissfully unaware of the danger her parents had been in just
a short time ago. 'She came last night. Uncle Ince stopped the car
and told us as we were driving through the village. Mummy, can Alfie
come and play with me soon? He's such fun.' Vicki went on chatting
nineteen to the dozen and Spencer groaned and reached for his pills.

'Off the bed, Vicki,' Laura said sternly.

'But I want to tell you—'

'Now, Vicki! Daddy's got a headache and Mummy has to get out of
bed and fetch some water for his pills.' Vicki climbed down obediently.
'Sorry, Daddy.'

'You weren't to know, pipkin,' he murmured drowsily.

'Daddy needs some rest. Perhaps if Grandma wouldn't mind, it
would be a good idea if she took you back to Hawksmoor House
for another night. You can help her prepare Uncle Harry's room for
when he comes out of hospital.'

Felicity was delighted. 'Of course I'd love to have her. Come along,
darling.'

'But I want to stay here with Mummy,' and Vicki wound her arms round Laura's legs and looked up at her beguilingly. 'I want you to put up those new curtains you made for my playhouse.'

For a moment Laura's heart was torn. She looked down at the beautiful, golden-haired little girl, then at the handsome man lying weakly on the pillows. Then she was resolute. 'It won't hurt you to go with Grandma today, Vicki. Mummy has to look after Daddy. He needs me.'

After a little more fuss, Vicki was taken downstairs, kissed goodbye and packed off in Felicity's car.

'It's not like you not to put Vicki first,' Spencer said. He was groggy but he had been thinking hard while Laura was fetching the glass of water for him.

She kissed him softly on the cheek then held his head lovingly against her breast as he took the pills. 'It's just a matter of getting your priorities right.'

'Oh? Am I now high on your list then?'

Laura slipped back into bed beside Spencer and cuddled in close. 'When I thought you'd been killed last night I realised that you're right at the very top. I do love you, Spencer.'

'I've been hoping for ages that one day you would say that to me. I love you too, Laura.' He grinned boyishly.

'This could put Vicki's nose out of joint though. She's used to you running to her first every time.'

Laura took his hand and put it on the gentle swell of her stomach. 'It will be better for this little one and it will be better for Vicki. Right now, it's nice just being the two of us.'

Then they snuggled down together and drifted off into a peaceful sleep.

The Kilgarthen Sagas

Kilgarthen
Rosemerryn